Kingdoms

A Biblical Epic

The Coming Storm

ERVAN®

Storm
2007 by Lamp Post, Inc.

for information should be addressed to:
van, Grand Rapids, Michigan 49530

ary of Congress Cataloging-in-Publication Data

ery, Ben, 1974–
    Josiah: the coming storm: a biblical fiction / by Ben Avery; illustrated by Mat Broome.
        p. cm. -- (Kingdoms: a biblical epic; v. #1)
    ISBN-13: 978-0-310-71353-1 (softcover)
    ISBN-10: 0-310-71353-6 (softcover)
    1. Graphic novels. I. Broome, Mat. II. Title.
    PN6727.A945J67 2007
    741.5'973--dc22

                                                              2007003148

This book published in conjunction with Lamp Post, Inc.; 8367 Lemon Avenue, La Mesa, CA 91941

Series Editor: Bud Rogers
Managing Editor: Bruce Nuffer
Managing Art Director: Sarah Molegraaf

Printed in the United States of America

07 08 09 10 11 12 • 8 7 6 5 4 3 2

A Biblical Epic
Kingdoms™
The Coming Storm

Series Editor: Bud Rogers
Story by Ben Avery
Art by Mat Broome

ZONDERVAN®

ZONDERVAN.com/
AUTHORTRACKER
follow your favorite authors

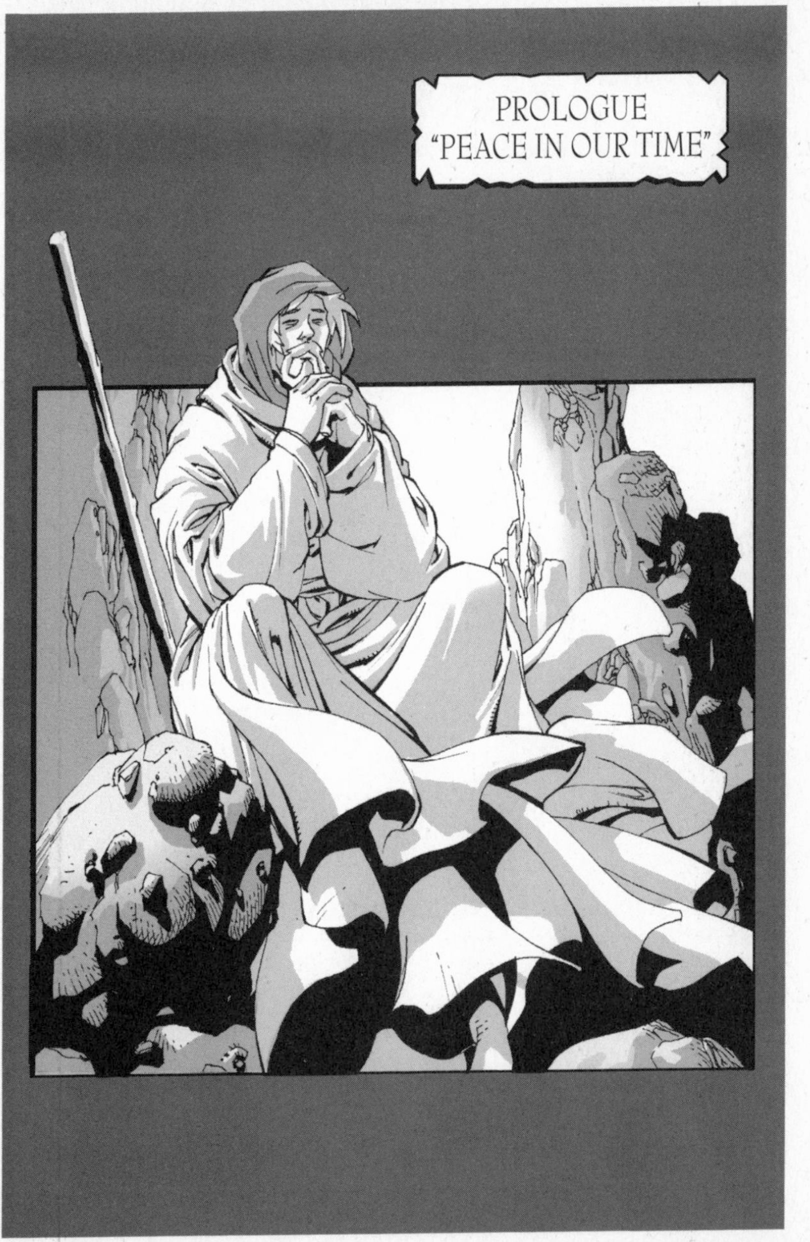
PROLOGUE
"PEACE IN OUR TIME"

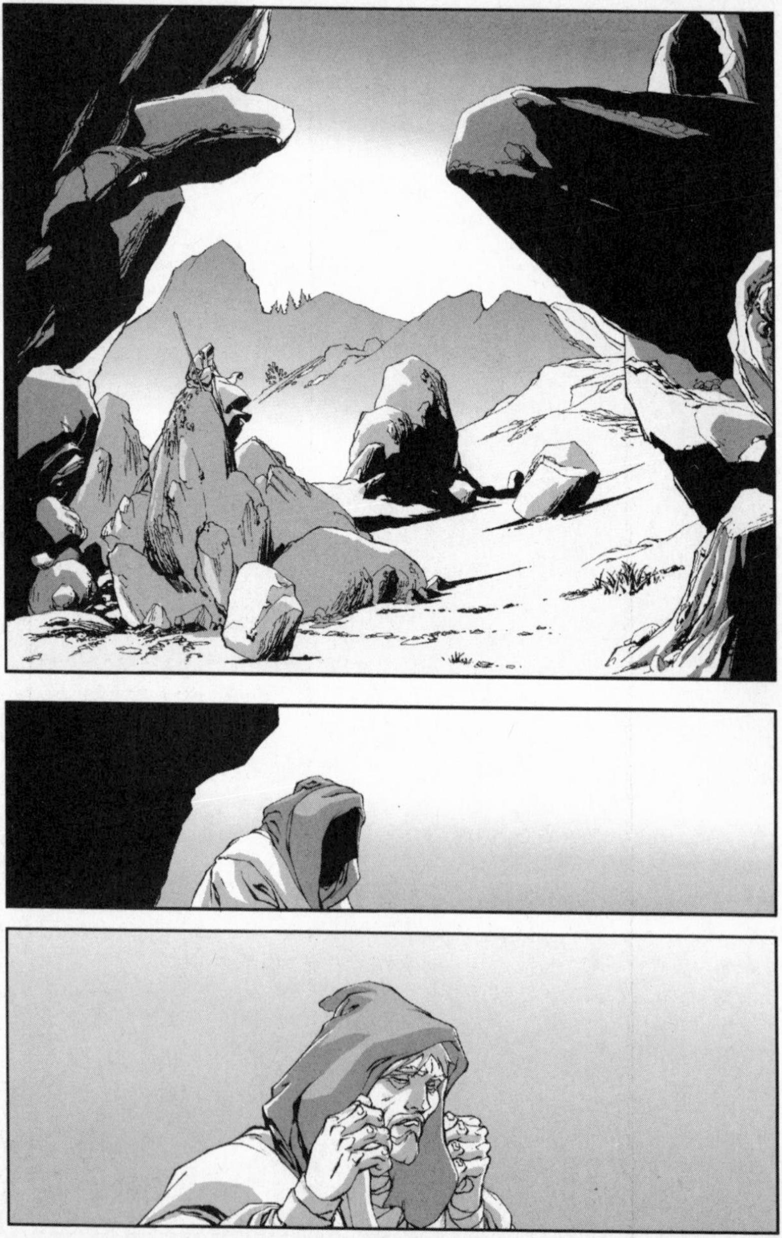

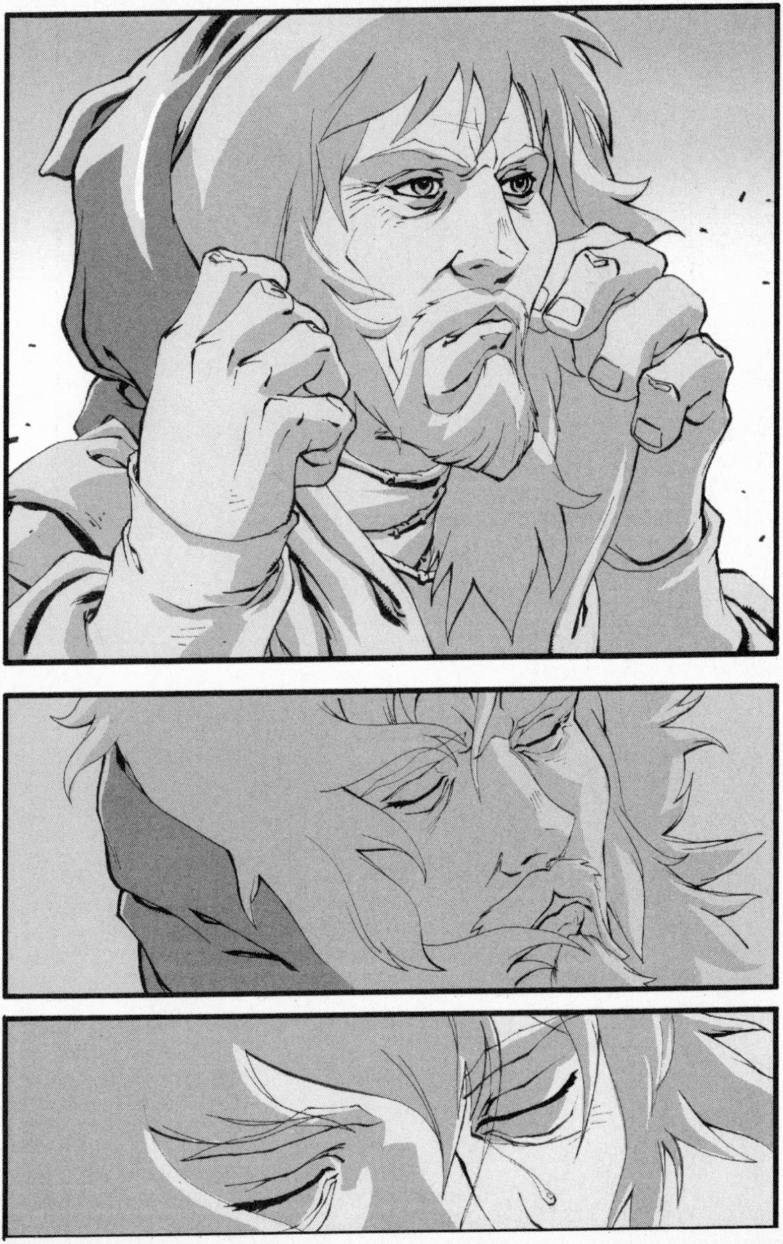

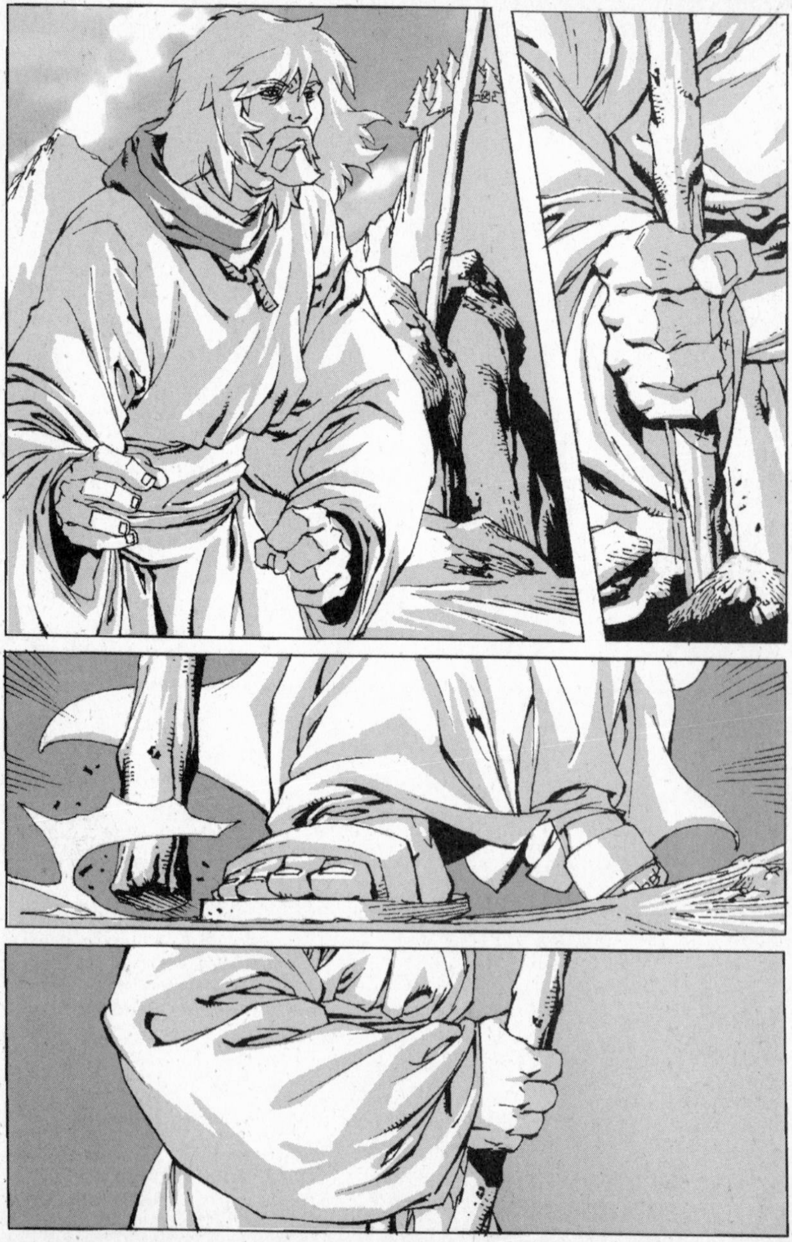

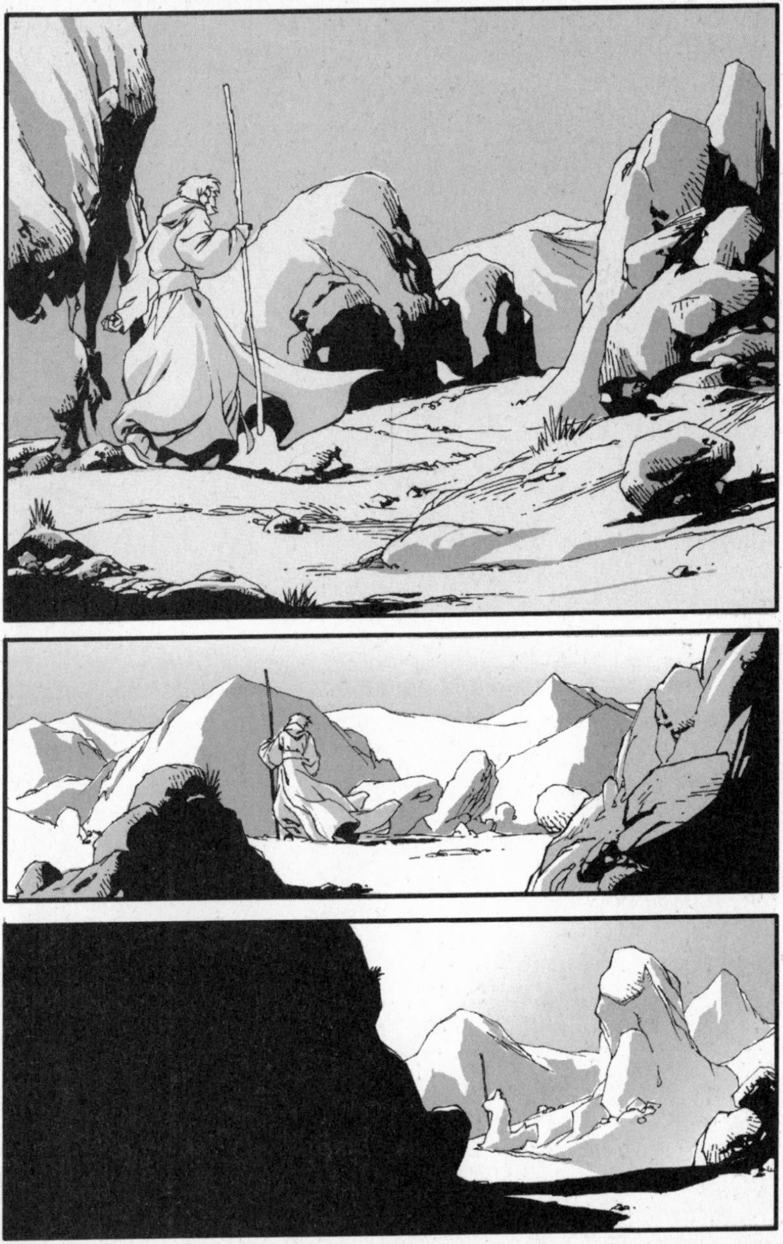

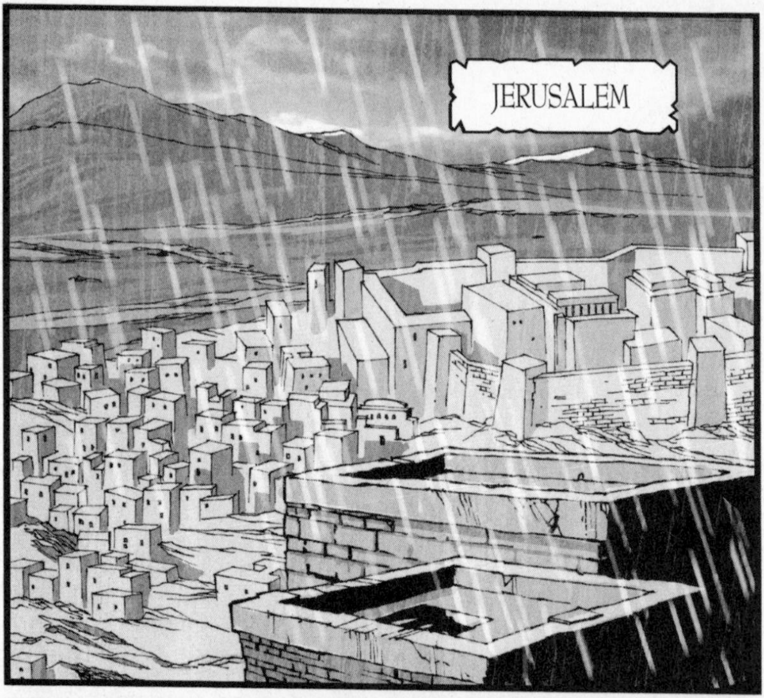
JERUSALEM
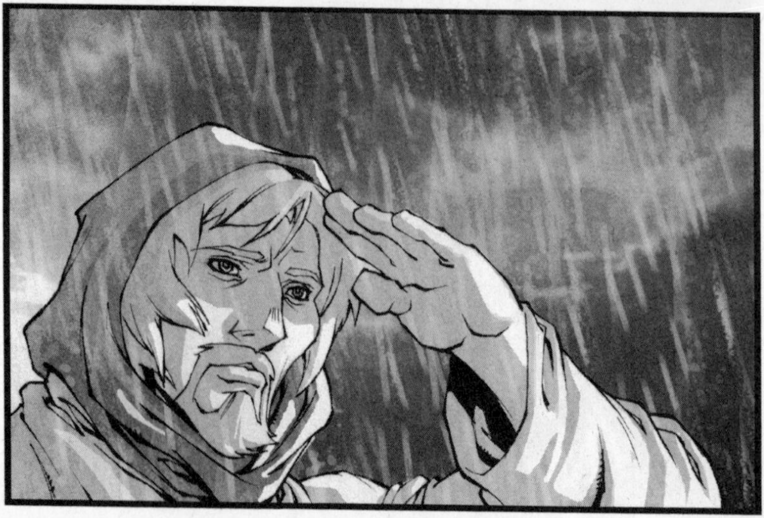

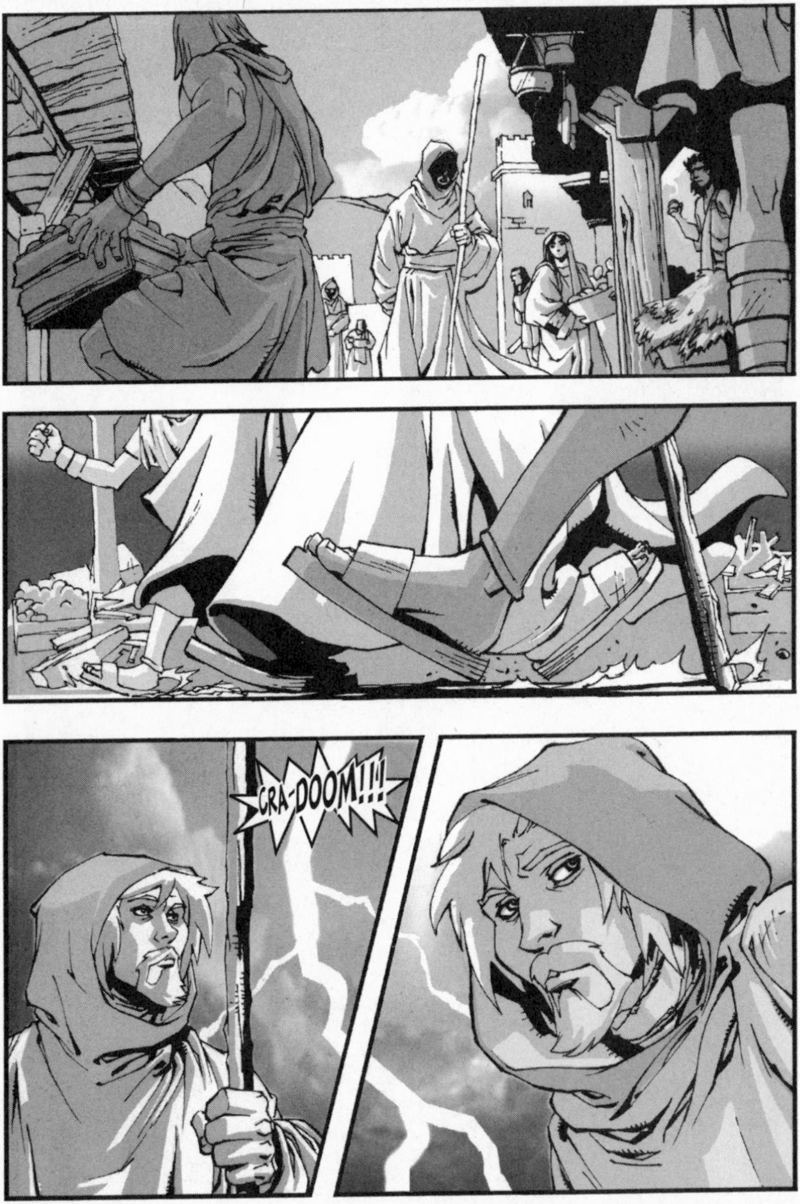
CRA-DOOM!!!!

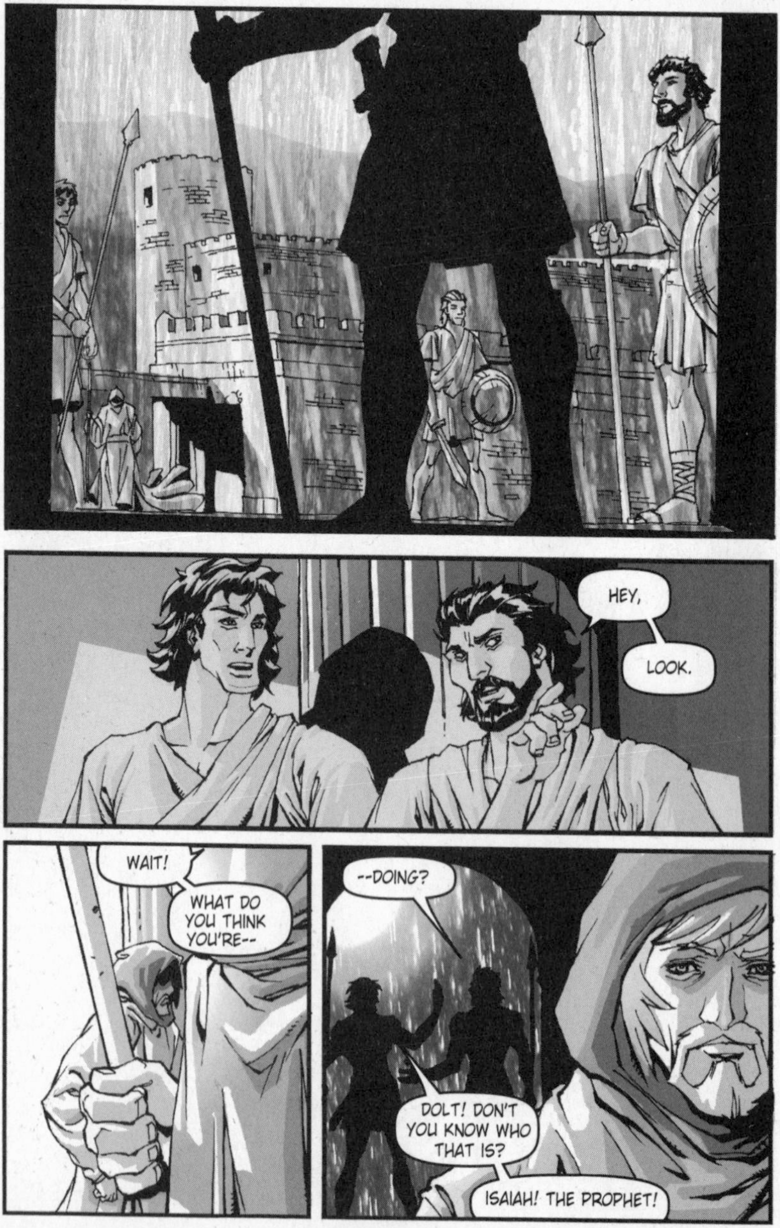
HEY,
LOOK.
WAIT!
WHAT DO YOU THINK YOU'RE--
--DOING?
DOLT! DON'T YOU KNOW WHO THAT IS?
ISAIAH! THE PROPHET!

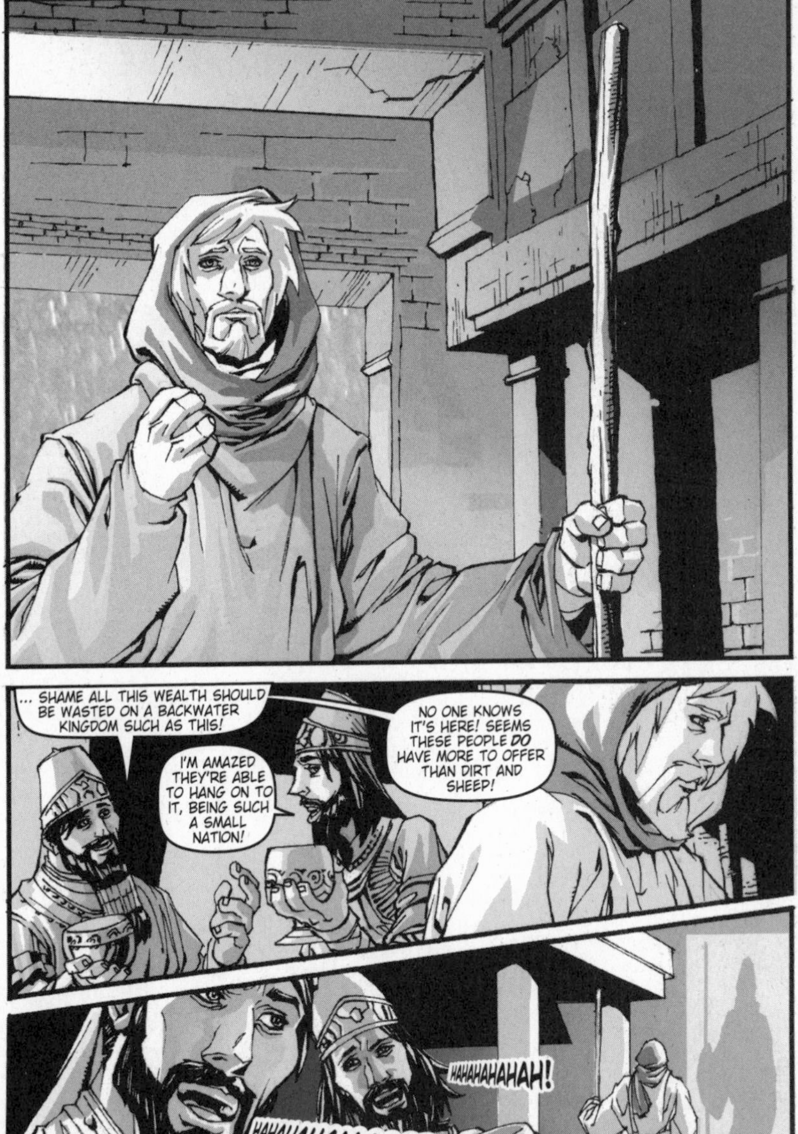
... SHAME ALL THIS WEALTH SHOULD BE WASTED ON A BACKWATER KINGDOM SUCH AS THIS!
I'M AMAZED THEY'RE ABLE TO HANG ON TO IT, BEING SUCH A SMALL NATION!
NO ONE KNOWS IT'S HERE! SEEMS THESE PEOPLE DO HAVE MORE TO OFFER THAN DIRT AND SHEEP!
HAHAHAHAHAH!
HAHAHAHAHAH!

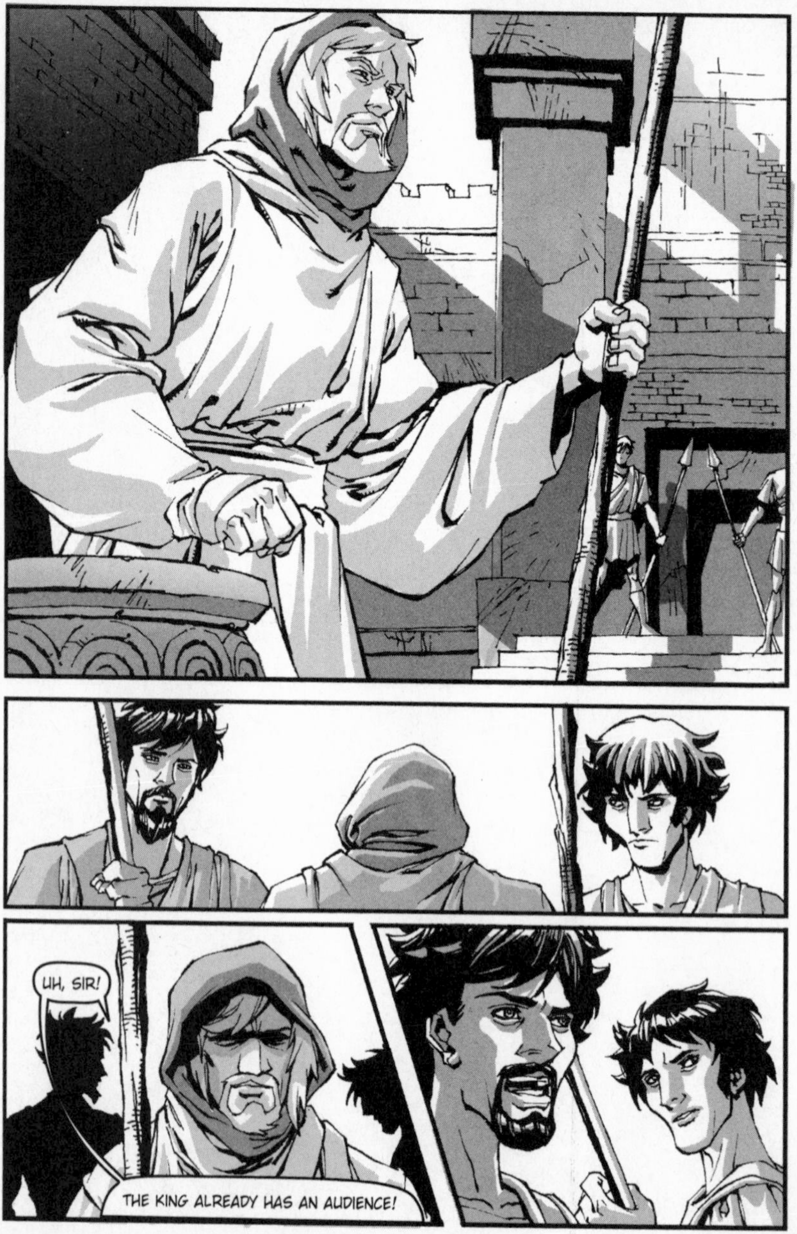
UH, SIR!
THE KING ALREADY HAS AN AUDIENCE!

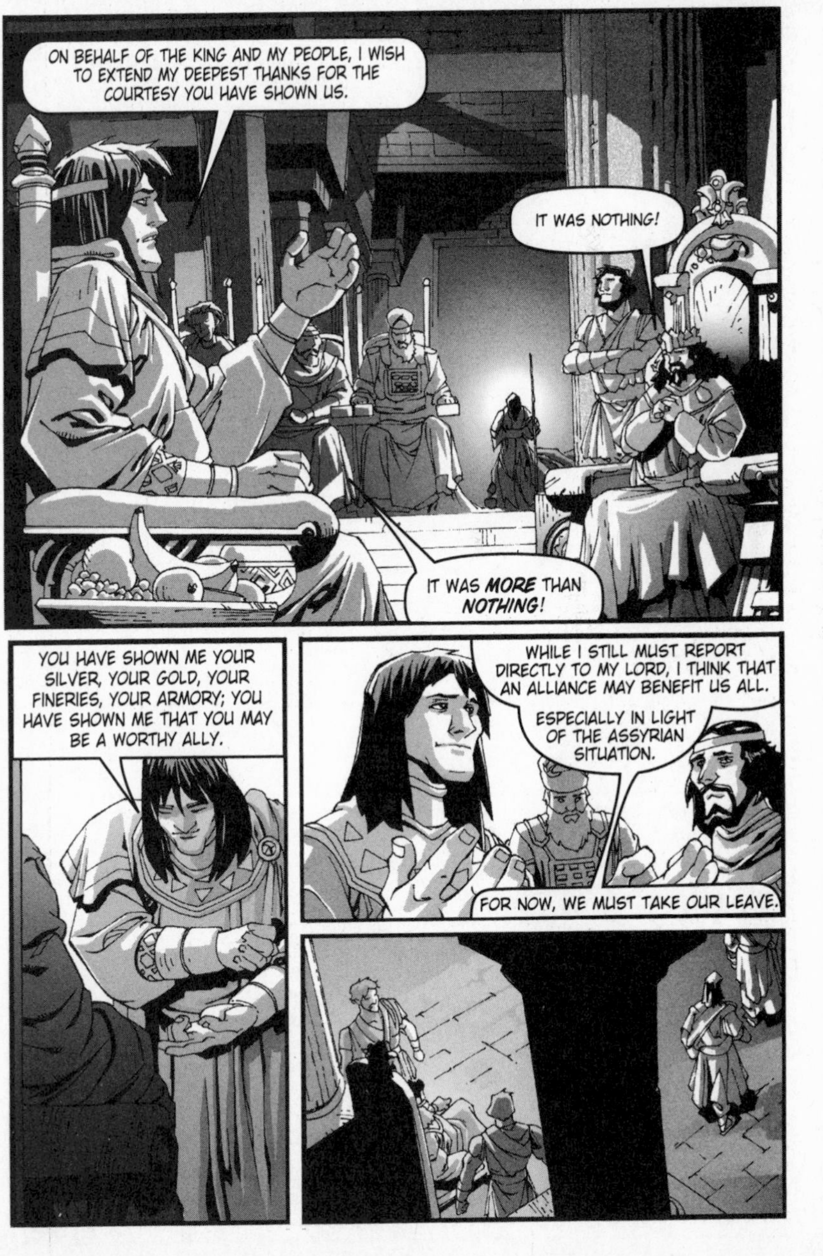
ON BEHALF OF THE KING AND MY PEOPLE, I WISH TO EXTEND MY DEEPEST THANKS FOR THE COURTESY YOU HAVE SHOWN US.
IT WAS NOTHING!
IT WAS *MORE* THAN *NOTHING*!
YOU HAVE SHOWN ME YOUR SILVER, YOUR GOLD, YOUR FINERIES, YOUR ARMORY; YOU HAVE SHOWN ME THAT YOU MAY BE A WORTHY ALLY.
WHILE I STILL MUST REPORT DIRECTLY TO MY LORD, I THINK THAT AN ALLIANCE MAY BENEFIT US ALL.
ESPECIALLY IN LIGHT OF THE ASSYRIAN SITUATION.
FOR NOW, WE MUST TAKE OUR LEAVE.

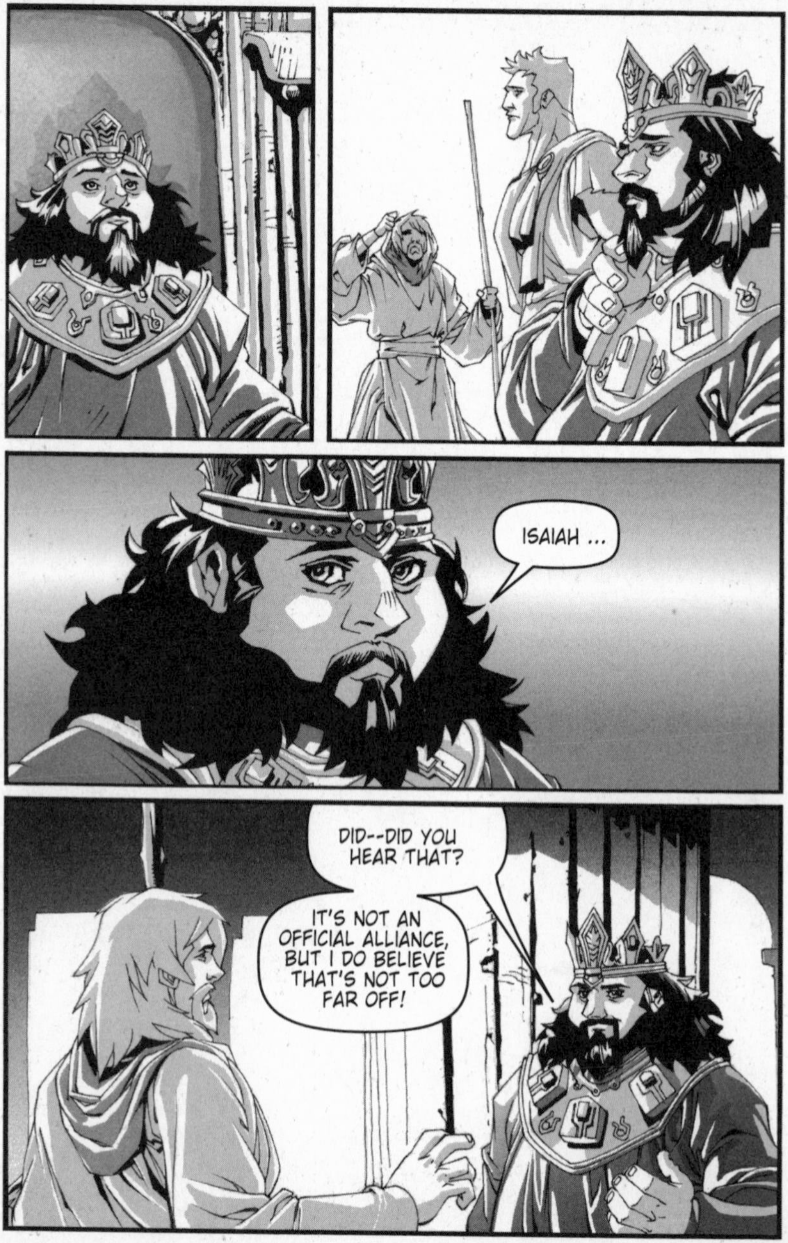
ISAIAH ...
DID--DID YOU HEAR THAT?
IT'S NOT AN OFFICIAL ALLIANCE, BUT I DO BELIEVE THAT'S NOT TOO FAR OFF!

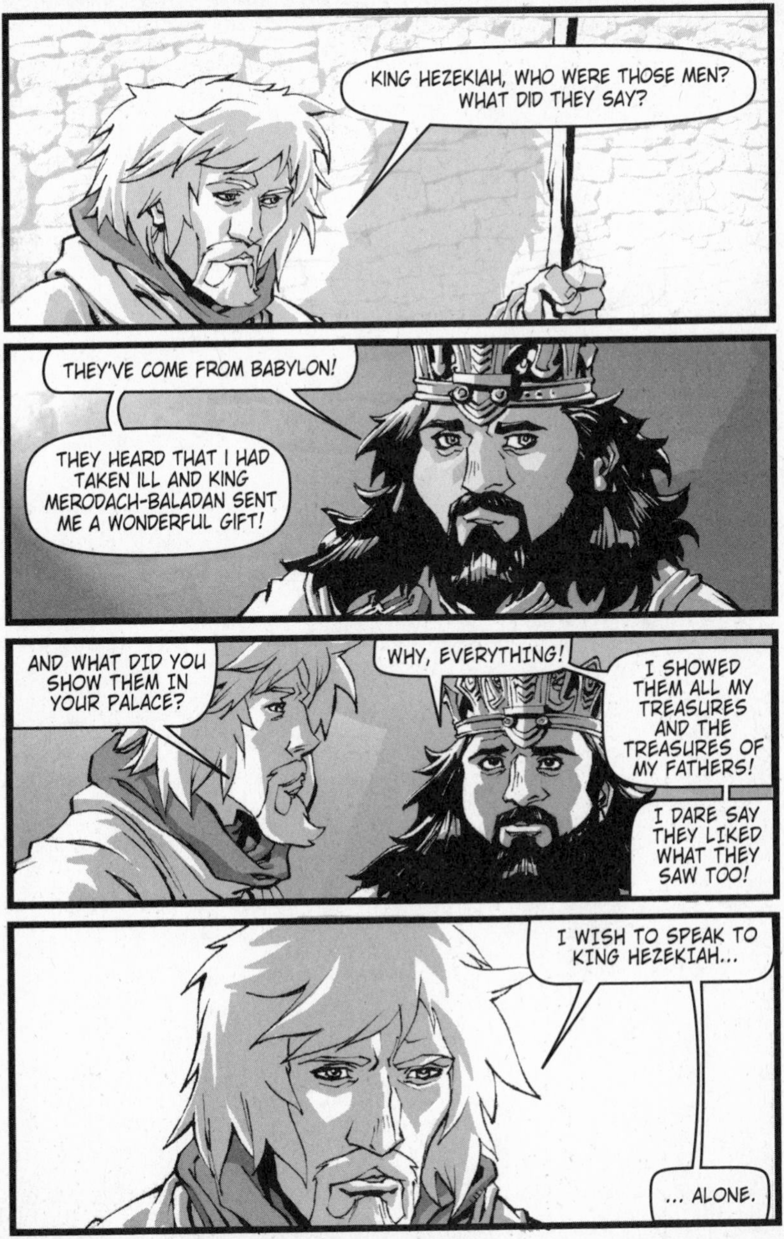
KING HEZEKIAH, WHO WERE THOSE MEN? WHAT DID THEY SAY?
THEY'VE COME FROM BABYLON!
THEY HEARD THAT I HAD TAKEN ILL AND KING MERODACH-BALADAN SENT ME A WONDERFUL GIFT!
AND WHAT DID YOU SHOW THEM IN YOUR PALACE?
WHY, EVERYTHING!
I SHOWED THEM ALL MY TREASURES AND THE TREASURES OF MY FATHERS!
I DARE SAY THEY LIKED WHAT THEY SAW TOO!
I WISH TO SPEAK TO KING HEZEKIAH...
... ALONE.

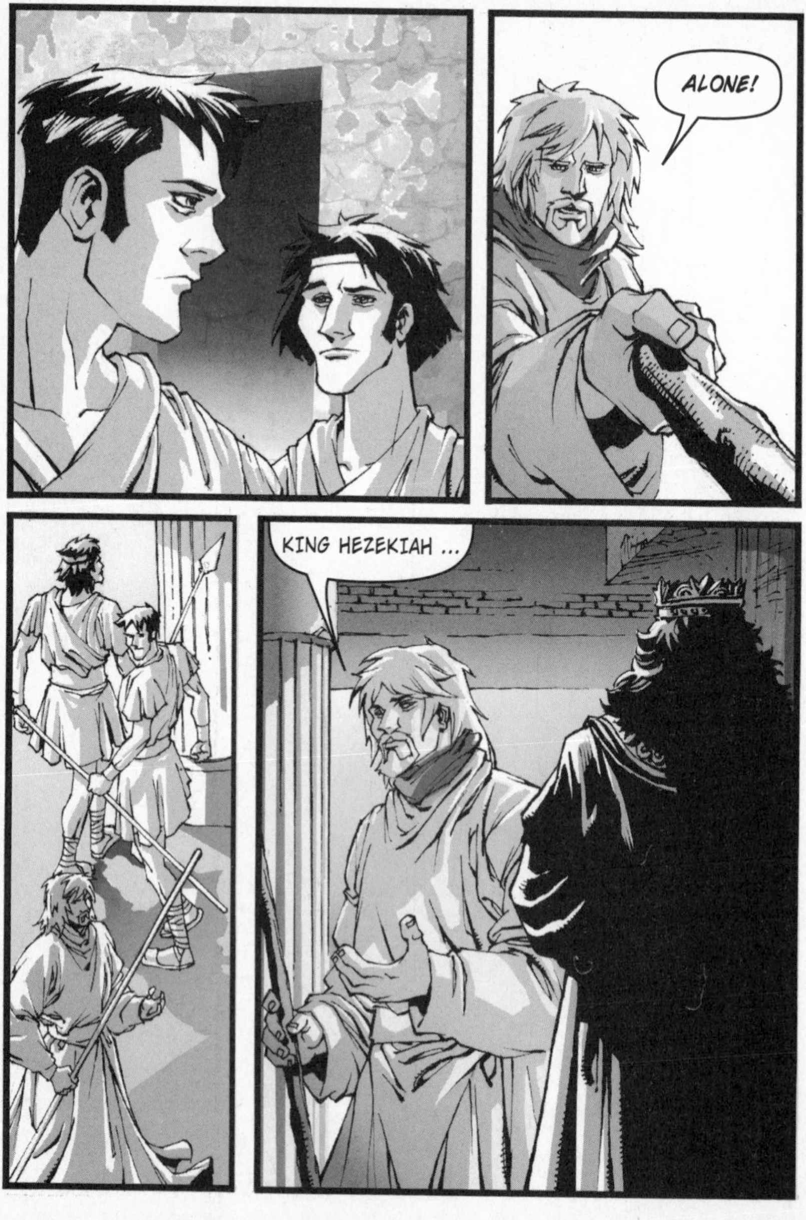
ALONE!
KING HEZEKIAH ...

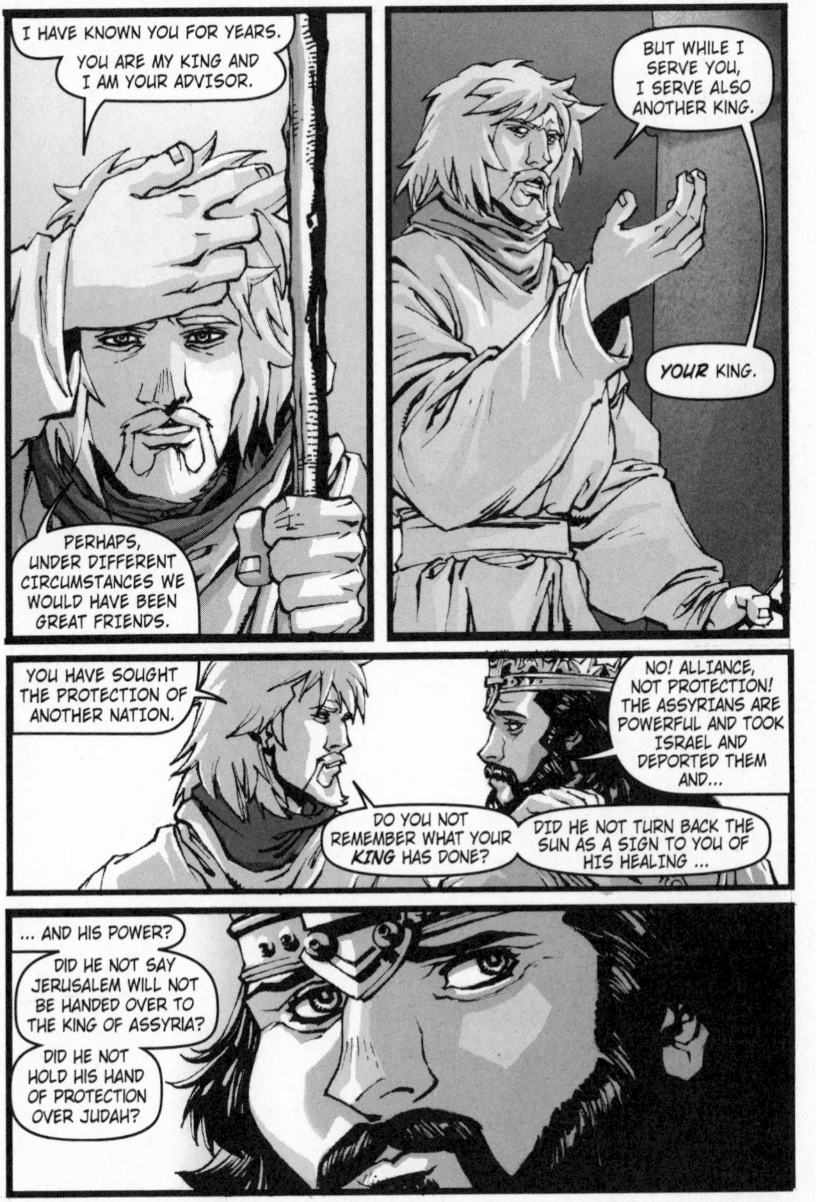I HAVE KNOWN YOU FOR YEARS.
YOU ARE MY KING AND I AM YOUR ADVISOR.
PERHAPS, UNDER DIFFERENT CIRCUMSTANCES WE WOULD HAVE BEEN GREAT FRIENDS.
BUT WHILE I SERVE YOU, I SERVE ALSO ANOTHER KING.
YOUR KING.
YOU HAVE SOUGHT THE PROTECTION OF ANOTHER NATION.
NO! ALLIANCE, NOT PROTECTION! THE ASSYRIANS ARE POWERFUL AND TOOK ISRAEL AND DEPORTED THEM AND...
DO YOU NOT REMEMBER WHAT YOUR *KING* HAS DONE?
DID HE NOT TURN BACK THE SUN AS A SIGN TO YOU OF HIS HEALING ...
... AND HIS POWER?
DID HE NOT SAY JERUSALEM WILL NOT BE HANDED OVER TO THE KING OF ASSYRIA?
DID HE NOT HOLD HIS HAND OF PROTECTION OVER JUDAH?

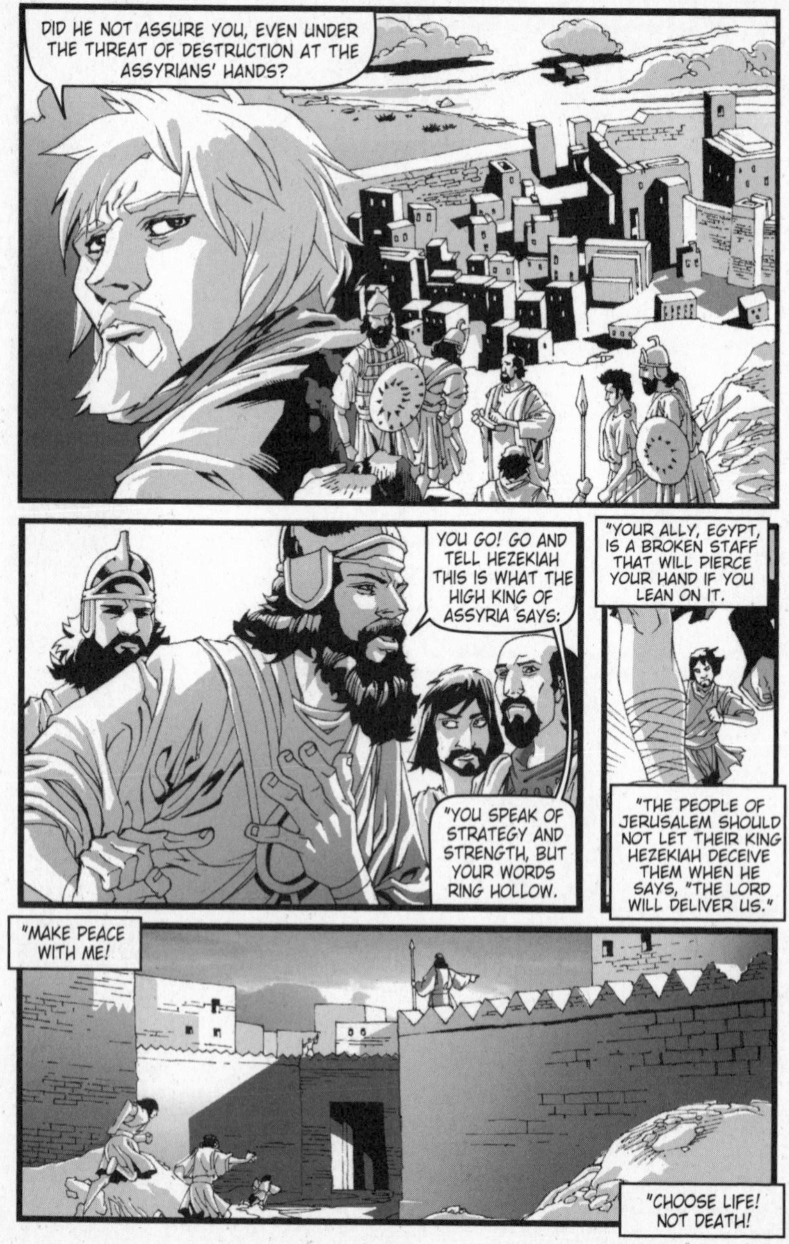
DID HE NOT ASSURE YOU, EVEN UNDER THE THREAT OF DESTRUCTION AT THE ASSYRIANS' HANDS?
YOU GO! GO AND TELL HEZEKIAH THIS IS WHAT THE HIGH KING OF ASSYRIA SAYS:
"YOU SPEAK OF STRATEGY AND STRENGTH, BUT YOUR WORDS RING HOLLOW.
"YOUR ALLY, EGYPT, IS A BROKEN STAFF THAT WILL PIERCE YOUR HAND IF YOU LEAN ON IT.
"THE PEOPLE OF JERUSALEM SHOULD NOT LET THEIR KING HEZEKIAH DECEIVE THEM WHEN HE SAYS, "THE LORD WILL DELIVER US."
"MAKE PEACE WITH ME!
"CHOOSE LIFE! NOT DEATH!

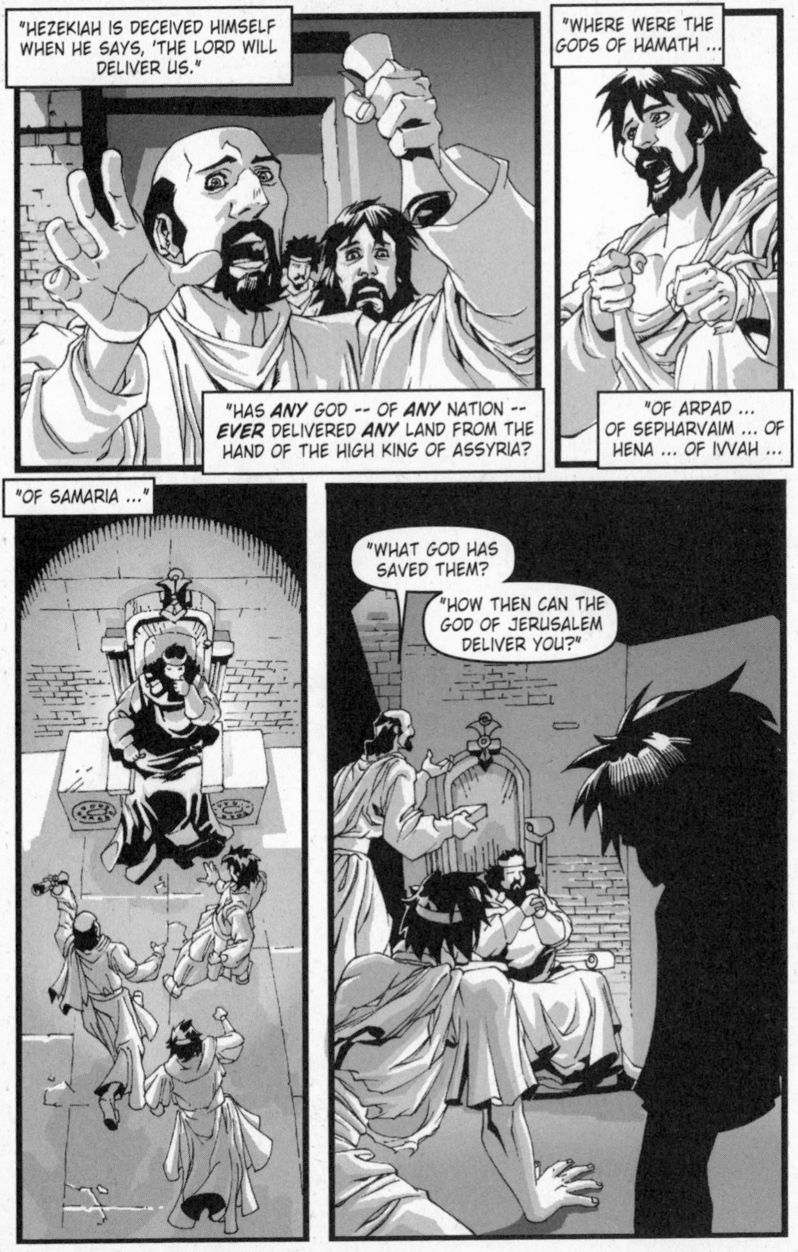
"HEZEKIAH IS DECEIVED HIMSELF WHEN HE SAYS, 'THE LORD WILL DELIVER US."
"HAS ANY GOD -- OF ANY NATION -- EVER DELIVERED ANY LAND FROM THE HAND OF THE HIGH KING OF ASSYRIA?
"WHERE WERE THE GODS OF HAMATH ...
"OF ARPAD ... OF SEPHARVAIM ... OF HENA ... OF IVVAH ...
"OF SAMARIA ..."
"WHAT GOD HAS SAVED THEM?
"HOW THEN CAN THE GOD OF JERUSALEM DELIVER YOU?"

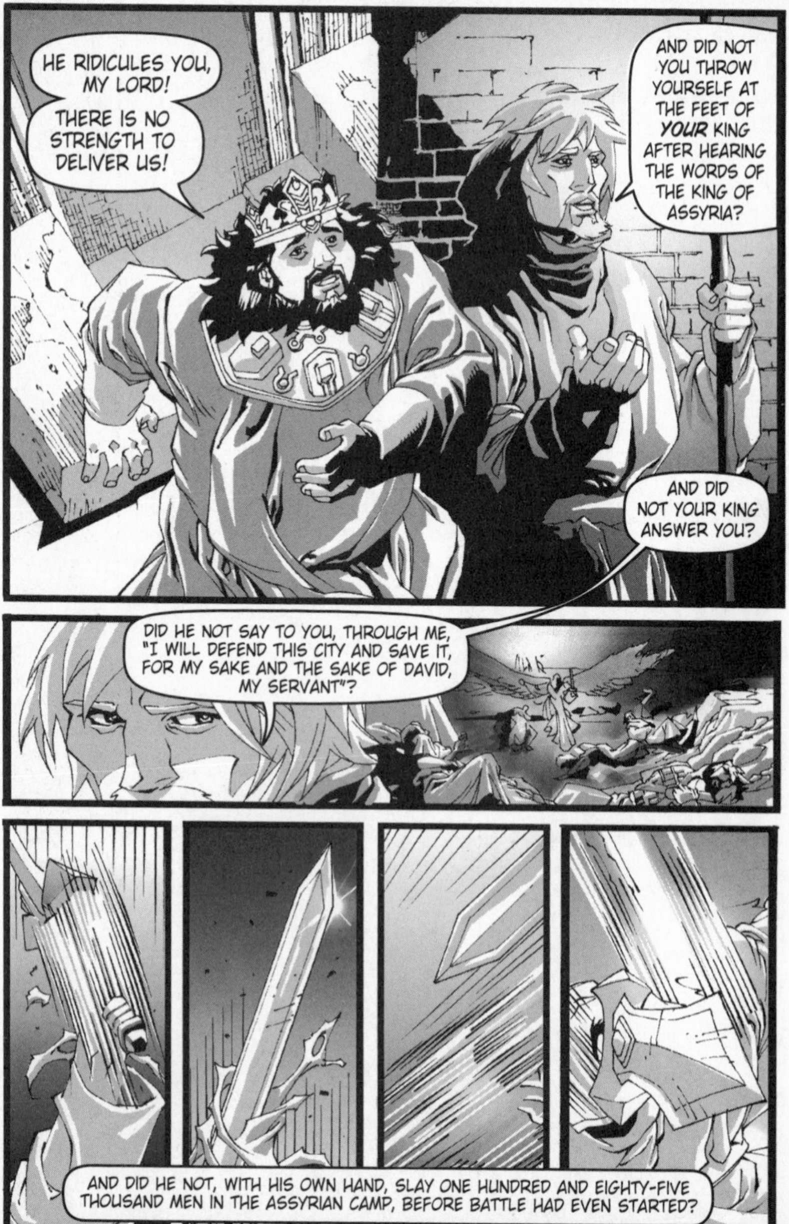
HE RIDICULES YOU, MY LORD!
THERE IS NO STRENGTH TO DELIVER US!
AND DID NOT YOU THROW YOURSELF AT THE FEET OF ***YOUR*** KING AFTER HEARING THE WORDS OF THE KING OF ASSYRIA?
AND DID NOT YOUR KING ANSWER YOU?
DID HE NOT SAY TO YOU, THROUGH ME, "I WILL DEFEND THIS CITY AND SAVE IT, FOR MY SAKE AND THE SAKE OF DAVID, MY SERVANT"?
AND DID HE NOT, WITH HIS OWN HAND, SLAY ONE HUNDRED AND EIGHTY-FIVE THOUSAND MEN IN THE ASSYRIAN CAMP, BEFORE BATTLE HAD EVEN STARTED?

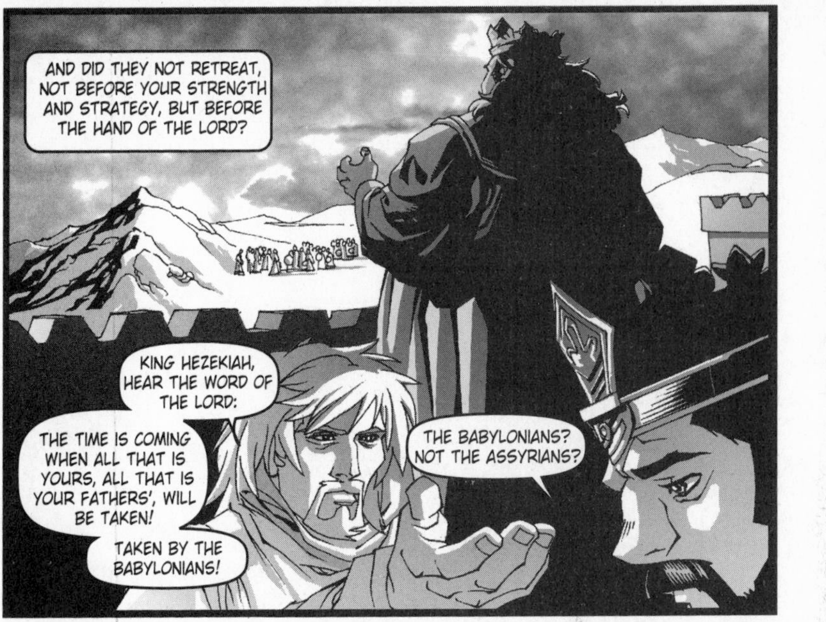
AND DID THEY NOT RETREAT, NOT BEFORE YOUR STRENGTH AND STRATEGY, BUT BEFORE THE HAND OF THE LORD?
KING HEZEKIAH, HEAR THE WORD OF THE LORD:
THE TIME IS COMING WHEN ALL THAT IS YOURS, ALL THAT IS YOUR FATHERS', WILL BE TAKEN!
TAKEN BY THE BABYLONIANS!
THE BABYLONIANS? NOT THE ASSYRIANS?

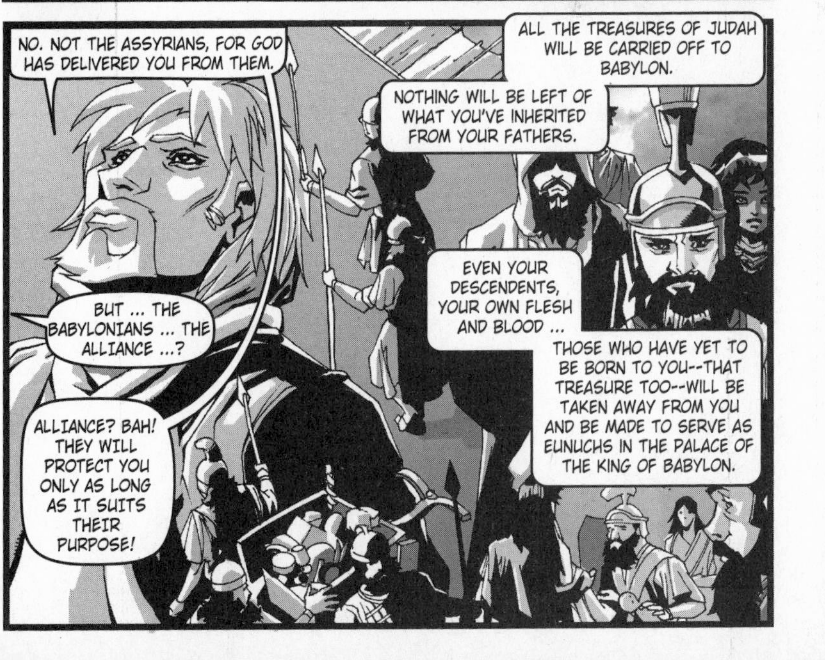
NO. NOT THE ASSYRIANS, FOR GOD HAS DELIVERED YOU FROM THEM.
ALL THE TREASURES OF JUDAH WILL BE CARRIED OFF TO BABYLON.
NOTHING WILL BE LEFT OF WHAT YOU'VE INHERITED FROM YOUR FATHERS.
EVEN YOUR DESCENDENTS, YOUR OWN FLESH AND BLOOD ...
BUT ... THE BABYLONIANS ... THE ALLIANCE ...?
THOSE WHO HAVE YET TO BE BORN TO YOU--THAT TREASURE TOO--WILL BE TAKEN AWAY FROM YOU AND BE MADE TO SERVE AS EUNUCHS IN THE PALACE OF THE KING OF BABYLON.
ALLIANCE? BAH! THEY WILL PROTECT YOU ONLY AS LONG AS IT SUITS THEIR PURPOSE!

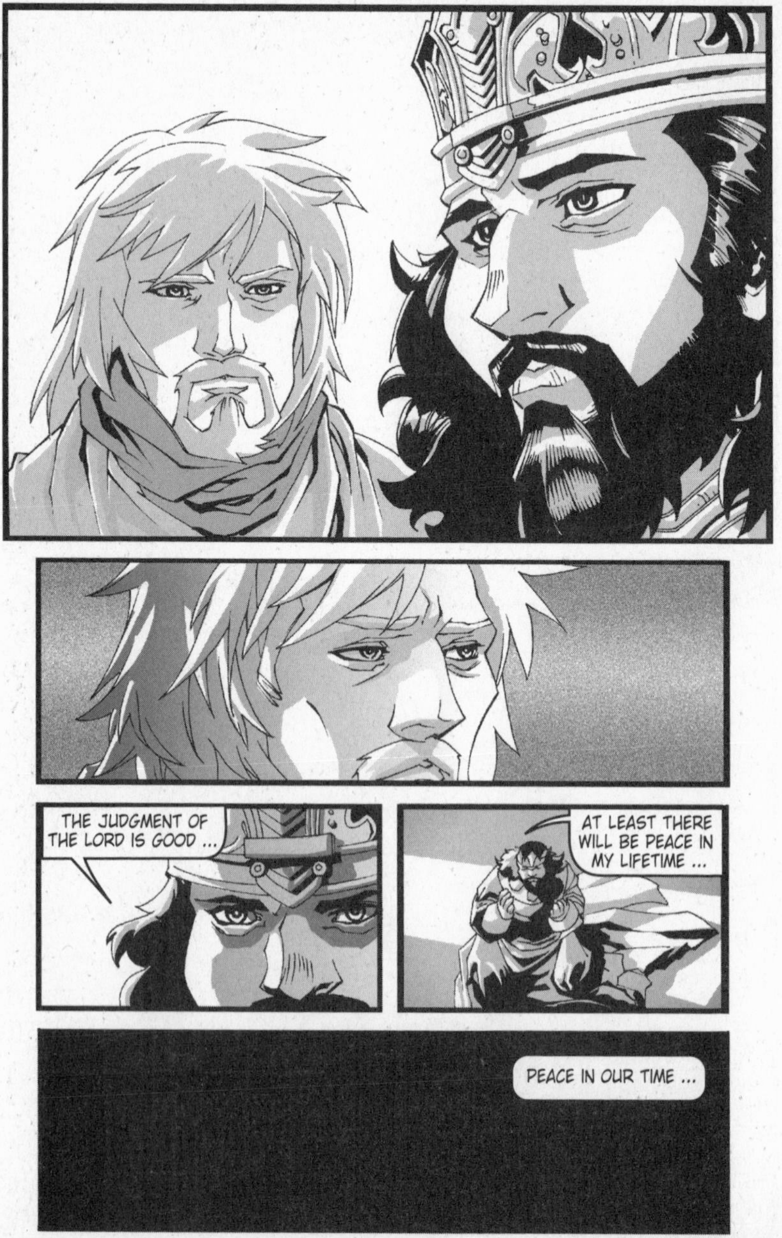
THE JUDGMENT OF THE LORD IS GOOD ...
AT LEAST THERE WILL BE PEACE IN MY LIFETIME ...
PEACE IN OUR TIME ...

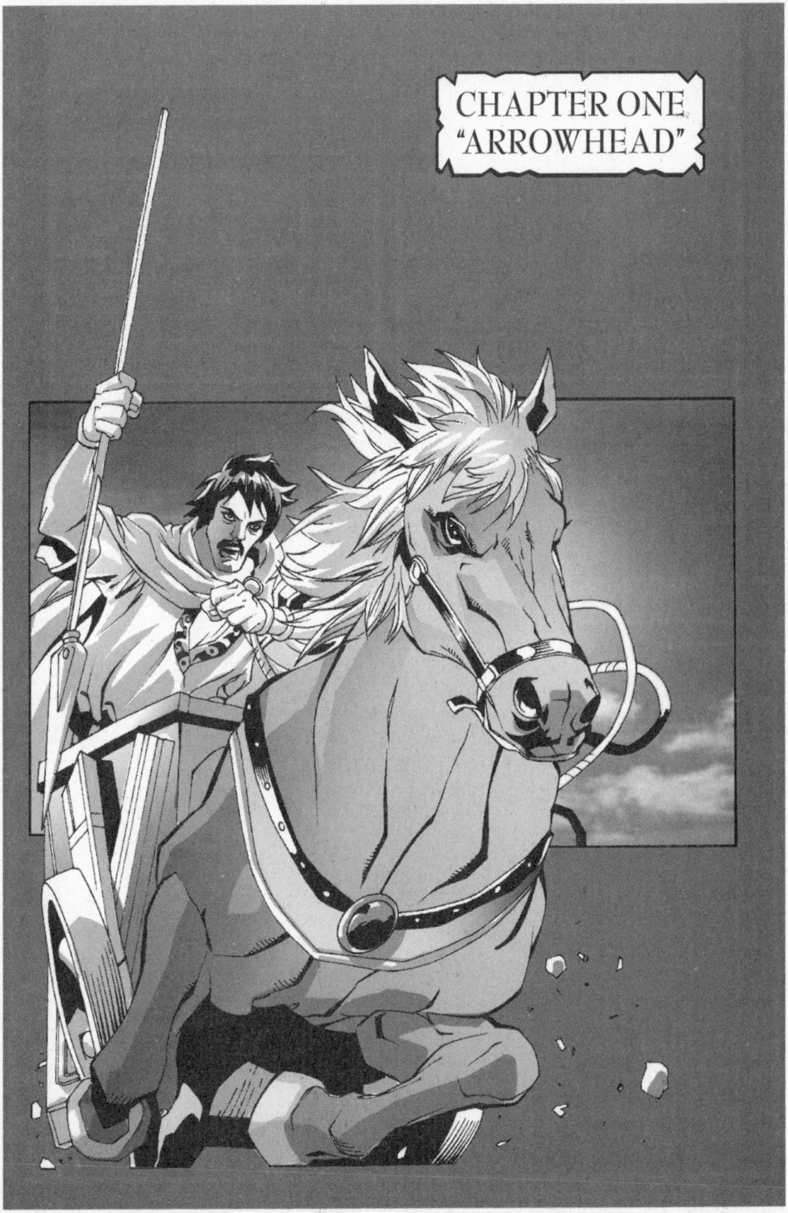
CHAPTER ONE
"ARROWHEAD"

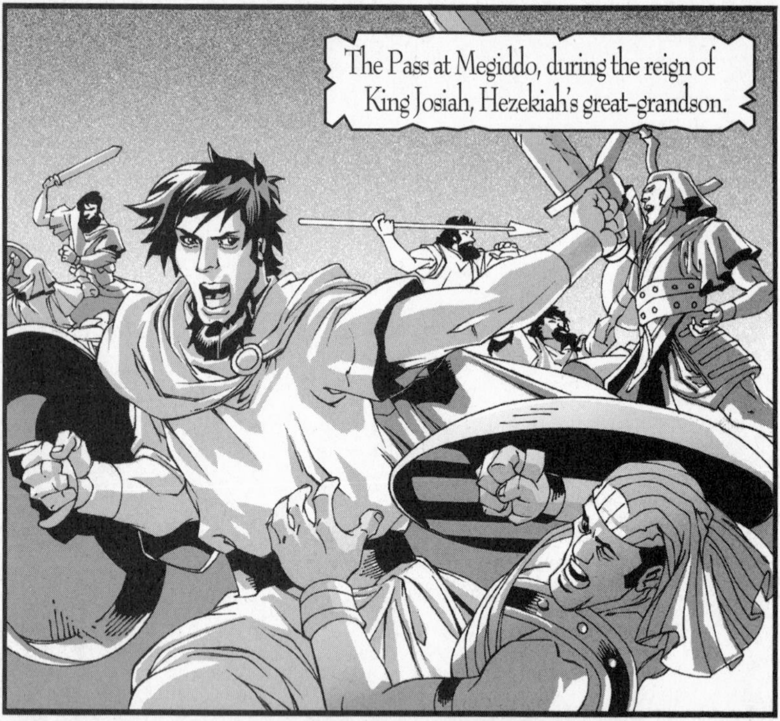
The Pass at Megiddo, during the reign of King Josiah, Hezekiah's great-grandson.

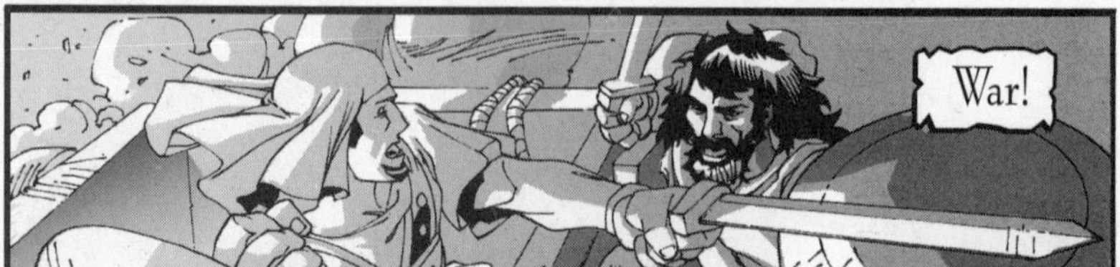
War!

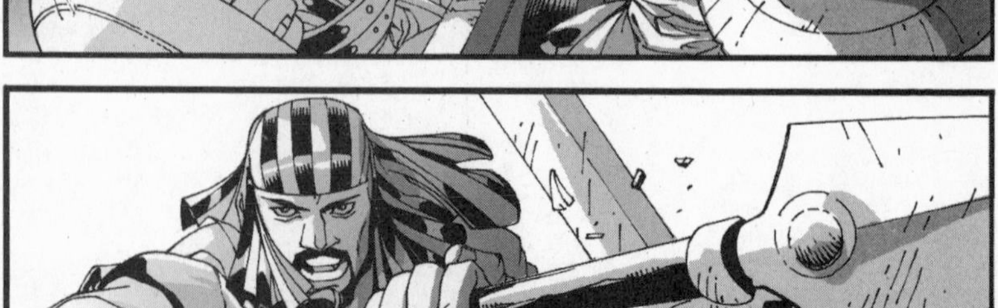

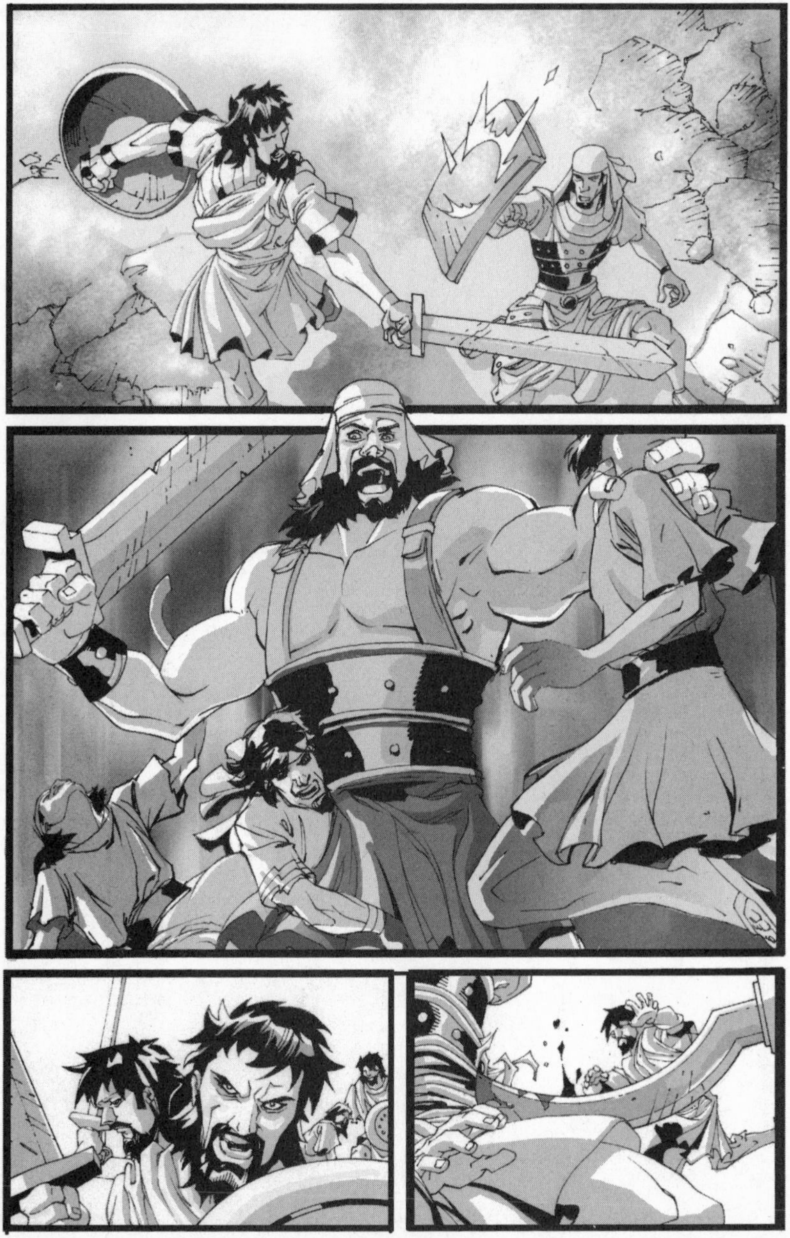

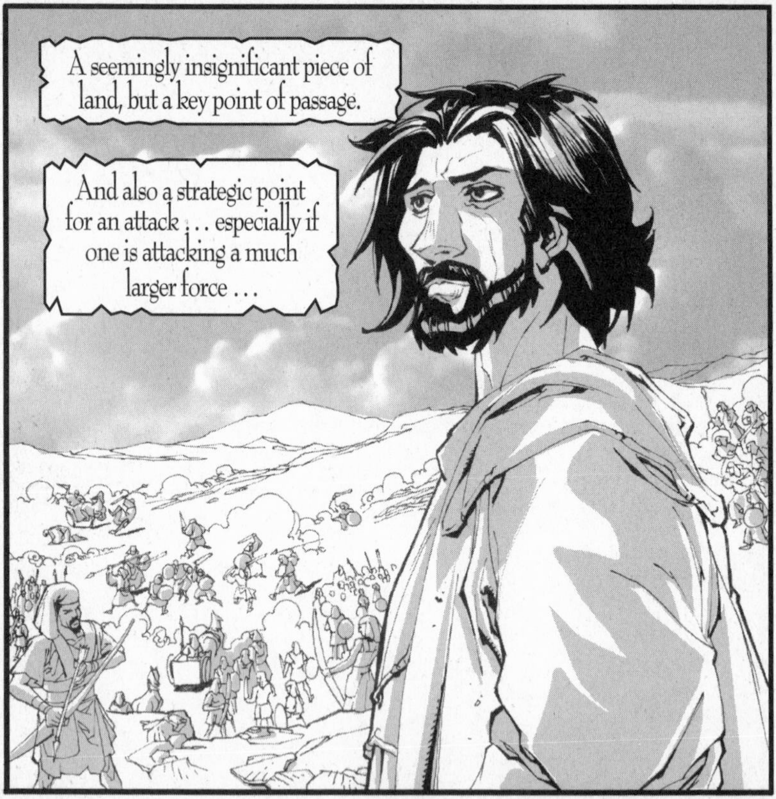
A seemingly insignificant piece of land, but a key point of passage.
And also a strategic point for an attack . . . especially if one is attacking a much larger force . . .

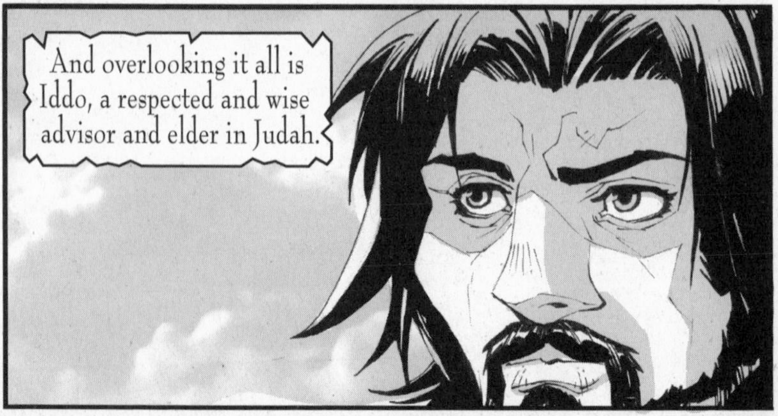
And overlooking it all is Iddo, a respected and wise advisor and elder in Judah.

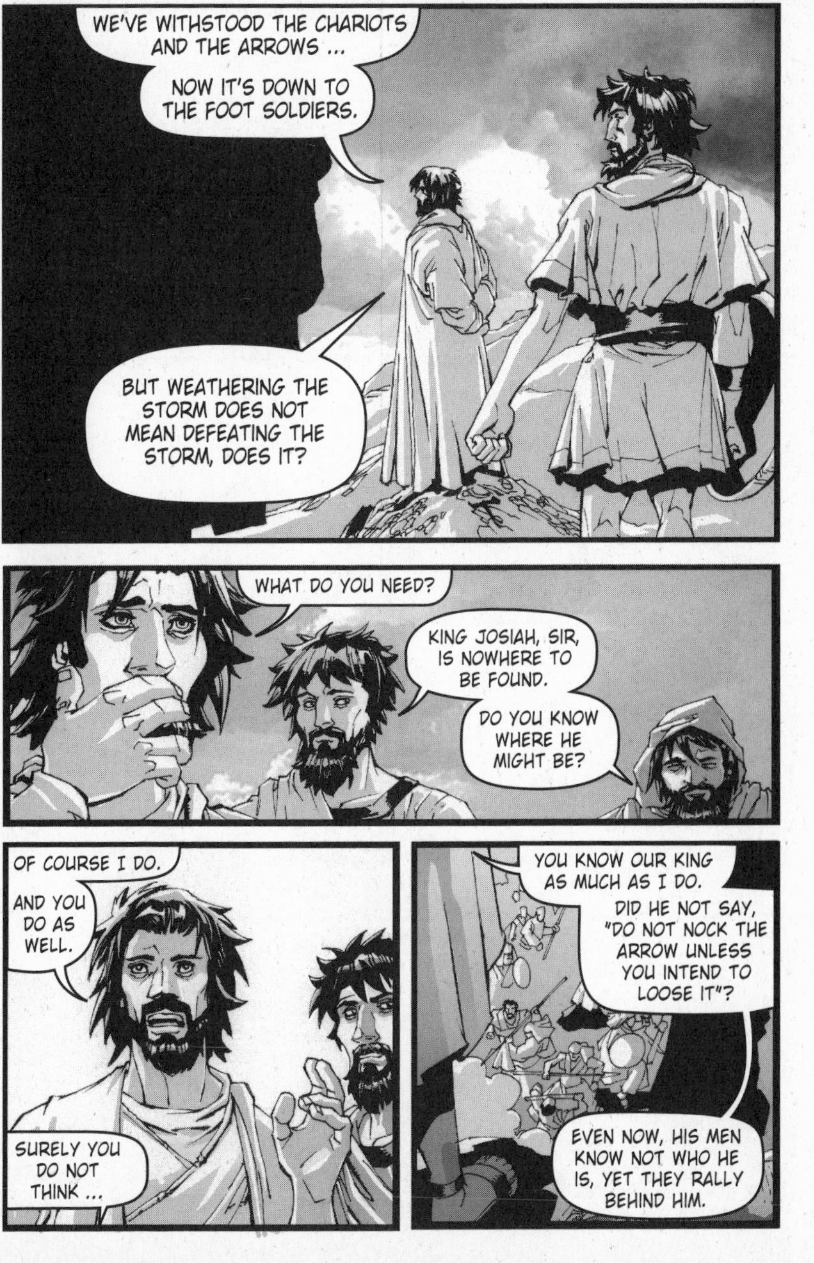
WE'VE WITHSTOOD THE CHARIOTS AND THE ARROWS ...
NOW IT'S DOWN TO THE FOOT SOLDIERS.
BUT WEATHERING THE STORM DOES NOT MEAN DEFEATING THE STORM, DOES IT?
WHAT DO YOU NEED?
KING JOSIAH, SIR, IS NOWHERE TO BE FOUND.
DO YOU KNOW WHERE HE MIGHT BE?
OF COURSE I DO.
AND YOU DO AS WELL.
SURELY YOU DO NOT THINK ...
YOU KNOW OUR KING AS MUCH AS I DO.
DID HE NOT SAY, "DO NOT NOCK THE ARROW UNLESS YOU INTEND TO LOOSE IT"?
EVEN NOW, HIS MEN KNOW NOT WHO HE IS, YET THEY RALLY BEHIND HIM.

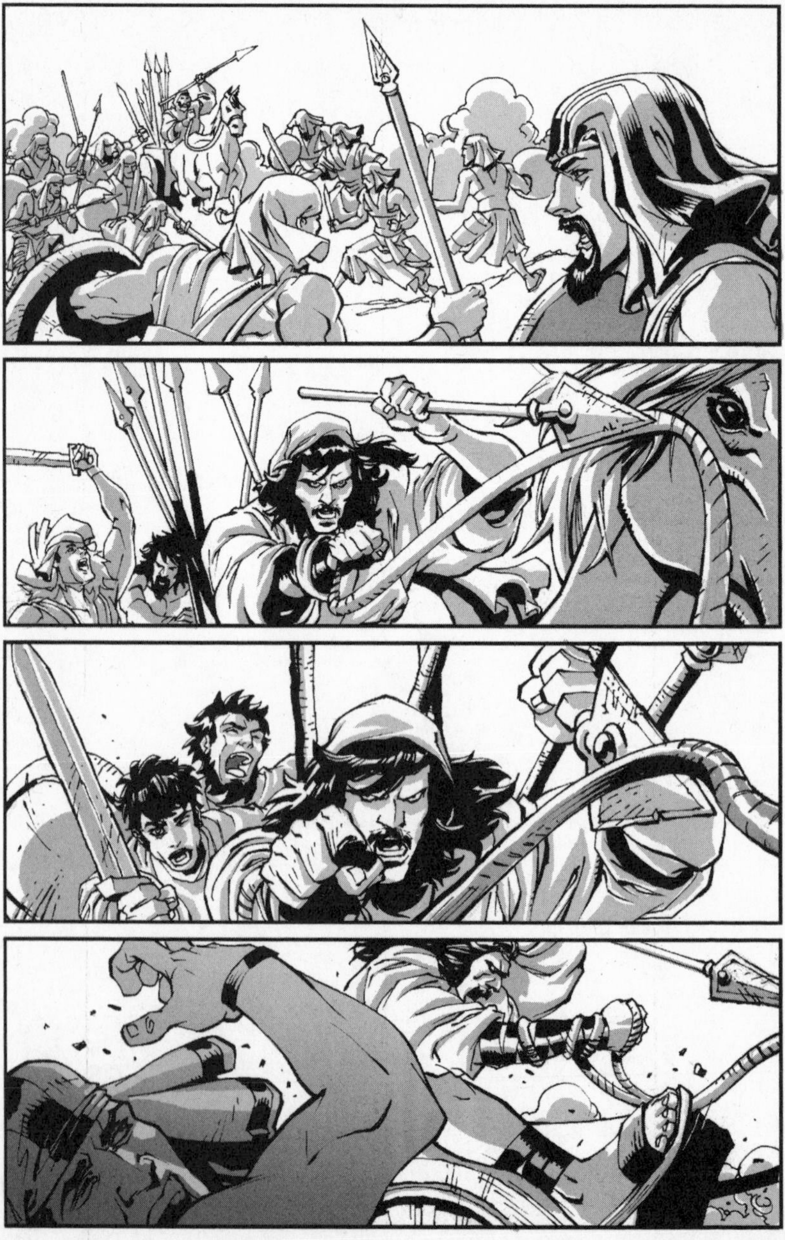

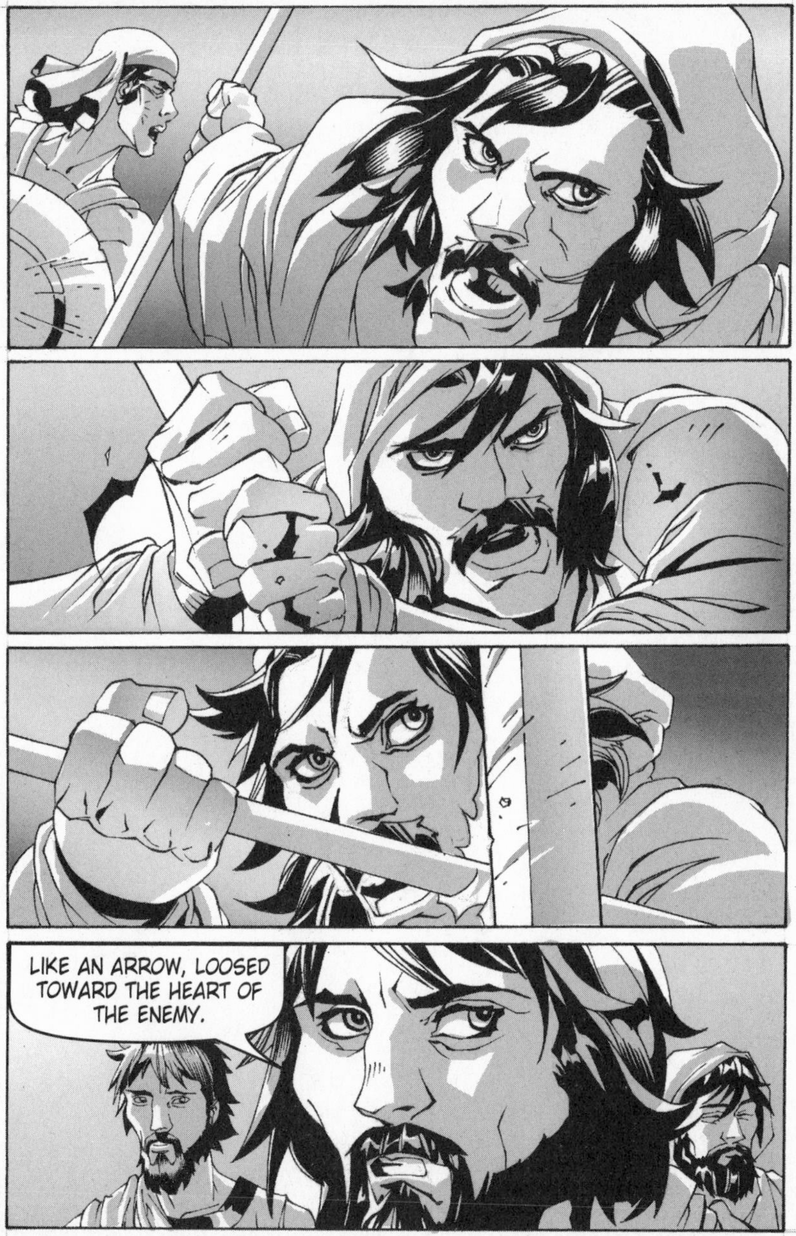
LIKE AN ARROW, LOOSED TOWARD THE HEART OF THE ENEMY.

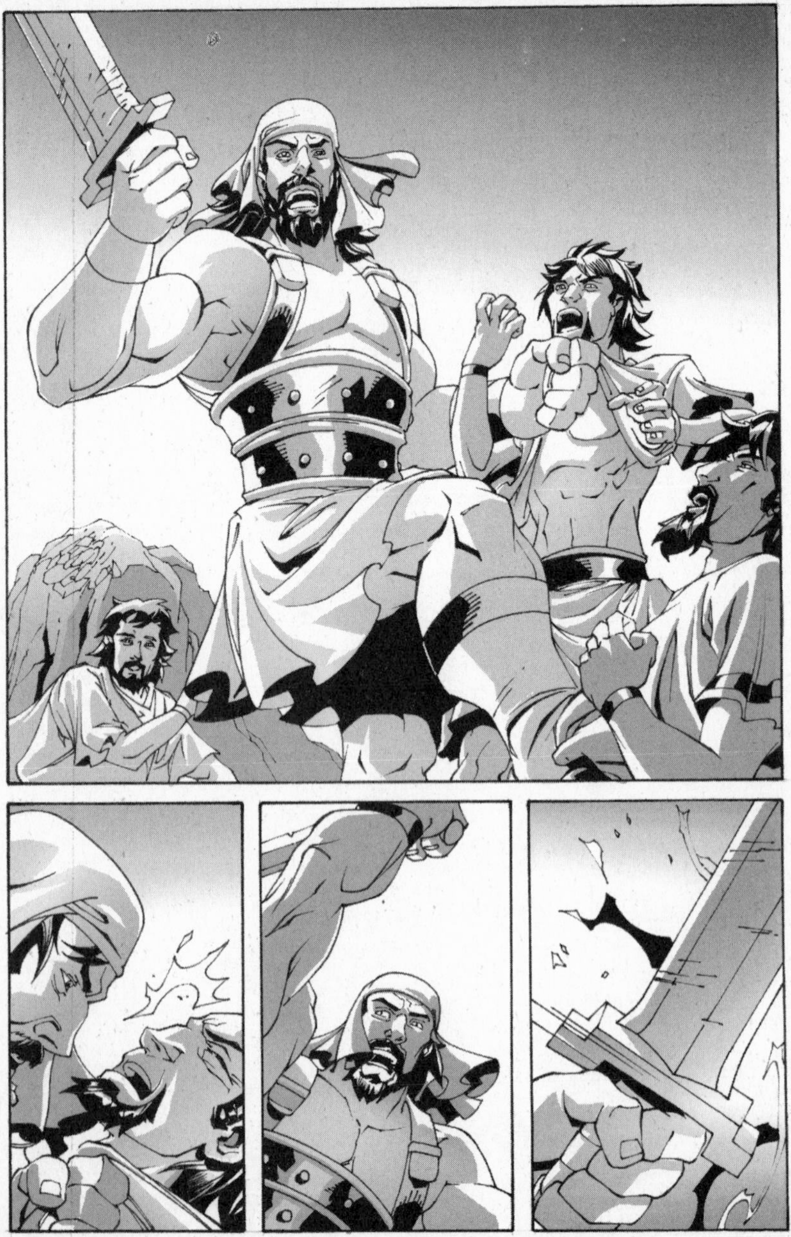

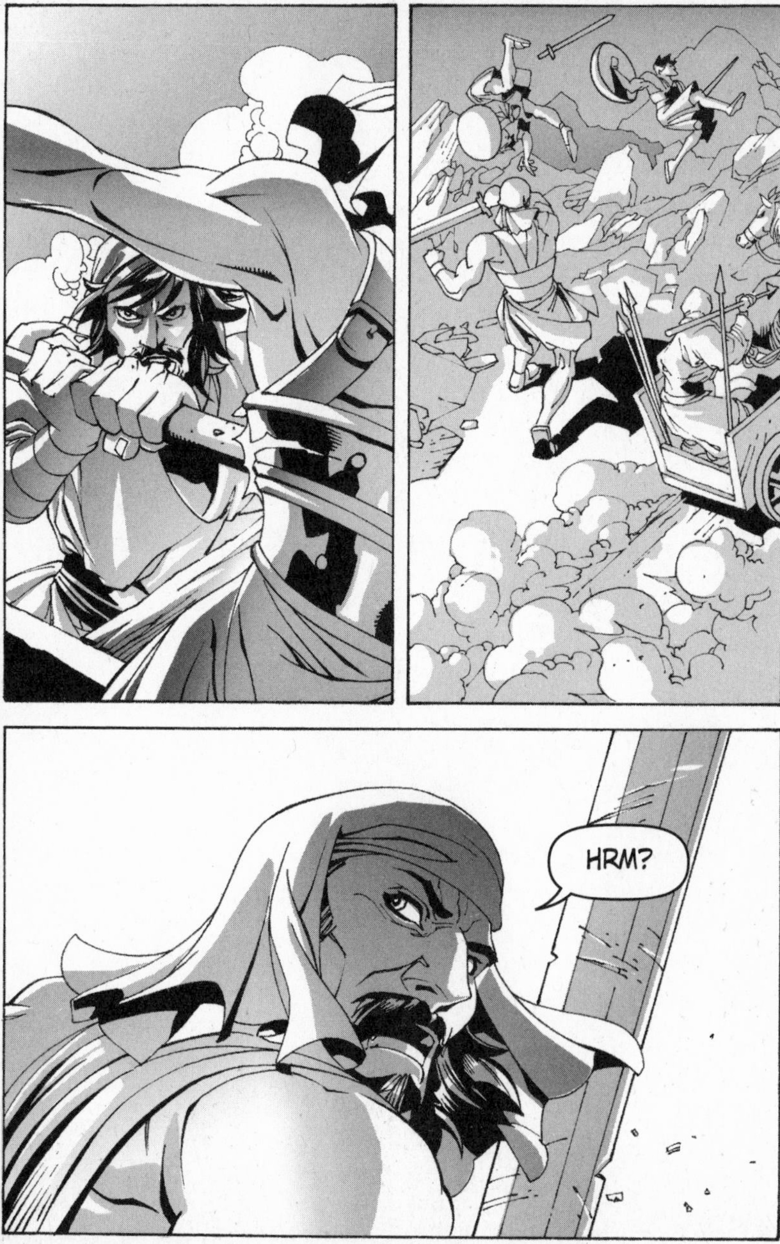
HRM?

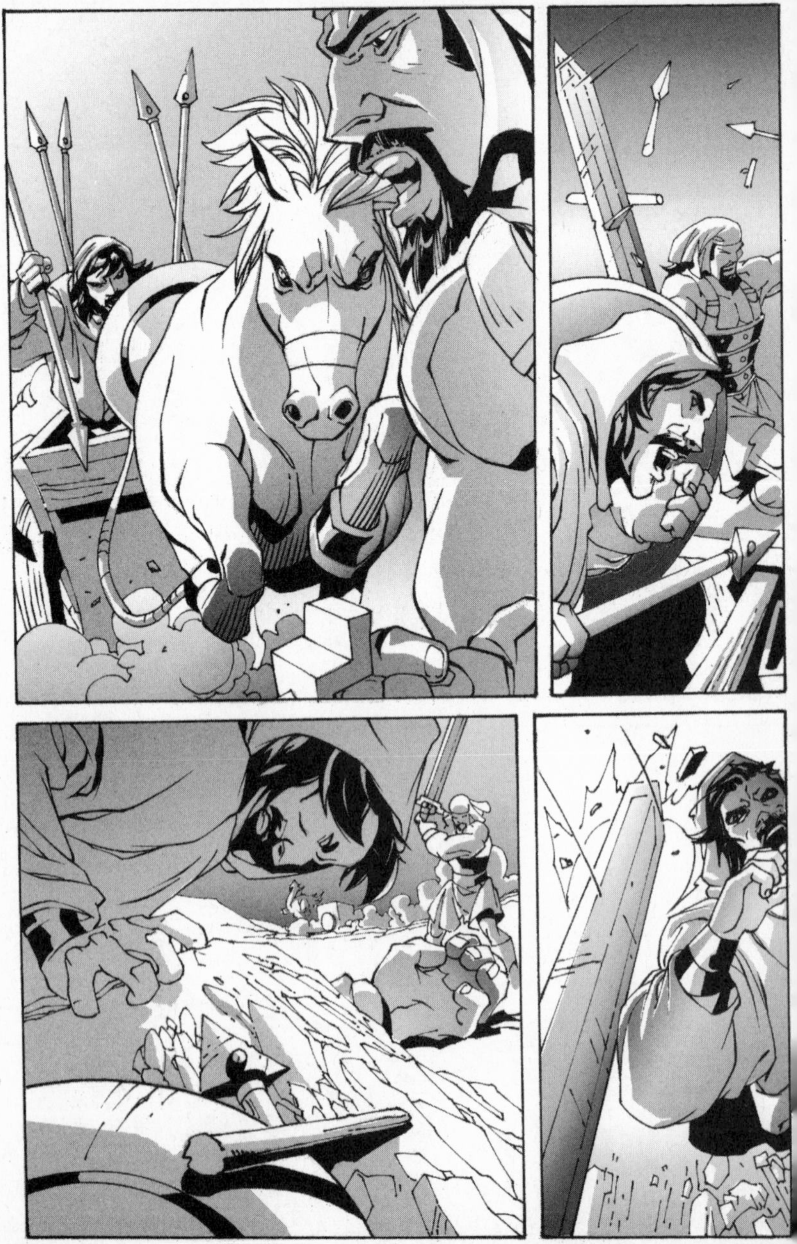

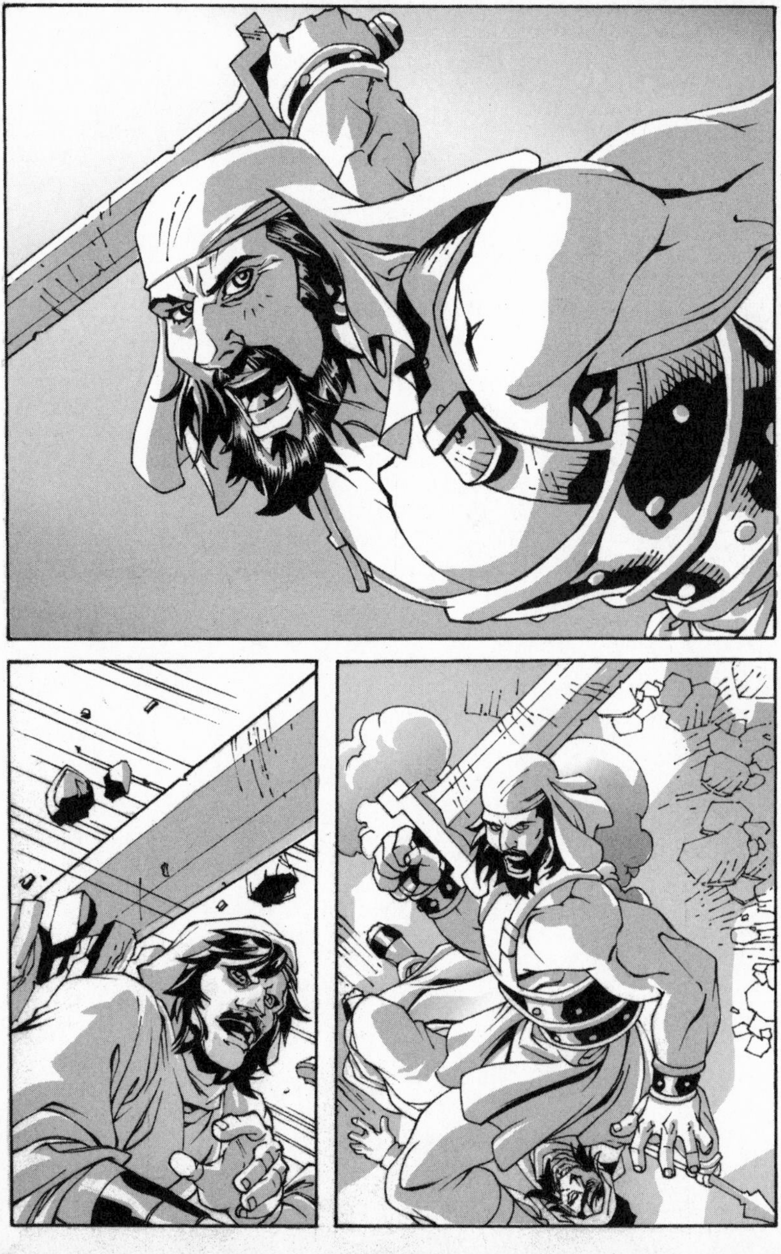

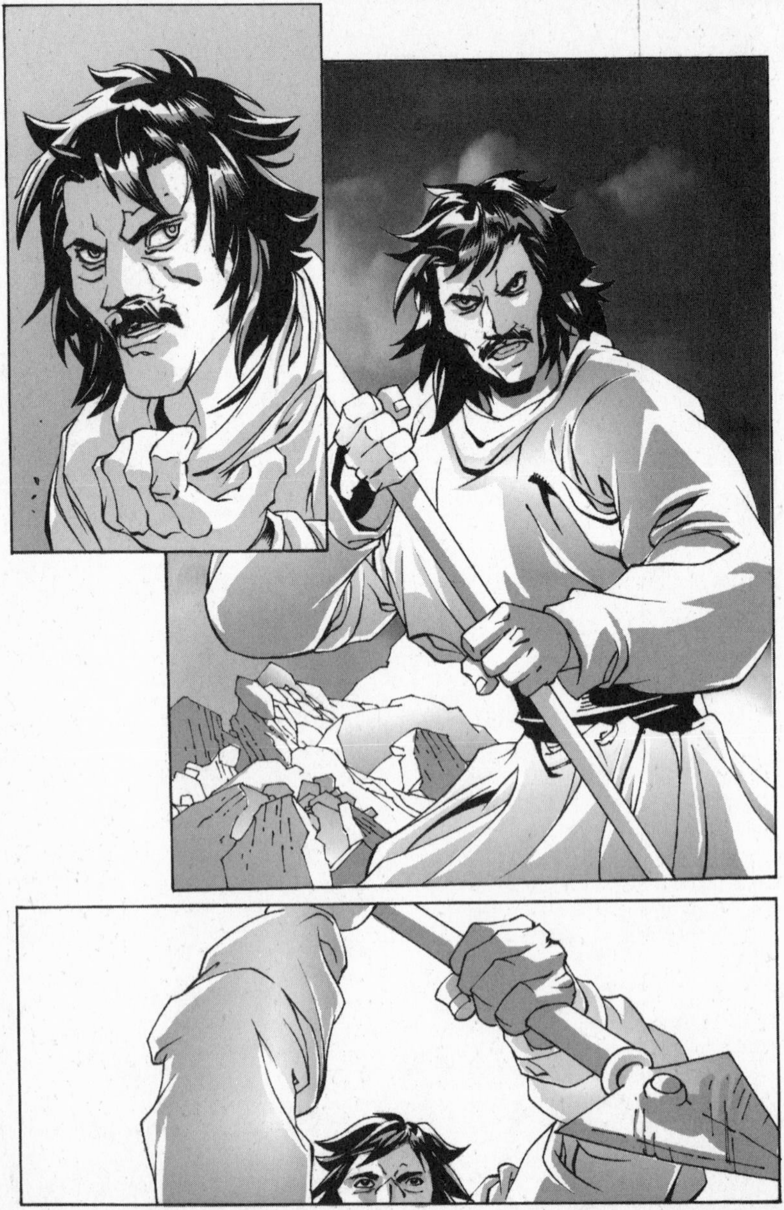

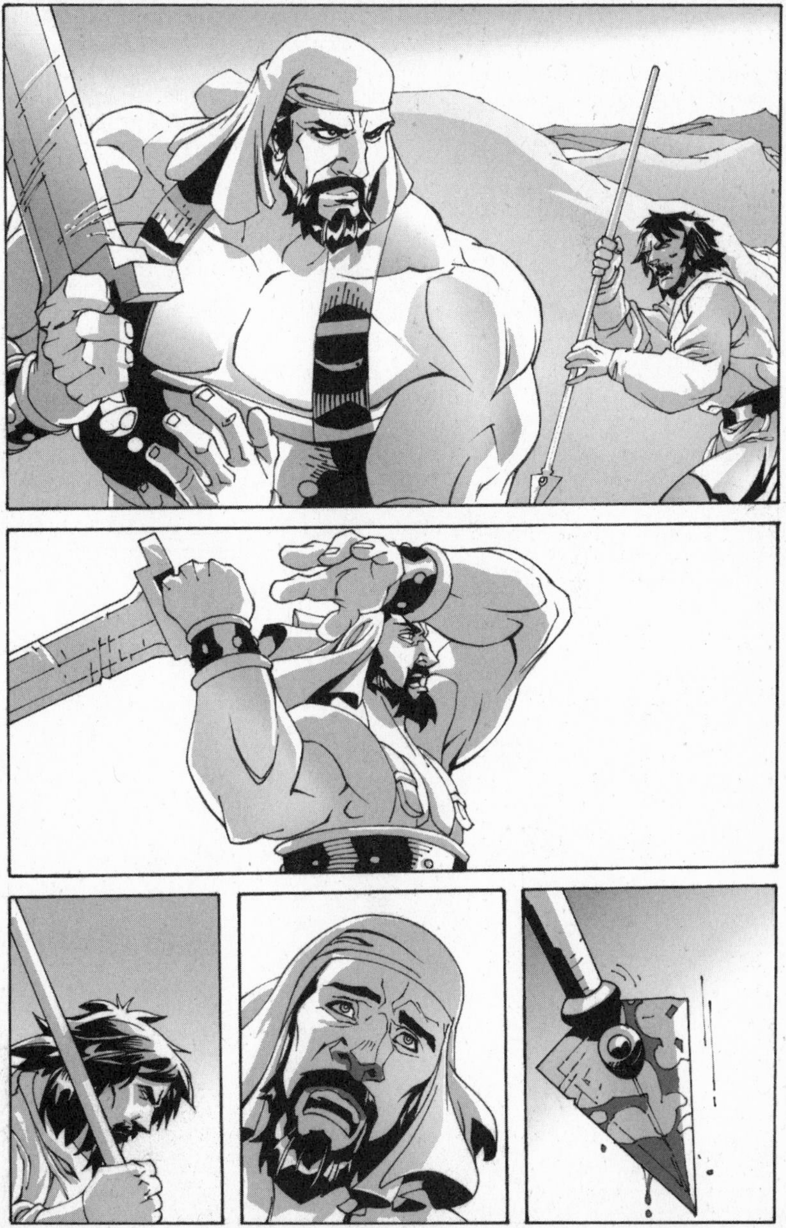

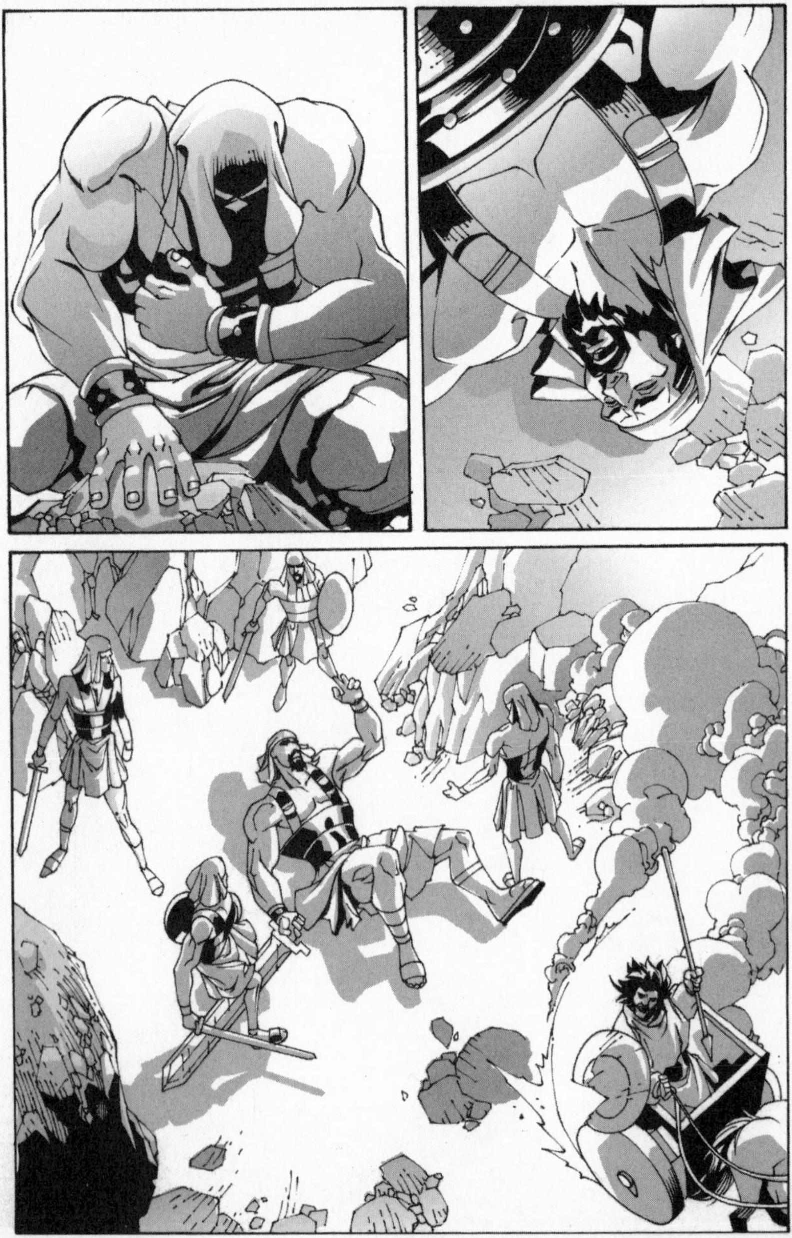

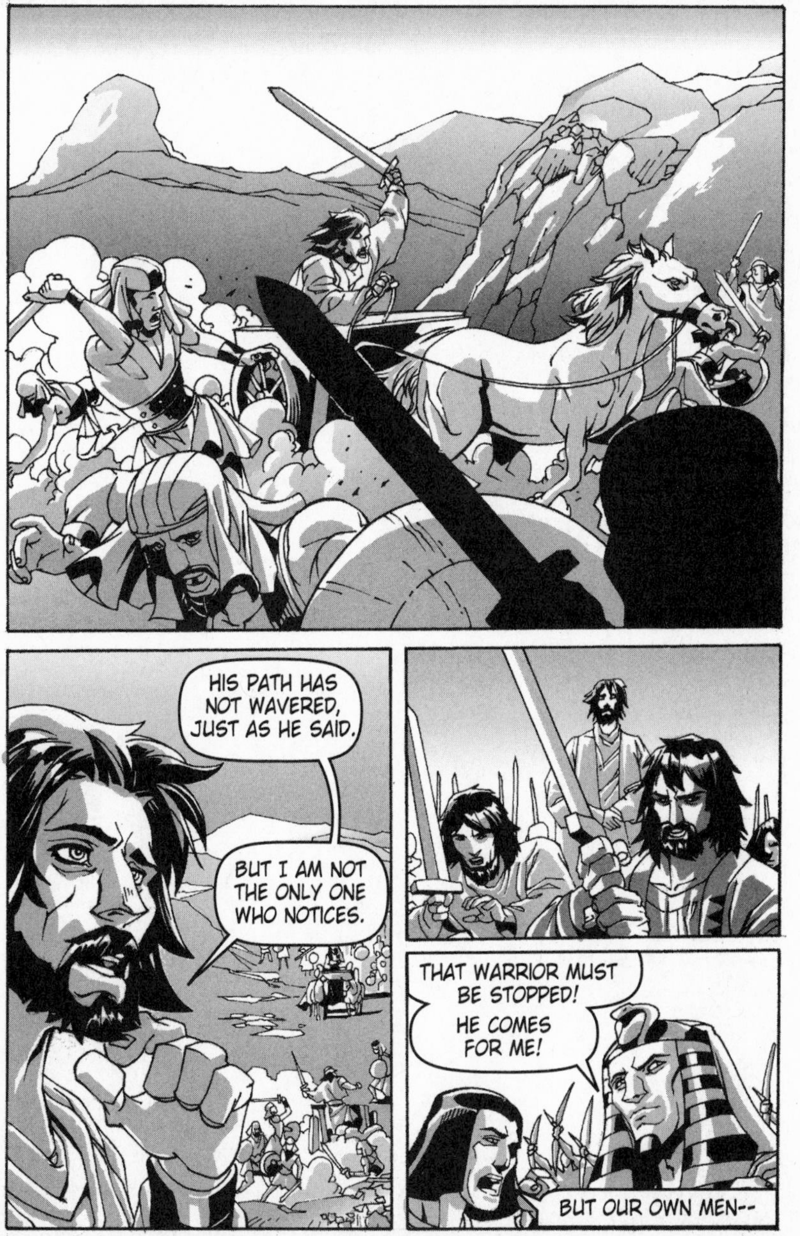
HIS PATH HAS NOT WAVERED, JUST AS HE SAID.
BUT I AM NOT THE ONLY ONE WHO NOTICES.
THAT WARRIOR MUST BE STOPPED!
HE COMES FOR ME!
BUT OUR OWN MEN--

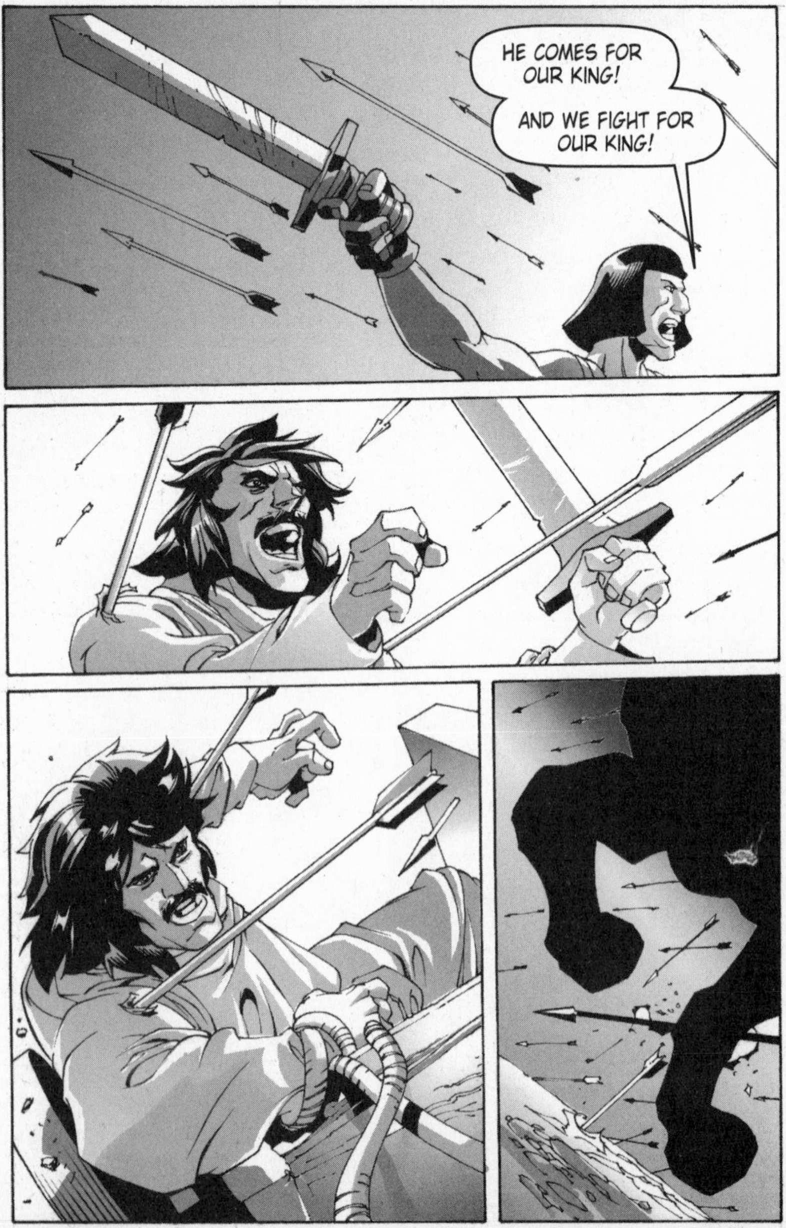
HE COMES FOR OUR KING!
AND WE FIGHT FOR OUR KING!

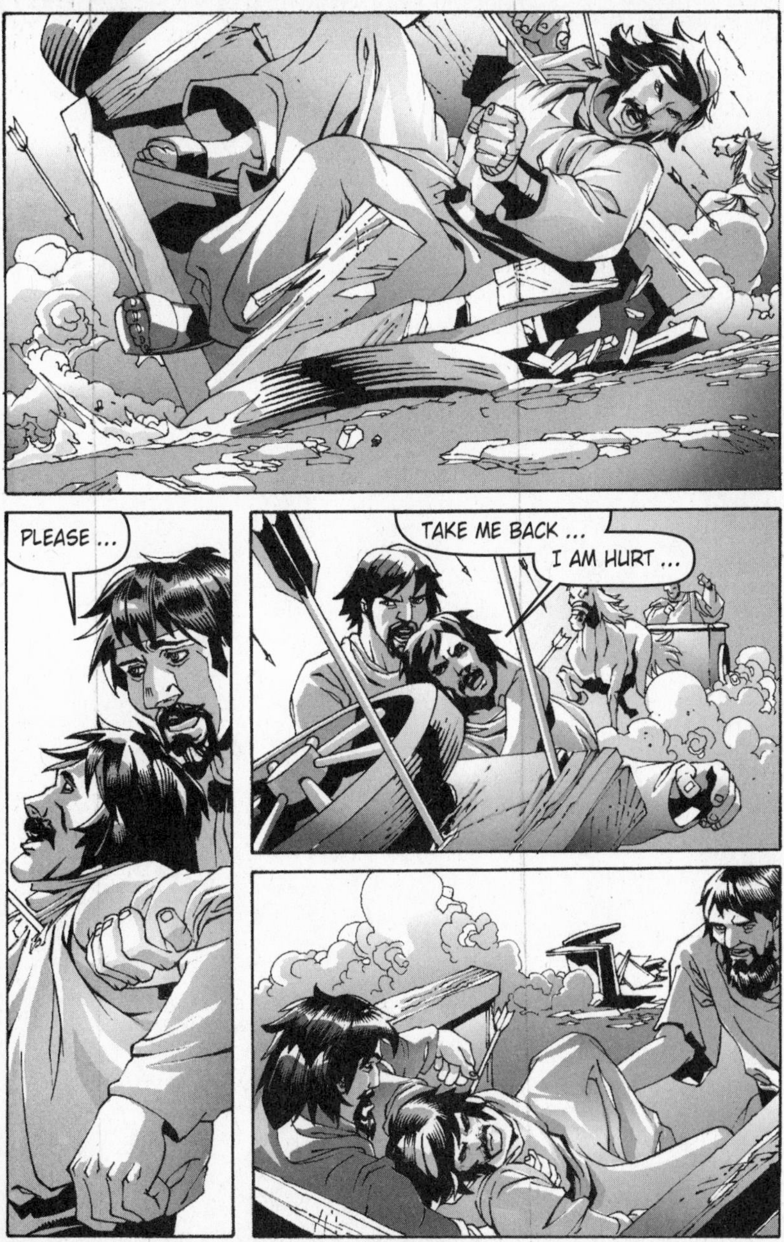
PLEASE ...
TAKE ME BACK ...
I AM HURT ...

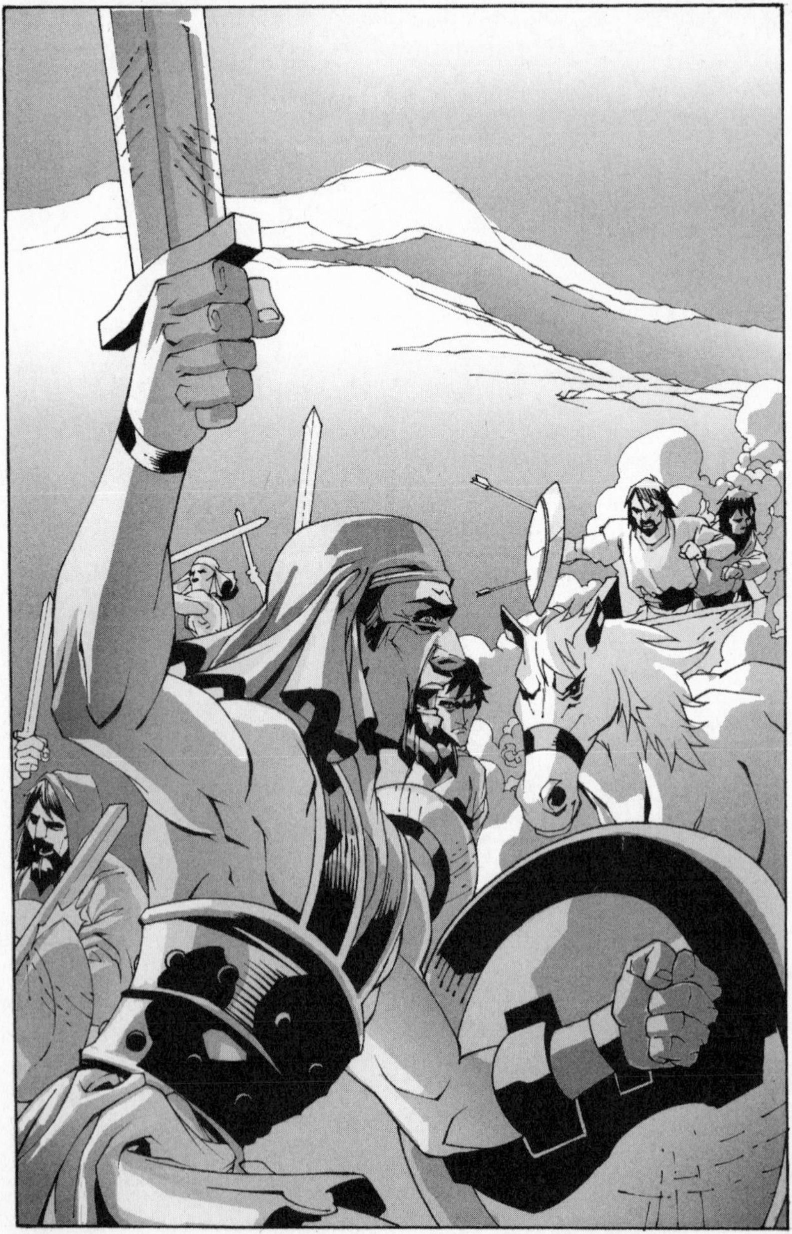

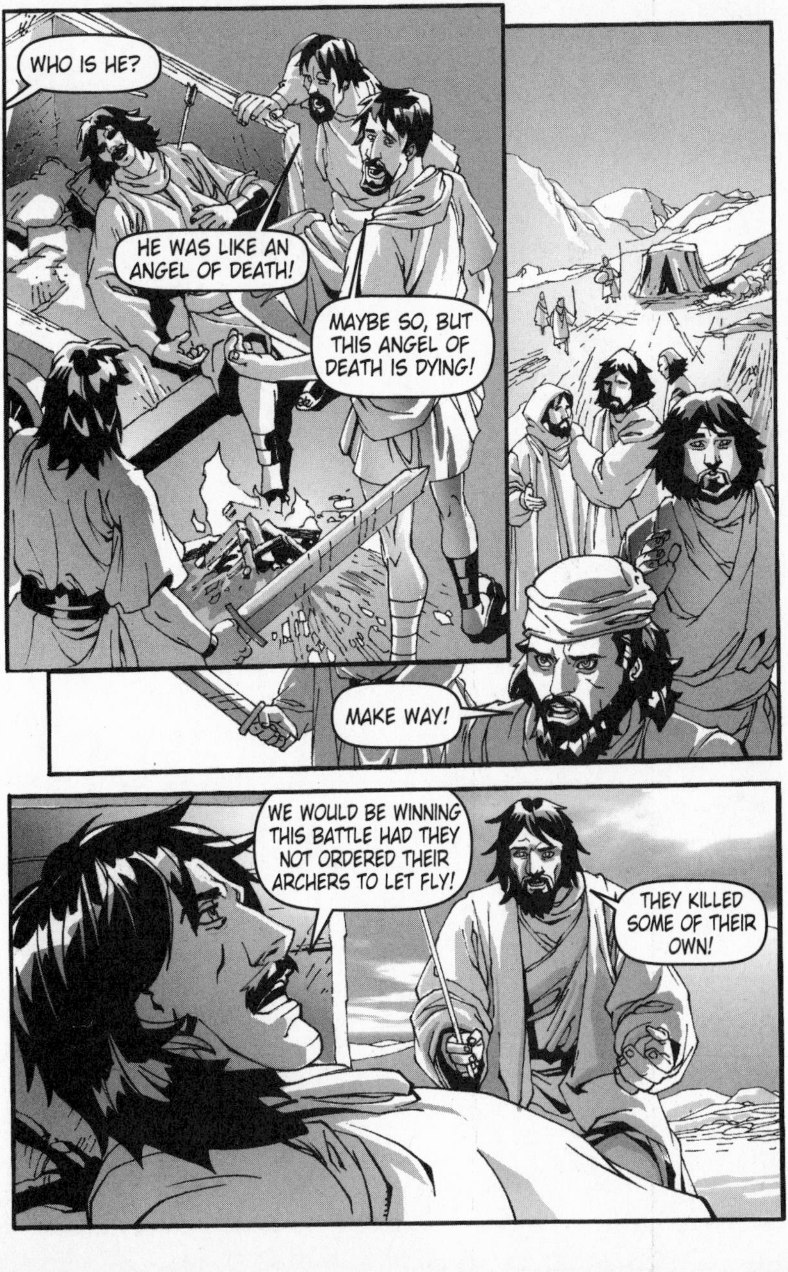
WHO IS HE?
HE WAS LIKE AN ANGEL OF DEATH!
MAYBE SO, BUT THIS ANGEL OF DEATH IS DYING!
MAKE WAY!
WE WOULD BE WINNING THIS BATTLE HAD THEY NOT ORDERED THEIR ARCHERS TO LET FLY!
THEY KILLED SOME OF THEIR OWN!

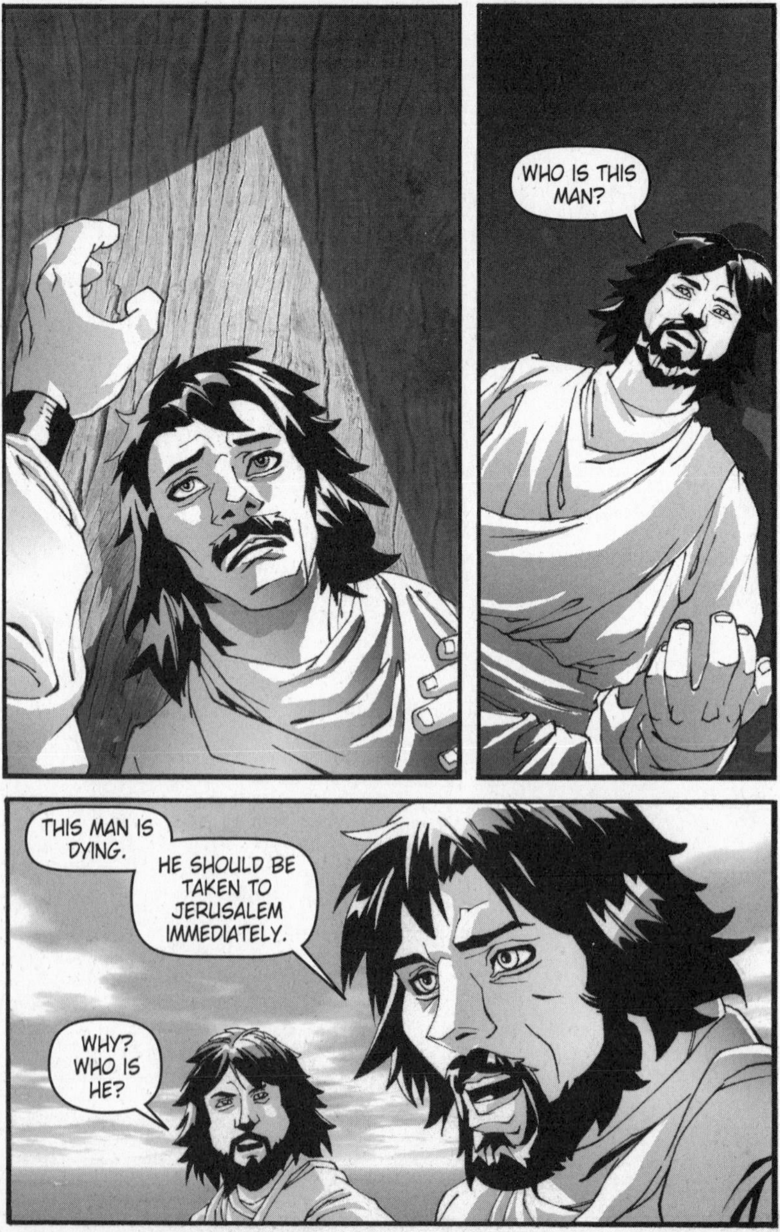
WHO IS THIS MAN?
THIS MAN IS DYING.
HE SHOULD BE TAKEN TO JERUSALEM IMMEDIATELY.
WHY? WHO IS HE?

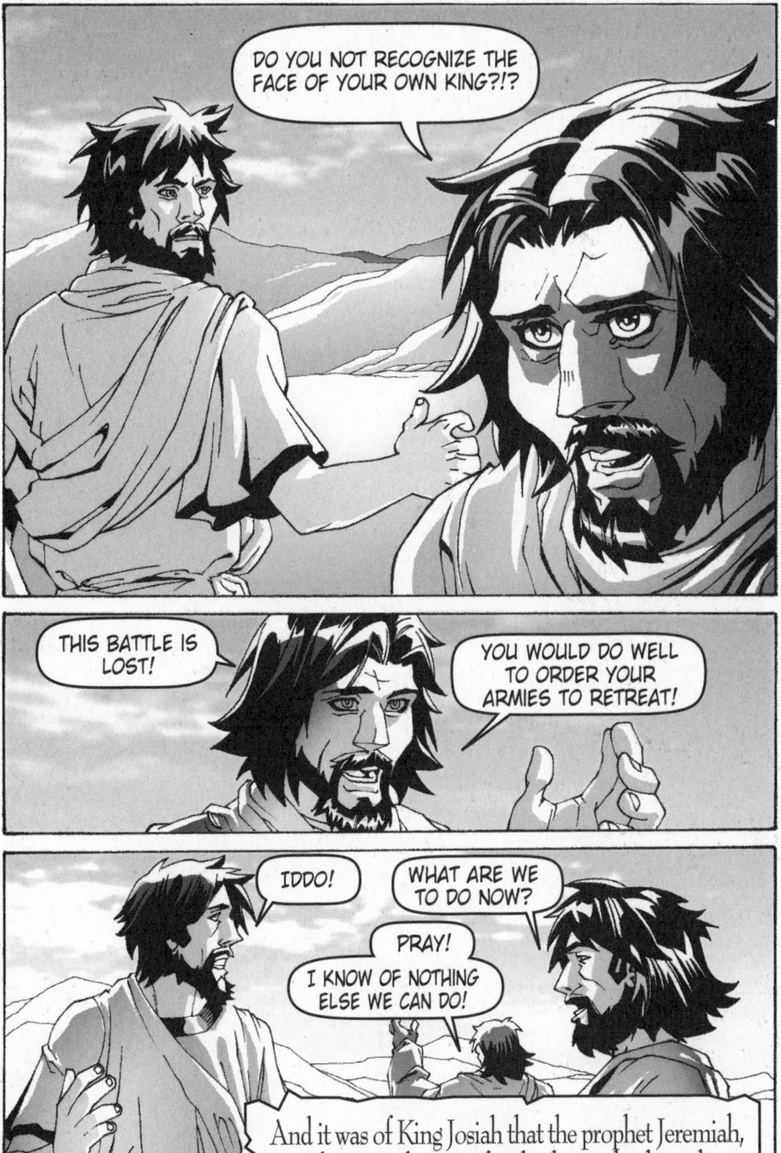
DO YOU NOT RECOGNIZE THE FACE OF YOUR OWN KING?!?
THIS BATTLE IS LOST!
YOU WOULD DO WELL TO ORDER YOUR ARMIES TO RETREAT!
IDDO!
WHAT ARE WE TO DO NOW?
PRAY!
I KNOW OF NOTHING ELSE WE CAN DO!
And it was of King Josiah that the prophet Jeremiah, who wrote laments for this king's death, said:

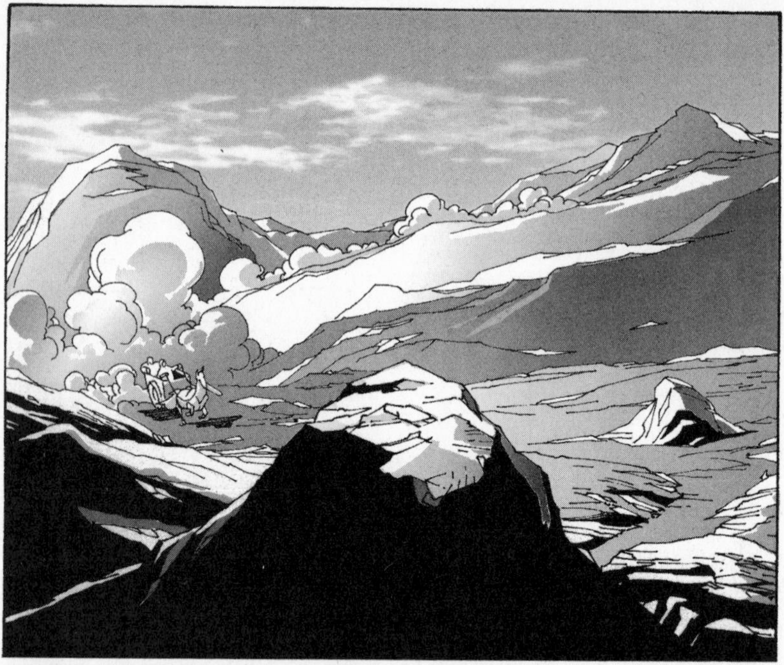
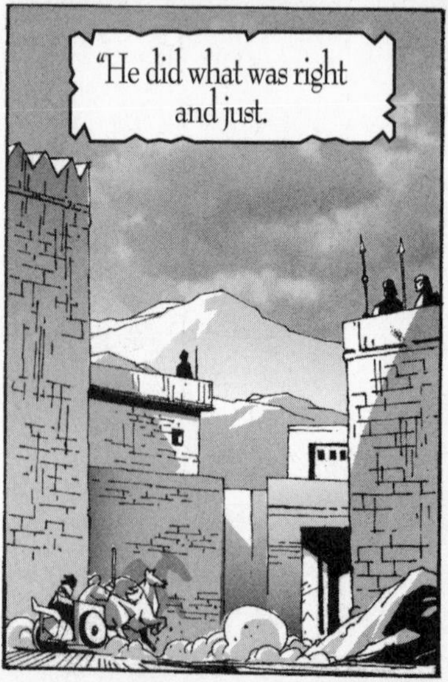
"He did what was right and just.
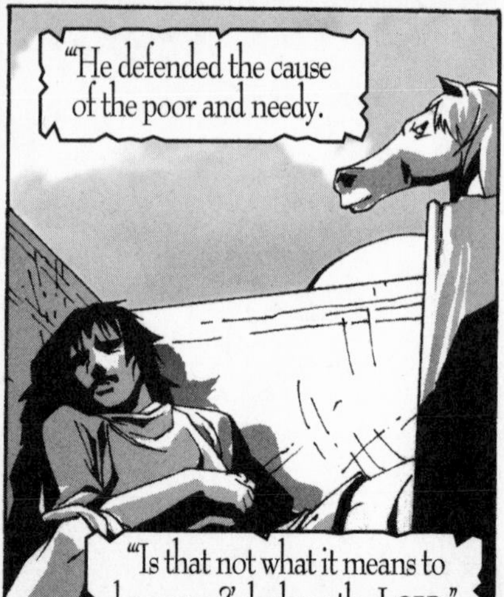
"'He defended the cause of the poor and needy.
"'Is that not what it means to know me?' declares the LORD."

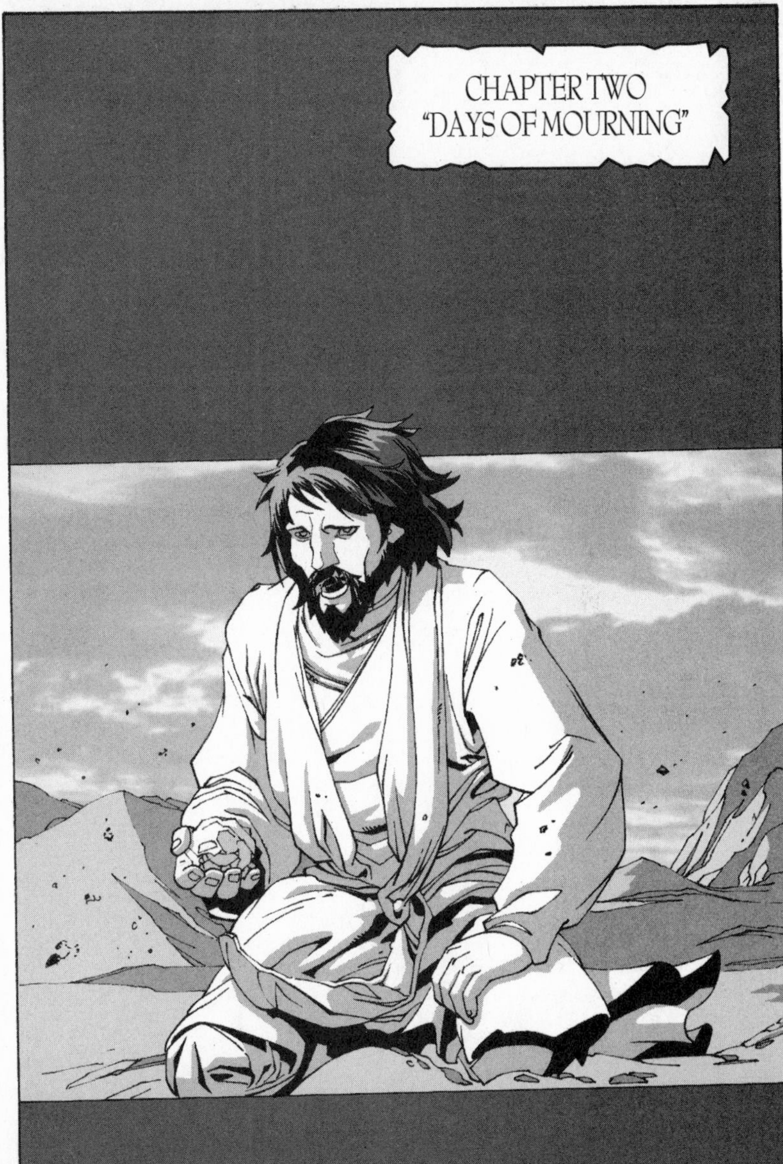
CHAPTER TWO
"DAYS OF MOURNING"

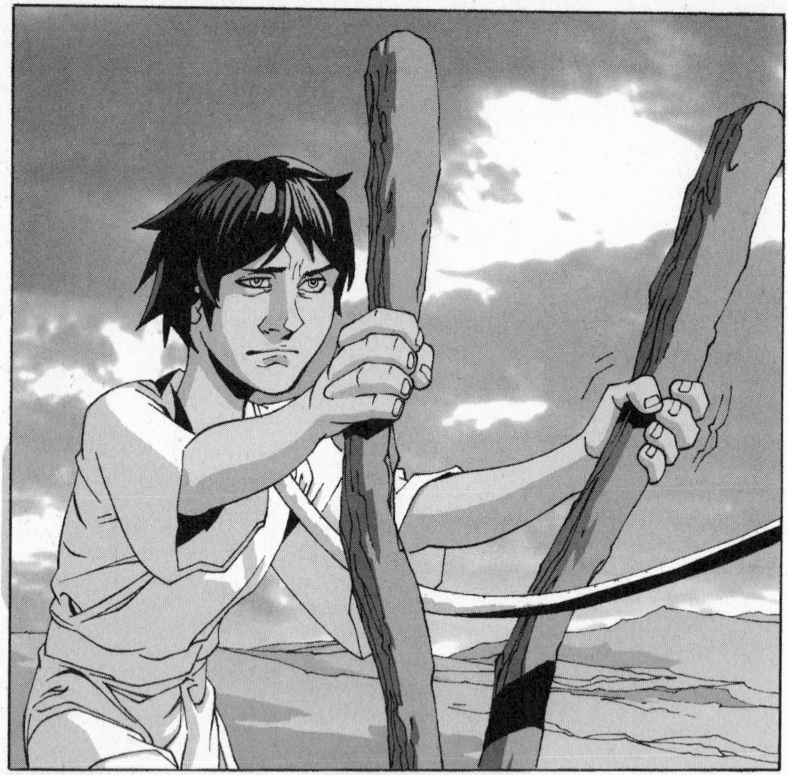
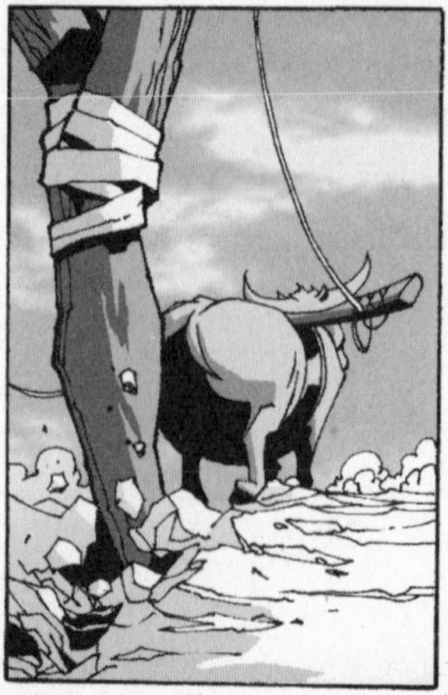
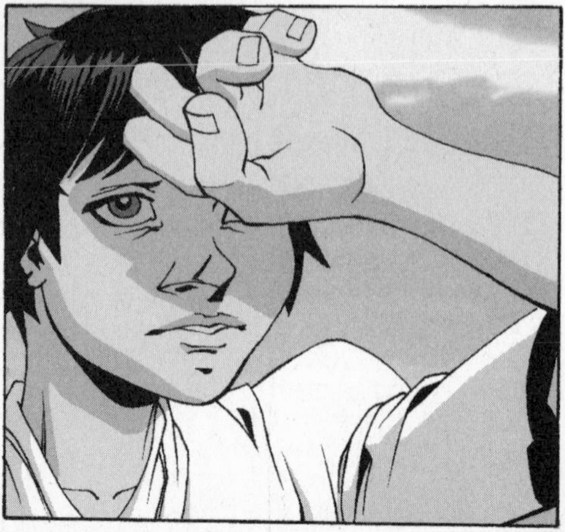

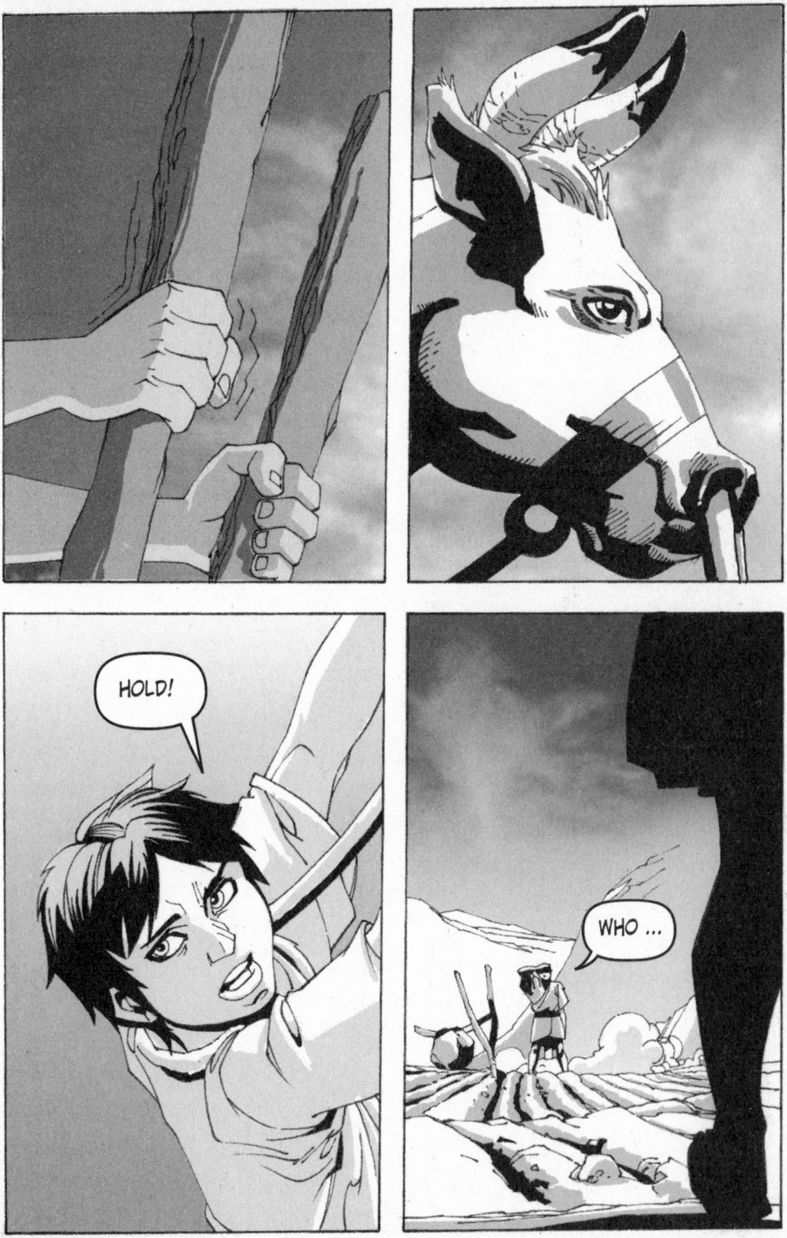
HOLD!
WHO ...

FATHER?

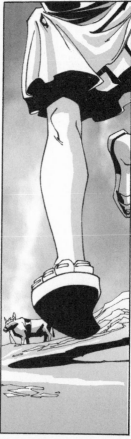

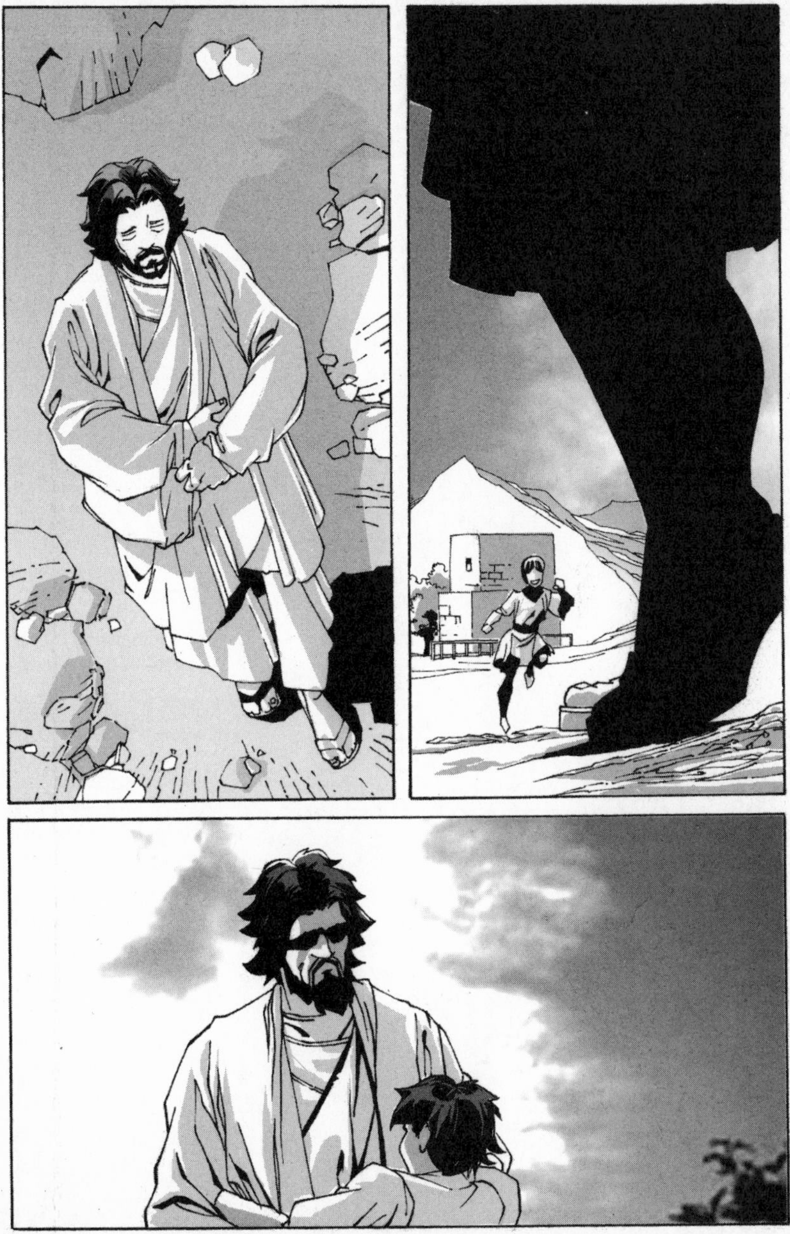

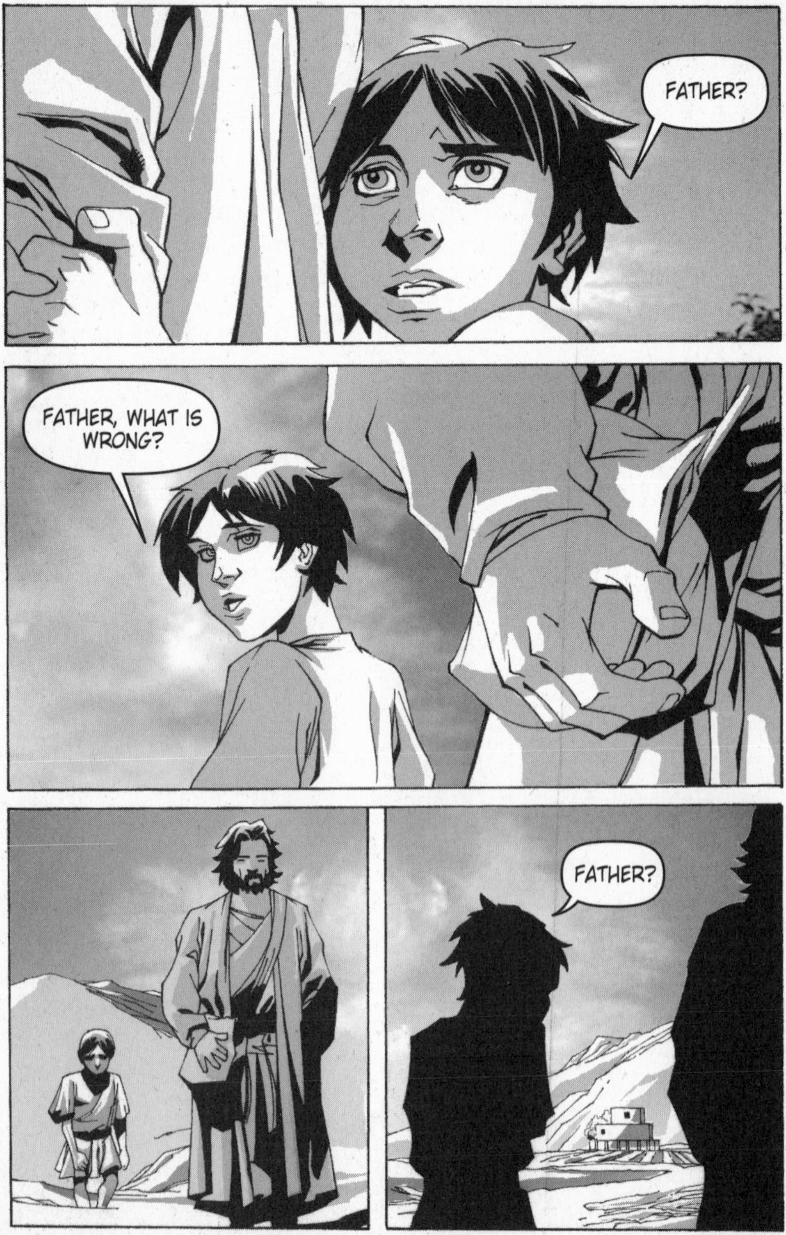
FATHER?
FATHER, WHAT IS WRONG?
FATHER?

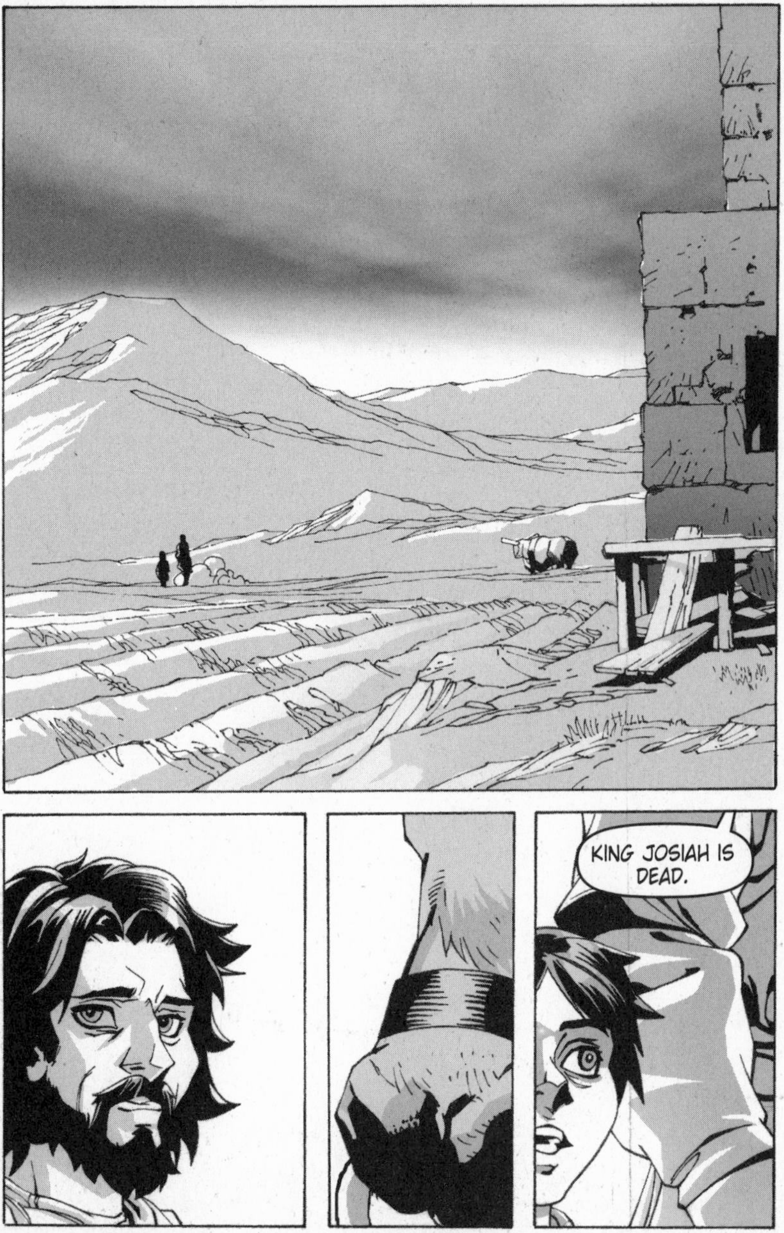
KING JOSIAH IS DEAD.

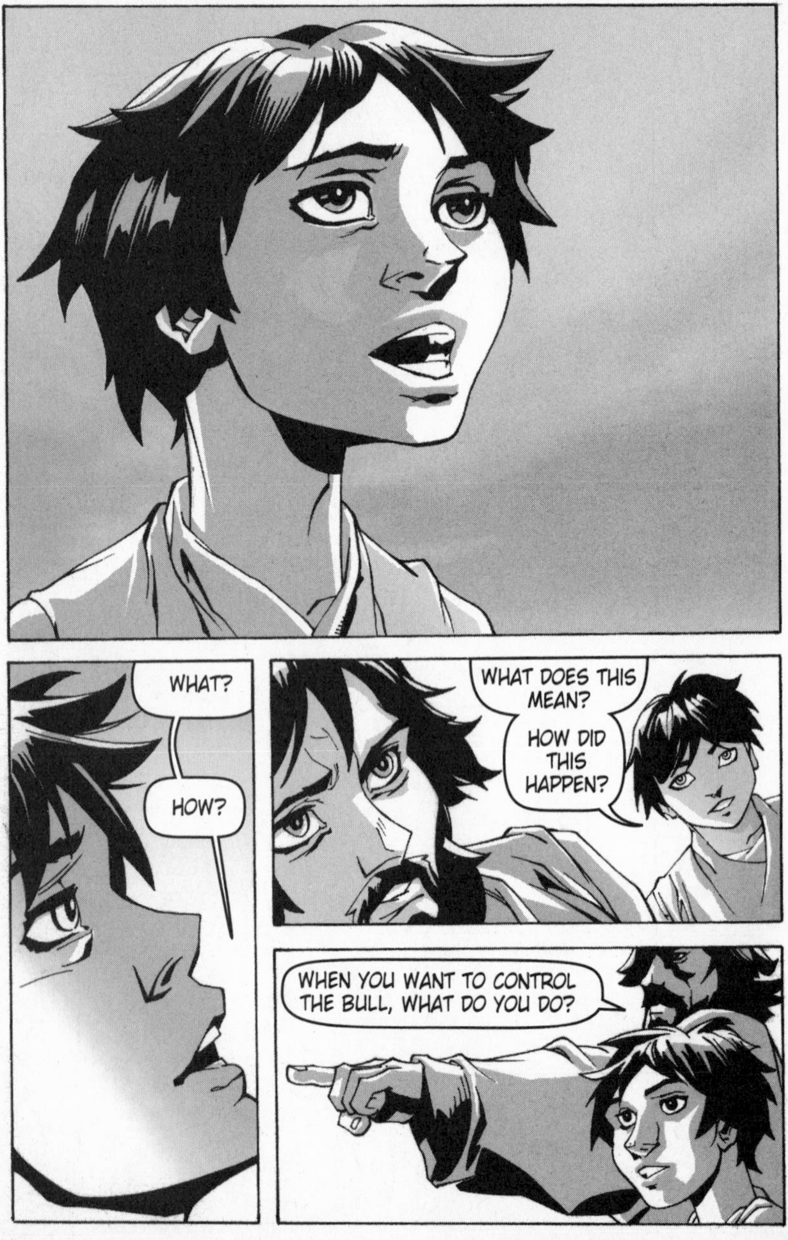
WHAT?
HOW?
WHAT DOES THIS MEAN?
HOW DID THIS HAPPEN?
WHEN YOU WANT TO CONTROL THE BULL, WHAT DO YOU DO?

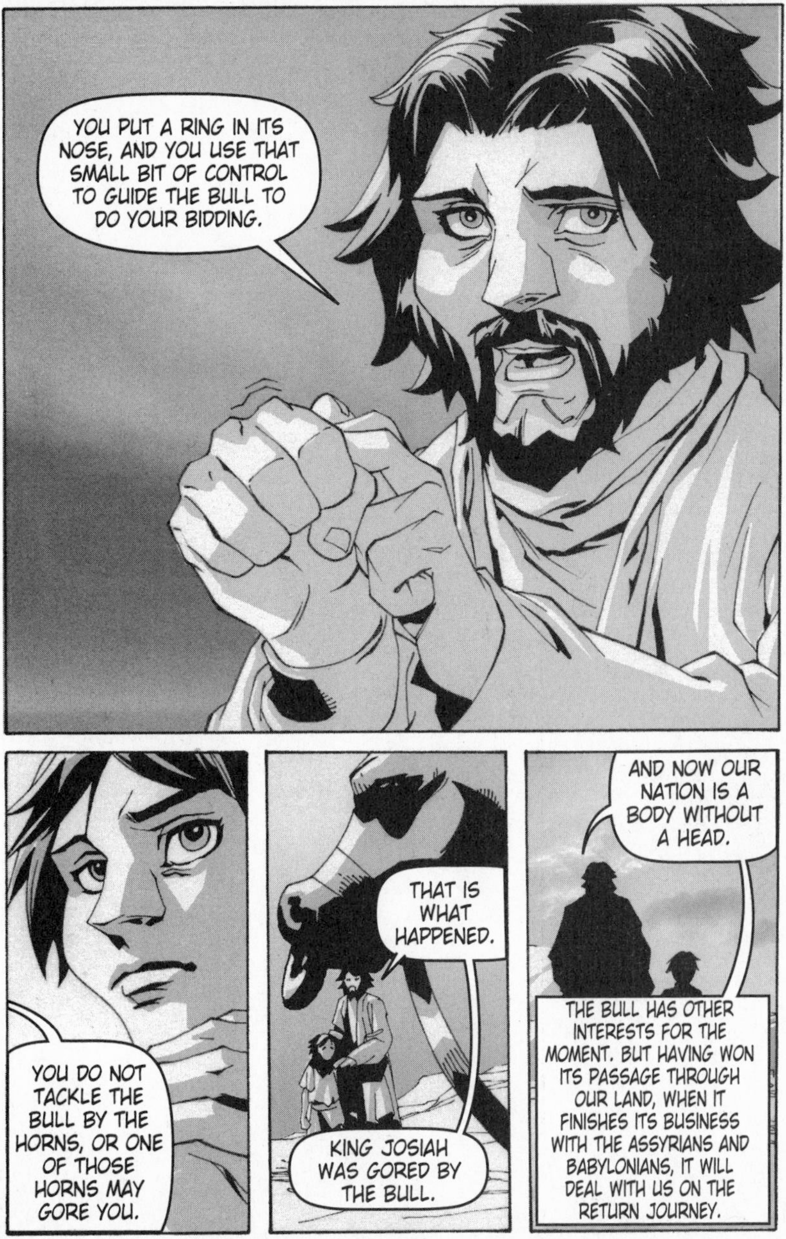
YOU PUT A RING IN ITS NOSE, AND YOU USE THAT SMALL BIT OF CONTROL TO GUIDE THE BULL TO DO YOUR BIDDING.
YOU DO NOT TACKLE THE BULL BY THE HORNS, OR ONE OF THOSE HORNS MAY GORE YOU.
THAT IS WHAT HAPPENED.
KING JOSIAH WAS GORED BY THE BULL.
AND NOW OUR NATION IS A BODY WITHOUT A HEAD.
THE BULL HAS OTHER INTERESTS FOR THE MOMENT. BUT HAVING WON ITS PASSAGE THROUGH OUR LAND, WHEN IT FINISHES ITS BUSINESS WITH THE ASSYRIANS AND BABYLONIANS, IT WILL DEAL WITH US ON THE RETURN JOURNEY.

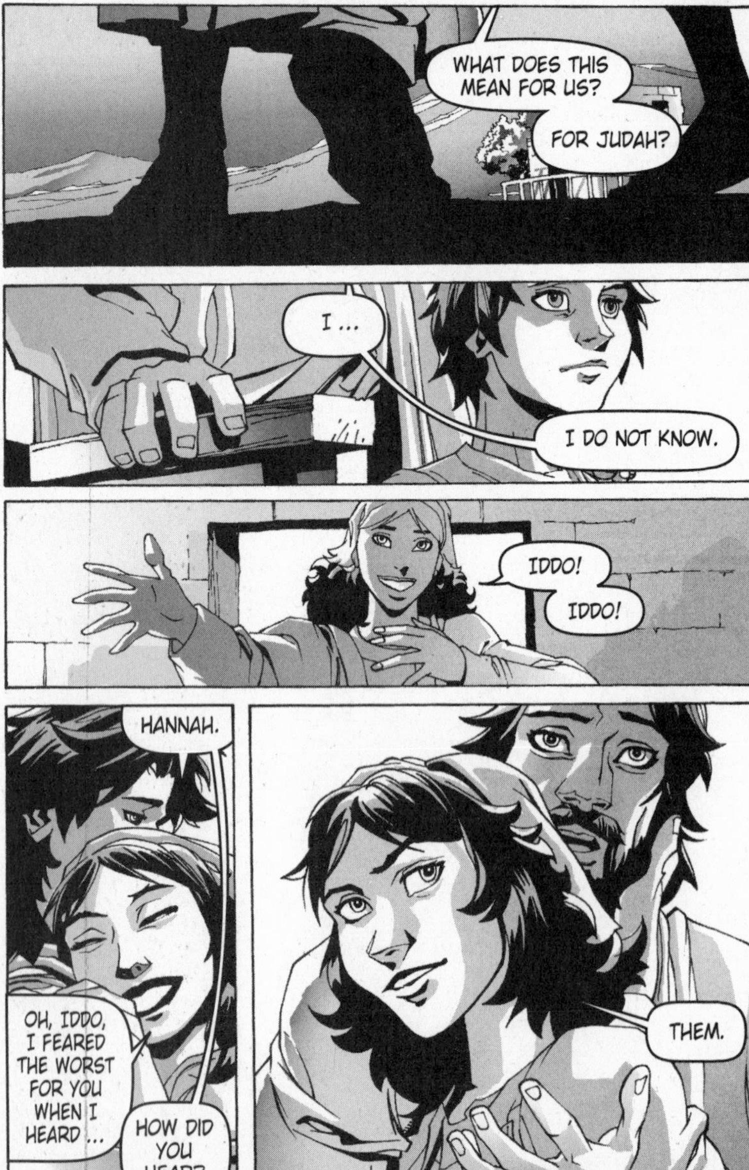

WHAT DOES THIS MEAN FOR US?
FOR JUDAH?
I ...
I DO NOT KNOW.
IDDO!
IDDO!
HANNAH.
OH, IDDO, I FEARED THE WORST FOR YOU WHEN I HEARD ...
HOW DID YOU HEAR?
THEM.

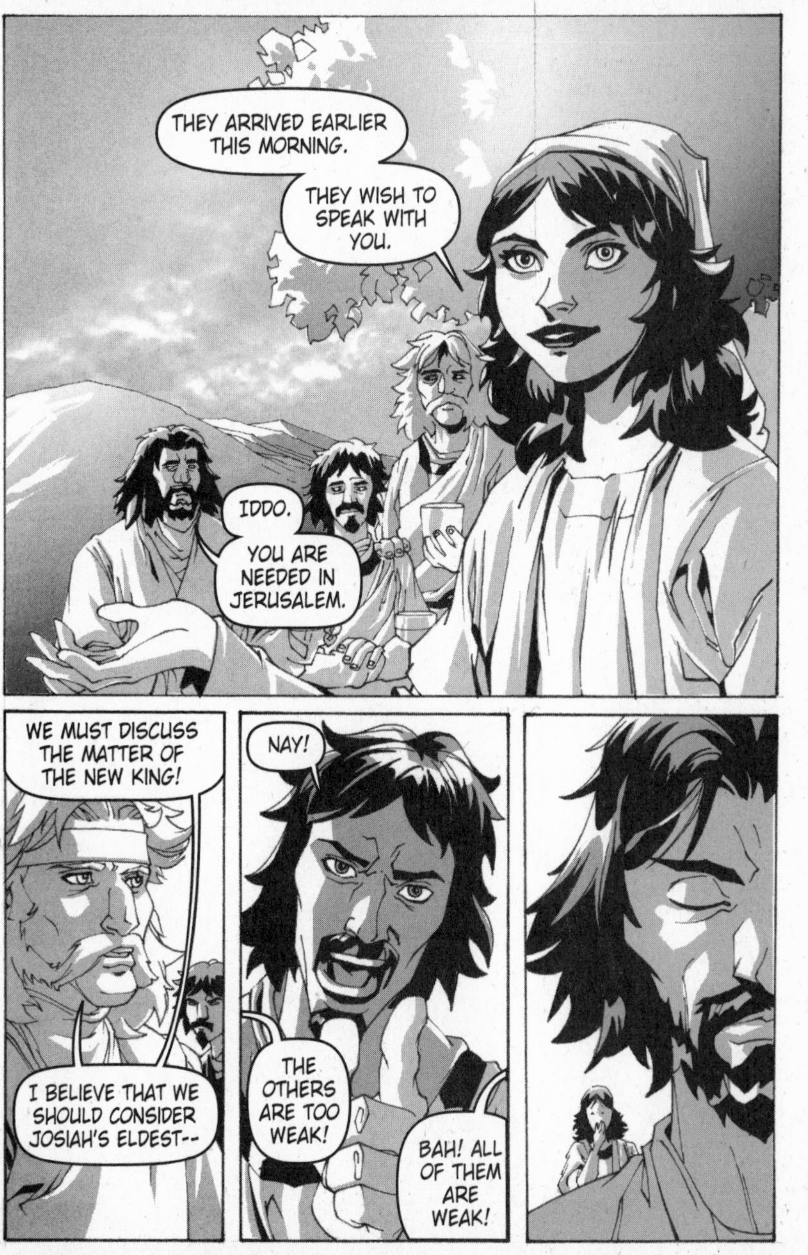
THEY ARRIVED EARLIER THIS MORNING.
THEY WISH TO SPEAK WITH YOU.
IDDO.
YOU ARE NEEDED IN JERUSALEM.
WE MUST DISCUSS THE MATTER OF THE NEW KING!
I BELIEVE THAT WE SHOULD CONSIDER JOSIAH'S ELDEST--
NAY!
THE OTHERS ARE TOO WEAK!
BAH! ALL OF THEM ARE WEAK!

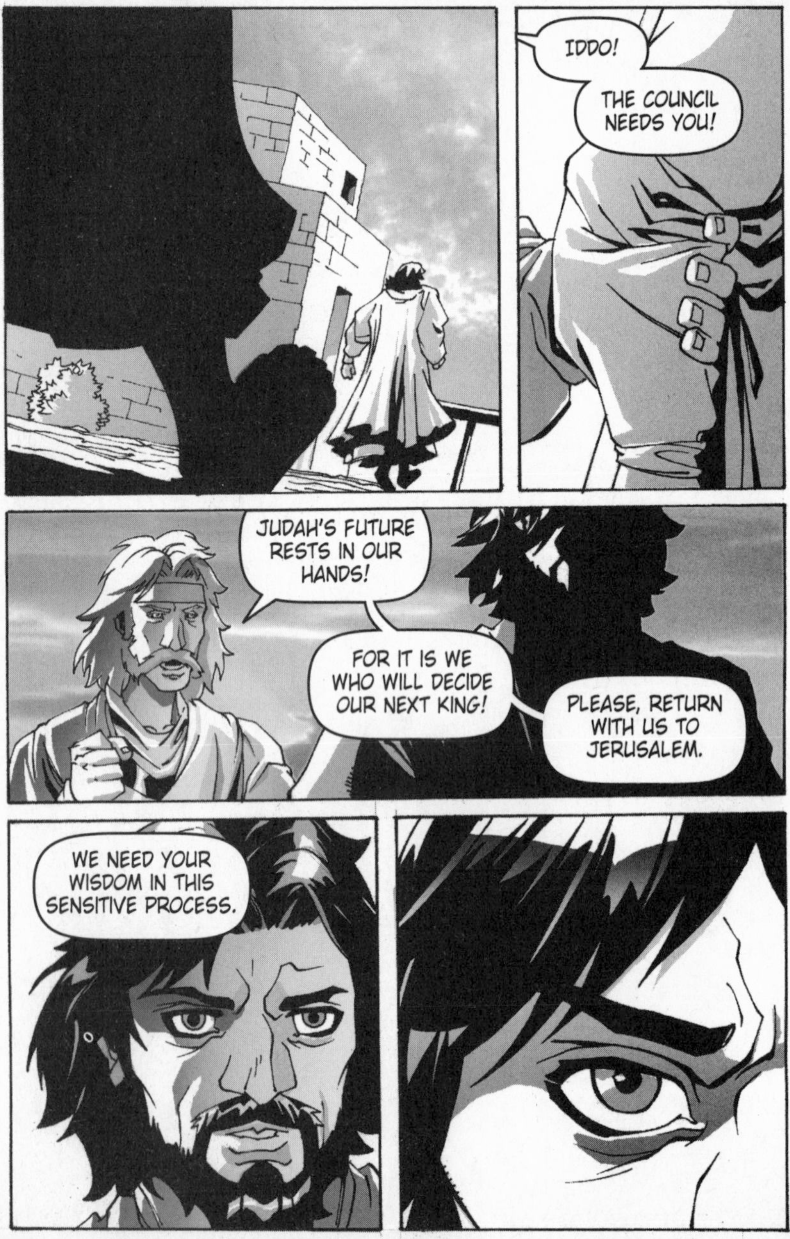
IDDO!
THE COUNCIL NEEDS YOU!
JUDAH'S FUTURE RESTS IN OUR HANDS!
FOR IT IS WE WHO WILL DECIDE OUR NEXT KING!
PLEASE, RETURN WITH US TO JERUSALEM.
WE NEED YOUR WISDOM IN THIS SENSITIVE PROCESS.

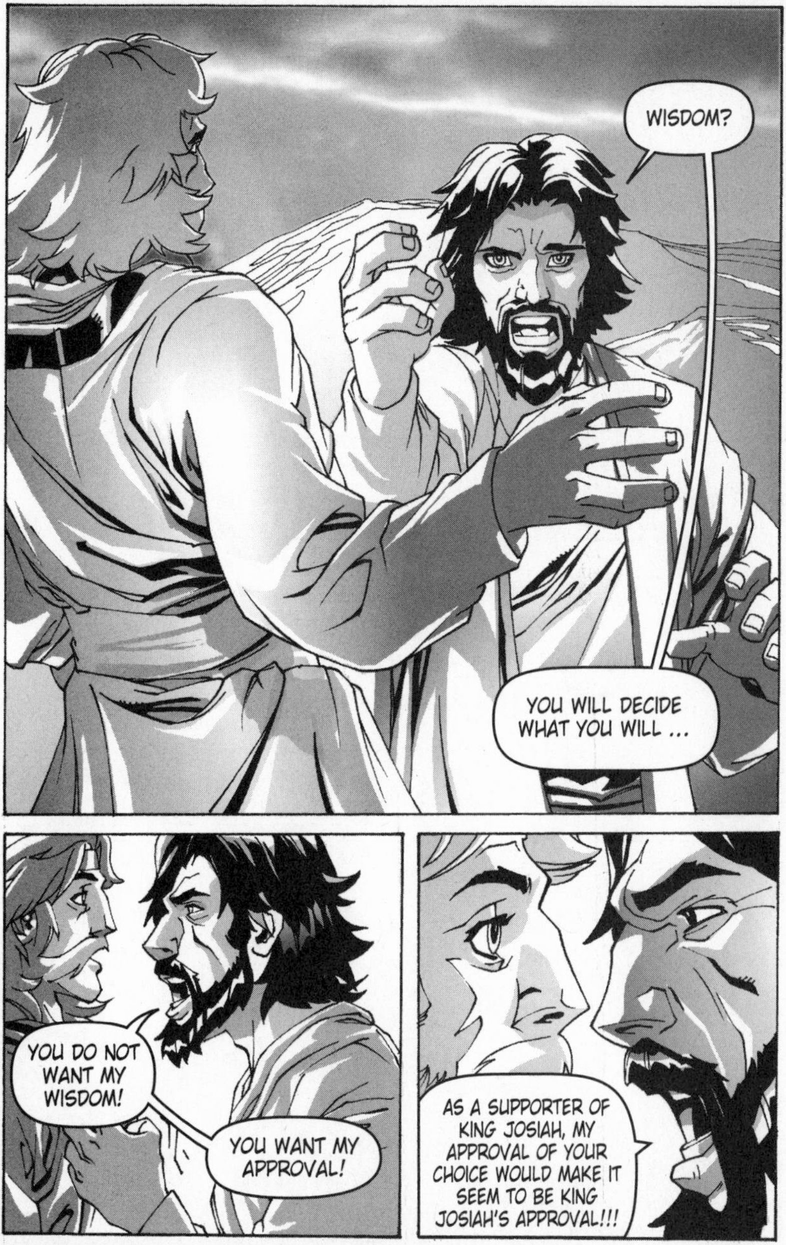
WISDOM?
YOU WILL DECIDE WHAT YOU WILL ...
YOU DO NOT WANT MY WISDOM!
YOU WANT MY APPROVAL!
AS A SUPPORTER OF KING JOSIAH, MY APPROVAL OF YOUR CHOICE WOULD MAKE IT SEEM TO BE KING JOSIAH'S APPROVAL!!!

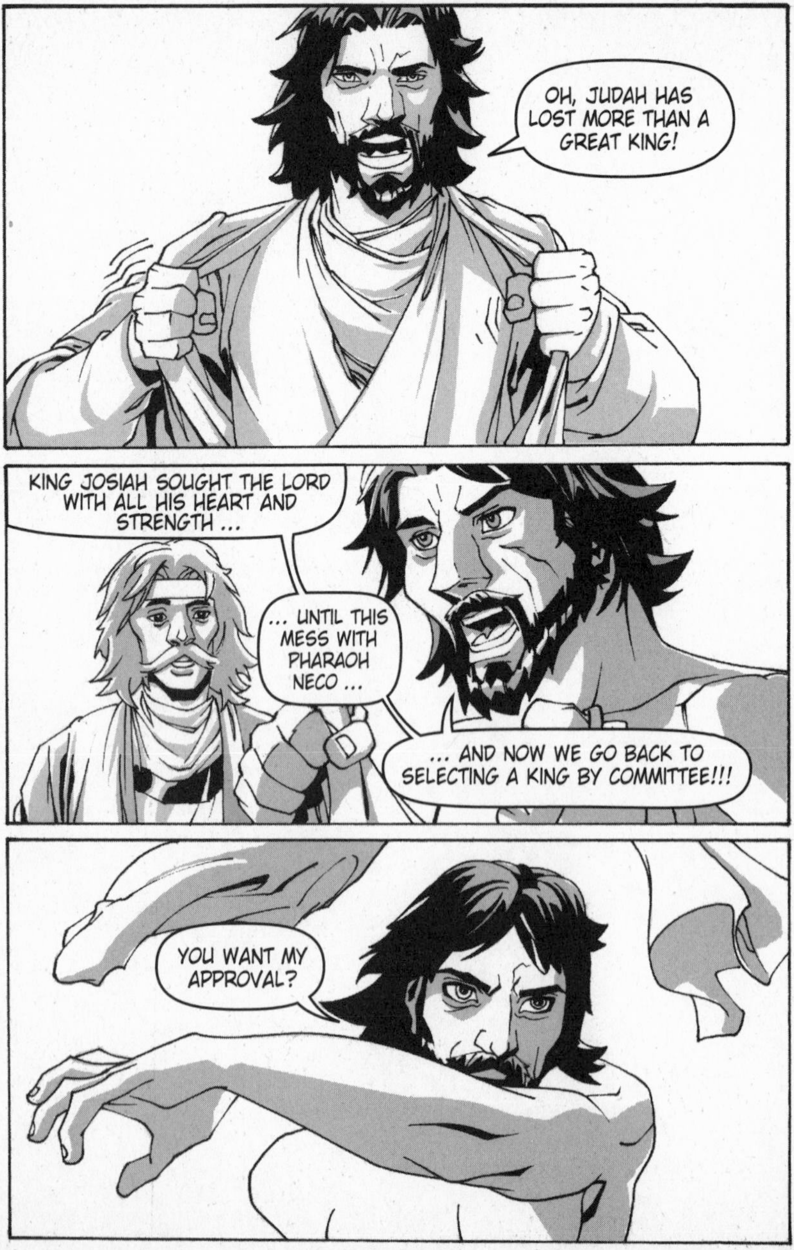
OH, JUDAH HAS LOST MORE THAN A GREAT KING!
KING JOSIAH SOUGHT THE LORD WITH ALL HIS HEART AND STRENGTH ...
... UNTIL THIS MESS WITH PHARAOH NECO ...
... AND NOW WE GO BACK TO SELECTING A KING BY COMMITTEE!!!
YOU WANT MY APPROVAL?

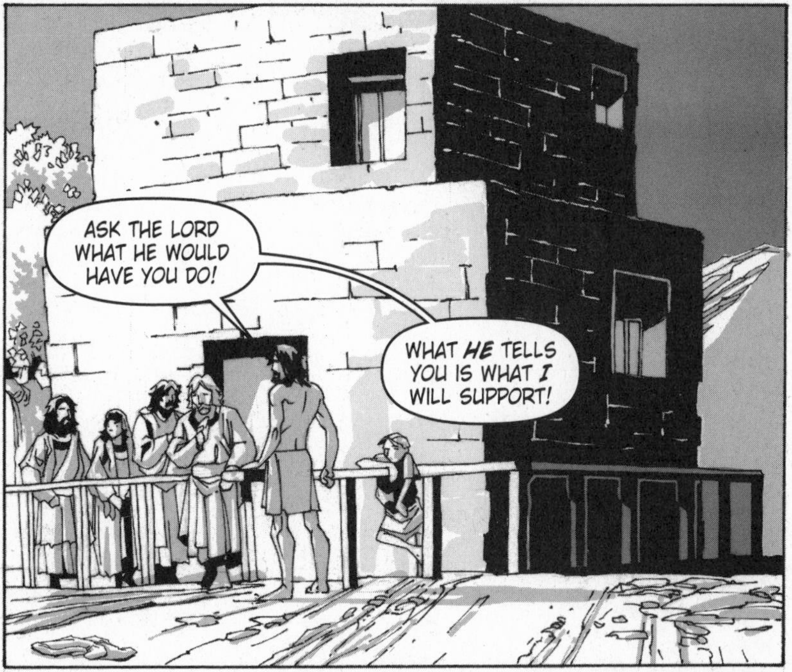
ASK THE LORD WHAT HE WOULD HAVE YOU DO!
WHAT *HE* TELLS YOU IS WHAT *I* WILL SUPPORT!

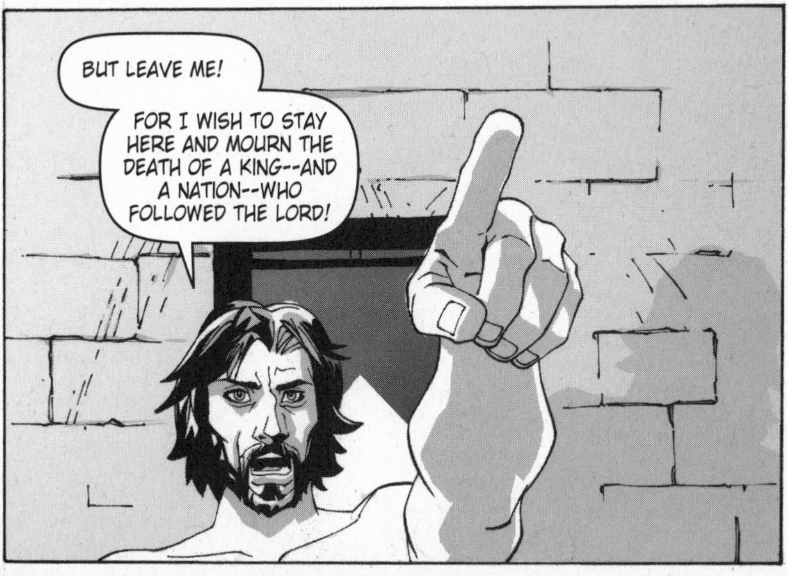
BUT LEAVE ME!
FOR I WISH TO STAY HERE AND MOURN THE DEATH OF A KING--AND A NATION--WHO FOLLOWED THE LORD!

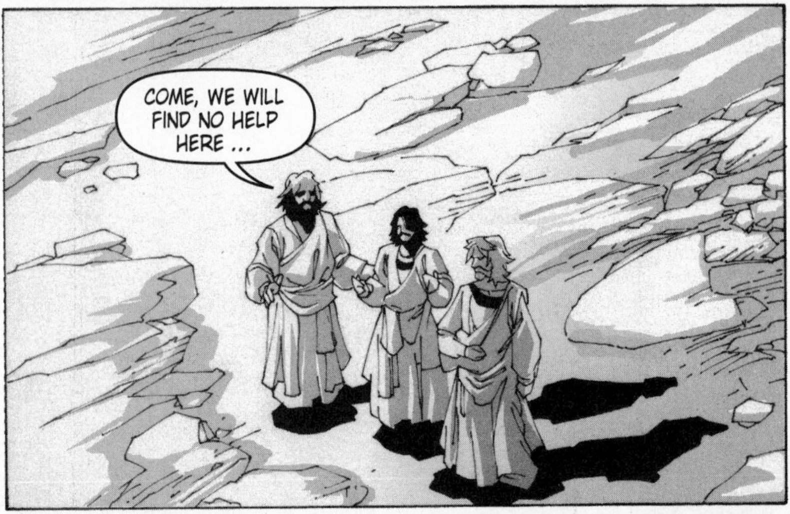
COME, WE WILL FIND NO HELP HERE ...
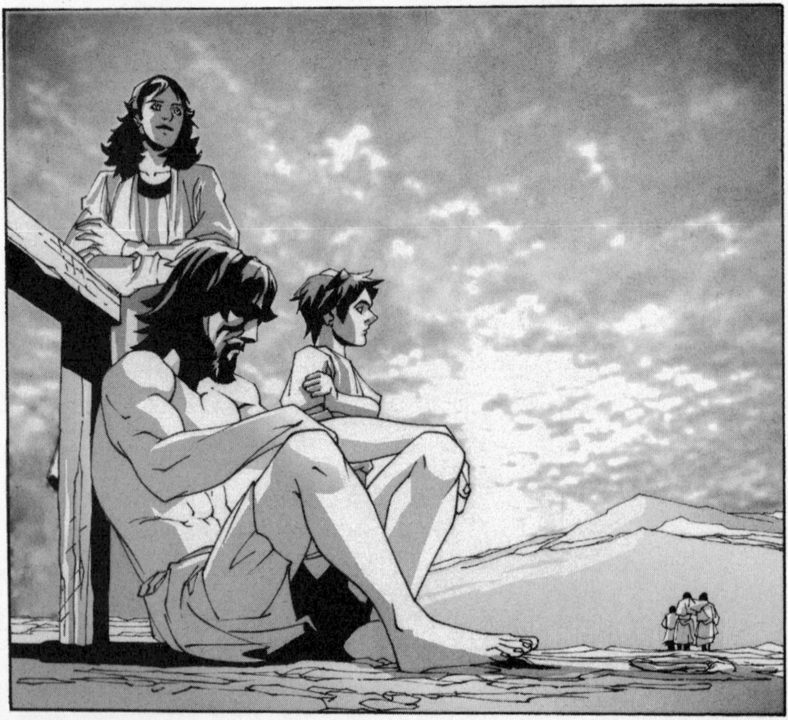

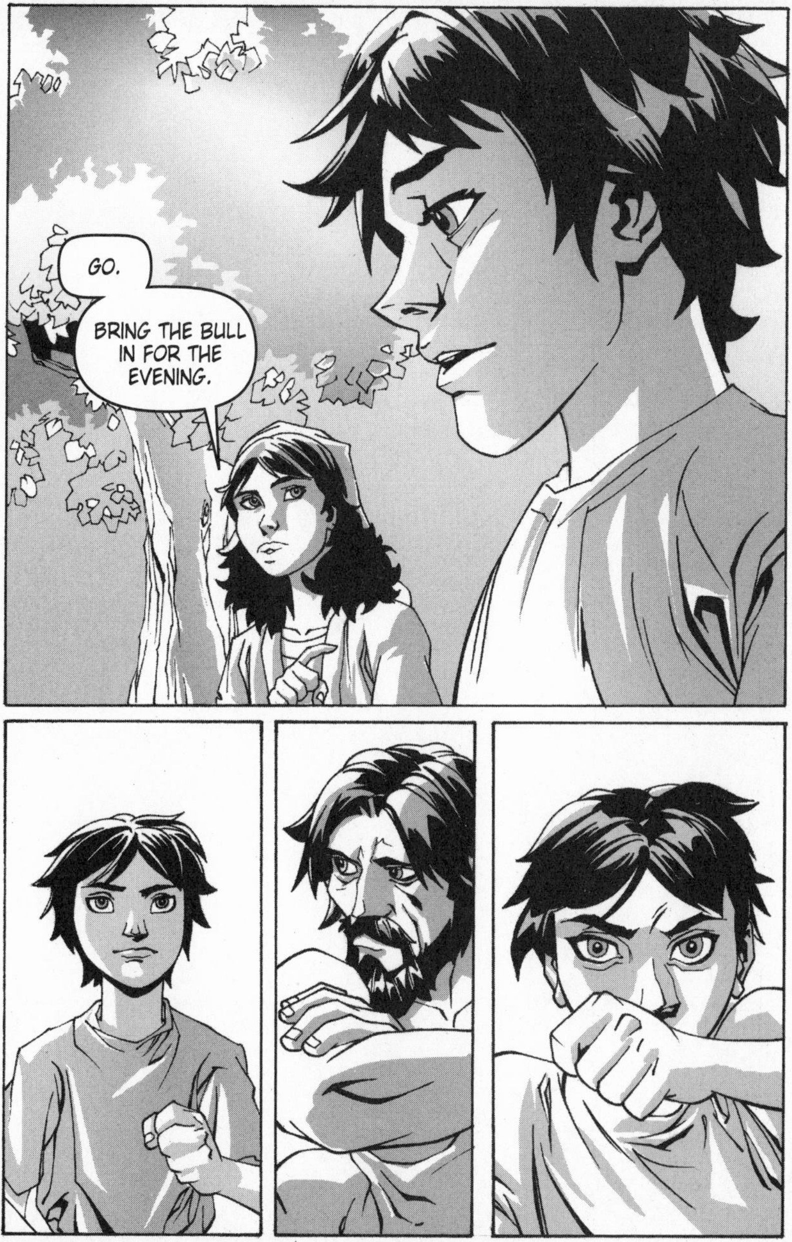
GO.
BRING THE BULL IN FOR THE EVENING.

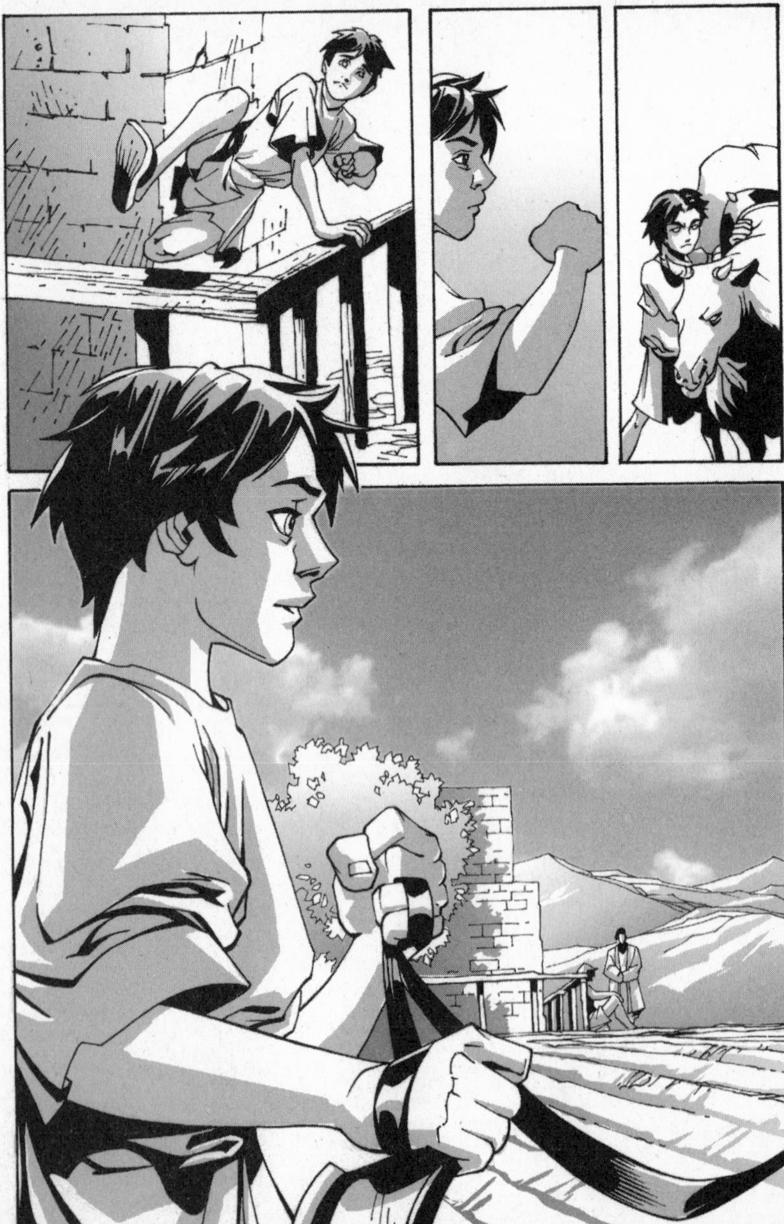

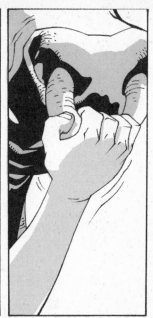

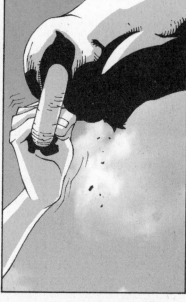

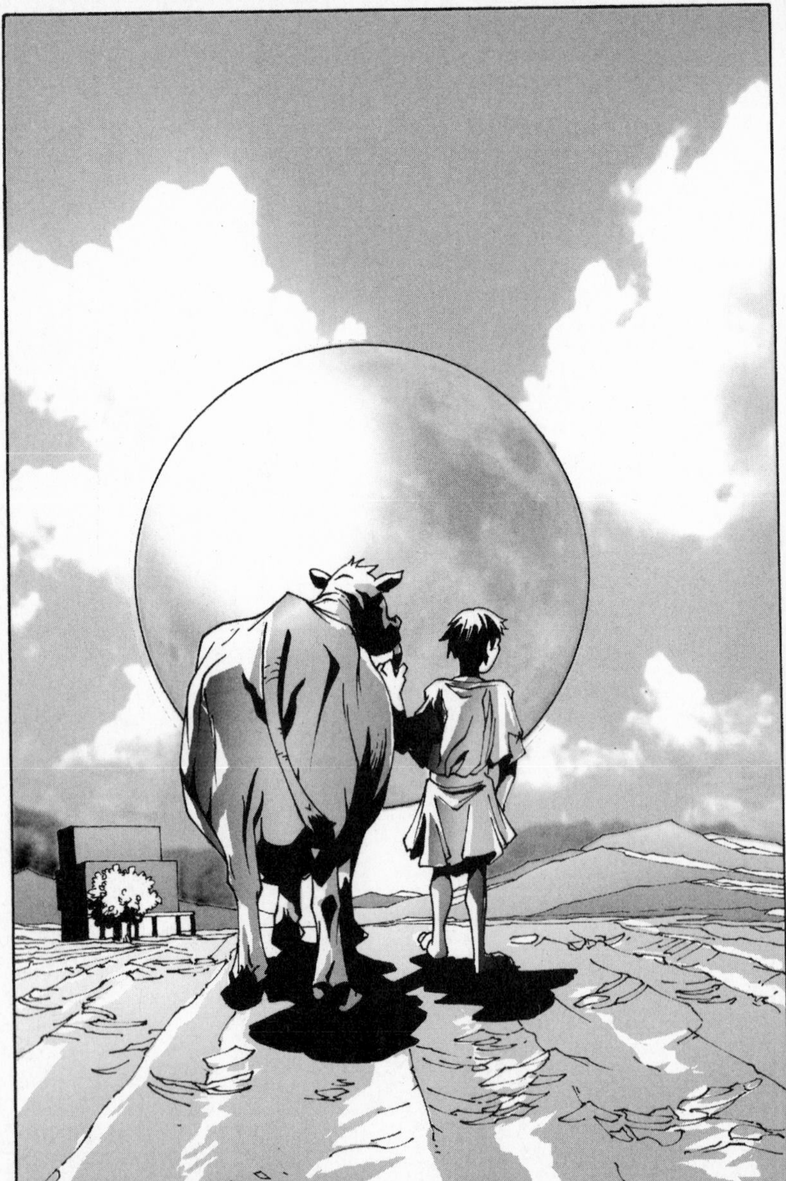

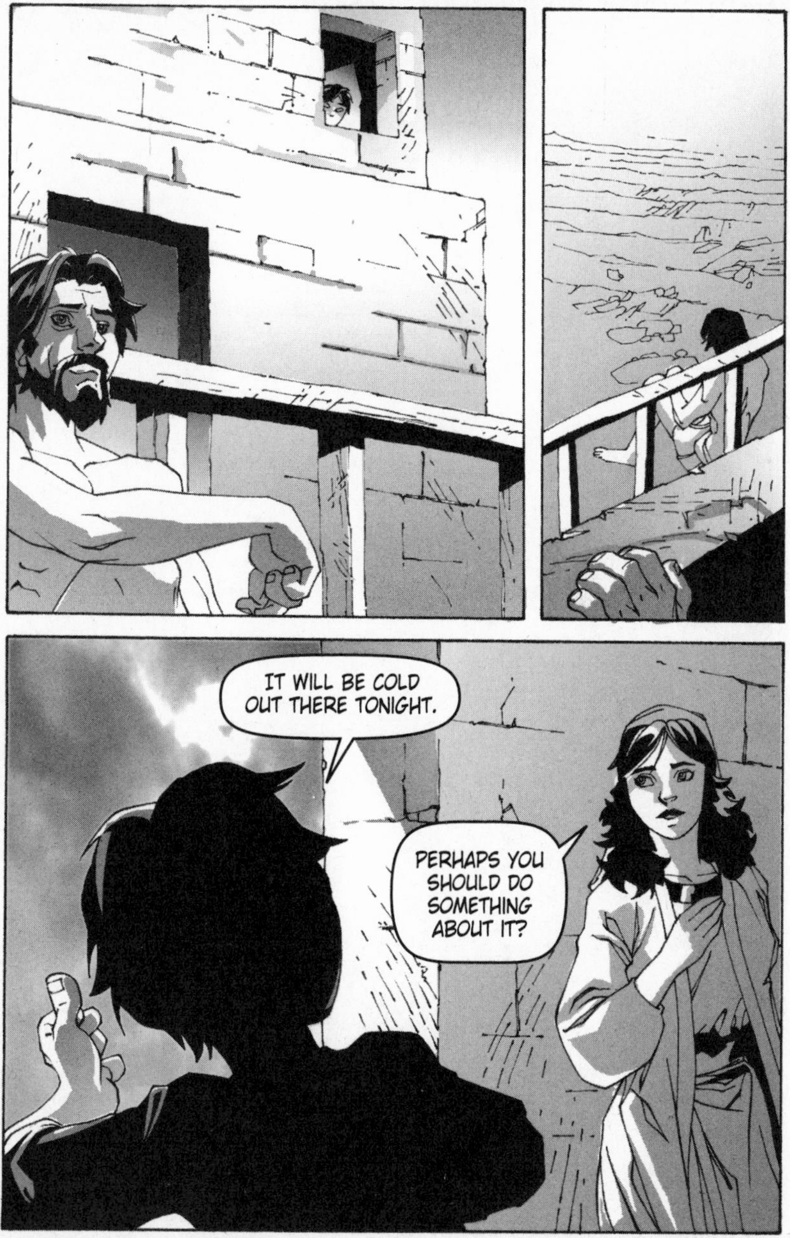
IT WILL BE COLD OUT THERE TONIGHT.
PERHAPS YOU SHOULD DO SOMETHING ABOUT IT?

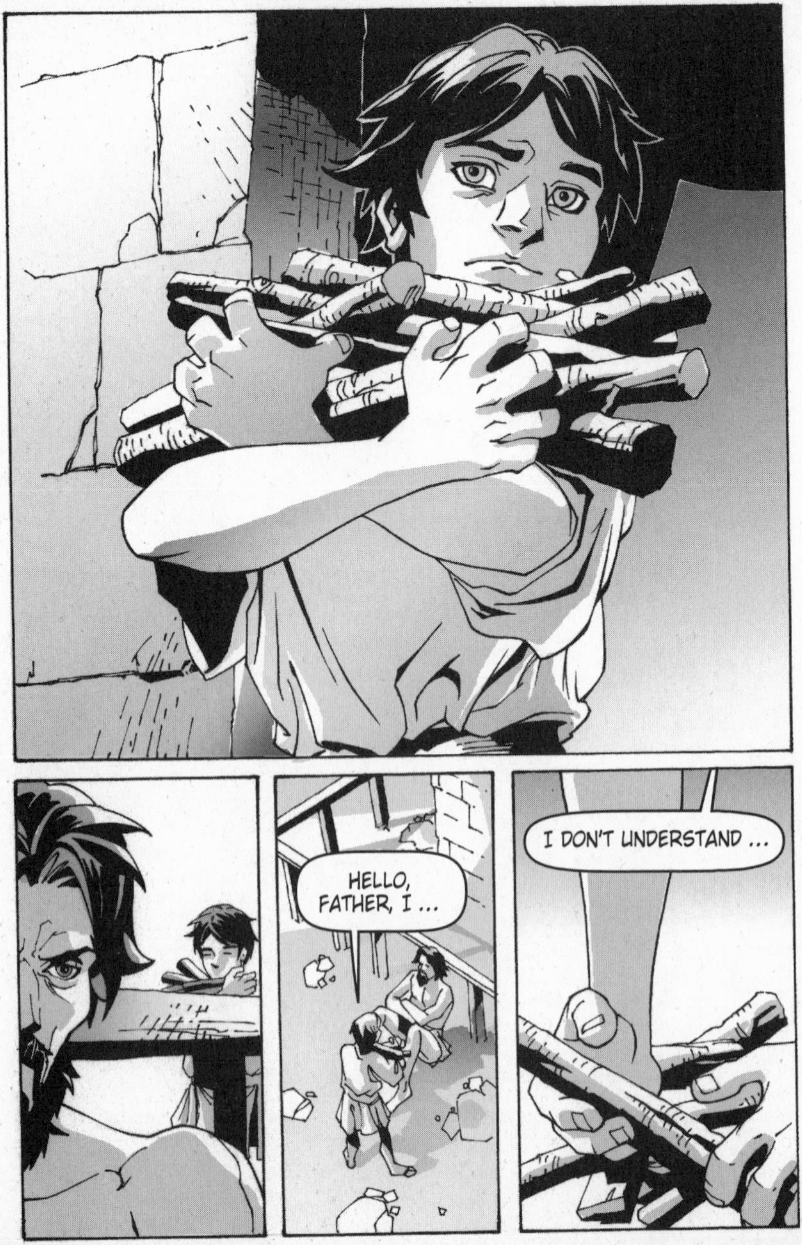
HELLO, FATHER, I ...
I DON'T UNDERSTAND ...

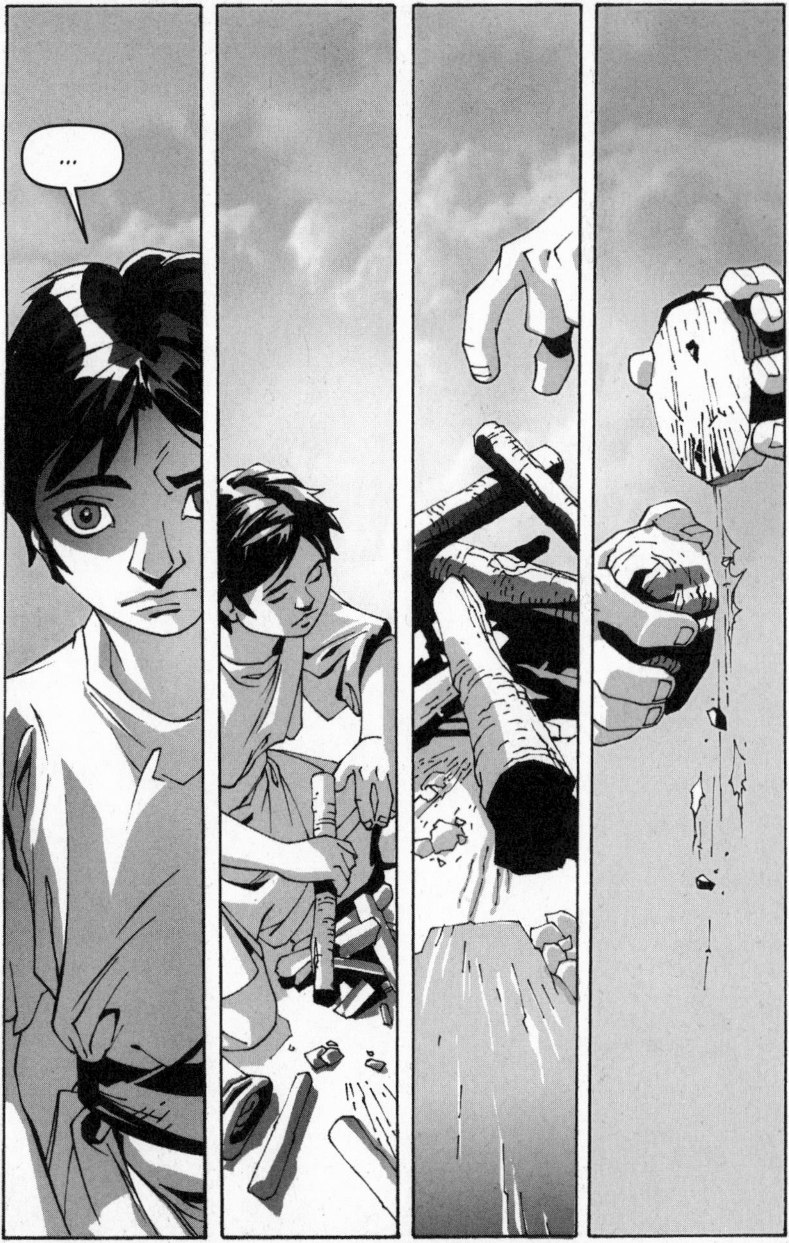
...

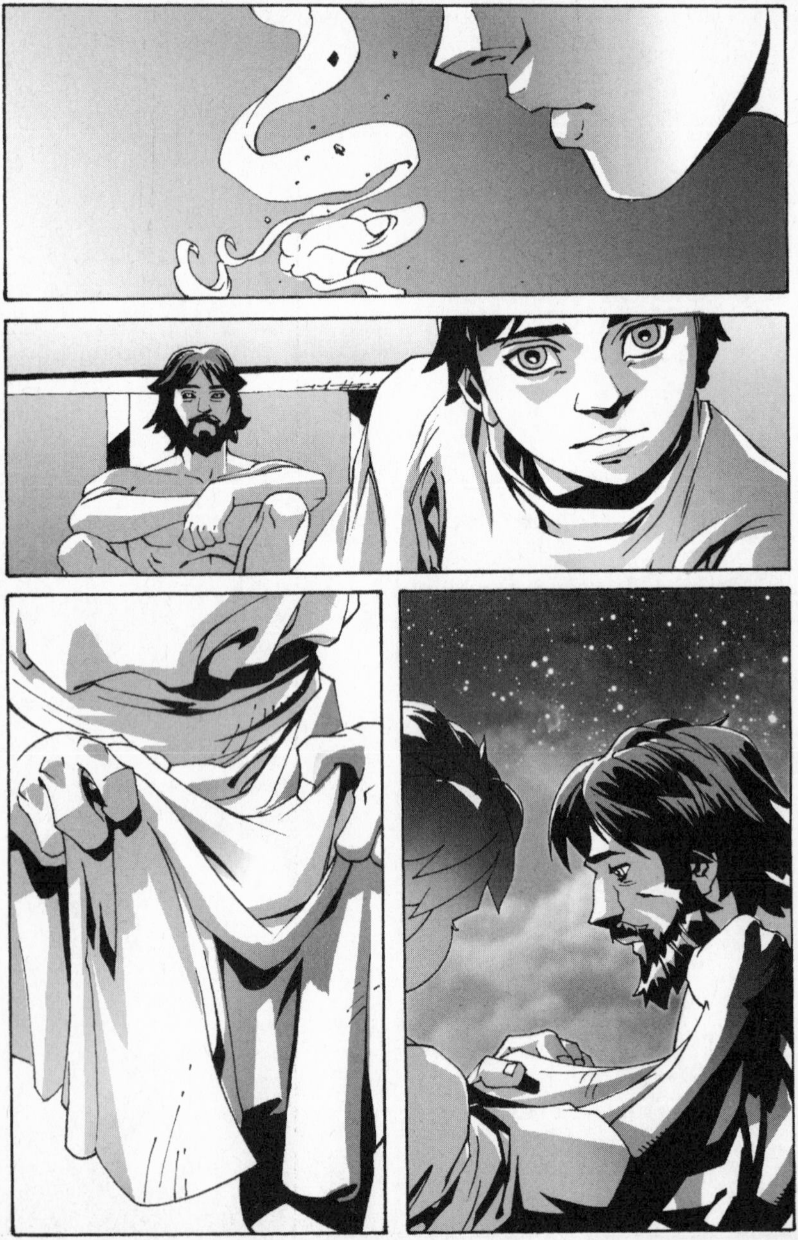

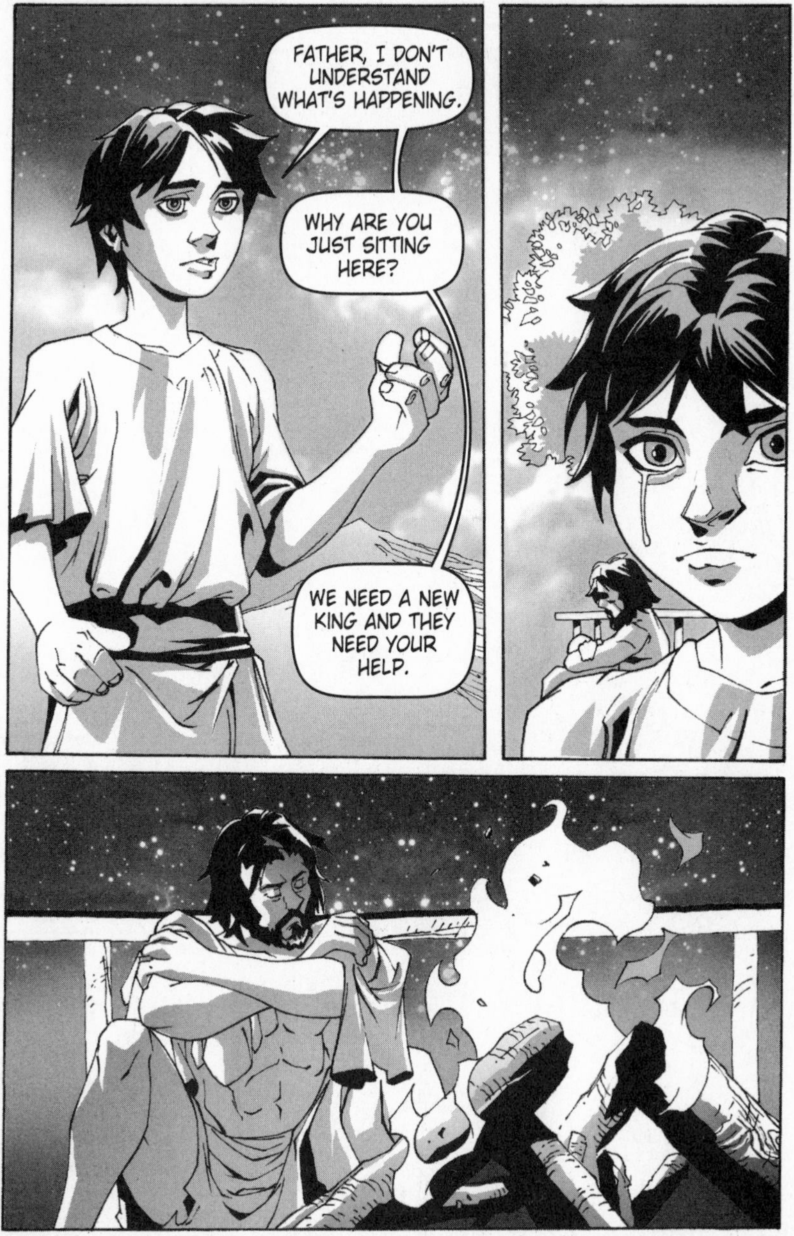
FATHER, I DON'T UNDERSTAND WHAT'S HAPPENING.
WHY ARE YOU JUST SITTING HERE?
WE NEED A NEW KING AND THEY NEED YOUR HELP.

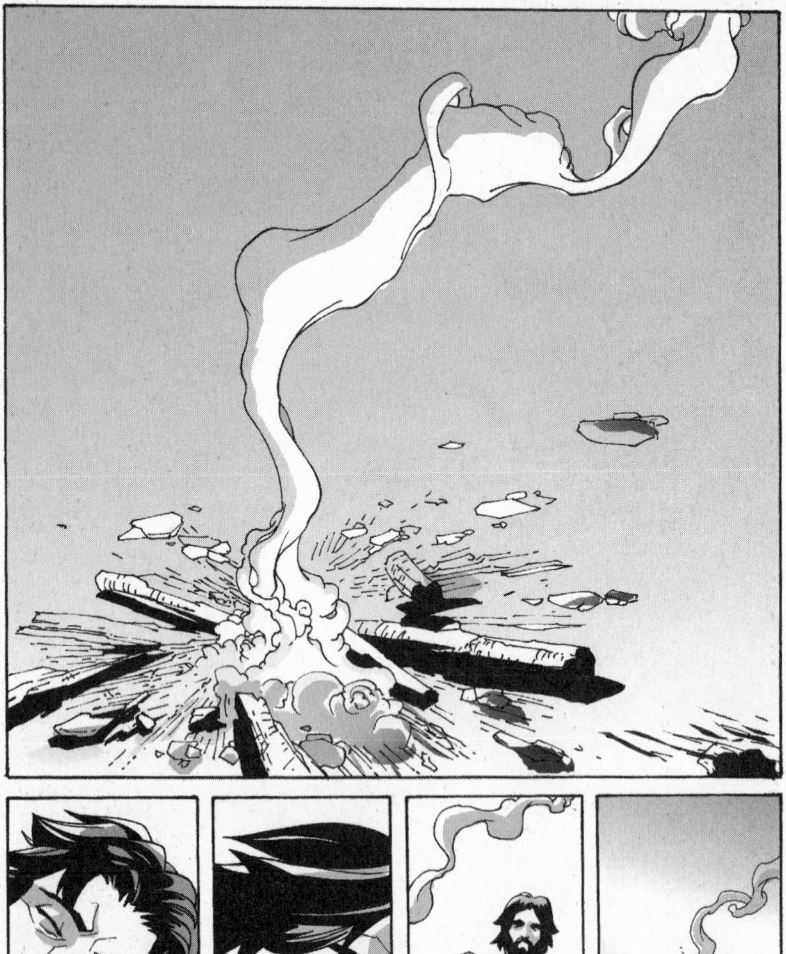
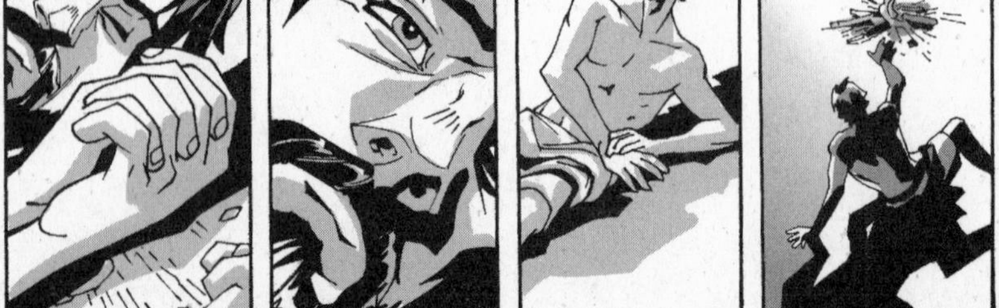

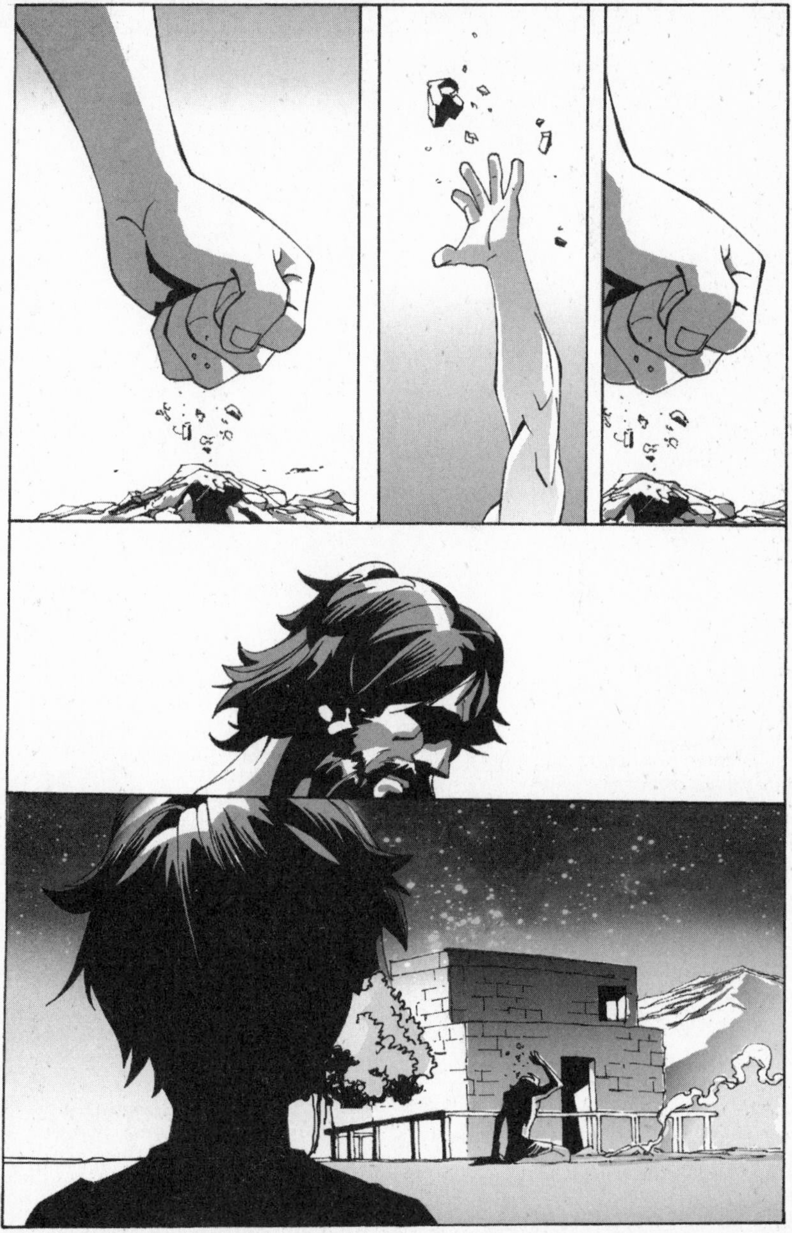

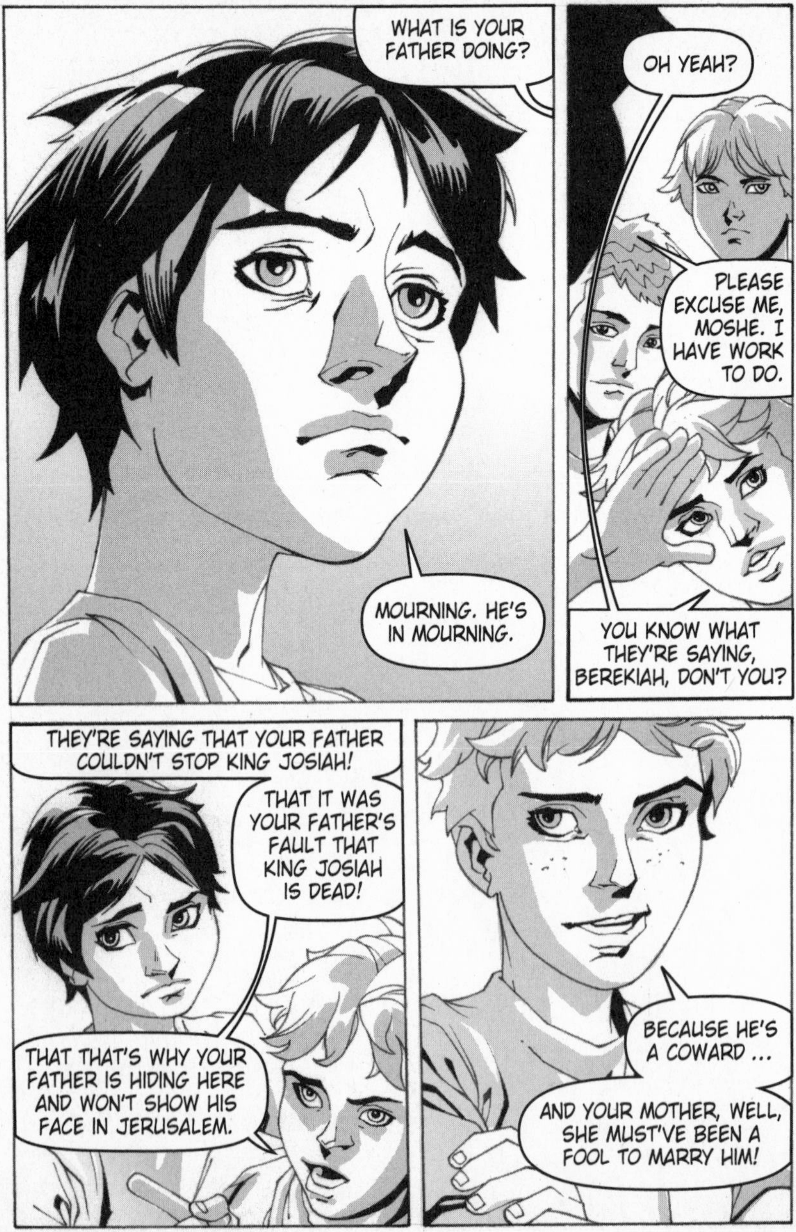
WHAT IS YOUR FATHER DOING?
MOURNING. HE'S IN MOURNING.
OH YEAH?
PLEASE EXCUSE ME, MOSHE. I HAVE WORK TO DO.
YOU KNOW WHAT THEY'RE SAYING, BEREKIAH, DON'T YOU?
THEY'RE SAYING THAT YOUR FATHER COULDN'T STOP KING JOSIAH!
THAT IT WAS YOUR FATHER'S FAULT THAT KING JOSIAH IS DEAD!
THAT THAT'S WHY YOUR FATHER IS HIDING HERE AND WON'T SHOW HIS FACE IN JERUSALEM.
BECAUSE HE'S A COWARD ...
AND YOUR MOTHER, WELL, SHE MUST'VE BEEN A FOOL TO MARRY HIM!

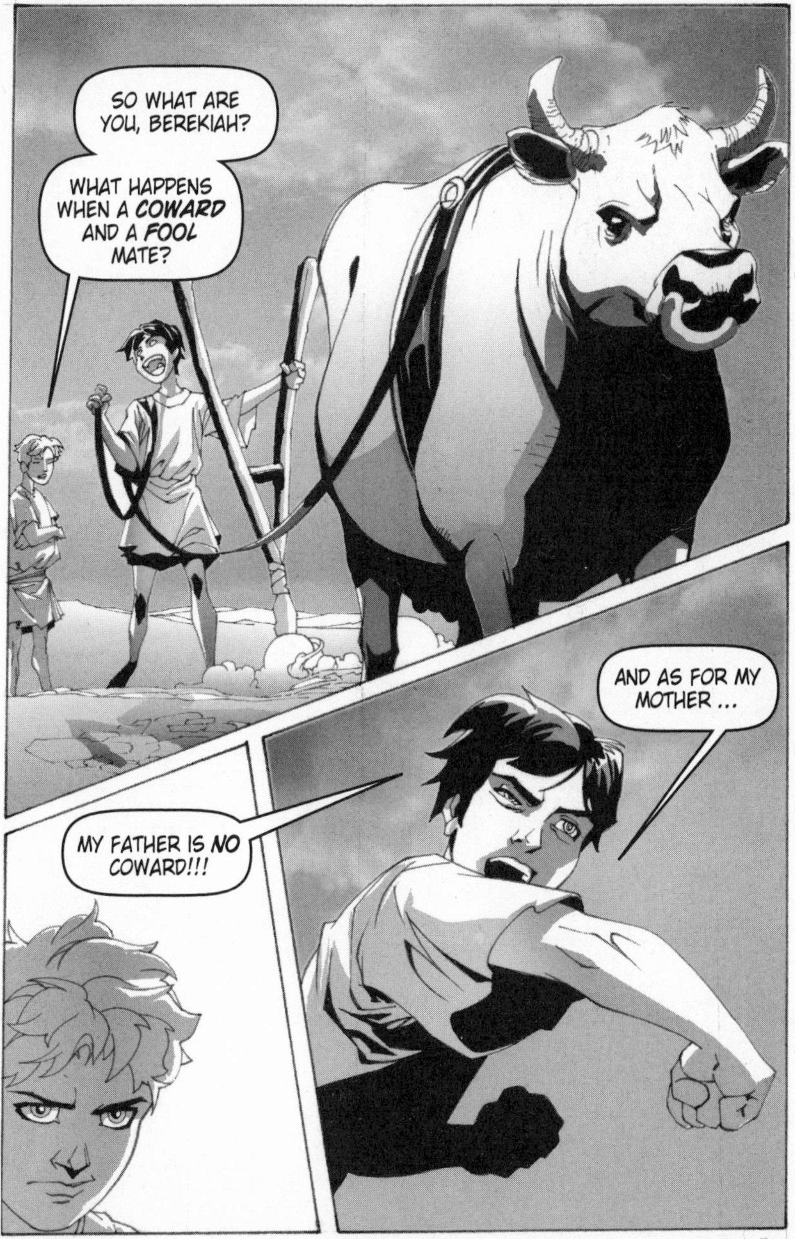
SO WHAT ARE YOU, BEREKIAH?
WHAT HAPPENS WHEN A ***COWARD*** AND A ***FOOL*** MATE?
MY FATHER IS ***NO*** COWARD!!!
AND AS FOR MY MOTHER ...

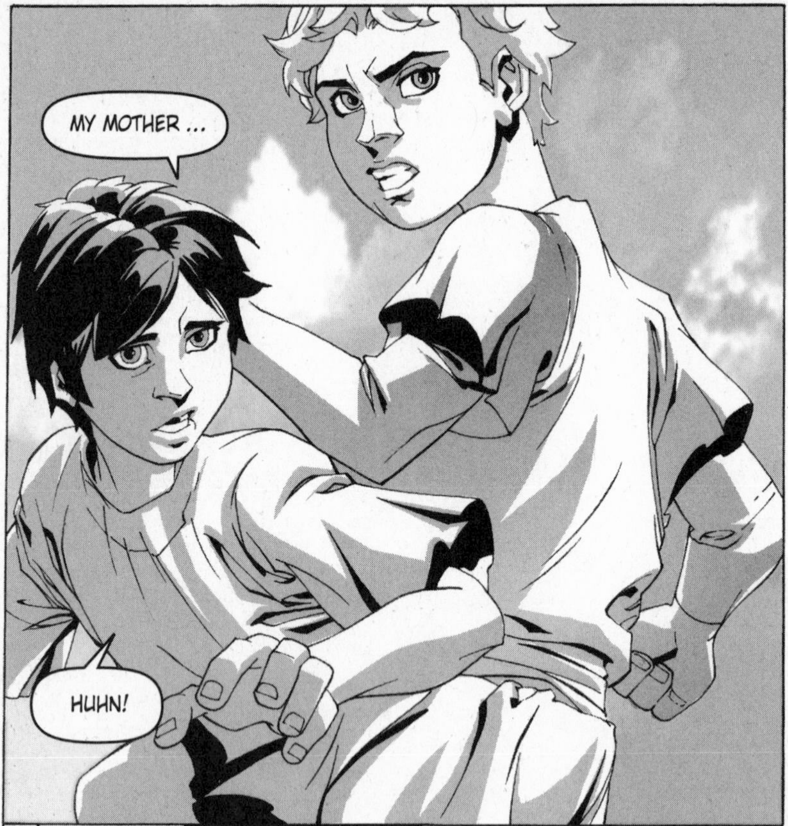
MY MOTHER ...
HUHN!

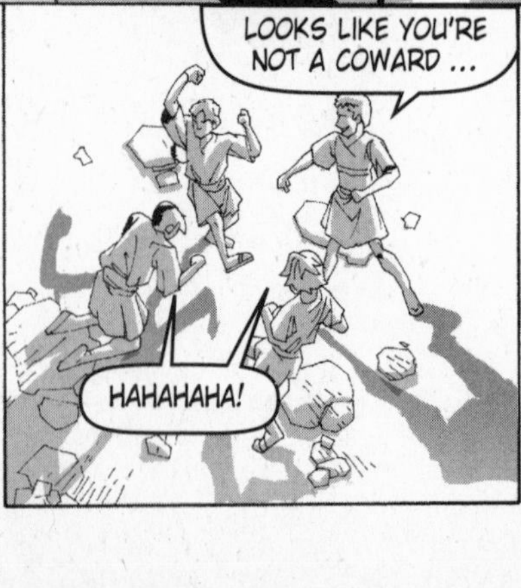
LOOKS LIKE YOU'RE NOT A COWARD ...
HAHAHAHA!

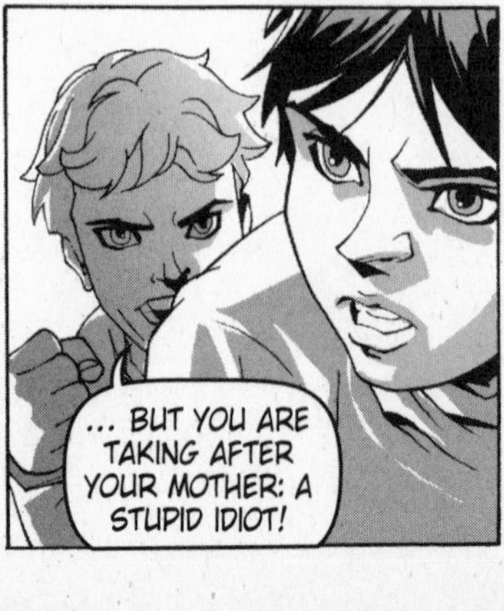
... BUT YOU ARE TAKING AFTER YOUR MOTHER: A STUPID IDIOT!

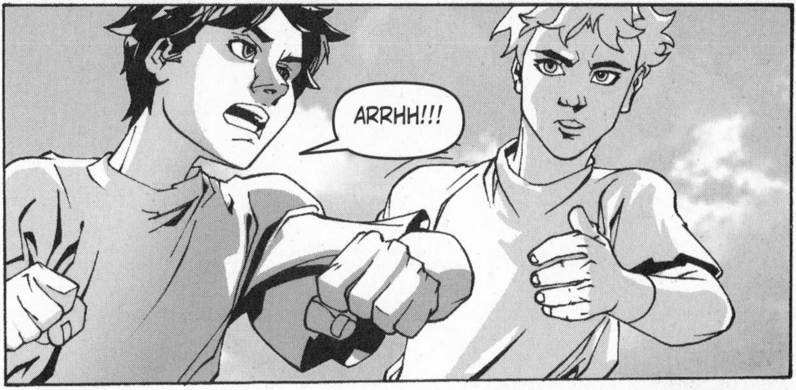
ARRHH!!!
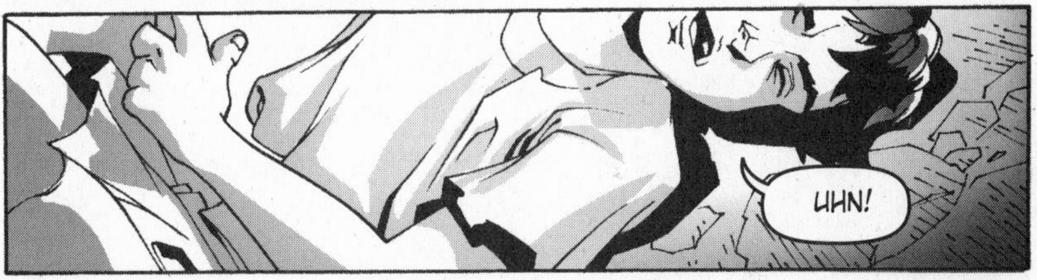
UHN!
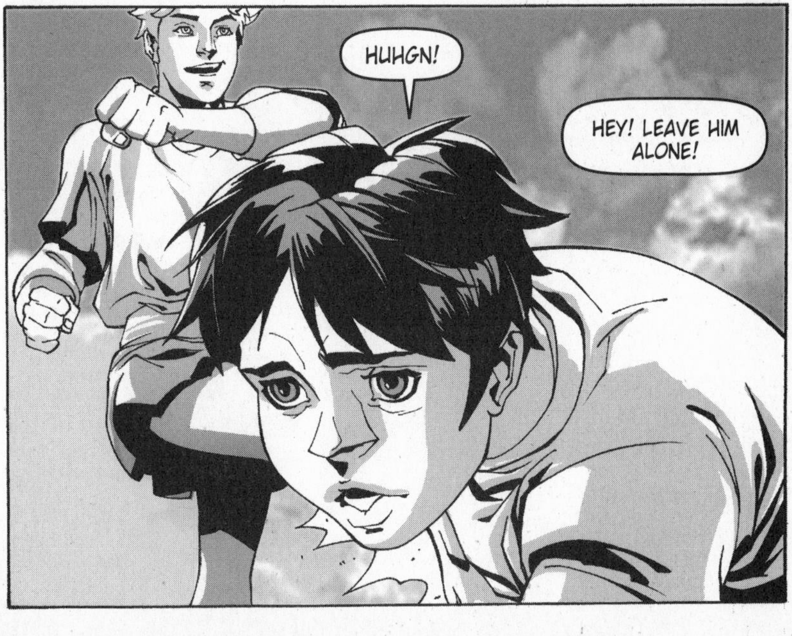
HUHGN!
HEY! LEAVE HIM ALONE!

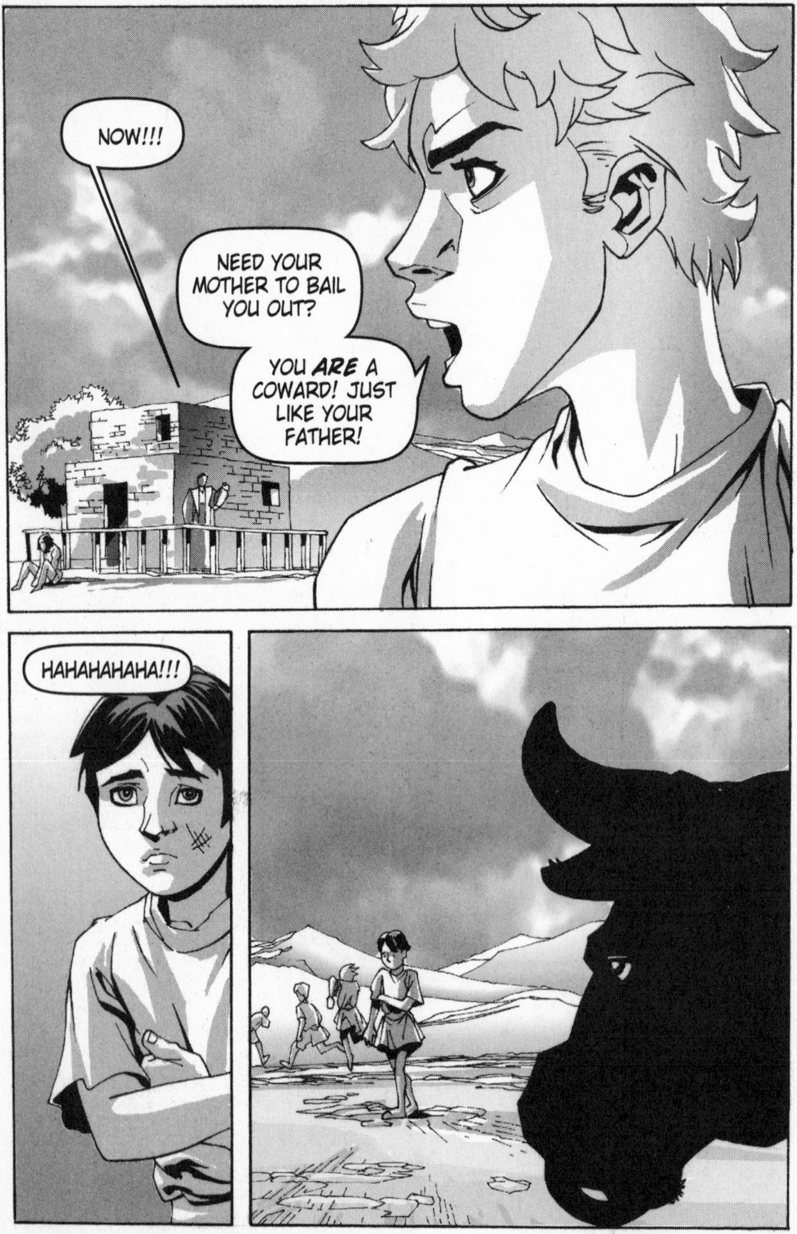
NOW!!!
NEED YOUR MOTHER TO BAIL YOU OUT?
YOU ARE A COWARD! JUST LIKE YOUR FATHER!
HAHAHAHAHA!!!

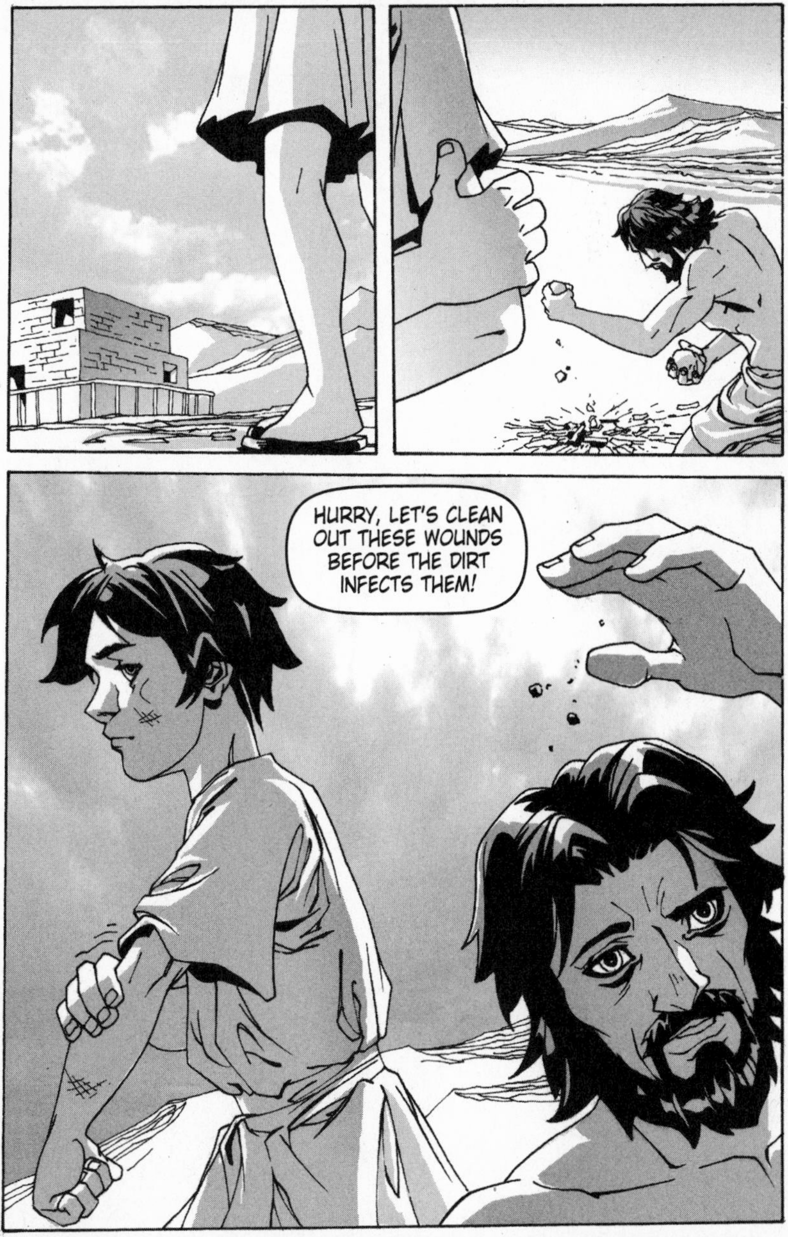
HURRY, LET'S CLEAN OUT THESE WOUNDS BEFORE THE DIRT INFECTS THEM!

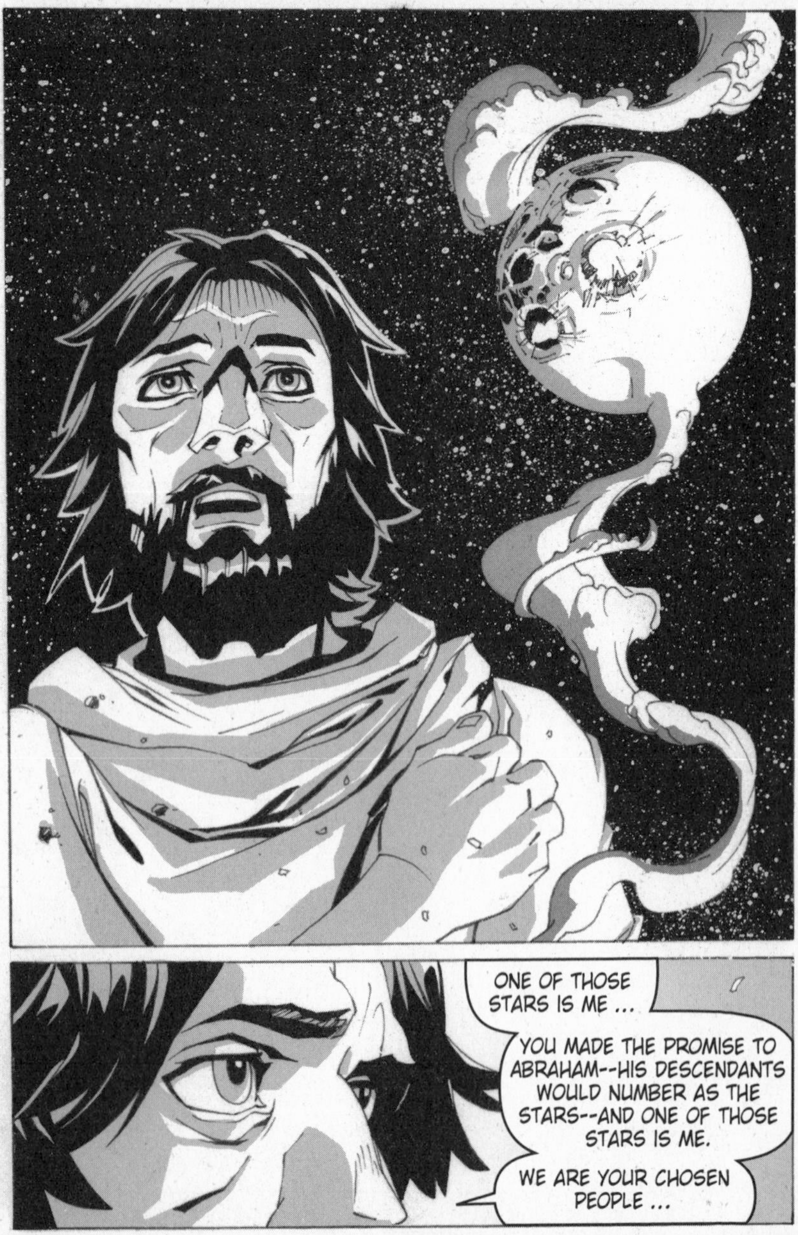
ONE OF THOSE STARS IS ME ...
YOU MADE THE PROMISE TO ABRAHAM--HIS DESCENDANTS WOULD NUMBER AS THE STARS--AND ONE OF THOSE STARS IS ME.
WE ARE YOUR CHOSEN PEOPLE ...

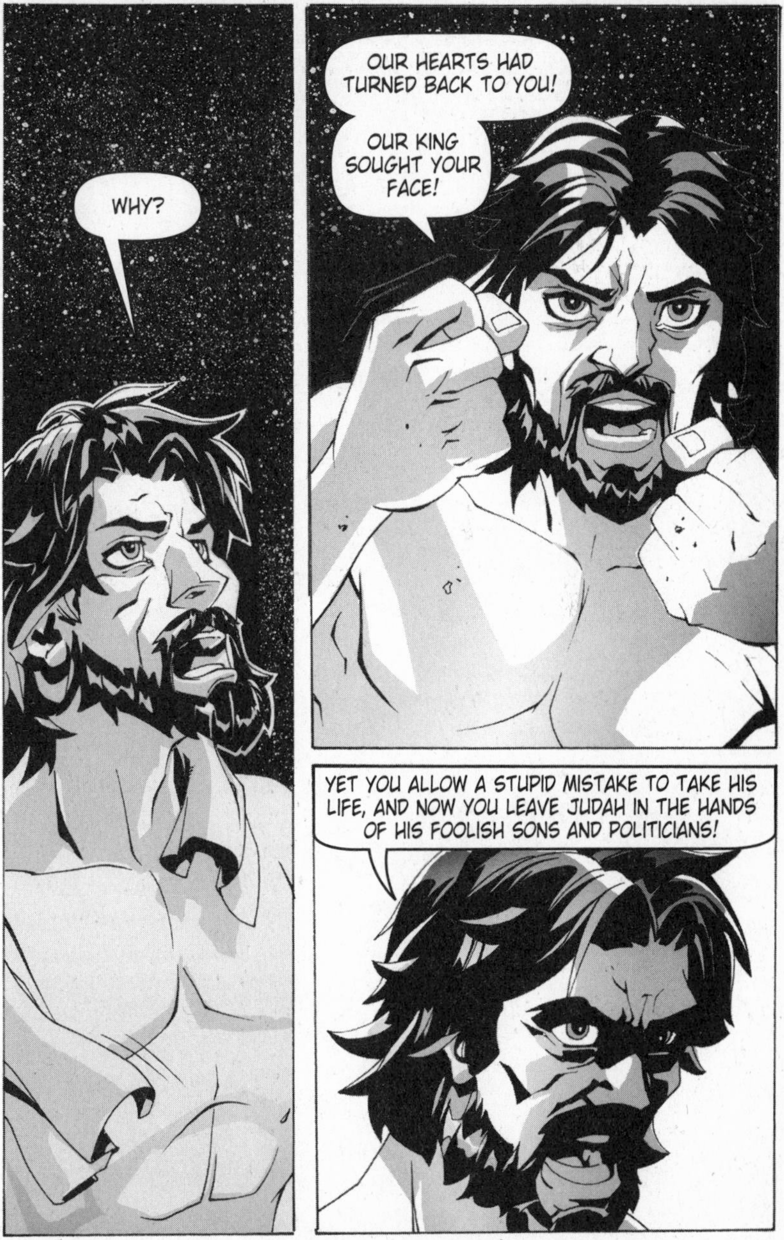
WHY?
OUR HEARTS HAD TURNED BACK TO YOU!
OUR KING SOUGHT YOUR FACE!
YET YOU ALLOW A STUPID MISTAKE TO TAKE HIS LIFE, AND NOW YOU LEAVE JUDAH IN THE HANDS OF HIS FOOLISH SONS AND POLITICIANS!

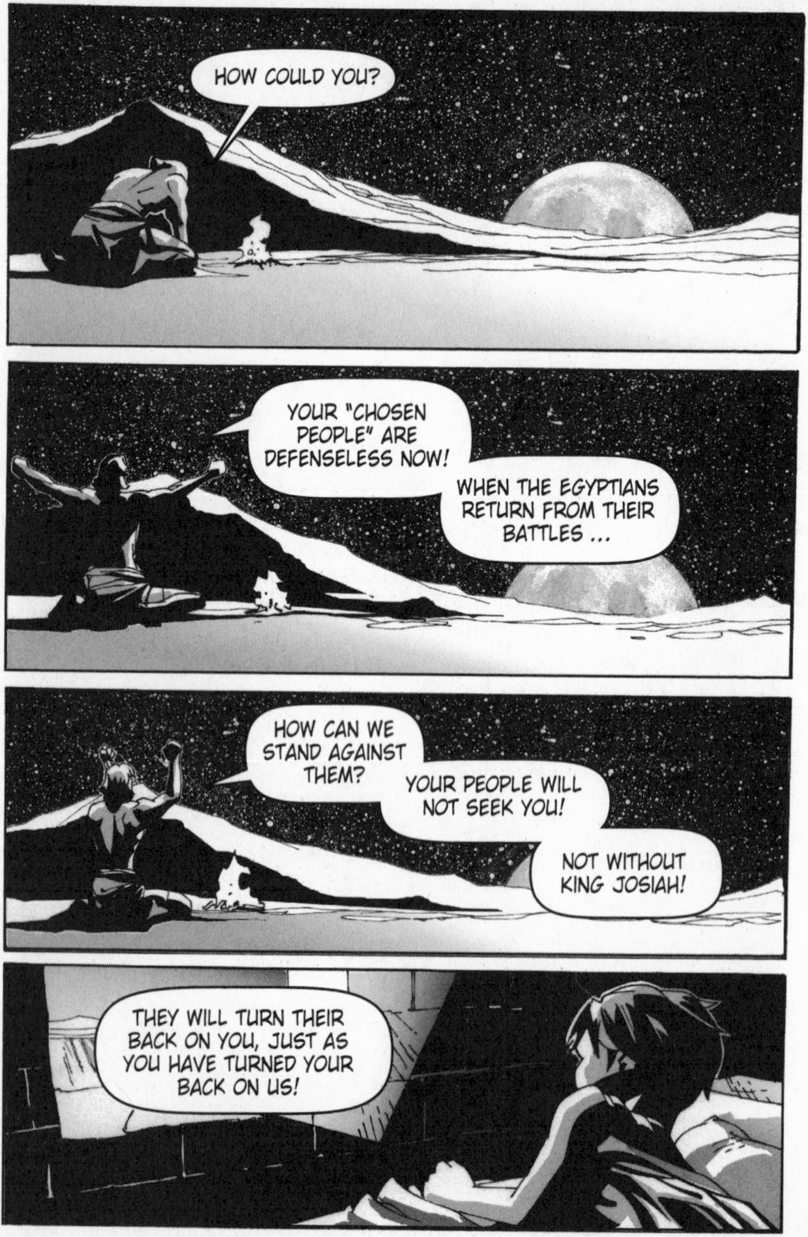
HOW COULD YOU?
YOUR "CHOSEN PEOPLE" ARE DEFENSELESS NOW!
WHEN THE EGYPTIANS RETURN FROM THEIR BATTLES ...
HOW CAN WE STAND AGAINST THEM?
YOUR PEOPLE WILL NOT SEEK YOU!
NOT WITHOUT KING JOSIAH!
THEY WILL TURN THEIR BACK ON YOU, JUST AS YOU HAVE TURNED YOUR BACK ON US!

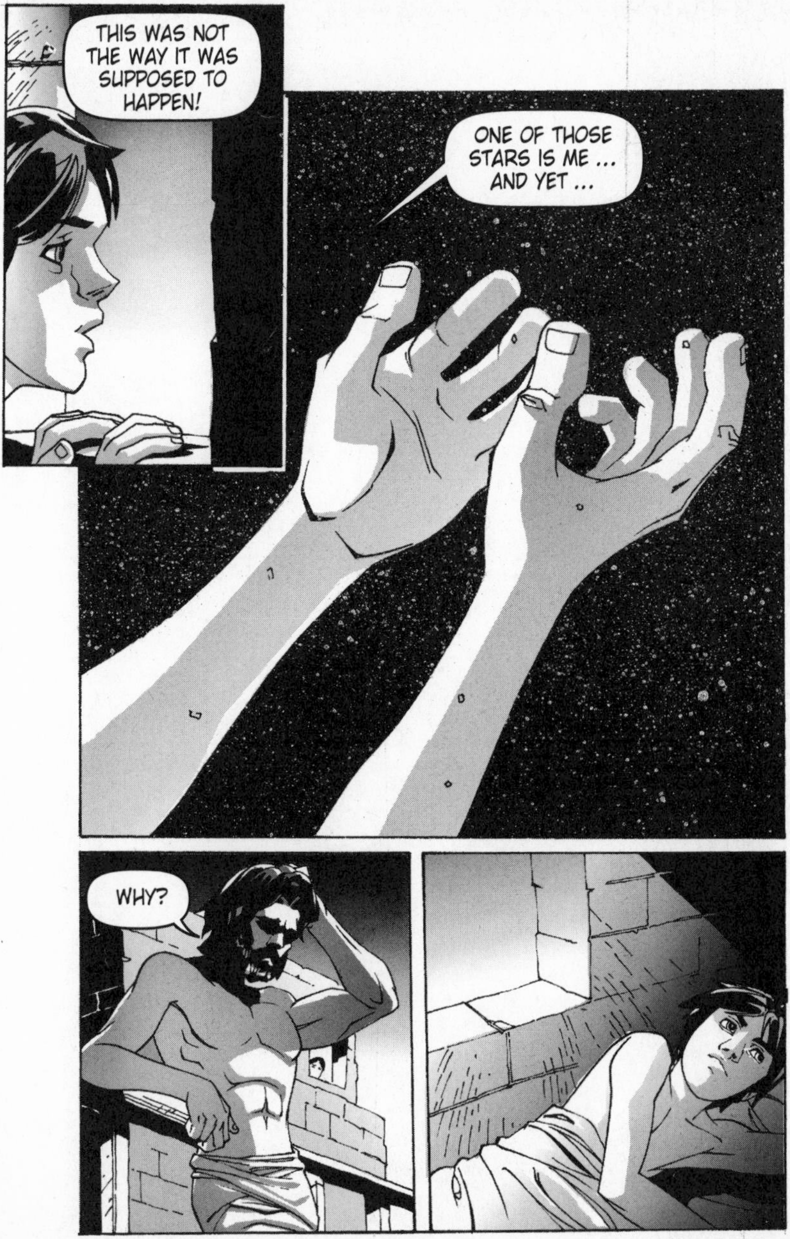
THIS WAS NOT THE WAY IT WAS SUPPOSED TO HAPPEN!
ONE OF THOSE STARS IS ME ... AND YET ...
WHY?

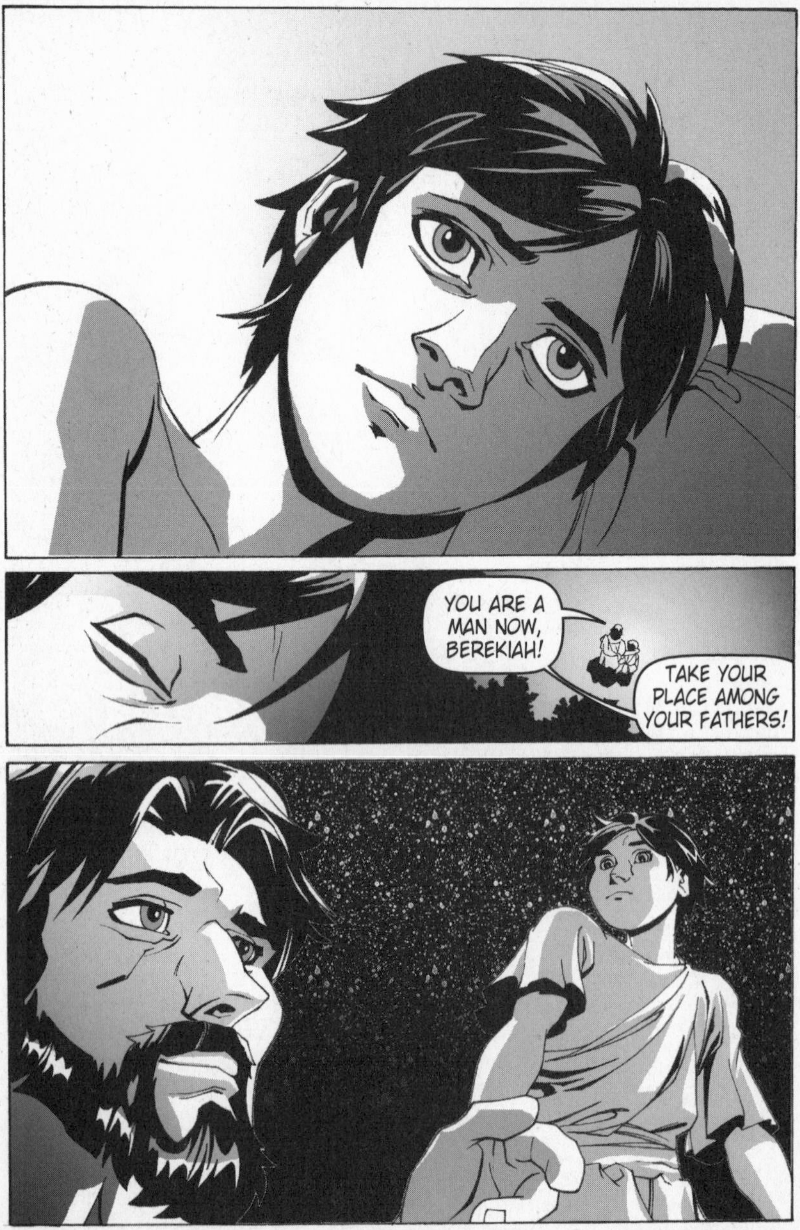
YOU ARE A MAN NOW, BEREKIAH!
TAKE YOUR PLACE AMONG YOUR FATHERS!

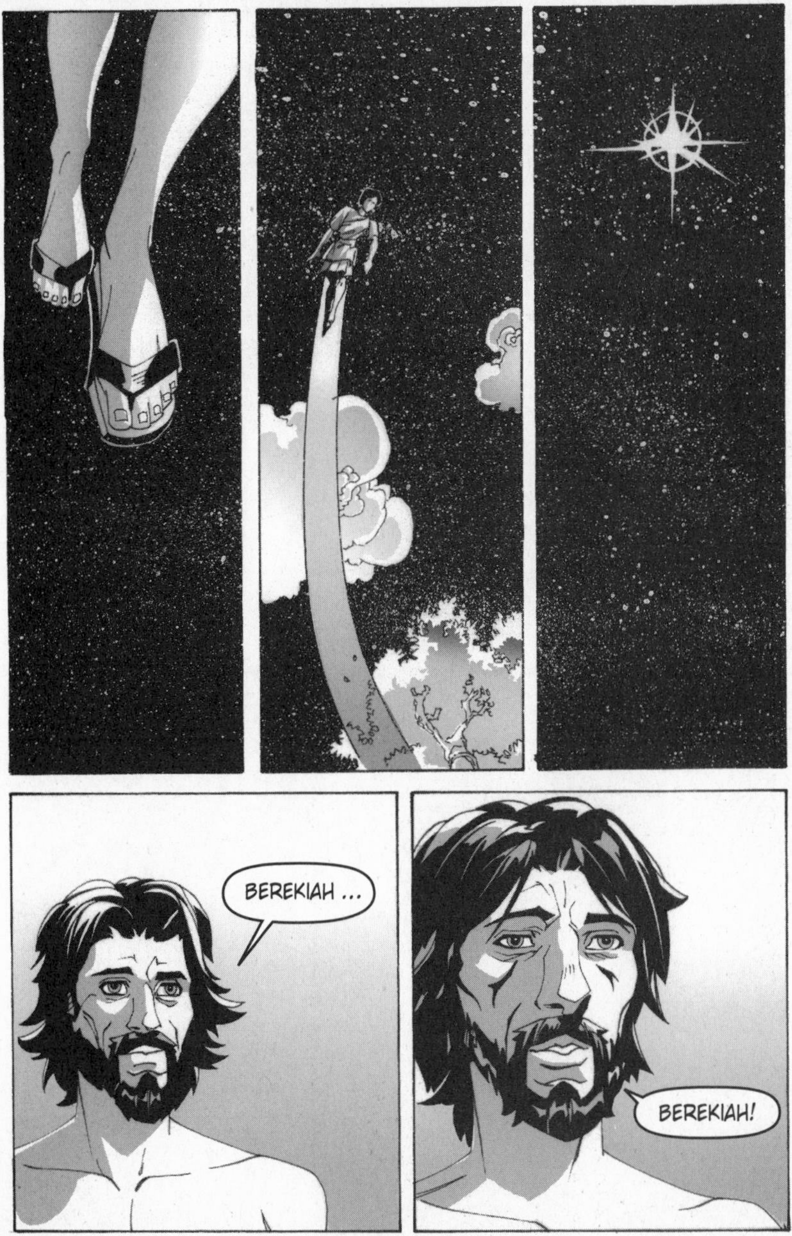
BEREKIAH ...
BEREKIAH!

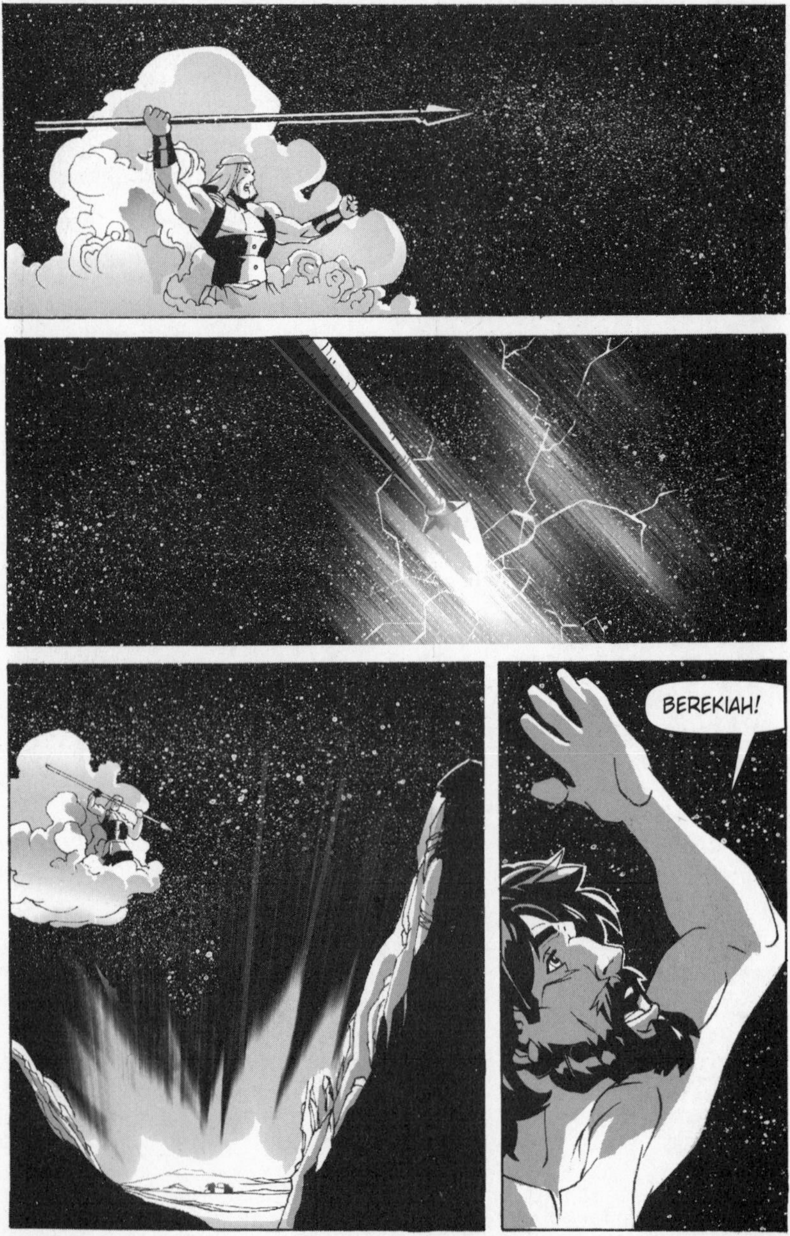
BEREKIAH!

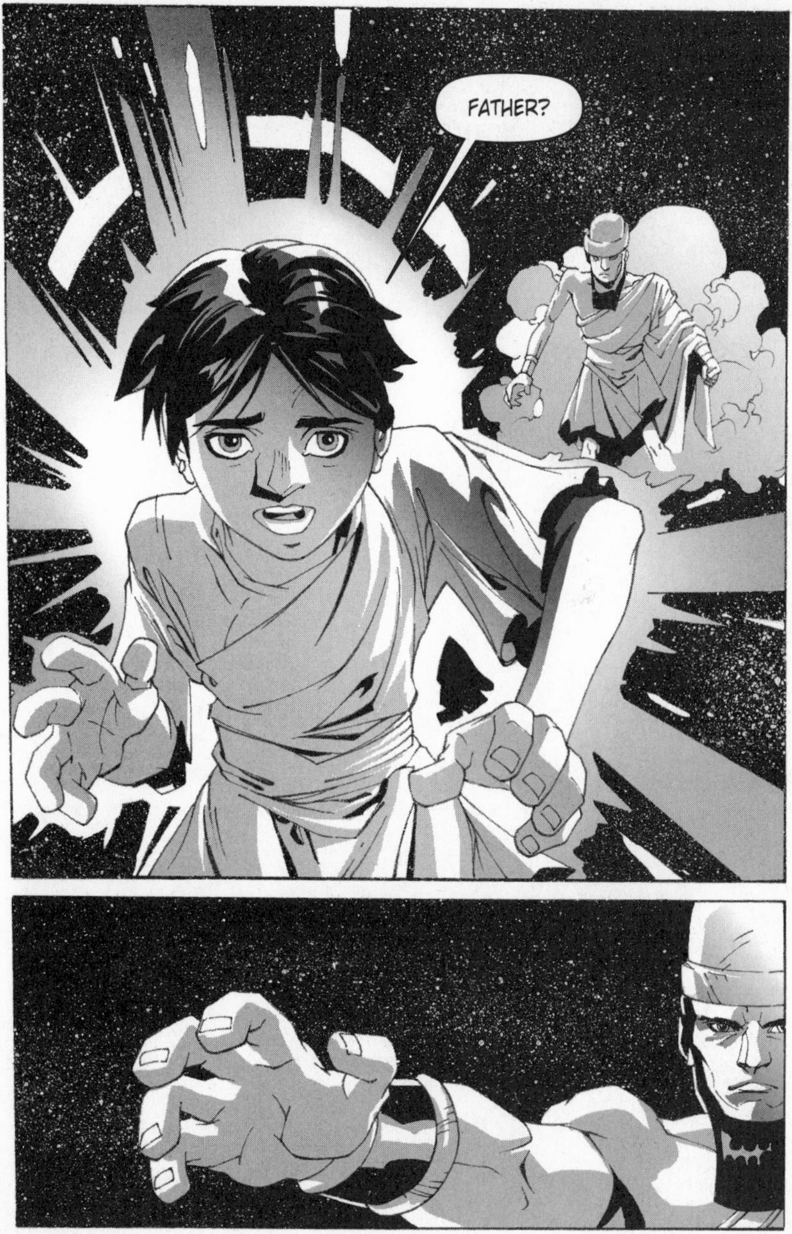
FATHER?

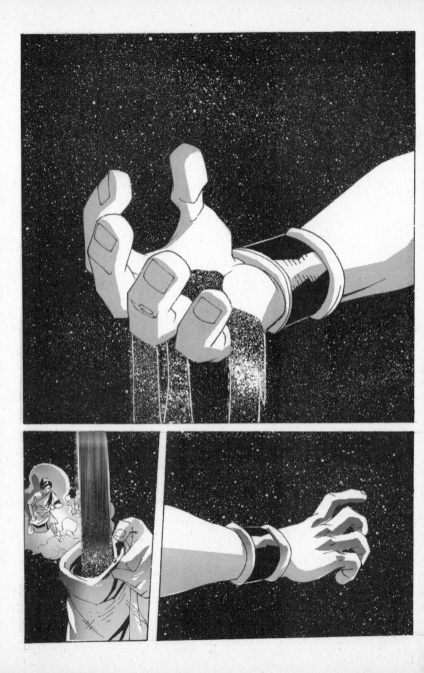

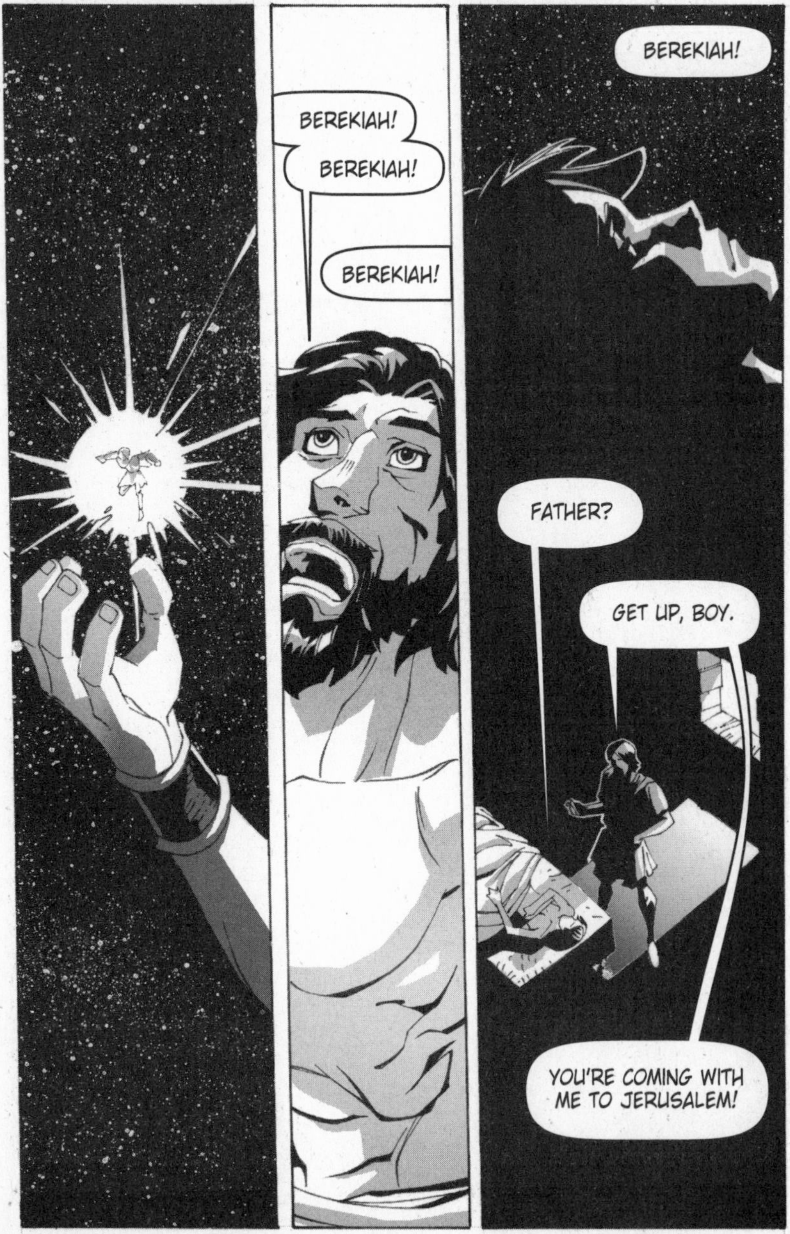
BEREKIAH!
BEREKIAH!
BEREKIAH!
BEREKIAH!
FATHER?
GET UP, BOY.
YOU'RE COMING WITH ME TO JERUSALEM!

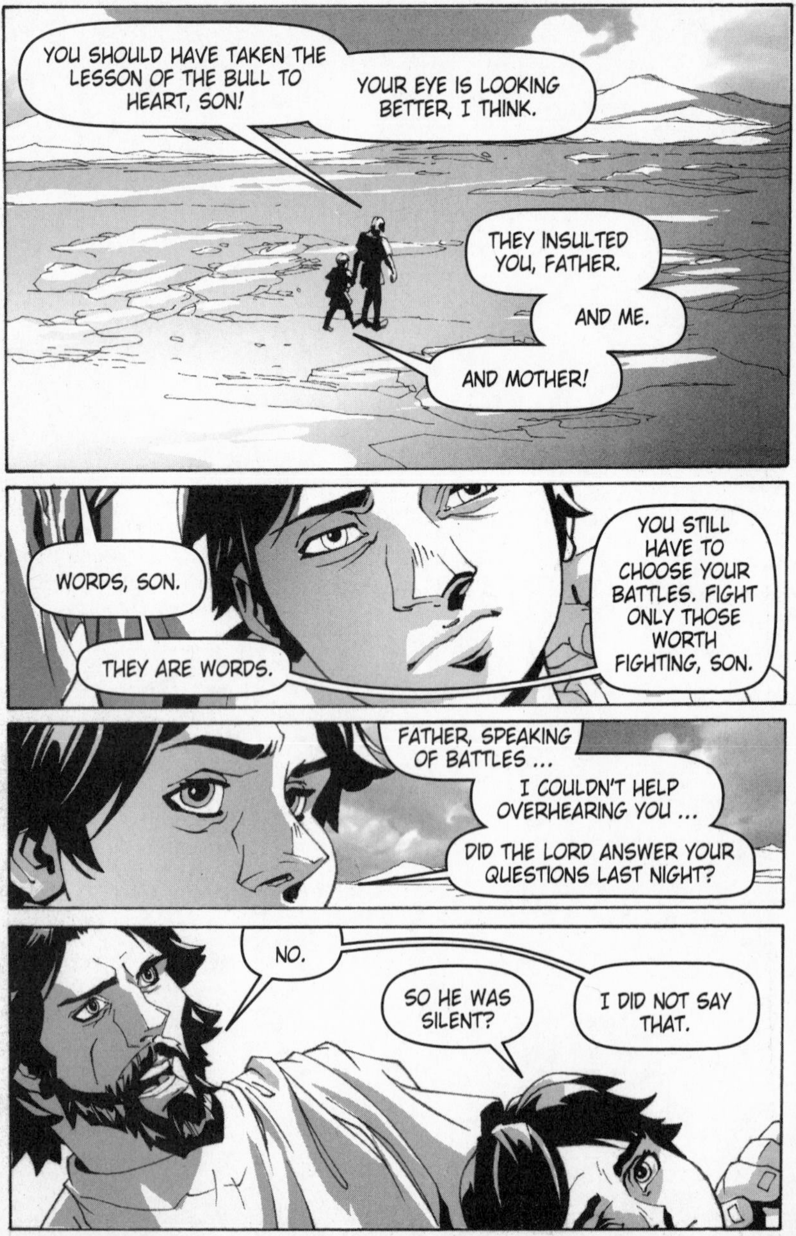
YOU SHOULD HAVE TAKEN THE LESSON OF THE BULL TO HEART, SON!
YOUR EYE IS LOOKING BETTER, I THINK.
THEY INSULTED YOU, FATHER.
AND ME.
AND MOTHER!
WORDS, SON.
THEY ARE WORDS.
YOU STILL HAVE TO CHOOSE YOUR BATTLES. FIGHT ONLY THOSE WORTH FIGHTING, SON.
FATHER, SPEAKING OF BATTLES ...
I COULDN'T HELP OVERHEARING YOU ...
DID THE LORD ANSWER YOUR QUESTIONS LAST NIGHT?
NO.
SO HE WAS SILENT?
I DID NOT SAY THAT.

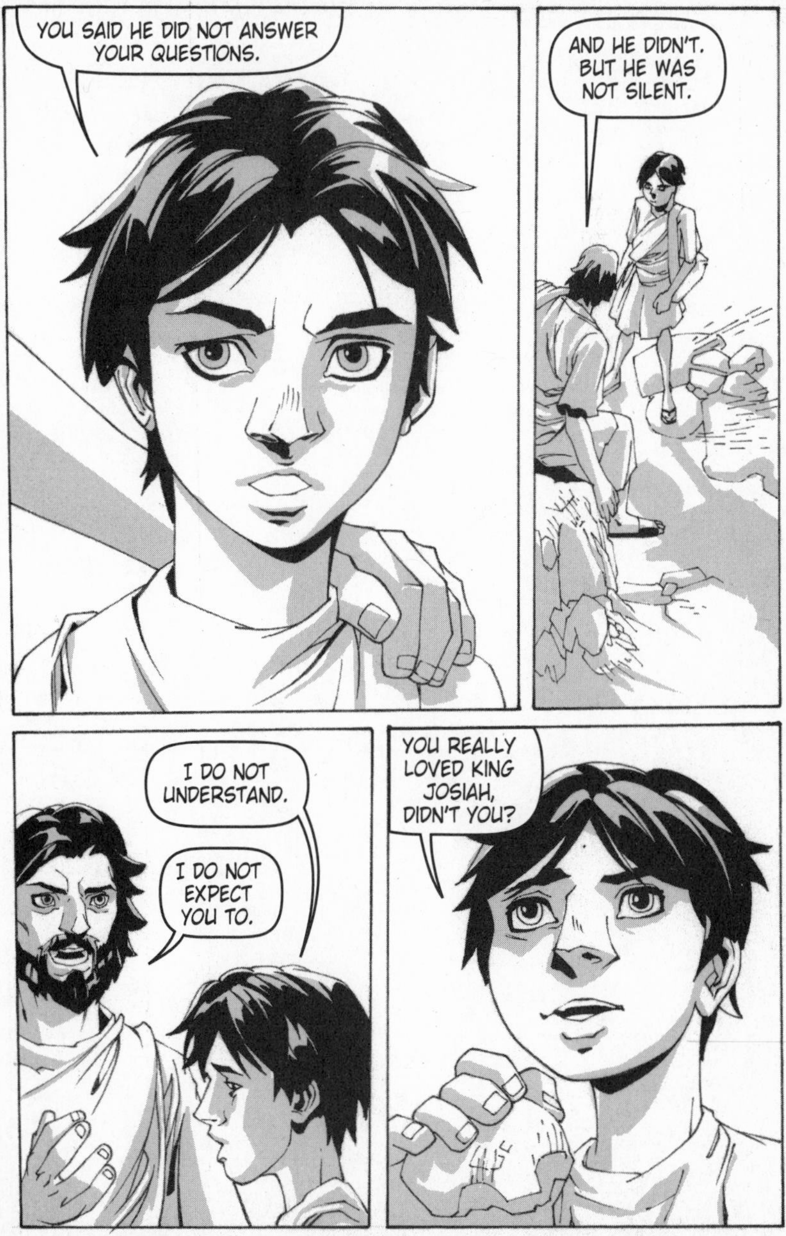
YOU SAID HE DID NOT ANSWER YOUR QUESTIONS.
AND HE DIDN'T. BUT HE WAS NOT SILENT.
I DO NOT UNDERSTAND.
I DO NOT EXPECT YOU TO.
YOU REALLY LOVED KING JOSIAH, DIDN'T YOU?

HE'S THE ONLY KING YOU'VE KNOWN, BEREKIAH.

HE WAS THE GREATEST KING WE'VE SEEN SINCE DAVID, MAKE NO MISTAKE.

I WANT THE SAME THING FOR JUDAH AS KING JOSIAH WANTED.

FOR HER TO KEEP HER EYES ON OUR LORD.

AND THAT'S WHY WE'RE GOING TO JERUSALEM.

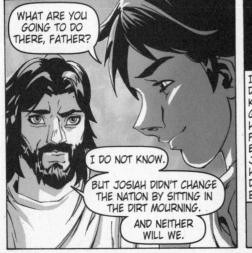

WHAT ARE YOU GOING TO DO THERE, FATHER?

I DO NOT KNOW.

BUT JOSIAH DIDN'T CHANGE THE NATION BY SITTING IN THE DIRT MOURNING.

AND NEITHER WILL WE.

COME, BOY ...

WHO DO YOU THINK SHOULD BE KING, FATHER?

IT WILL BE DIFFICULT TO REPLACE KING JOSIAH. HE WAS A GIFT TO JUDAH FROM THE HAND OF THE LORD. HIS FATHER AMON WAS AN EVIL KING, AND YET JOSIAH ... HE ... HE WAS A DIFFERENT BREED.

CHAPTER THREE
"AND A CHILD SHALL LEAD THEM"

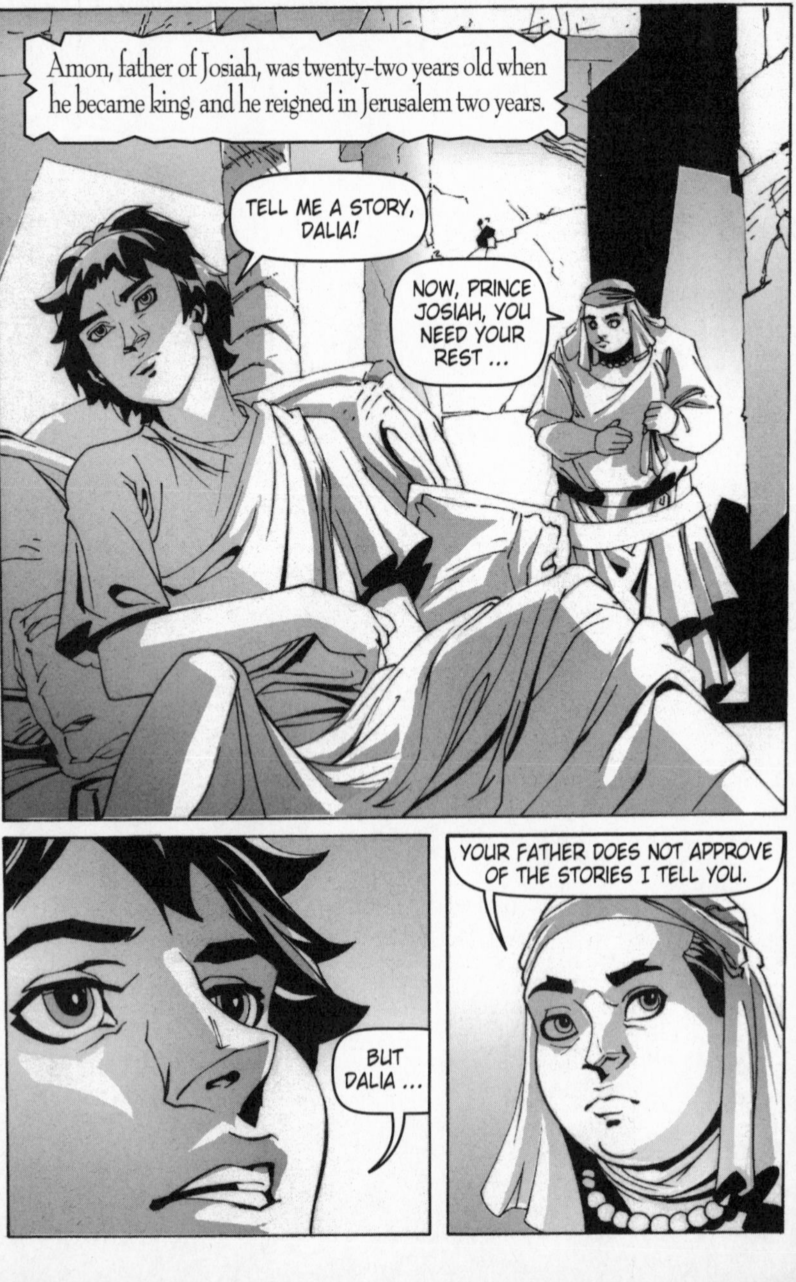
Amon, father of Josiah, was twenty-two years old when he became king, and he reigned in Jerusalem two years.
TELL ME A STORY, DALIA!
NOW, PRINCE JOSIAH, YOU NEED YOUR REST ...
BUT DALIA ...
YOUR FATHER DOES NOT APPROVE OF THE STORIES I TELL YOU.

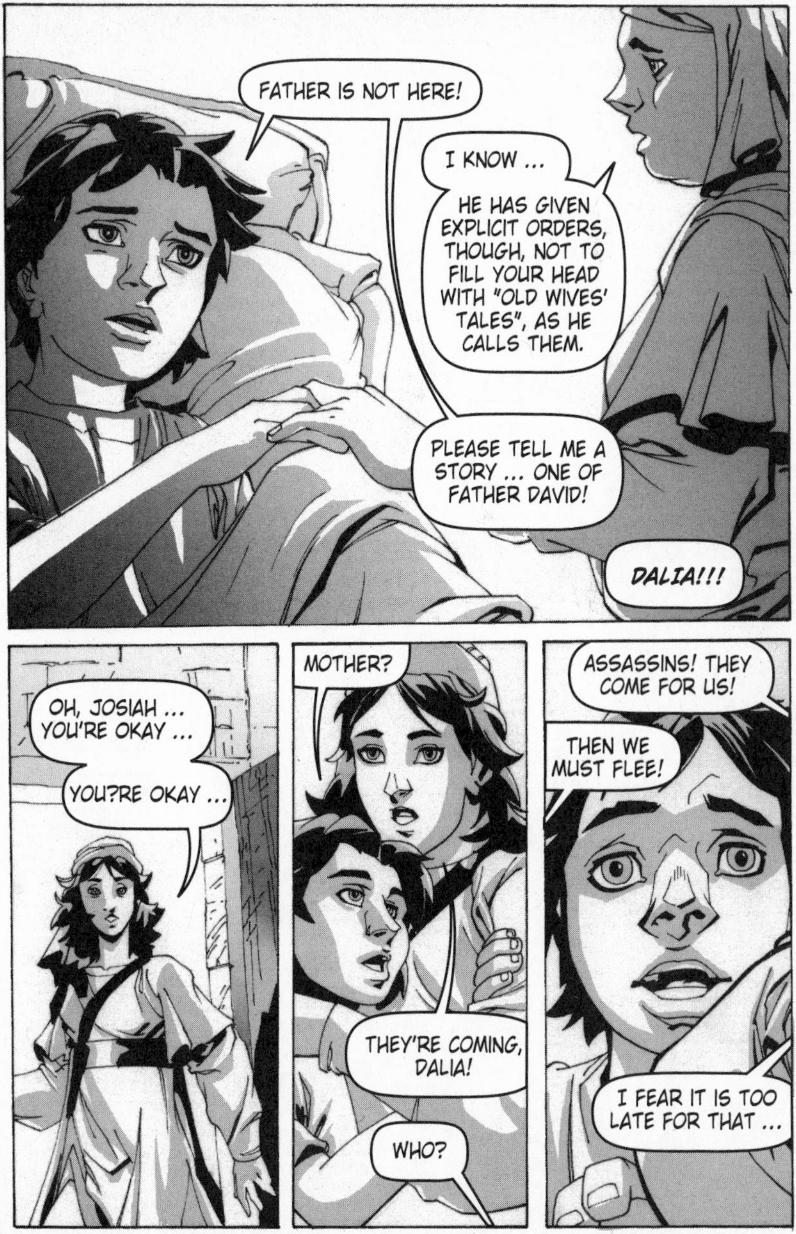
FATHER IS NOT HERE!
I KNOW ...
HE HAS GIVEN EXPLICIT ORDERS, THOUGH, NOT TO FILL YOUR HEAD WITH "OLD WIVES' TALES", AS HE CALLS THEM.
PLEASE TELL ME A STORY ... ONE OF FATHER DAVID!
DALIA!!!
OH, JOSIAH ... YOU'RE OKAY ...
YOU?RE OKAY ...
MOTHER?
THEY'RE COMING, DALIA!
WHO?
ASSASSINS! THEY COME FOR US!
THEN WE MUST FLEE!
I FEAR IT IS TOO LATE FOR THAT ...

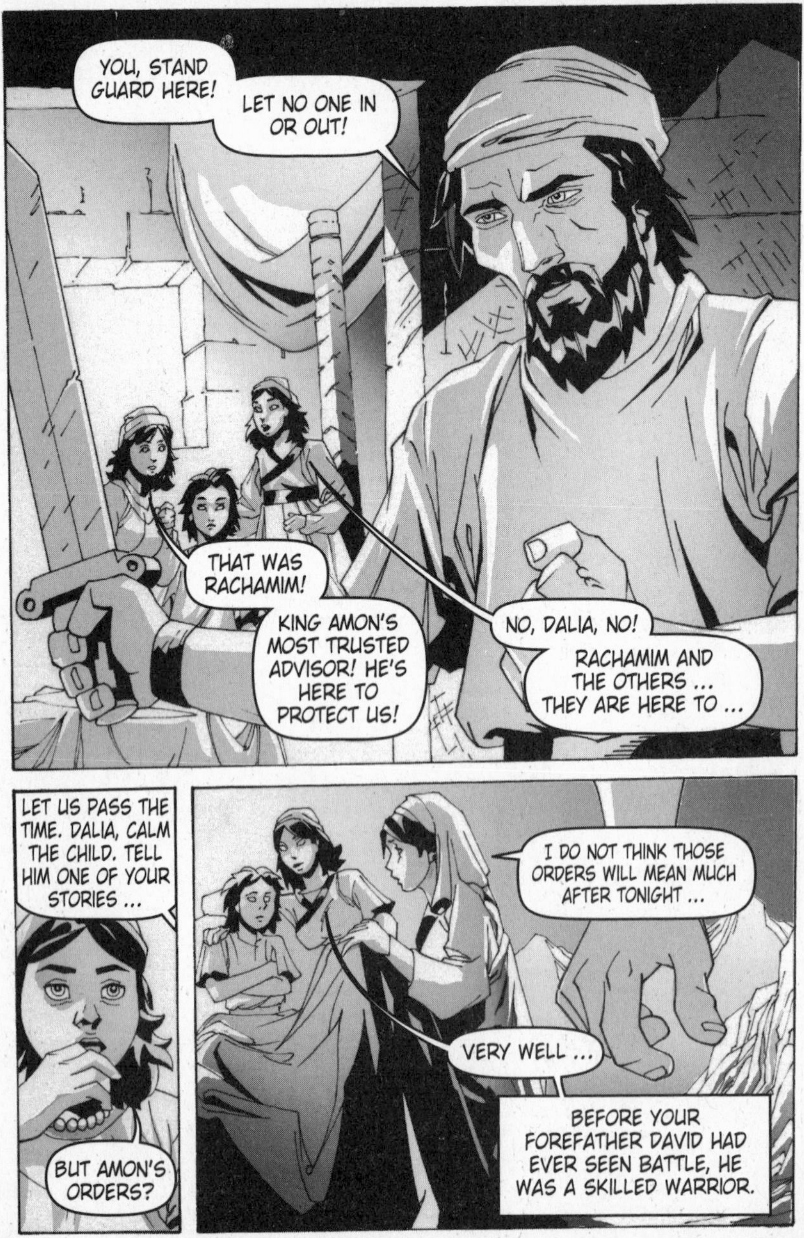
YOU, STAND GUARD HERE!
LET NO ONE IN OR OUT!
THAT WAS RACHAMIM!
KING AMON'S MOST TRUSTED ADVISOR! HE'S HERE TO PROTECT US!
NO, DALIA, NO!
RACHAMIM AND THE OTHERS ... THEY ARE HERE TO ...
LET US PASS THE TIME. DALIA, CALM THE CHILD. TELL HIM ONE OF YOUR STORIES ...
BUT AMON'S ORDERS?
I DO NOT THINK THOSE ORDERS WILL MEAN MUCH AFTER TONIGHT ...
VERY WELL ...
BEFORE YOUR FOREFATHER DAVID HAD EVER SEEN BATTLE, HE WAS A SKILLED WARRIOR.

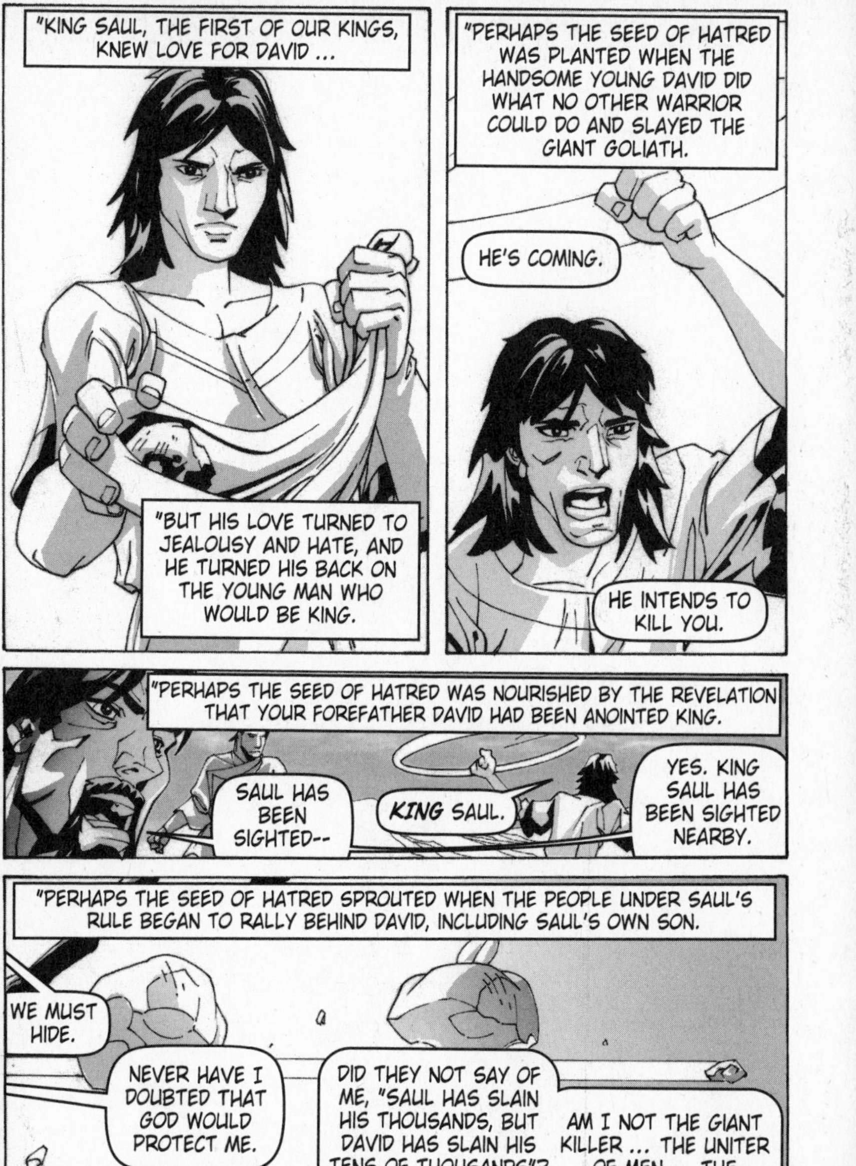
"KING SAUL, THE FIRST OF OUR KINGS, KNEW LOVE FOR DAVID ...
"BUT HIS LOVE TURNED TO JEALOUSY AND HATE, AND HE TURNED HIS BACK ON THE YOUNG MAN WHO WOULD BE KING.
"PERHAPS THE SEED OF HATRED WAS PLANTED WHEN THE HANDSOME YOUNG DAVID DID WHAT NO OTHER WARRIOR COULD DO AND SLAYED THE GIANT GOLIATH.
HE'S COMING.
HE INTENDS TO KILL YOU.
"PERHAPS THE SEED OF HATRED WAS NOURISHED BY THE REVELATION THAT YOUR FOREFATHER DAVID HAD BEEN ANOINTED KING.
SAUL HAS BEEN SIGHTED--
KING SAUL.
YES. KING SAUL HAS BEEN SIGHTED NEARBY.
"PERHAPS THE SEED OF HATRED SPROUTED WHEN THE PEOPLE UNDER SAUL'S RULE BEGAN TO RALLY BEHIND DAVID, INCLUDING SAUL'S OWN SON.
WE MUST HIDE.
NEVER HAVE I DOUBTED THAT GOD WOULD PROTECT ME.
DID THEY NOT SAY OF ME, "SAUL HAS SLAIN HIS THOUSANDS, BUT DAVID HAS SLAIN HIS TENS OF THOUSANDS"?
AM I NOT THE GIANT KILLER ... THE UNITER OF MEN ... THE ANOINTED KING?

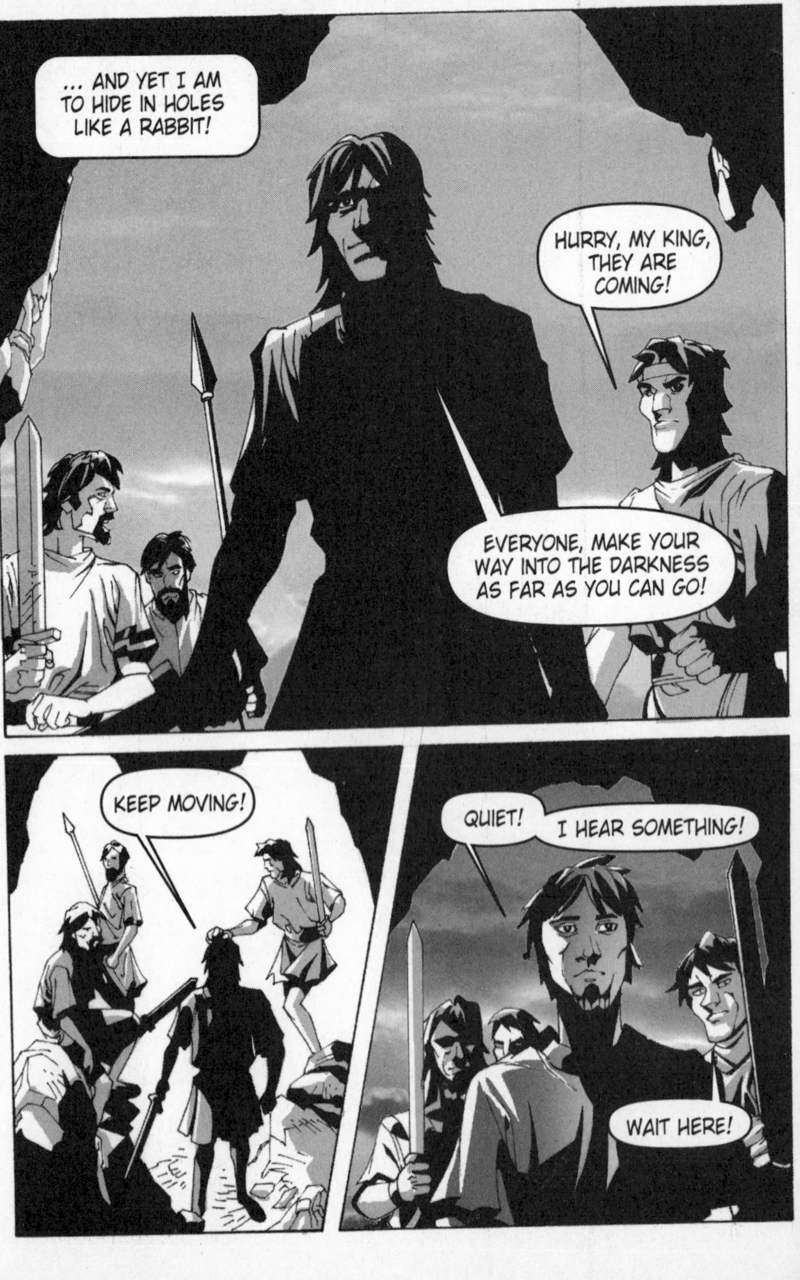
... AND YET I AM TO HIDE IN HOLES LIKE A RABBIT!
HURRY, MY KING, THEY ARE COMING!
EVERYONE, MAKE YOUR WAY INTO THE DARKNESS AS FAR AS YOU CAN GO!
KEEP MOVING!
QUIET!
I HEAR SOMETHING!
WAIT HERE!

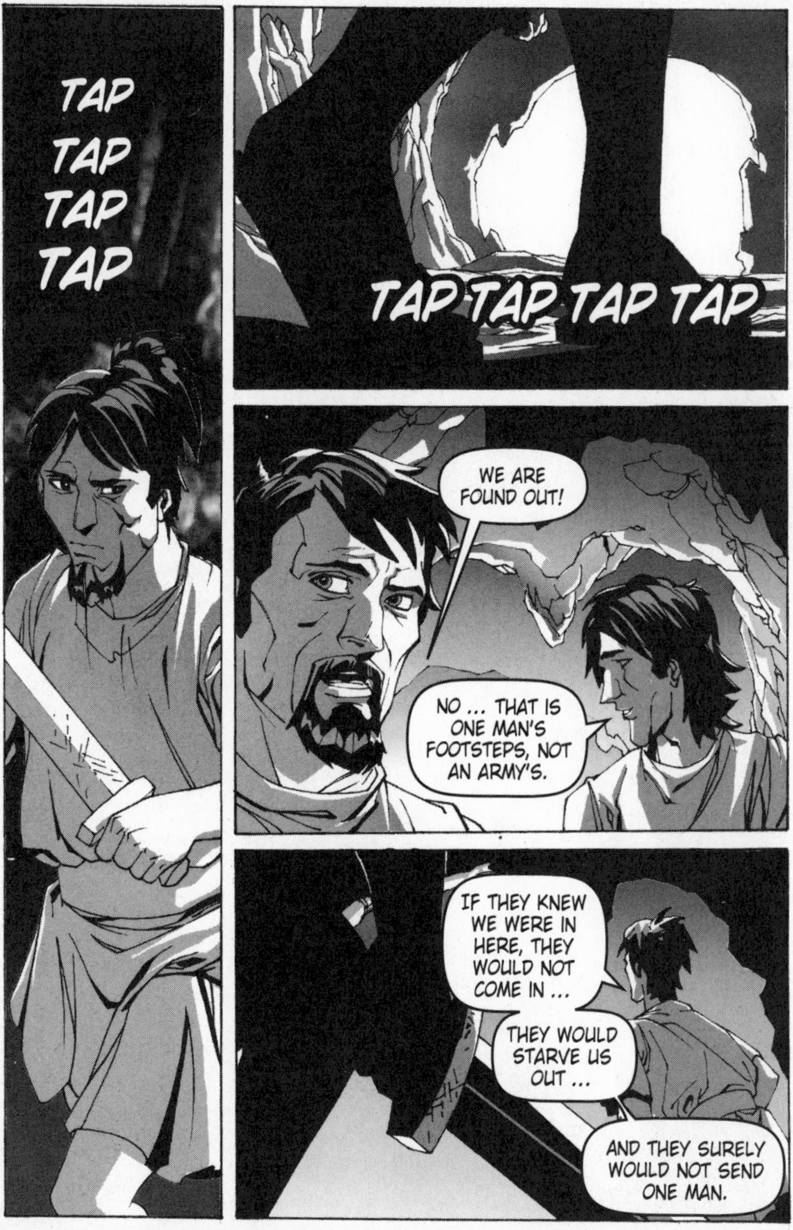
TAP TAP TAP TAP
TAP TAP TAP TAP
WE ARE FOUND OUT!
NO ... THAT IS ONE MAN'S FOOTSTEPS, NOT AN ARMY'S.
IF THEY KNEW WE WERE IN HERE, THEY WOULD NOT COME IN ...
THEY WOULD STARVE US OUT ...
AND THEY SURELY WOULD NOT SEND ONE MAN.

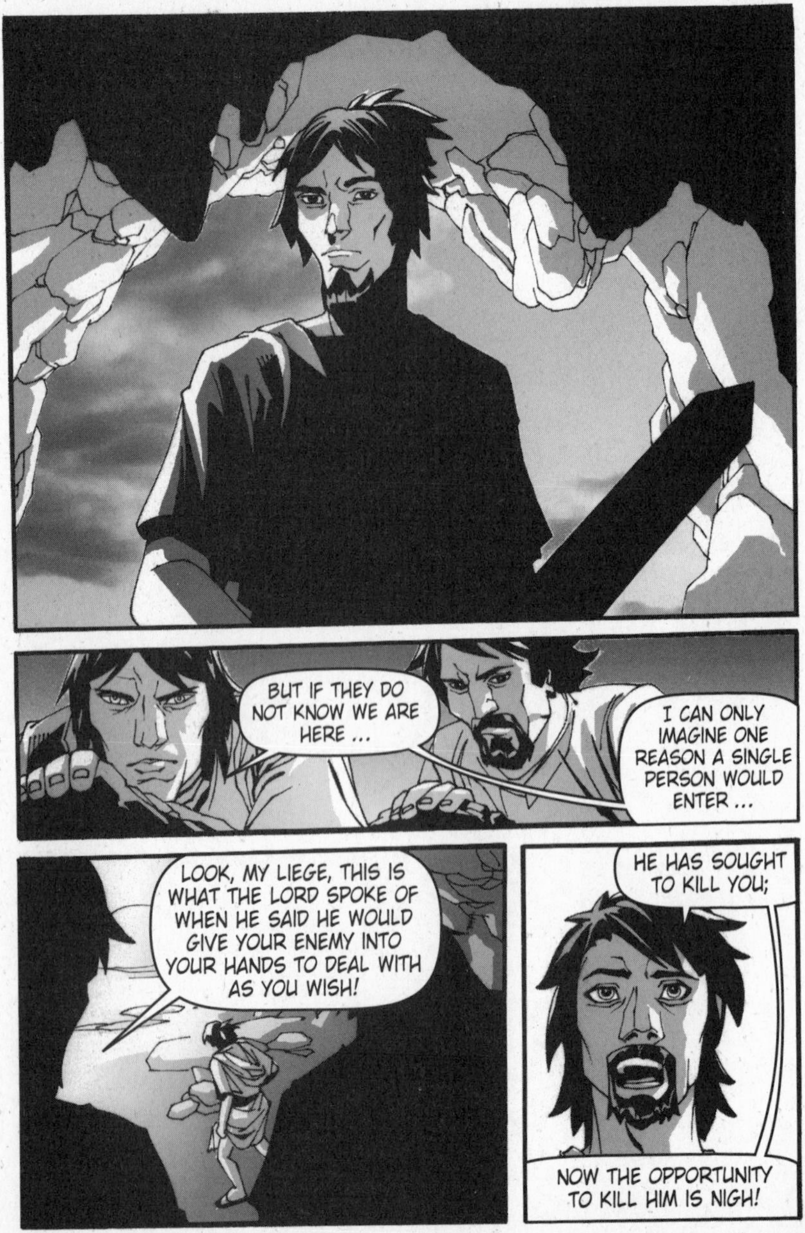
BUT IF THEY DO NOT KNOW WE ARE HERE ...
I CAN ONLY IMAGINE ONE REASON A SINGLE PERSON WOULD ENTER ...
LOOK, MY LIEGE, THIS IS WHAT THE LORD SPOKE OF WHEN HE SAID HE WOULD GIVE YOUR ENEMY INTO YOUR HANDS TO DEAL WITH AS YOU WISH!
HE HAS SOUGHT TO KILL YOU;
NOW THE OPPORTUNITY TO KILL HIM IS NIGH!

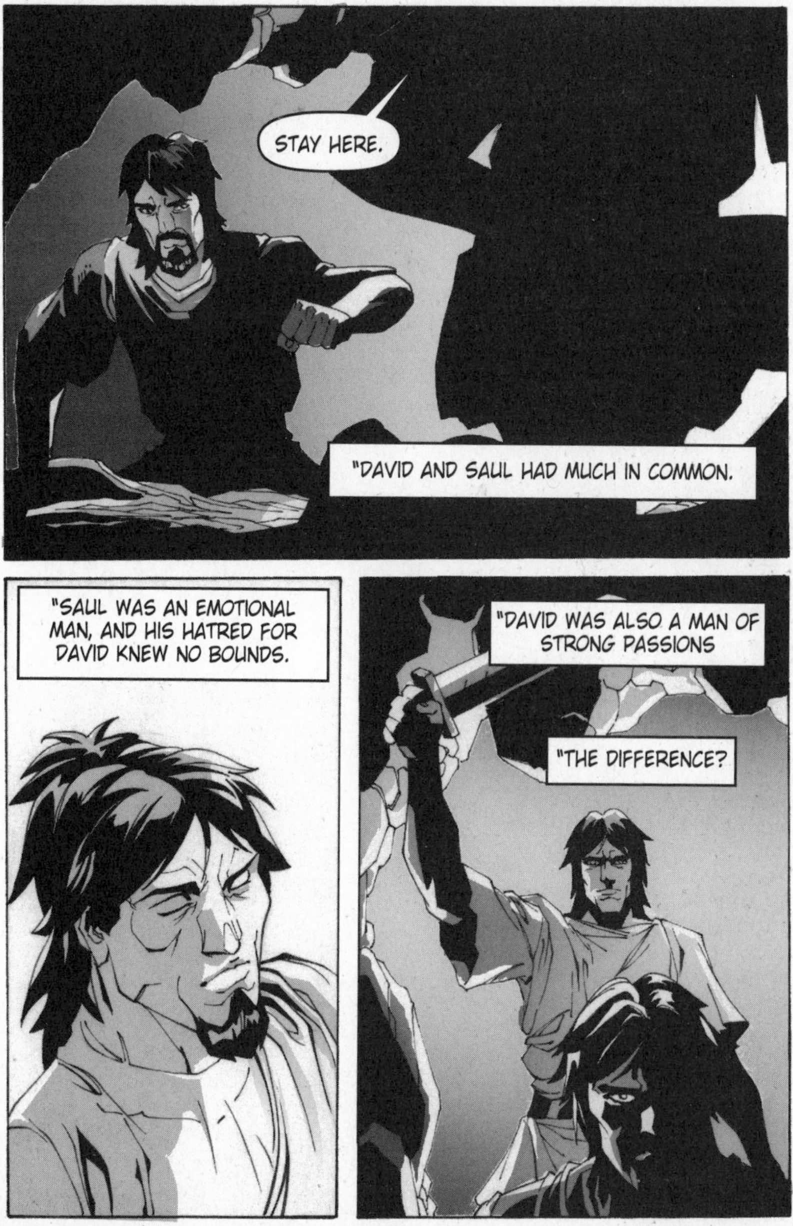
STAY HERE.
"DAVID AND SAUL HAD MUCH IN COMMON.
"SAUL WAS AN EMOTIONAL MAN, AND HIS HATRED FOR DAVID KNEW NO BOUNDS.
"DAVID WAS ALSO A MAN OF STRONG PASSIONS
"THE DIFFERENCE?

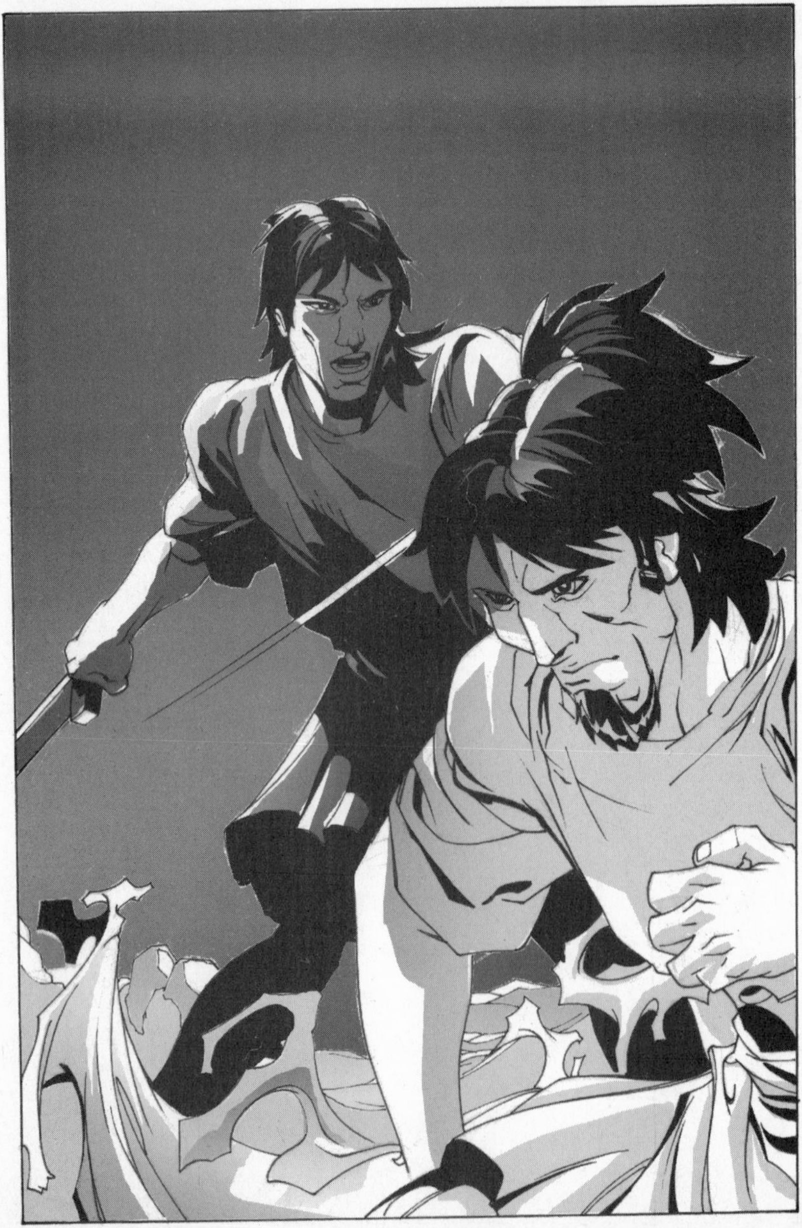

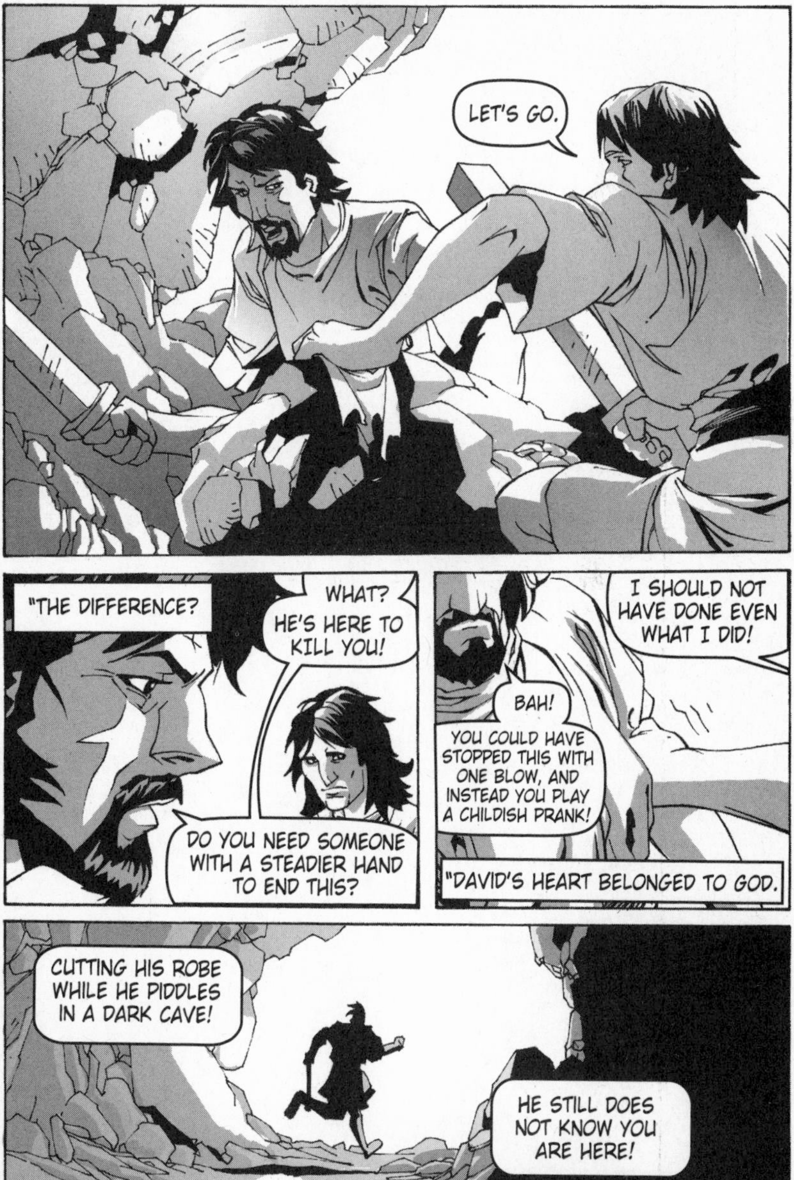
LET'S GO.
"THE DIFFERENCE?
WHAT? HE'S HERE TO KILL YOU!
DO YOU NEED SOMEONE WITH A STEADIER HAND TO END THIS?
I SHOULD NOT HAVE DONE EVEN WHAT I DID!
BAH!
YOU COULD HAVE STOPPED THIS WITH ONE BLOW, AND INSTEAD YOU PLAY A CHILDISH PRANK!
"DAVID'S HEART BELONGED TO GOD.
CUTTING HIS ROBE WHILE HE PIDDLES IN A DARK CAVE!
HE STILL DOES NOT KNOW YOU ARE HERE!

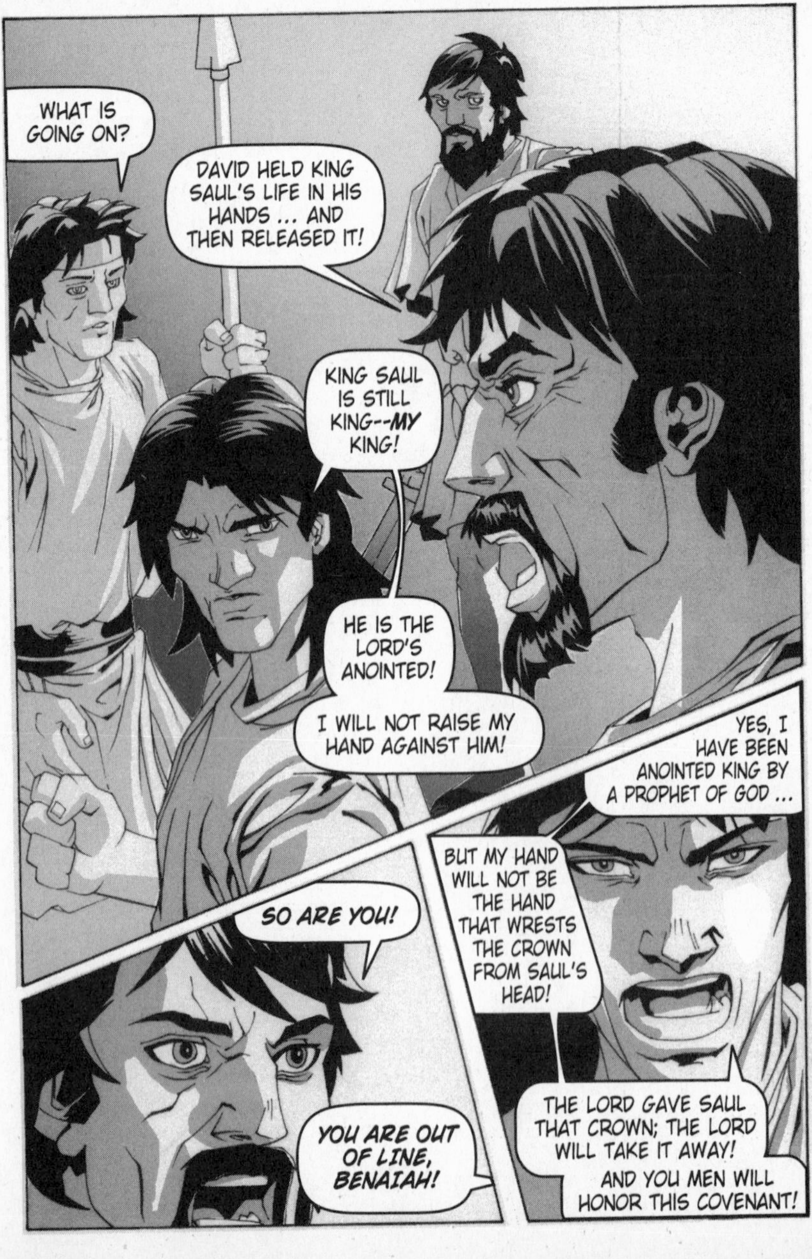
WHAT IS GOING ON?
DAVID HELD KING SAUL'S LIFE IN HIS HANDS ... AND THEN RELEASED IT!
KING SAUL IS STILL KING--*MY* KING!
HE IS THE LORD'S ANOINTED!
I WILL NOT RAISE MY HAND AGAINST HIM!
SO ARE YOU!
YOU ARE OUT OF LINE, BENAIAH!
YES, I HAVE BEEN ANOINTED KING BY A PROPHET OF GOD ...
BUT MY HAND WILL NOT BE THE HAND THAT WRESTS THE CROWN FROM SAUL'S HEAD!
THE LORD GAVE SAUL THAT CROWN; THE LORD WILL TAKE IT AWAY!
AND YOU MEN WILL HONOR THIS COVENANT!

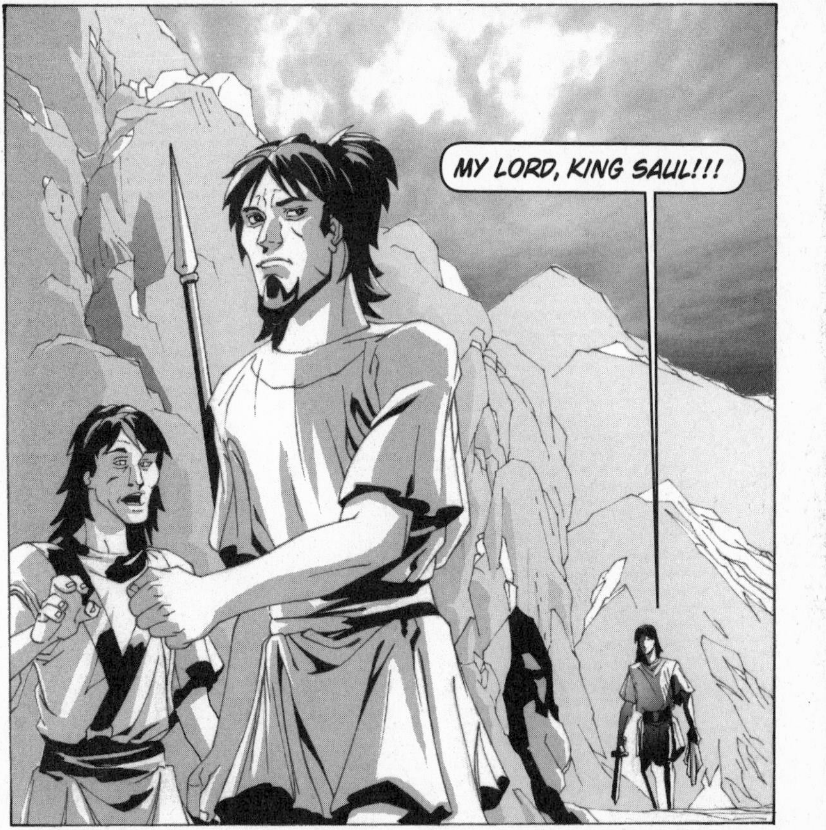
MY LORD, KING SAUL!!!

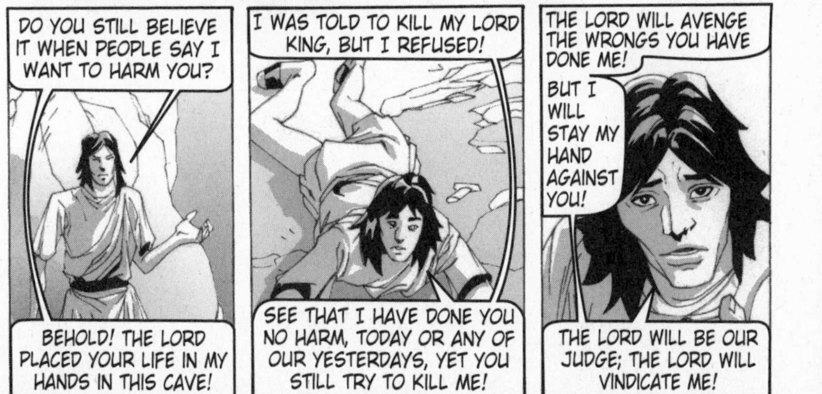
DO YOU STILL BELIEVE IT WHEN PEOPLE SAY I WANT TO HARM YOU?
BEHOLD! THE LORD PLACED YOUR LIFE IN MY HANDS IN THIS CAVE!
I WAS TOLD TO KILL MY LORD KING, BUT I REFUSED!
SEE THAT I HAVE DONE YOU NO HARM, TODAY OR ANY OF OUR YESTERDAYS, YET YOU STILL TRY TO KILL ME!
THE LORD WILL AVENGE THE WRONGS YOU HAVE DONE ME!
BUT I WILL STAY MY HAND AGAINST YOU!
THE LORD WILL BE OUR JUDGE; THE LORD WILL VINDICATE ME!

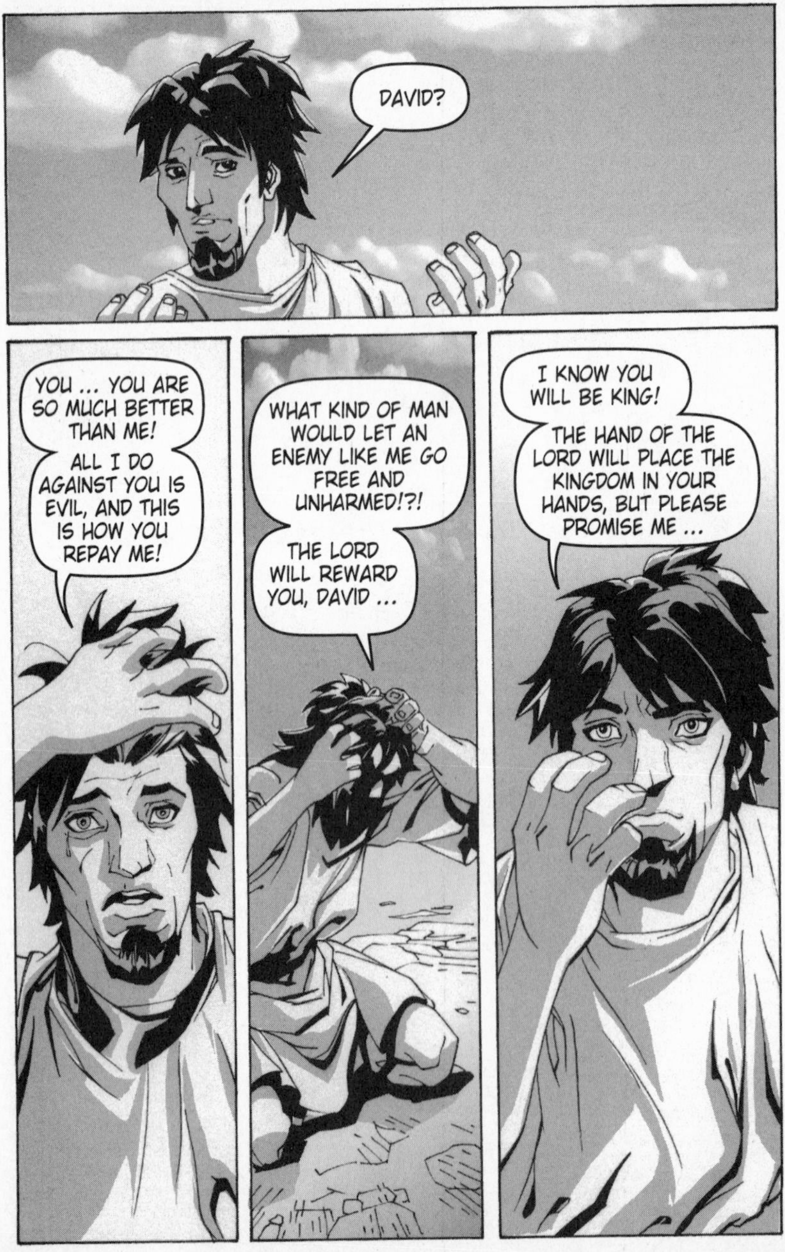

DAVID?
YOU ... YOU ARE SO MUCH BETTER THAN ME!
ALL I DO AGAINST YOU IS EVIL, AND THIS IS HOW YOU REPAY ME!
WHAT KIND OF MAN WOULD LET AN ENEMY LIKE ME GO FREE AND UNHARMED!?!
THE LORD WILL REWARD YOU, DAVID ...
I KNOW YOU WILL BE KING!
THE HAND OF THE LORD WILL PLACE THE KINGDOM IN YOUR HANDS, BUT PLEASE PROMISE ME ...

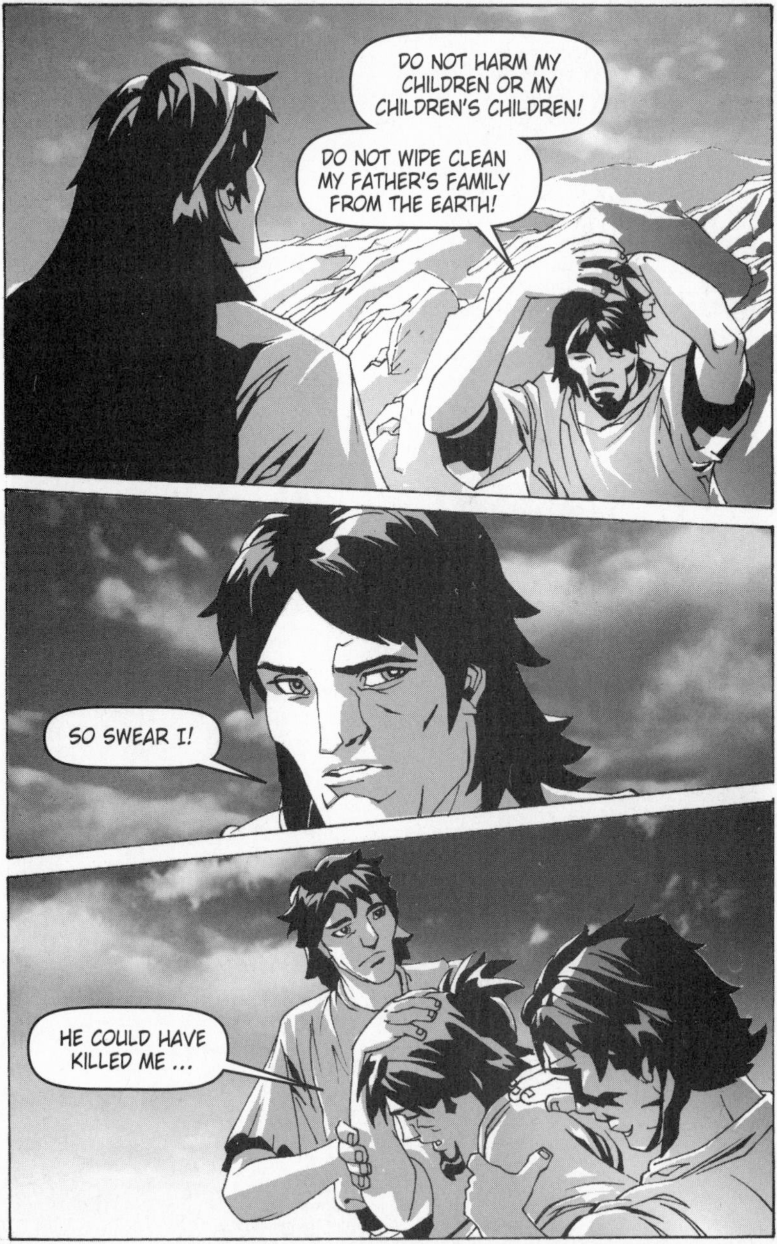
DO NOT HARM MY CHILDREN OR MY CHILDREN'S CHILDREN!
DO NOT WIPE CLEAN MY FATHER'S FAMILY FROM THE EARTH!
SO SWEAR I!
HE COULD HAVE KILLED ME ...

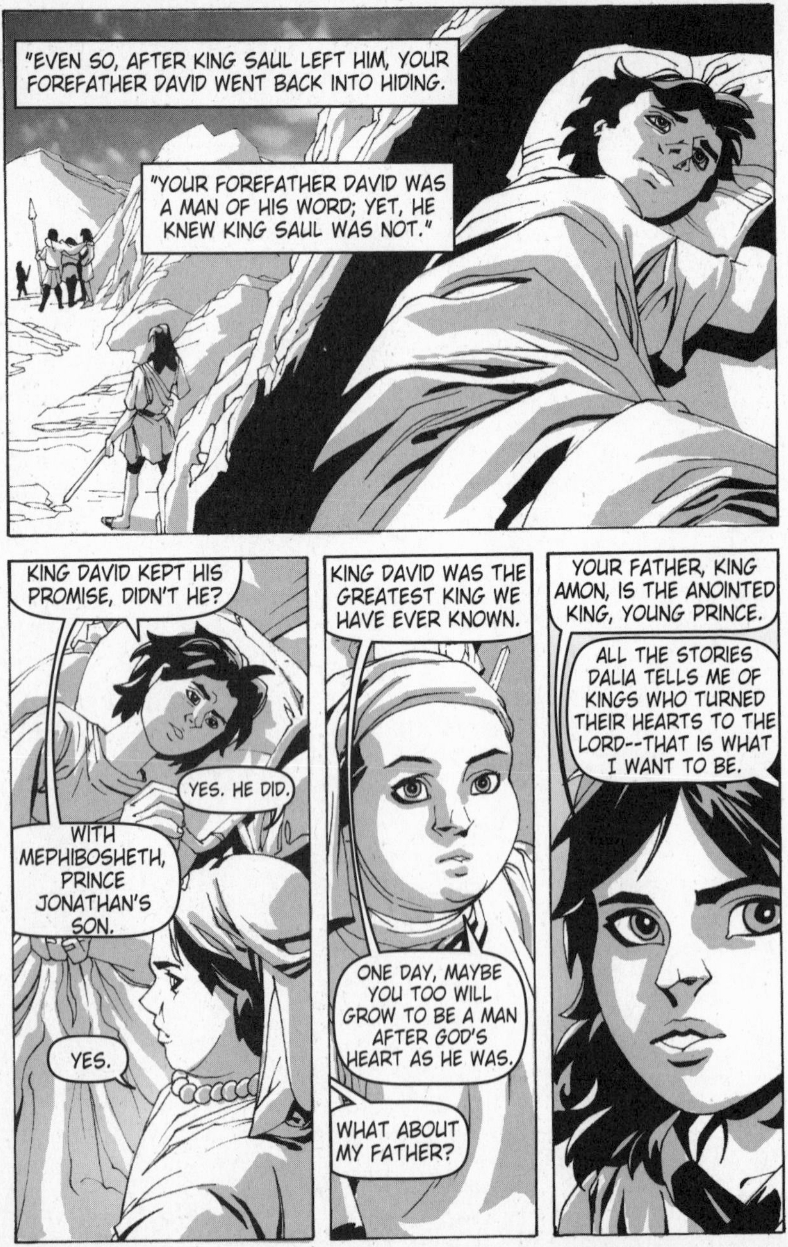
"EVEN SO, AFTER KING SAUL LEFT HIM, YOUR FOREFATHER DAVID WENT BACK INTO HIDING.
"YOUR FOREFATHER DAVID WAS A MAN OF HIS WORD; YET, HE KNEW KING SAUL WAS NOT."
KING DAVID KEPT HIS PROMISE, DIDN'T HE?
YES. HE DID.
WITH MEPHIBOSHETH, PRINCE JONATHAN'S SON.
YES.
KING DAVID WAS THE GREATEST KING WE HAVE EVER KNOWN.
ONE DAY, MAYBE YOU TOO WILL GROW TO BE A MAN AFTER GOD'S HEART AS HE WAS.
WHAT ABOUT MY FATHER?
YOUR FATHER, KING AMON, IS THE ANOINTED KING, YOUNG PRINCE.
ALL THE STORIES DALIA TELLS ME OF KINGS WHO TURNED THEIR HEARTS TO THE LORD--THAT IS WHAT I WANT TO BE.

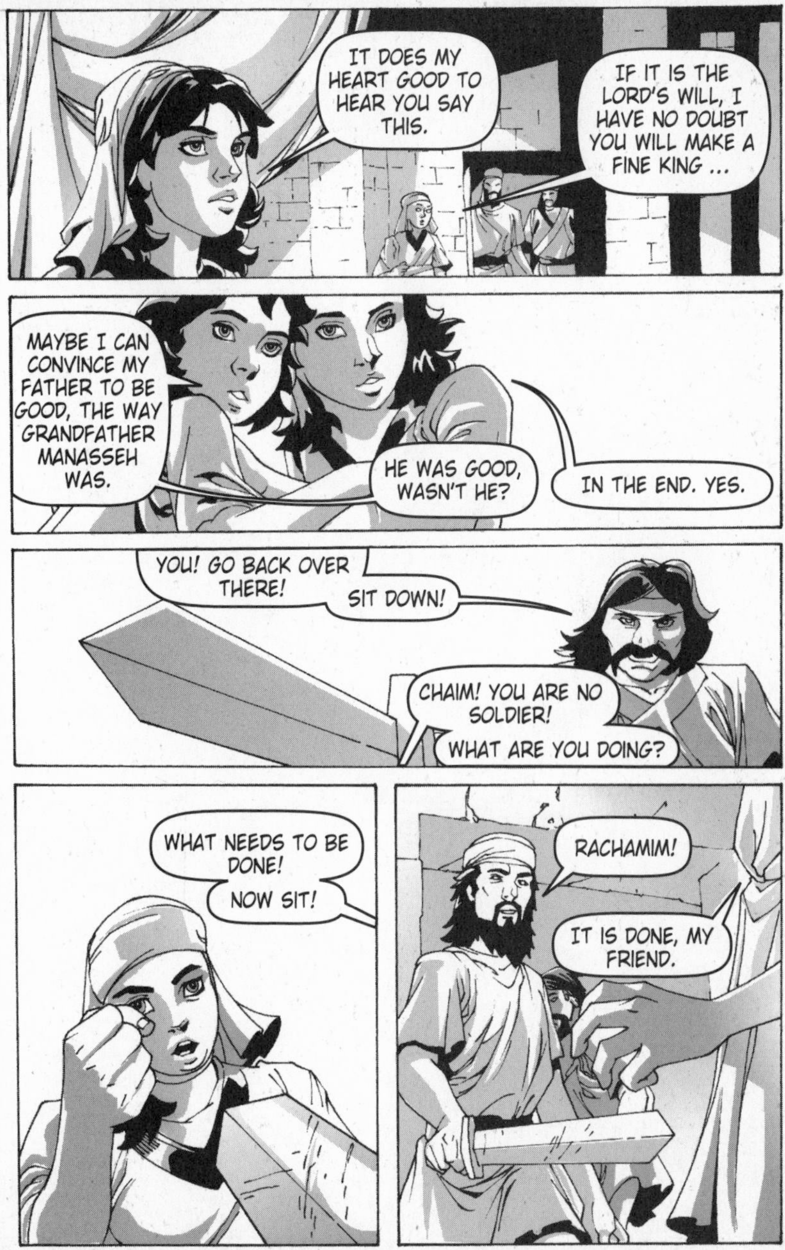
IT DOES MY HEART GOOD TO HEAR YOU SAY THIS.
IF IT IS THE LORD'S WILL, I HAVE NO DOUBT YOU WILL MAKE A FINE KING ...
MAYBE I CAN CONVINCE MY FATHER TO BE GOOD, THE WAY GRANDFATHER MANASSEH WAS.
HE WAS GOOD, WASN'T HE?
IN THE END. YES.
YOU! GO BACK OVER THERE!
SIT DOWN!
CHAIM! YOU ARE NO SOLDIER!
WHAT ARE YOU DOING?
WHAT NEEDS TO BE DONE!
NOW SIT!
RACHAMIM!
IT IS DONE, MY FRIEND.

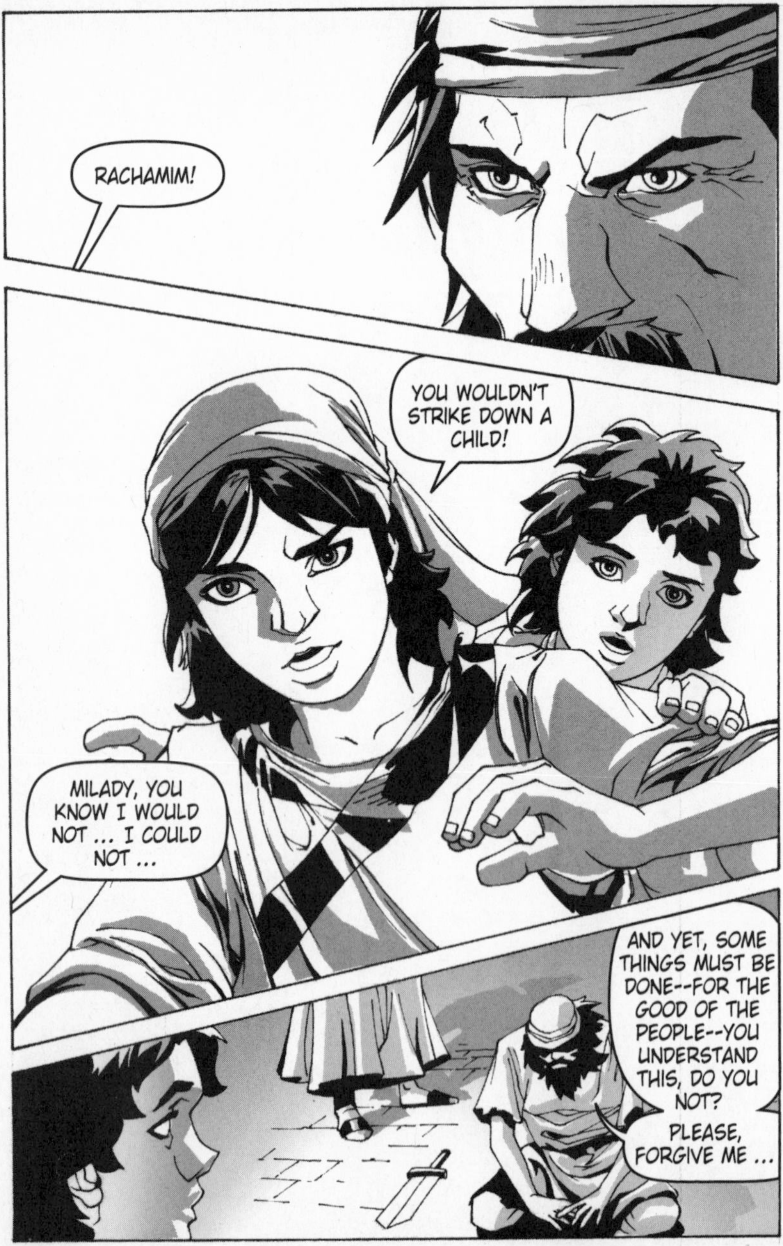
RACHAMIM!
YOU WOULDN'T STRIKE DOWN A CHILD!
MILADY, YOU KNOW I WOULD NOT ... I COULD NOT ...
AND YET, SOME THINGS MUST BE DONE--FOR THE GOOD OF THE PEOPLE--YOU UNDERSTAND THIS, DO YOU NOT?
PLEASE, FORGIVE ME ...

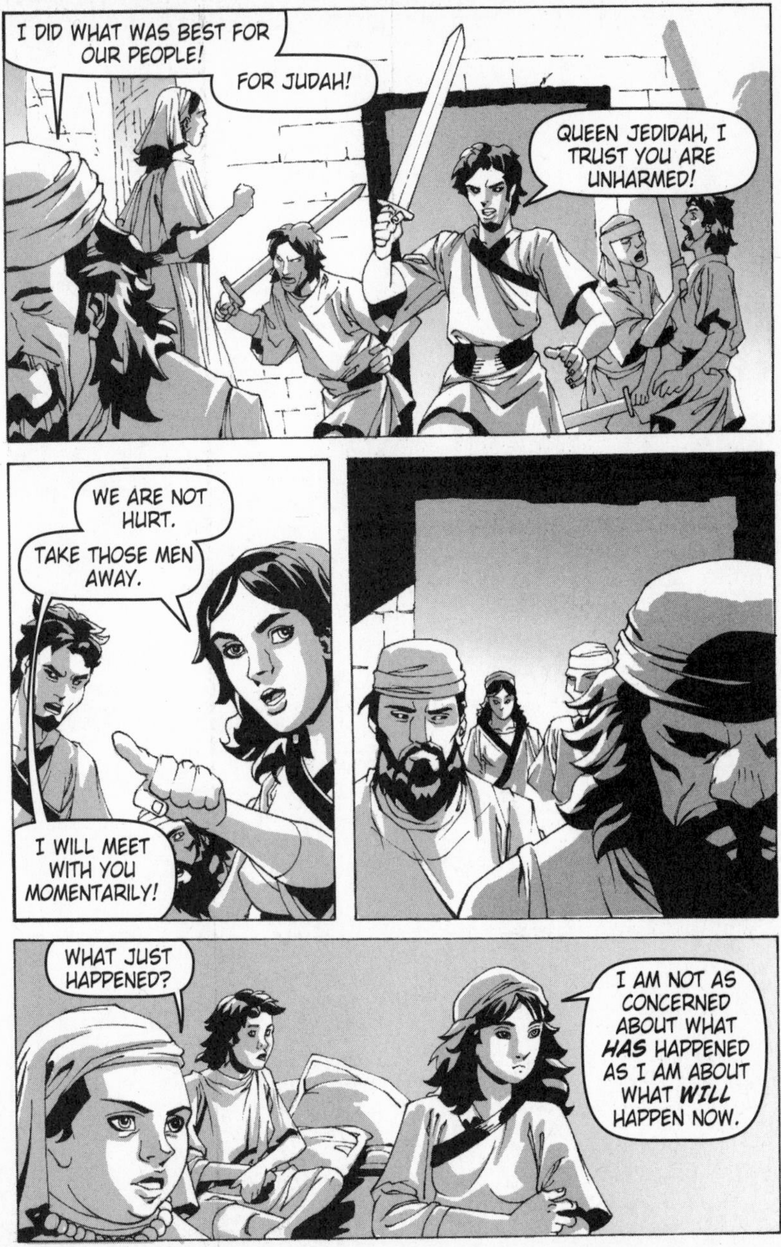
I DID WHAT WAS BEST FOR OUR PEOPLE!
FOR JUDAH!
QUEEN JEDIDAH, I TRUST YOU ARE UNHARMED!
WE ARE NOT HURT.
TAKE THOSE MEN AWAY.
I WILL MEET WITH YOU MOMENTARILY!
WHAT JUST HAPPENED?
I AM NOT AS CONCERNED ABOUT WHAT **HAS** HAPPENED AS I AM ABOUT WHAT **WILL** HAPPEN NOW.

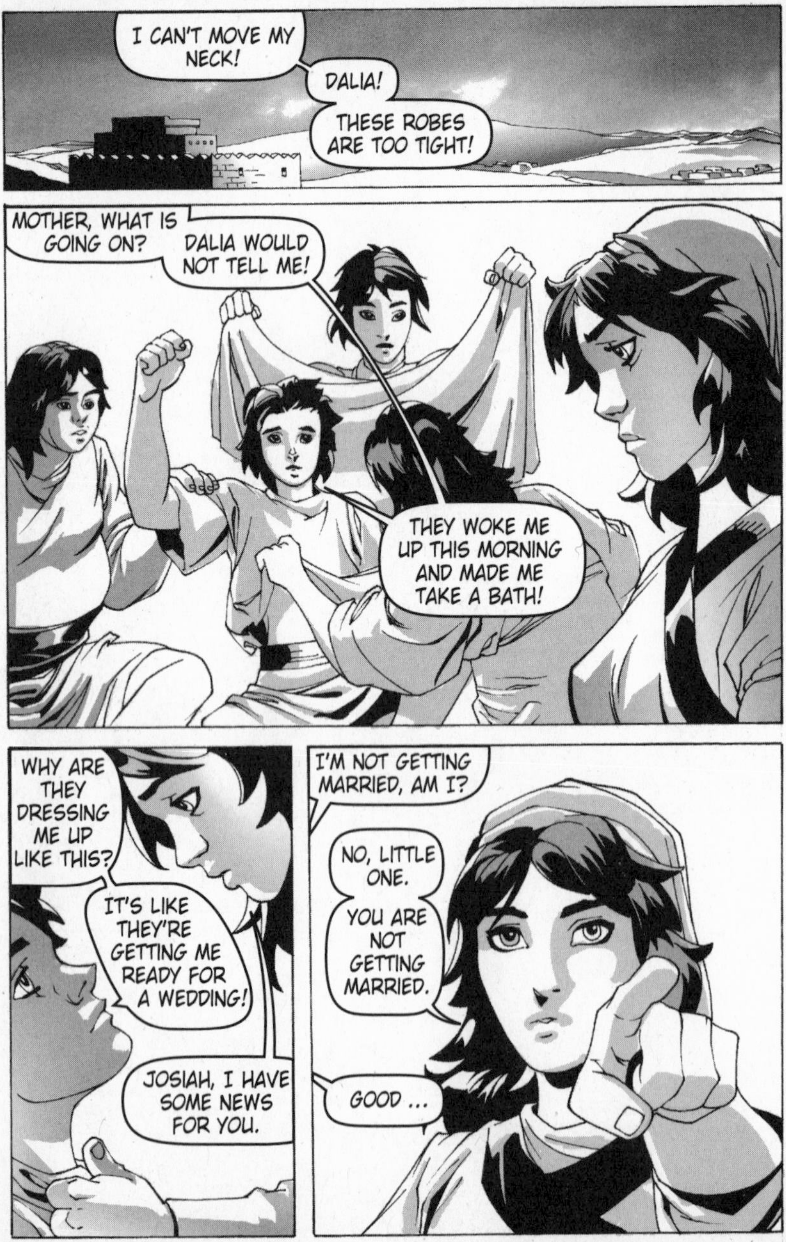
I CAN'T MOVE MY NECK!
DALIA!
THESE ROBES ARE TOO TIGHT!
MOTHER, WHAT IS GOING ON?
DALIA WOULD NOT TELL ME!
THEY WOKE ME UP THIS MORNING AND MADE ME TAKE A BATH!
WHY ARE THEY DRESSING ME UP LIKE THIS?
IT'S LIKE THEY'RE GETTING ME READY FOR A WEDDING!
JOSIAH, I HAVE SOME NEWS FOR YOU.
I'M NOT GETTING MARRIED, AM I?
NO, LITTLE ONE.
YOU ARE NOT GETTING MARRIED.
GOOD ...

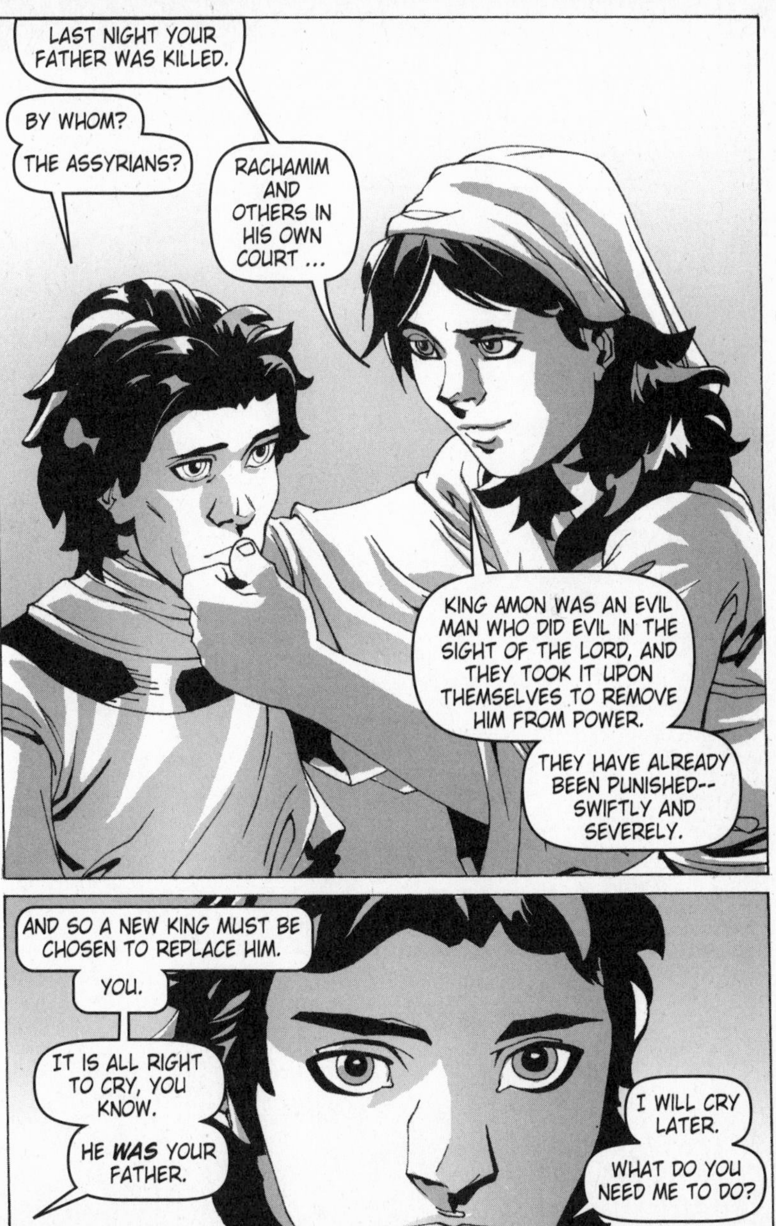
LAST NIGHT YOUR FATHER WAS KILLED.
BY WHOM?
THE ASSYRIANS?
RACHAMIM AND OTHERS IN HIS OWN COURT ...
KING AMON WAS AN EVIL MAN WHO DID EVIL IN THE SIGHT OF THE LORD, AND THEY TOOK IT UPON THEMSELVES TO REMOVE HIM FROM POWER.
THEY HAVE ALREADY BEEN PUNISHED-- SWIFTLY AND SEVERELY.
AND SO A NEW KING MUST BE CHOSEN TO REPLACE HIM.
YOU.
IT IS ALL RIGHT TO CRY, YOU KNOW.
HE *WAS* YOUR FATHER.
I WILL CRY LATER.
WHAT DO YOU NEED ME TO DO?

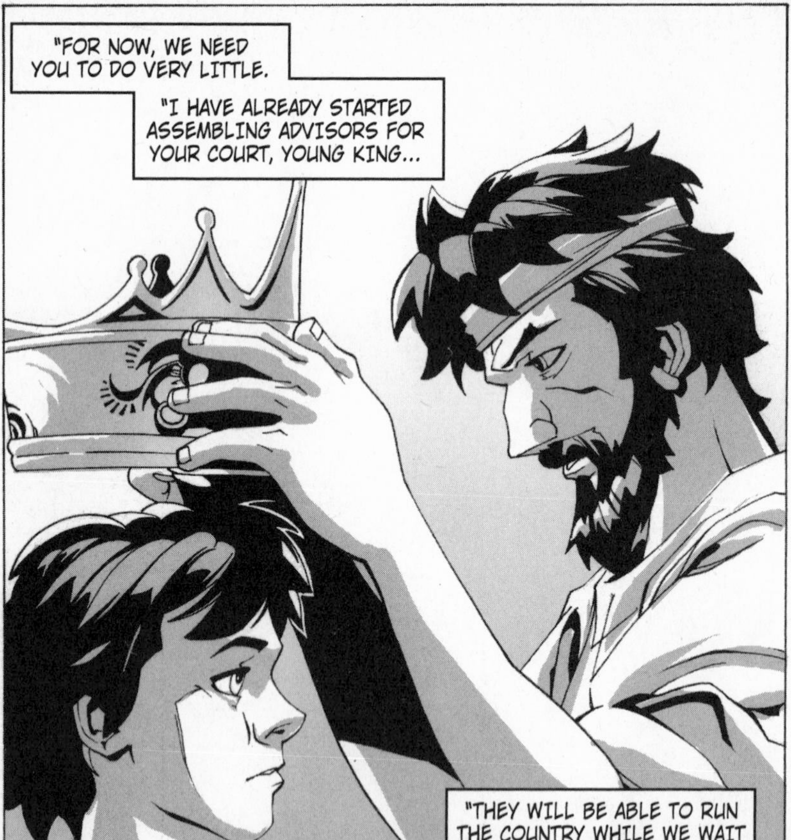
"FOR NOW, WE NEED YOU TO DO VERY LITTLE.
"I HAVE ALREADY STARTED ASSEMBLING ADVISORS FOR YOUR COURT, YOUNG KING...
"THEY WILL BE ABLE TO RUN THE COUNTRY WHILE WE WAIT FOR YOU TO COME OF AGE."

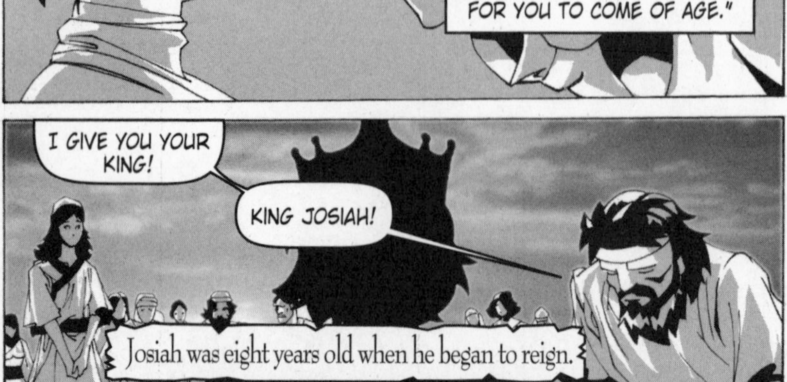
I GIVE YOU YOUR KING!
KING JOSIAH!
Josiah was eight years old when he began to reign.

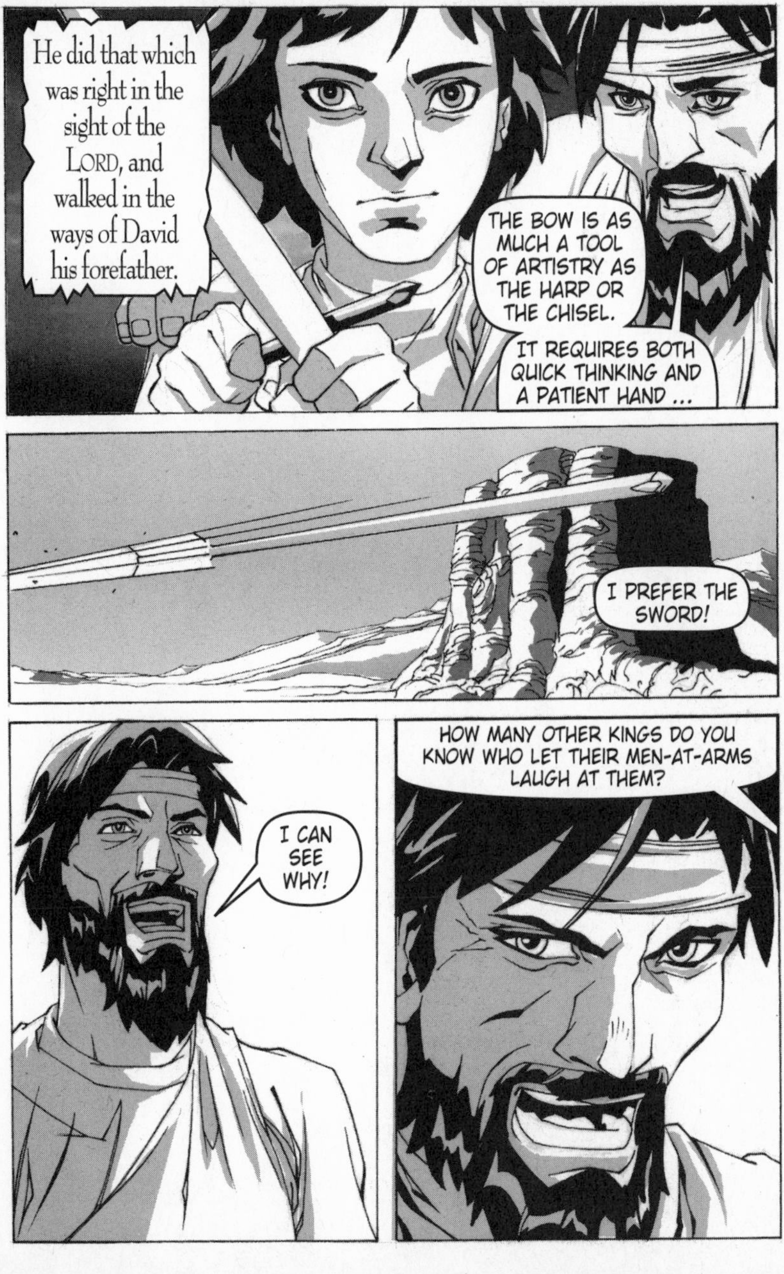
He did that which was right in the sight of the LORD, and walked in the ways of David his forefather.
THE BOW IS AS MUCH A TOOL OF ARTISTRY AS THE HARP OR THE CHISEL.
IT REQUIRES BOTH QUICK THINKING AND A PATIENT HAND ...
I PREFER THE SWORD!
I CAN SEE WHY!
HOW MANY OTHER KINGS DO YOU KNOW WHO LET THEIR MEN-AT-ARMS LAUGH AT THEM?

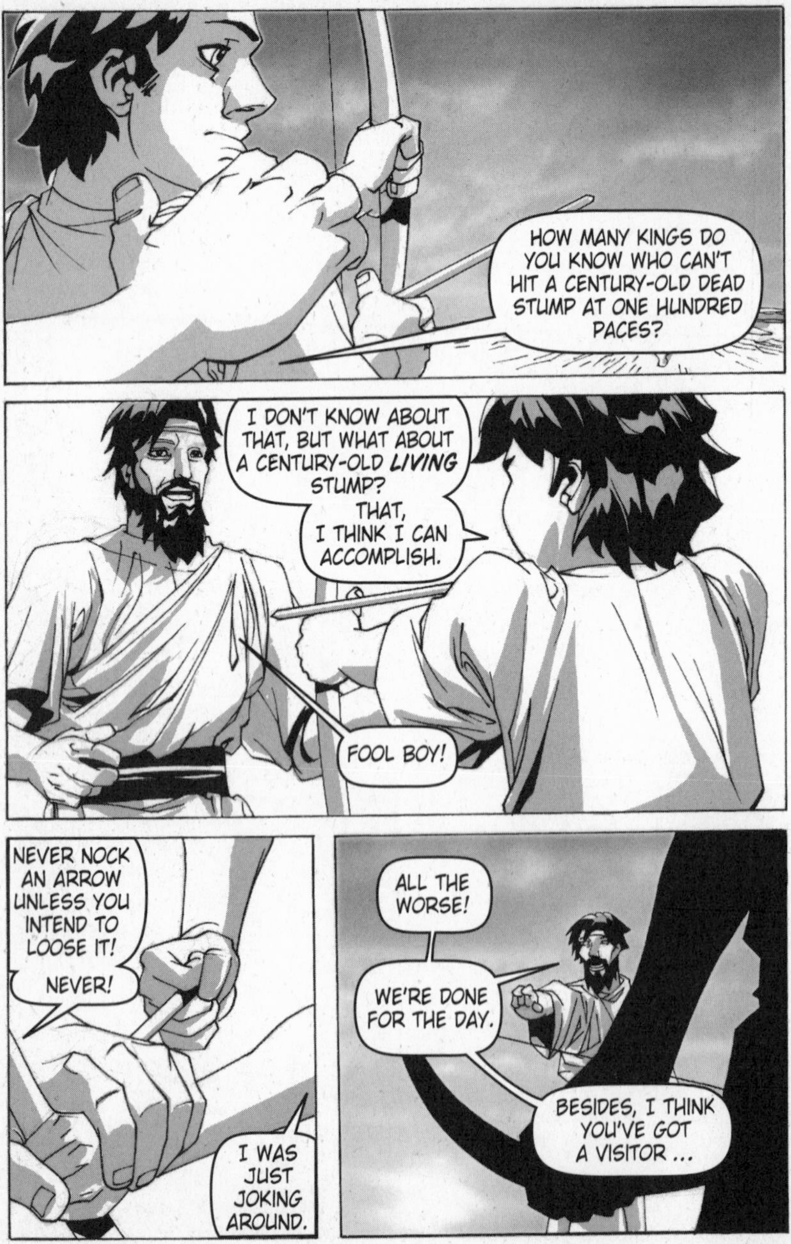
HOW MANY KINGS DO YOU KNOW WHO CAN'T HIT A CENTURY-OLD DEAD STUMP AT ONE HUNDRED PACES?
I DON'T KNOW ABOUT THAT, BUT WHAT ABOUT A CENTURY-OLD *LIVING* STUMP?
THAT, I THINK I CAN ACCOMPLISH.
FOOL BOY!
NEVER NOCK AN ARROW UNLESS YOU INTEND TO LOOSE IT!
NEVER!
I WAS JUST JOKING AROUND.
ALL THE WORSE!
WE'RE DONE FOR THE DAY.
BESIDES, I THINK YOU'VE GOT A VISITOR ...

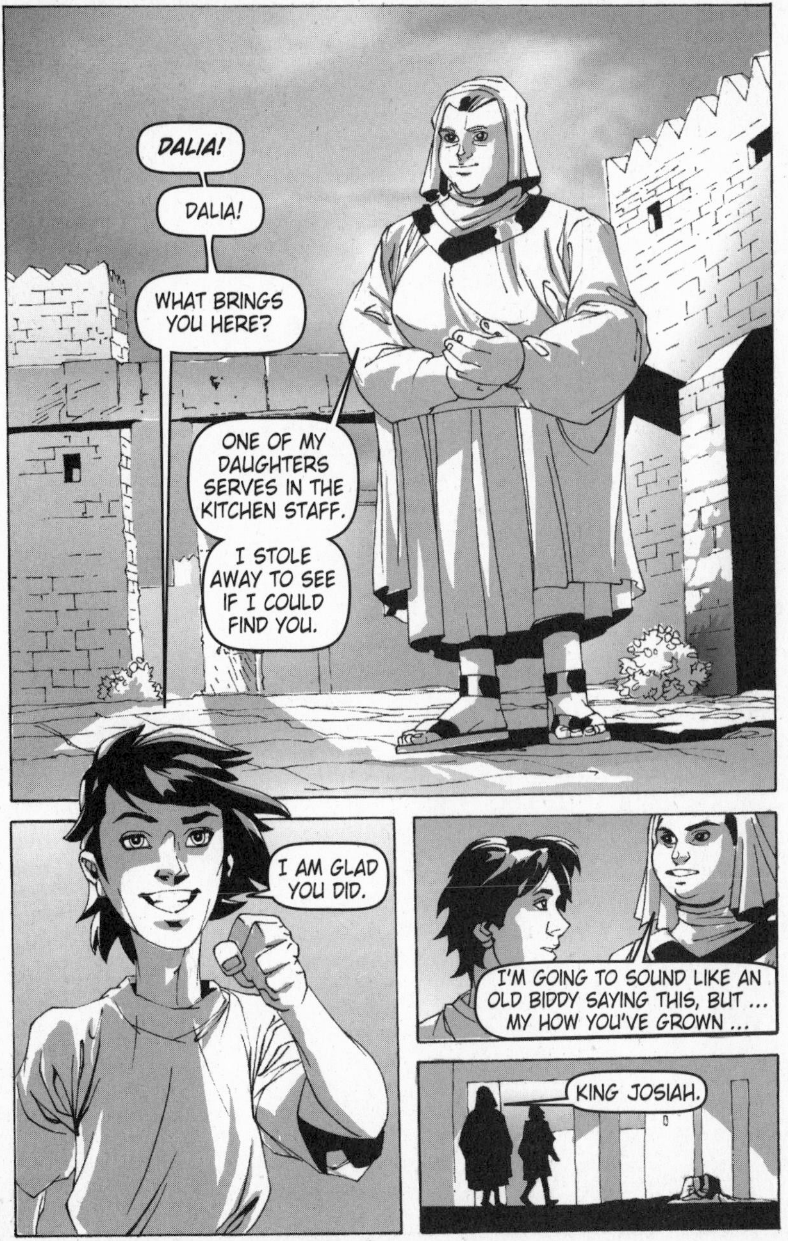
DALIA!
DALIA!
WHAT BRINGS YOU HERE?
ONE OF MY DAUGHTERS SERVES IN THE KITCHEN STAFF.
I STOLE AWAY TO SEE IF I COULD FIND YOU.
I AM GLAD YOU DID.
I'M GOING TO SOUND LIKE AN OLD BIDDY SAYING THIS, BUT ... MY HOW YOU'VE GROWN ...
KING JOSIAH.

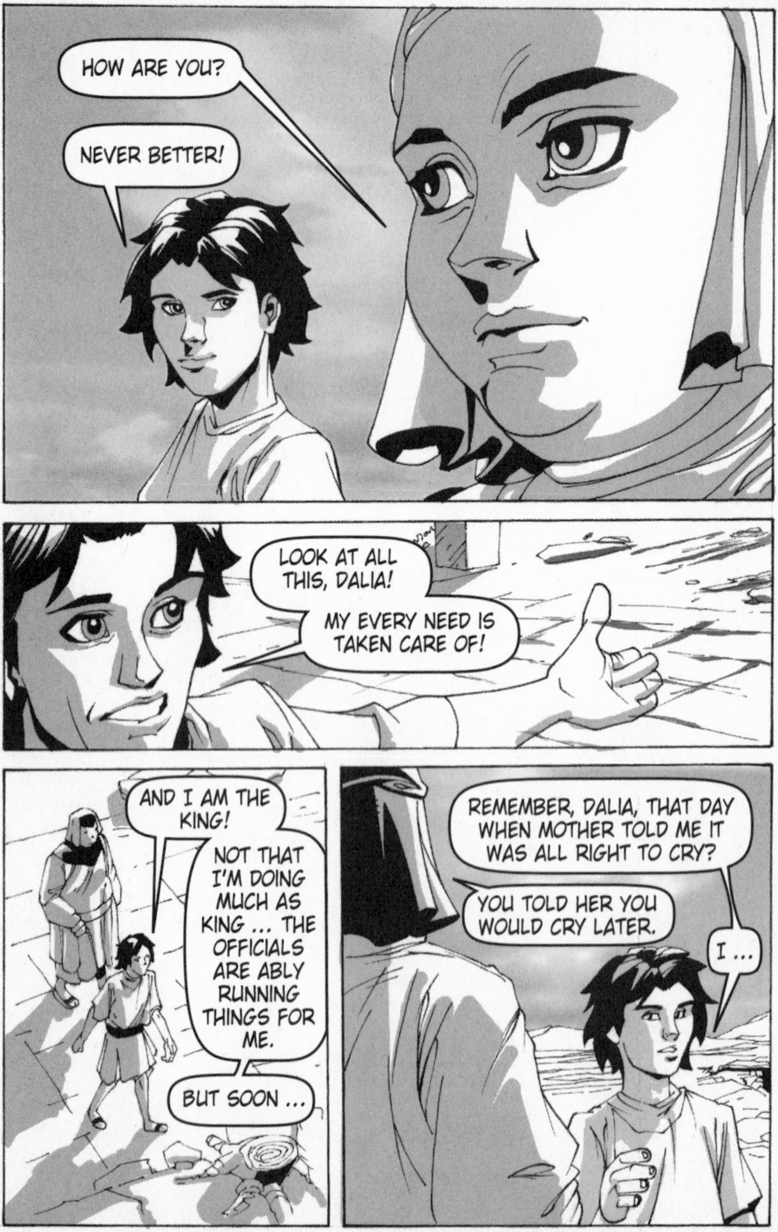
HOW ARE YOU?
NEVER BETTER!
LOOK AT ALL THIS, DALIA!
MY EVERY NEED IS TAKEN CARE OF!
AND I AM THE KING!
NOT THAT I'M DOING MUCH AS KING ... THE OFFICIALS ARE ABLY RUNNING THINGS FOR ME.
BUT SOON ...
REMEMBER, DALIA, THAT DAY WHEN MOTHER TOLD ME IT WAS ALL RIGHT TO CRY?
YOU TOLD HER YOU WOULD CRY LATER.
I ...

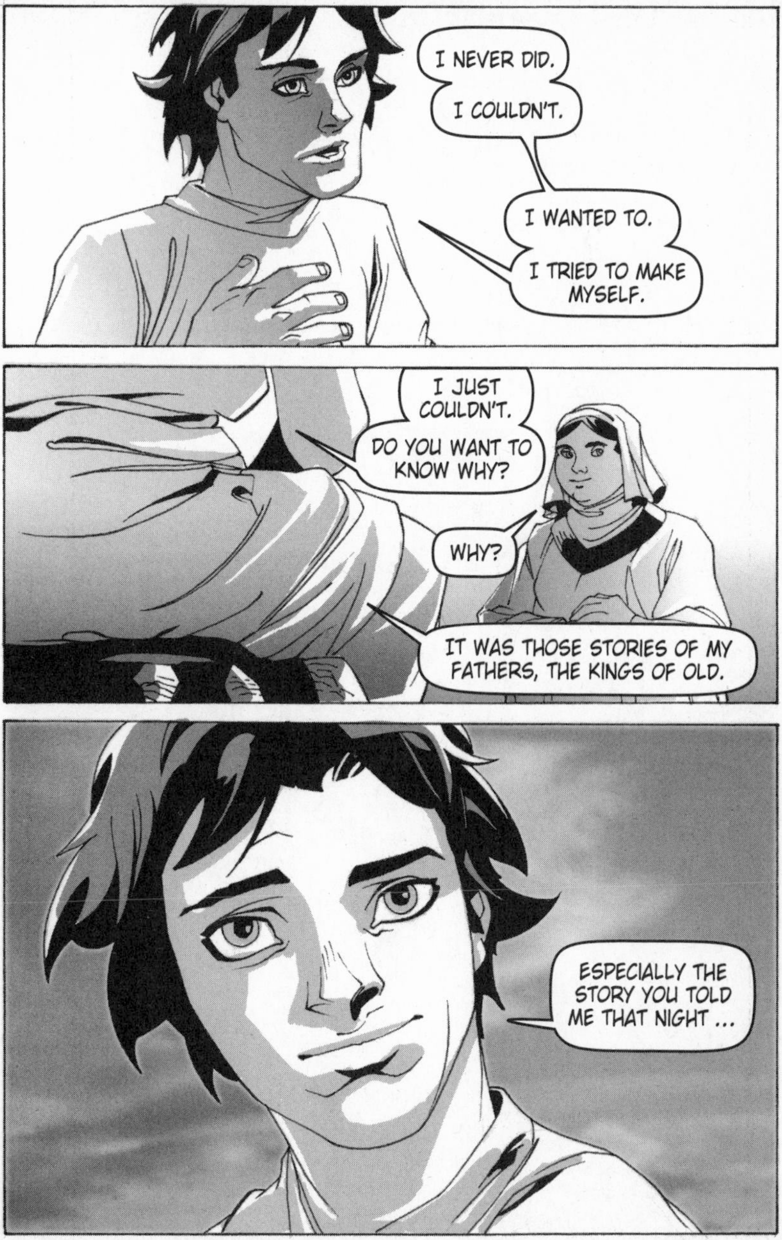
I NEVER DID.
I COULDN'T.
I WANTED TO.
I TRIED TO MAKE MYSELF.
I JUST COULDN'T.
DO YOU WANT TO KNOW WHY?
WHY?
IT WAS THOSE STORIES OF MY FATHERS, THE KINGS OF OLD.
ESPECIALLY THE STORY YOU TOLD ME THAT NIGHT ...

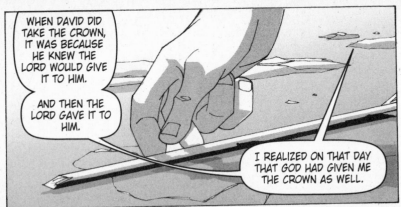

WHEN DAVID DID TAKE THE CROWN, IT WAS BECAUSE HE KNEW THE LORD WOULD GIVE IT TO HIM.

AND THEN THE LORD GAVE IT TO HIM.

I REALIZED ON THAT DAY THAT GOD HAD GIVEN ME THE CROWN AS WELL.

MY FATHER WAS AN EVIL MAN.

MY FAMILY HAS A HISTORY OF WICKEDNESS.

EVEN MY FOREFATHER KING DAVID DID EVIL WHEN HE TOOK SOLOMON'S MOTHER, KILLING HER FIRST HUSBAND TO DO SO!

I DID NOT CRY FOR HIM BECAUSE I KNEW HIS DEATH WAS RIGHT.

HIS WICKEDNESS WAS HURTING OUR LAND--AS ALL MY FAMILY'S WICKEDNESS HAS DONE.

SO WHAT DO YOU PROPOSE TO DO ABOUT IT?

I DON'T KNOW.

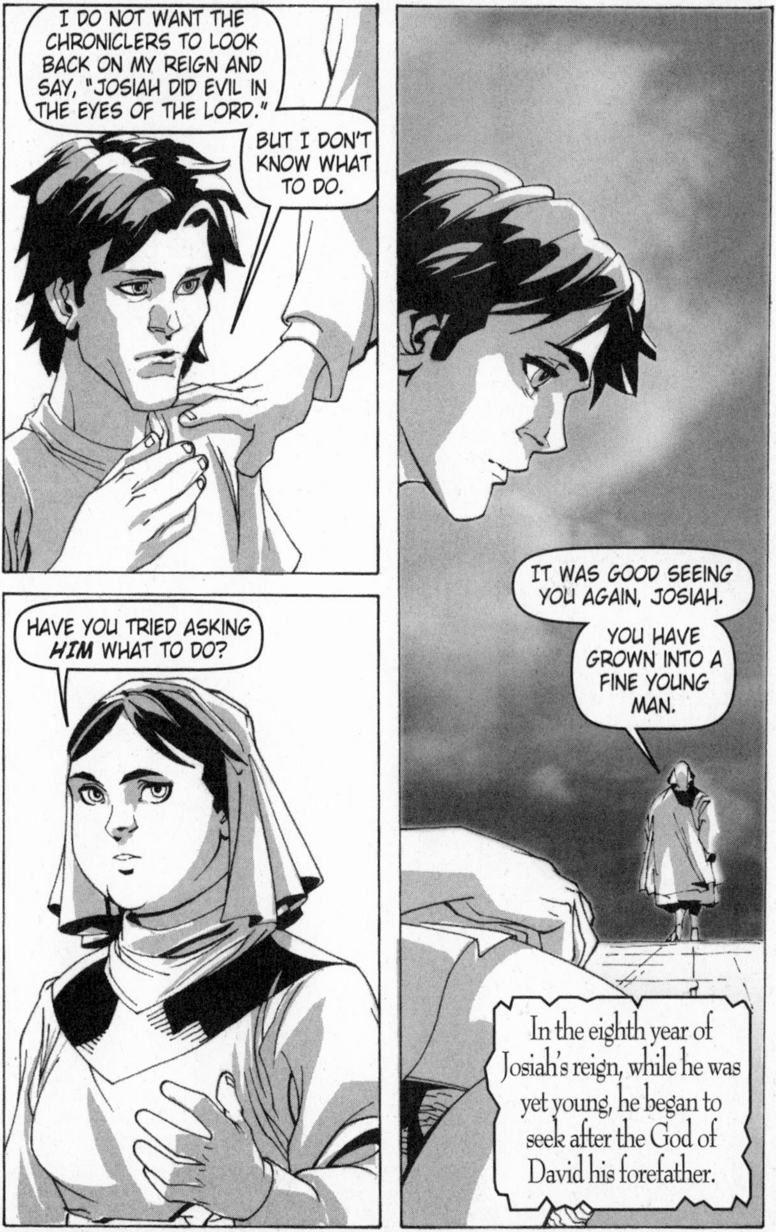
I DO NOT WANT THE CHRONICLERS TO LOOK BACK ON MY REIGN AND SAY, "JOSIAH DID EVIL IN THE EYES OF THE LORD."
BUT I DON'T KNOW WHAT TO DO.
HAVE YOU TRIED ASKING ***HIM*** WHAT TO DO?
IT WAS GOOD SEEING YOU AGAIN, JOSIAH.
YOU HAVE GROWN INTO A FINE YOUNG MAN.
In the eighth year of Josiah's reign, while he was yet young, he began to seek after the God of David his forefather.

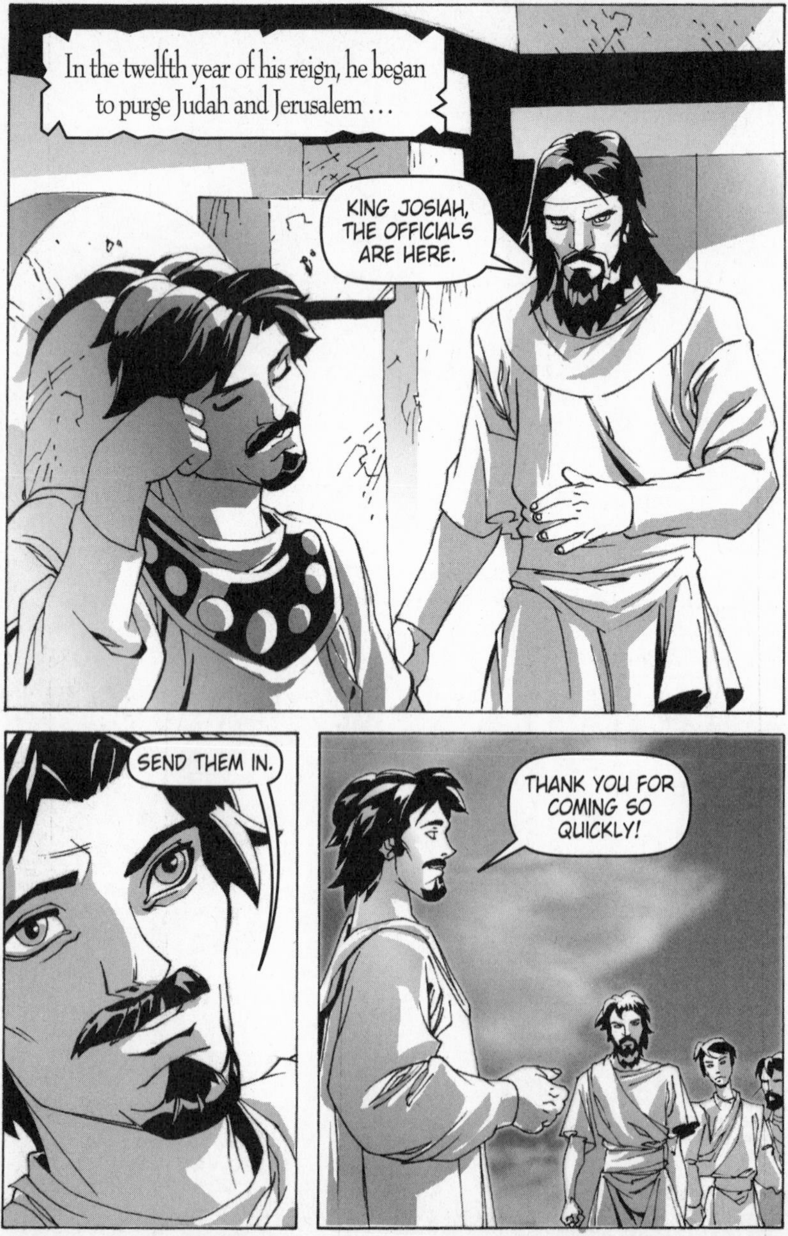
In the twelfth year of his reign, he began to purge Judah and Jerusalem …
KING JOSIAH, THE OFFICIALS ARE HERE.
SEND THEM IN.
THANK YOU FOR COMING SO QUICKLY!

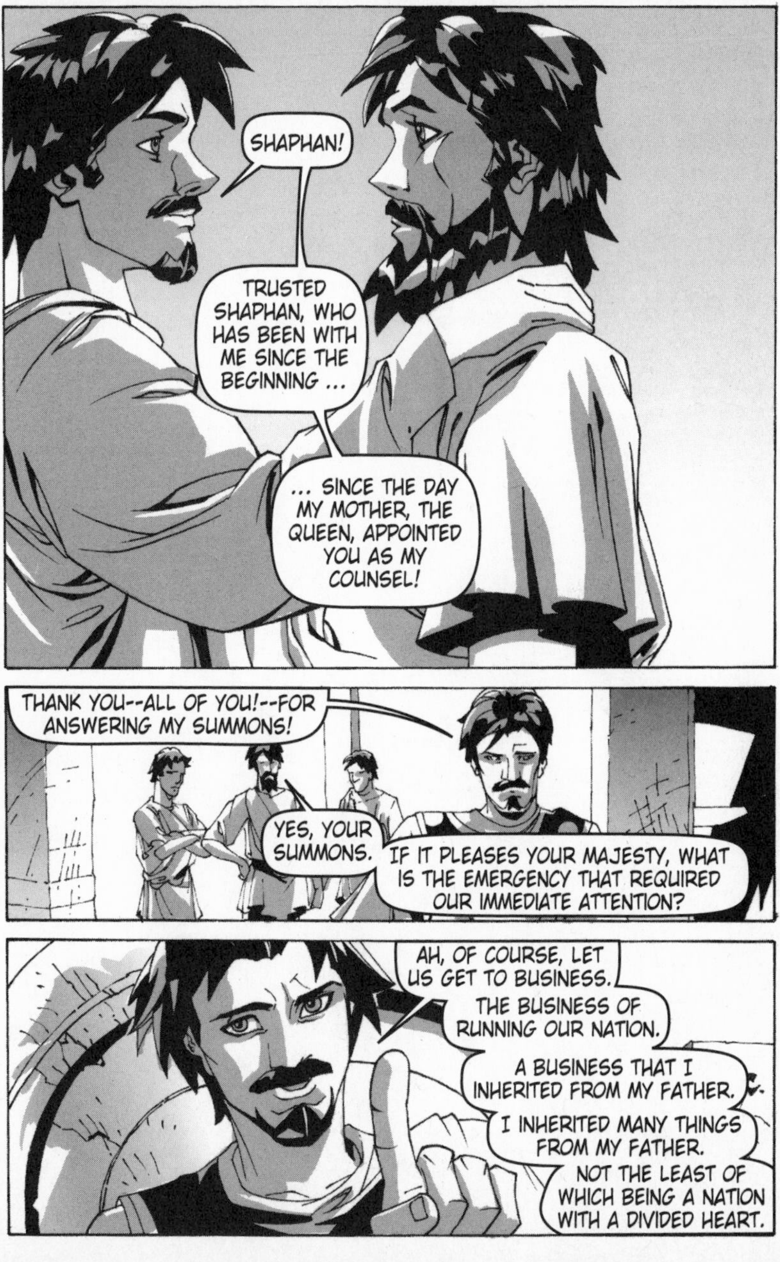
SHAPHAN!
TRUSTED SHAPHAN, WHO HAS BEEN WITH ME SINCE THE BEGINNING ...
... SINCE THE DAY MY MOTHER, THE QUEEN, APPOINTED YOU AS MY COUNSEL!
THANK YOU--ALL OF YOU!--FOR ANSWERING MY SUMMONS!
YES, YOUR SUMMONS.
IF IT PLEASES YOUR MAJESTY, WHAT IS THE EMERGENCY THAT REQUIRED OUR IMMEDIATE ATTENTION?
AH, OF COURSE, LET US GET TO BUSINESS.
THE BUSINESS OF RUNNING OUR NATION.
A BUSINESS THAT I INHERITED FROM MY FATHER.
I INHERITED MANY THINGS FROM MY FATHER.
NOT THE LEAST OF WHICH BEING A NATION WITH A DIVIDED HEART.

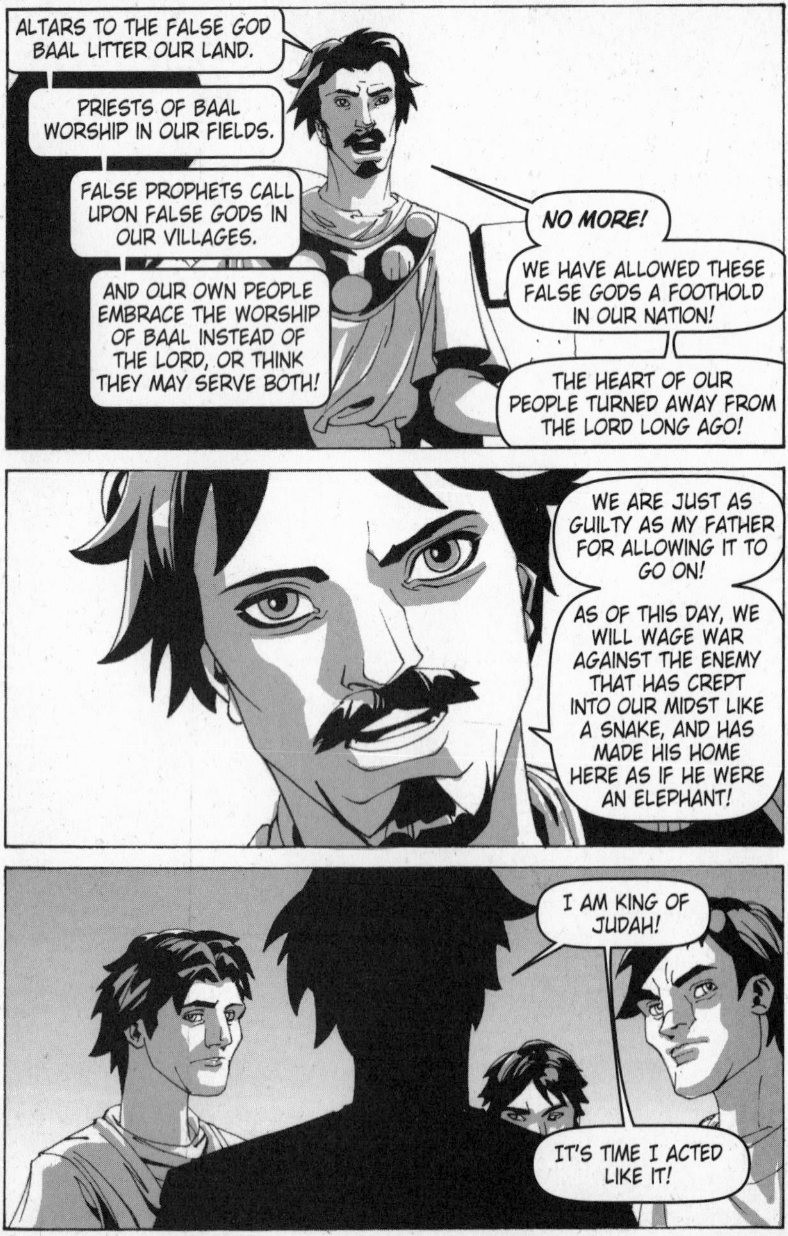
ALTARS TO THE FALSE GOD BAAL LITTER OUR LAND.
PRIESTS OF BAAL WORSHIP IN OUR FIELDS.
FALSE PROPHETS CALL UPON FALSE GODS IN OUR VILLAGES.
AND OUR OWN PEOPLE EMBRACE THE WORSHIP OF BAAL INSTEAD OF THE LORD, OR THINK THEY MAY SERVE BOTH!
NO MORE!
WE HAVE ALLOWED THESE FALSE GODS A FOOTHOLD IN OUR NATION!
THE HEART OF OUR PEOPLE TURNED AWAY FROM THE LORD LONG AGO!
WE ARE JUST AS GUILTY AS MY FATHER FOR ALLOWING IT TO GO ON!
AS OF THIS DAY, WE WILL WAGE WAR AGAINST THE ENEMY THAT HAS CREPT INTO OUR MIDST LIKE A SNAKE, AND HAS MADE HIS HOME HERE AS IF HE WERE AN ELEPHANT!
I AM KING OF JUDAH!
IT'S TIME I ACTED LIKE IT!

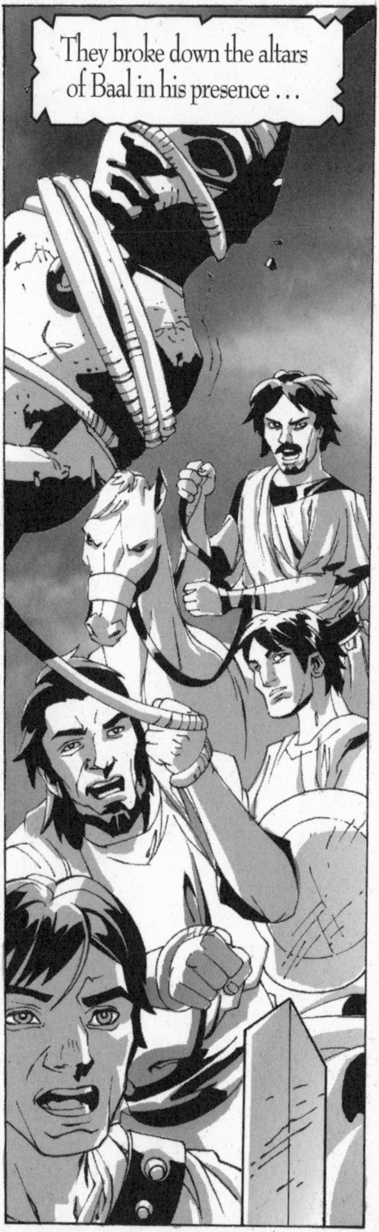
They broke down the altars of Baal in his presence ...
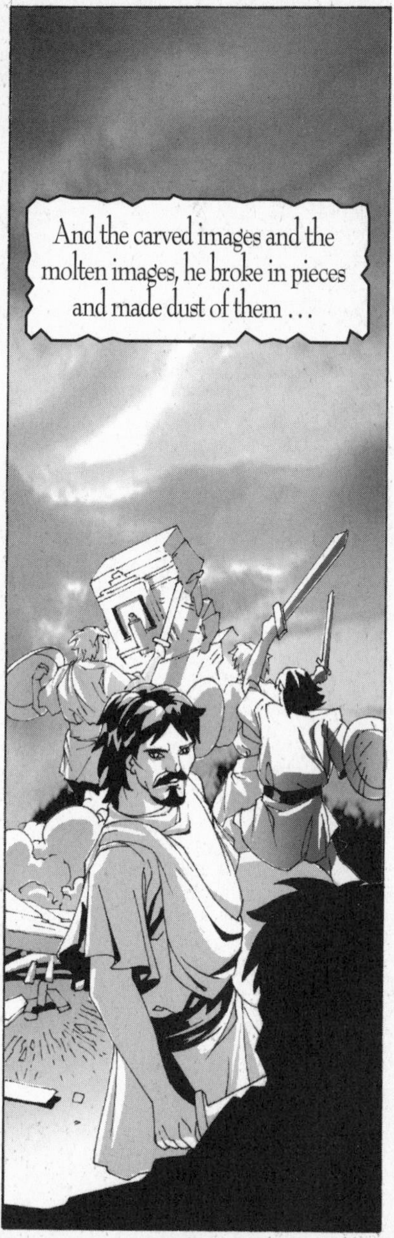
And the carved images and the molten images, he broke in pieces and made dust of them ...

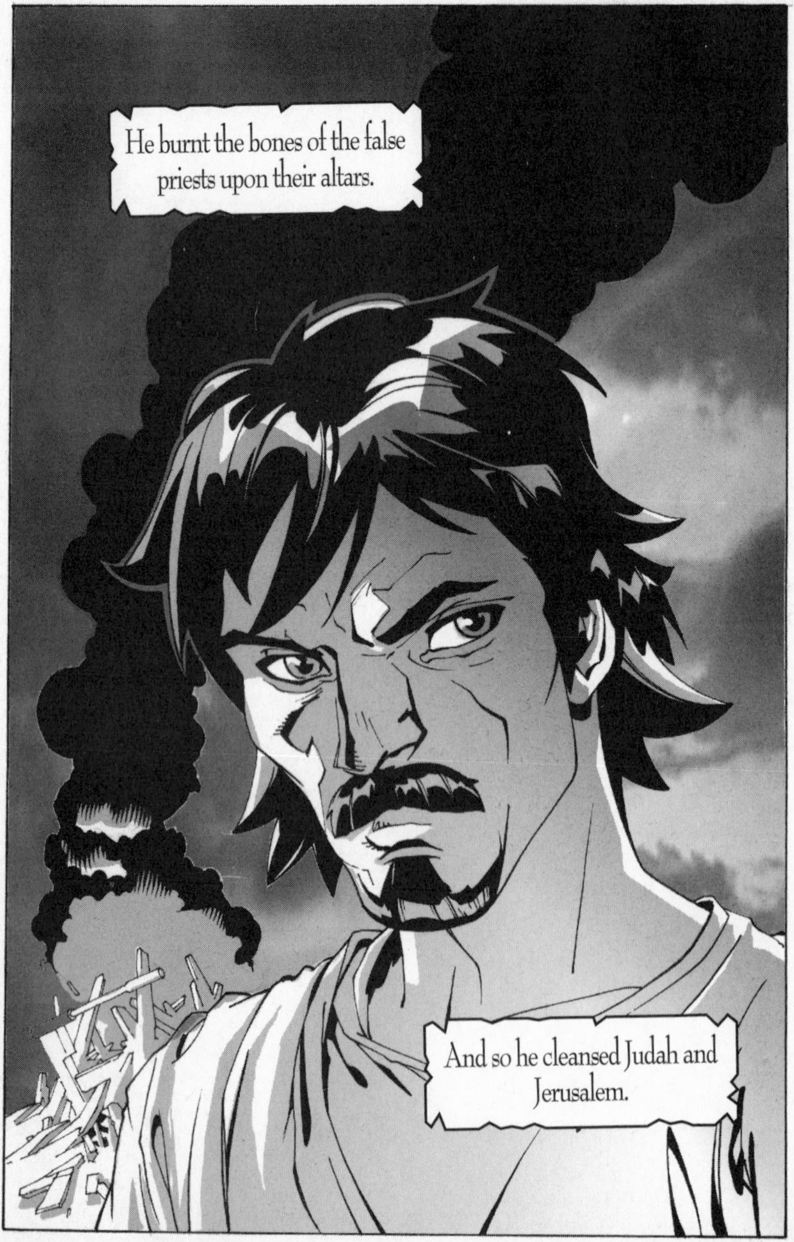
He burnt the bones of the false priests upon their altars.
And so he cleansed Judah and Jerusalem.

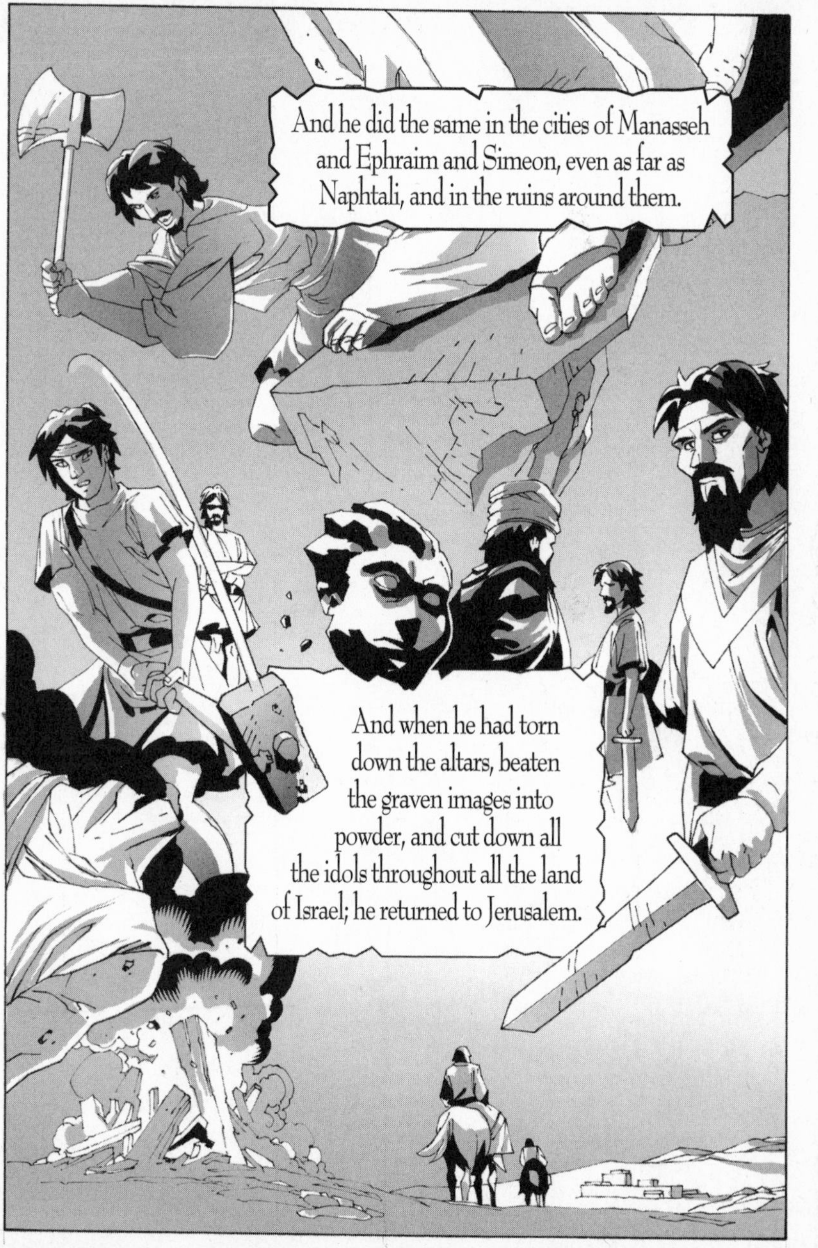
And he did the same in the cities of Manasseh and Ephraim and Simeon, even as far as Naphtali, and in the ruins around them.
And when he had torn down the altars, beaten the graven images into powder, and cut down all the idols throughout all the land of Israel; he returned to Jerusalem.

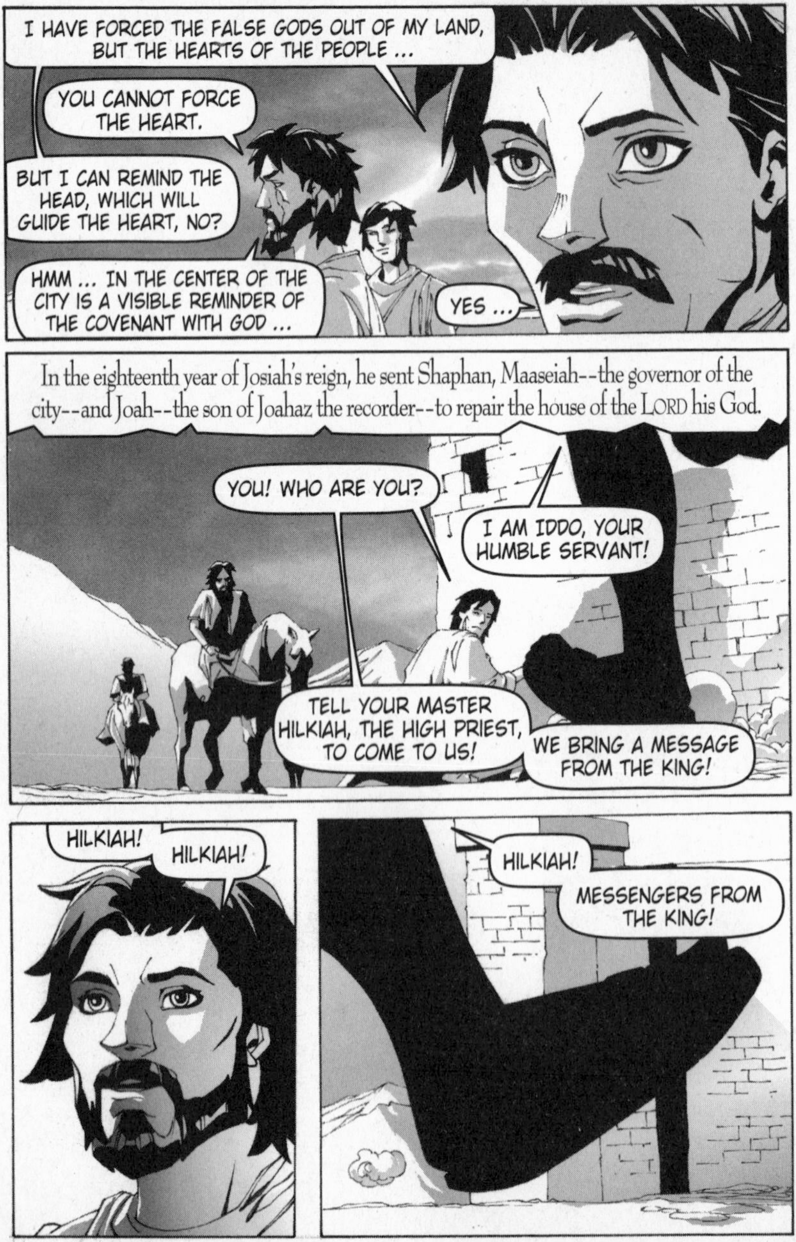
I HAVE FORCED THE FALSE GODS OUT OF MY LAND, BUT THE HEARTS OF THE PEOPLE ...
YOU CANNOT FORCE THE HEART.
BUT I CAN REMIND THE HEAD, WHICH WILL GUIDE THE HEART, NO?
HMM ... IN THE CENTER OF THE CITY IS A VISIBLE REMINDER OF THE COVENANT WITH GOD ...
YES ...
In the eighteenth year of Josiah's reign, he sent Shaphan, Maaseiah--the governor of the city--and Joah--the son of Joahaz the recorder--to repair the house of the LORD his God.
YOU! WHO ARE YOU?
I AM IDDO, YOUR HUMBLE SERVANT!
TELL YOUR MASTER HILKIAH, THE HIGH PRIEST, TO COME TO US!
WE BRING A MESSAGE FROM THE KING!
HILKIAH!
HILKIAH!
HILKIAH!
MESSENGERS FROM THE KING!

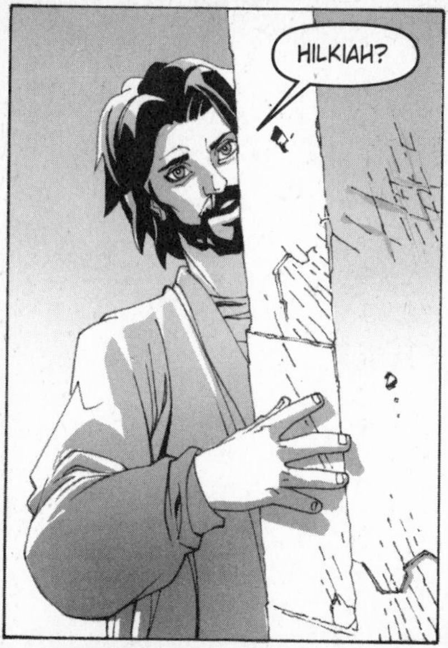
HILKIAH?

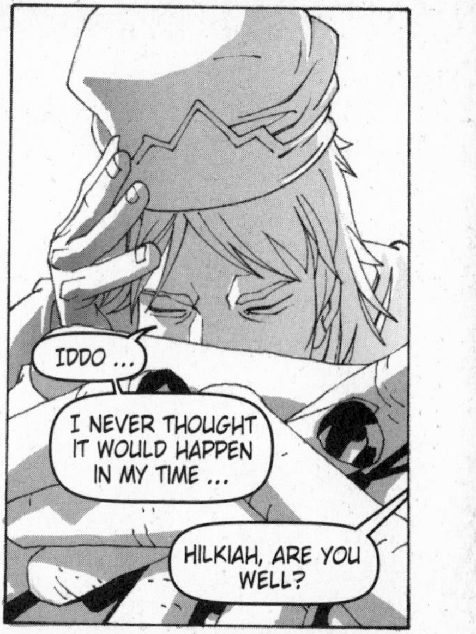
IDDO ...
I NEVER THOUGHT IT WOULD HAPPEN IN MY TIME ...
HILKIAH, ARE YOU WELL?

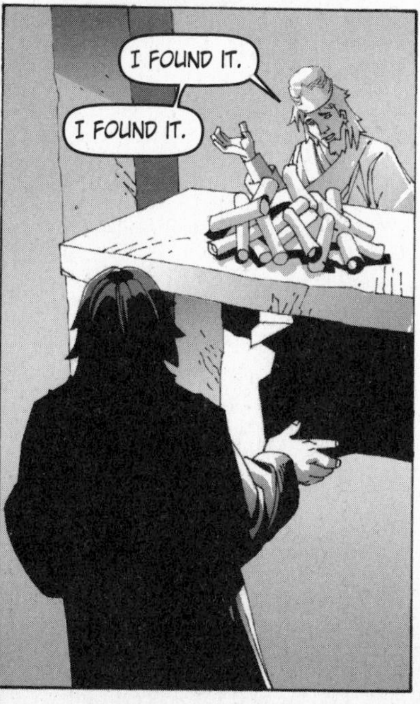
I FOUND IT.
I FOUND IT.

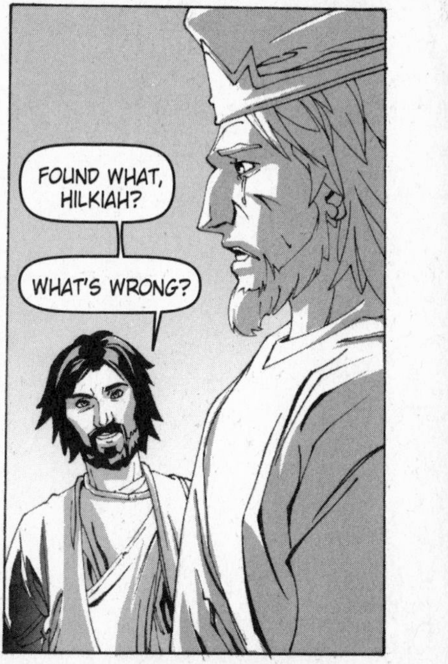
FOUND WHAT, HILKIAH?
WHAT'S WRONG?

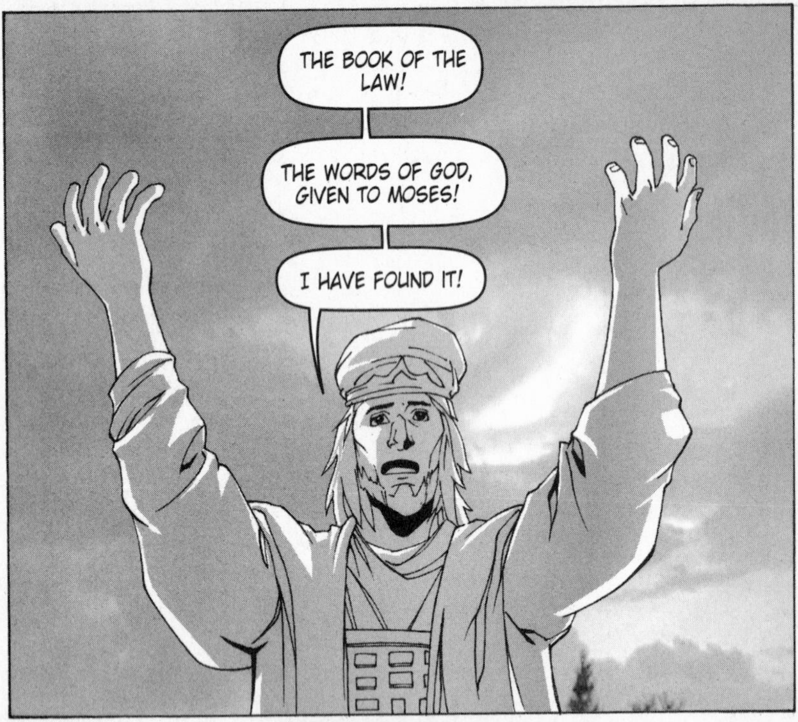
THE BOOK OF THE LAW!
THE WORDS OF GOD, GIVEN TO MOSES!
I HAVE FOUND IT!
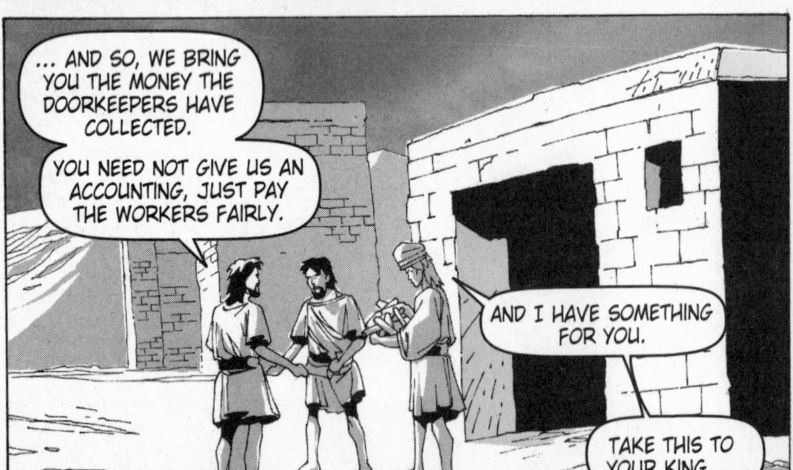
... AND SO, WE BRING YOU THE MONEY THE DOORKEEPERS HAVE COLLECTED.
YOU NEED NOT GIVE US AN ACCOUNTING, JUST PAY THE WORKERS FAIRLY.
AND I HAVE SOMETHING FOR YOU.
TAKE THIS TO YOUR KING ...

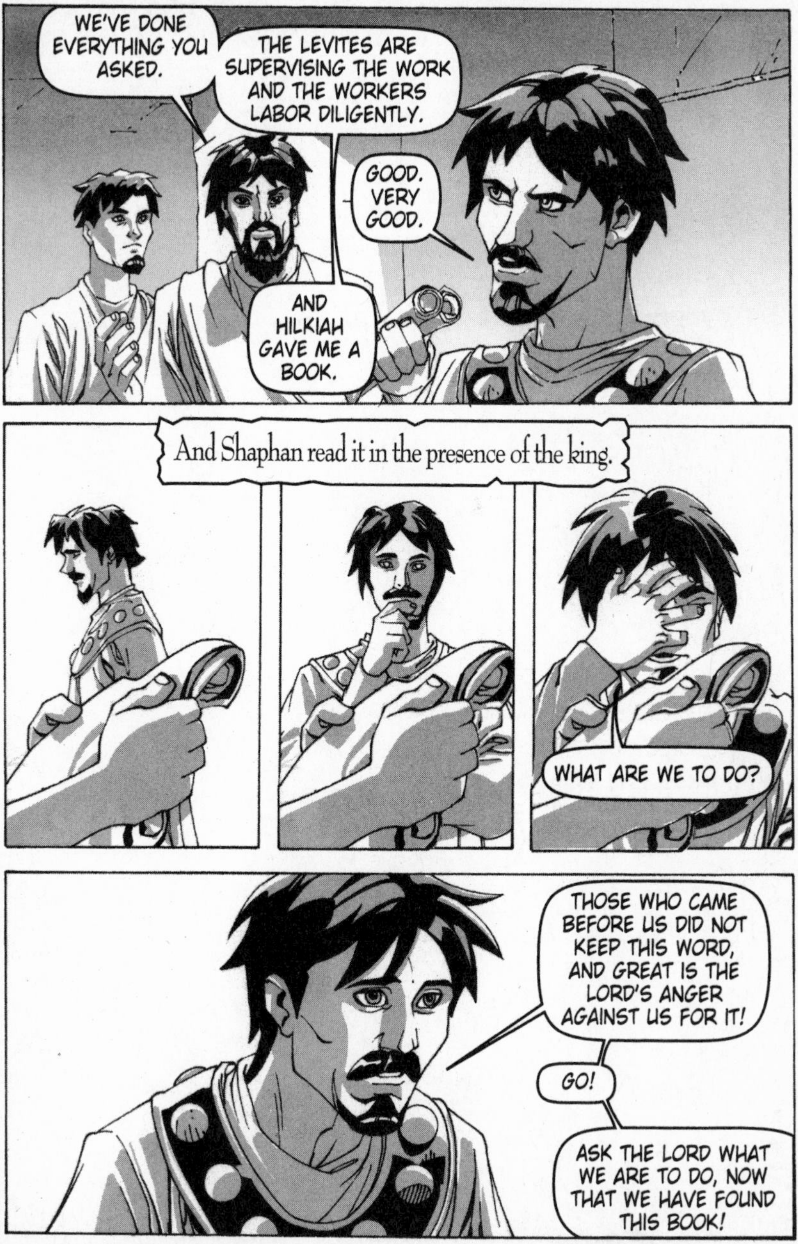
WE'VE DONE EVERYTHING YOU ASKED.
THE LEVITES ARE SUPERVISING THE WORK AND THE WORKERS LABOR DILIGENTLY.
GOOD. VERY GOOD.
AND HILKIAH GAVE ME A BOOK.
And Shaphan read it in the presence of the king.
WHAT ARE WE TO DO?
THOSE WHO CAME BEFORE US DID NOT KEEP THIS WORD, AND GREAT IS THE LORD'S ANGER AGAINST US FOR IT!
GO!
ASK THE LORD WHAT WE ARE TO DO, NOW THAT WE HAVE FOUND THIS BOOK!

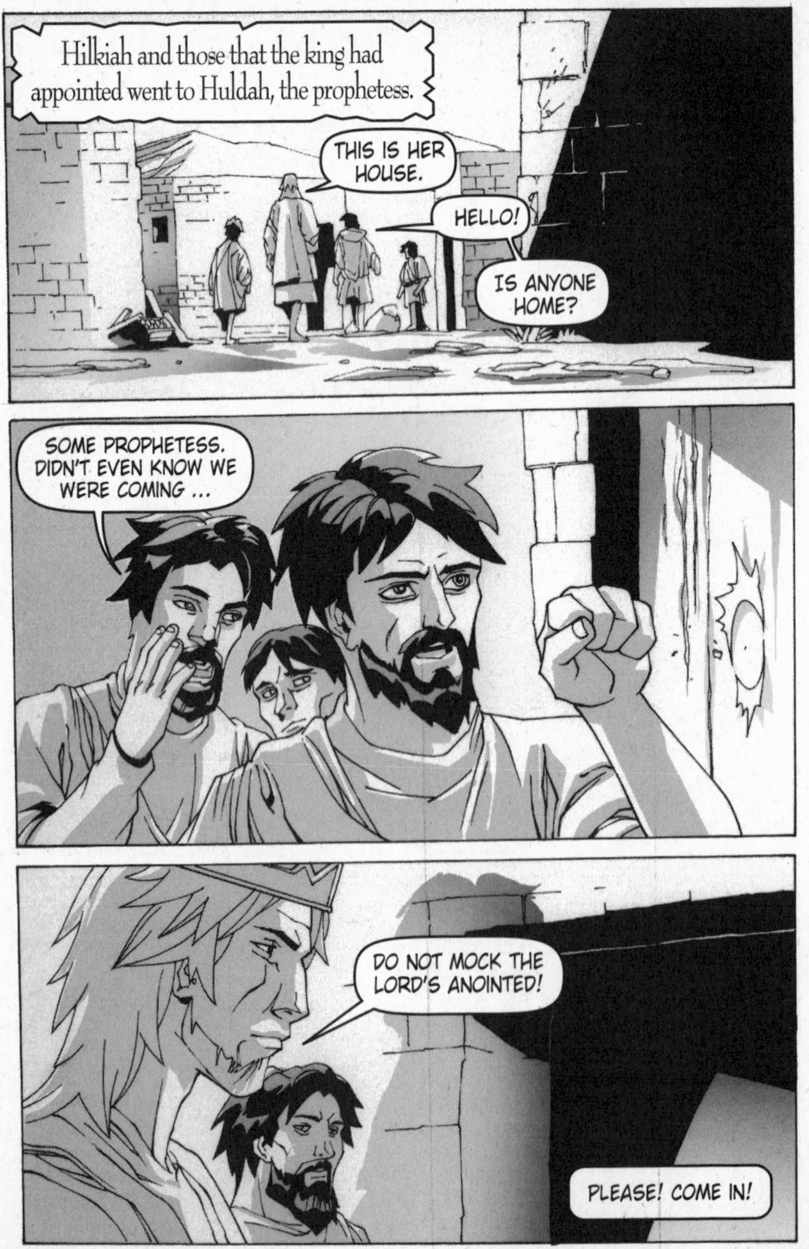
Hilkiah and those that the king had appointed went to Huldah, the prophetess.
THIS IS HER HOUSE.
HELLO!
IS ANYONE HOME?
SOME PROPHETESS. DIDN'T EVEN KNOW WE WERE COMING ...
DO NOT MOCK THE LORD'S ANOINTED!
PLEASE! COME IN!

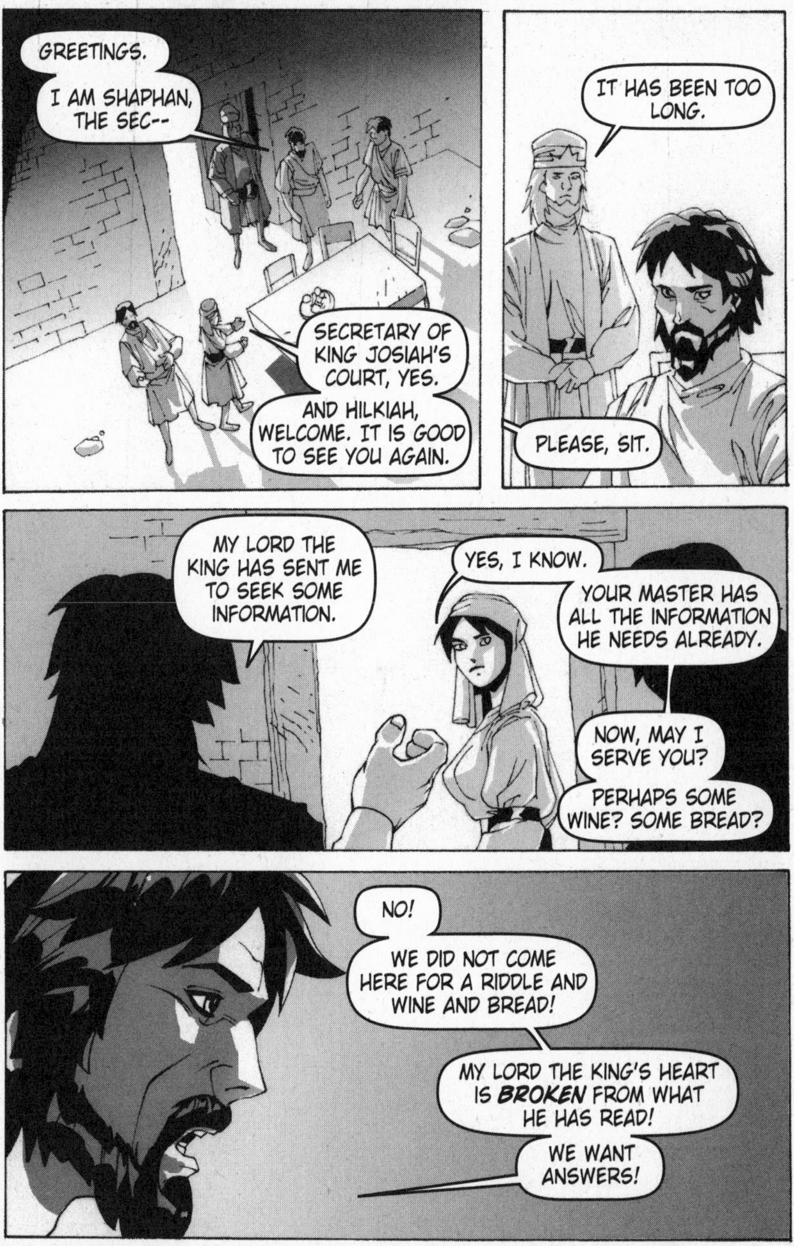
GREETINGS.
I AM SHAPHAN, THE SEC--
SECRETARY OF KING JOSIAH'S COURT, YES.
AND HILKIAH, WELCOME. IT IS GOOD TO SEE YOU AGAIN.
IT HAS BEEN TOO LONG.
PLEASE, SIT.
MY LORD THE KING HAS SENT ME TO SEEK SOME INFORMATION.
YES, I KNOW.
YOUR MASTER HAS ALL THE INFORMATION HE NEEDS ALREADY.
NOW, MAY I SERVE YOU?
PERHAPS SOME WINE? SOME BREAD?
NO!
WE DID NOT COME HERE FOR A RIDDLE AND WINE AND BREAD!
MY LORD THE KING'S HEART IS ***BROKEN*** FROM WHAT HE HAS READ!
WE WANT ANSWERS!

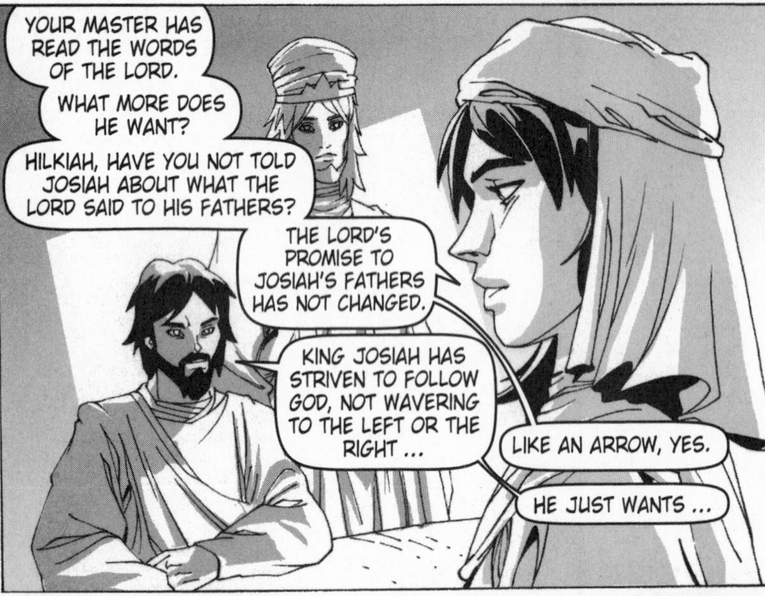
YOUR MASTER HAS READ THE WORDS OF THE LORD.
WHAT MORE DOES HE WANT?
HILKIAH, HAVE YOU NOT TOLD JOSIAH ABOUT WHAT THE LORD SAID TO HIS FATHERS?
THE LORD'S PROMISE TO JOSIAH'S FATHERS HAS NOT CHANGED.
KING JOSIAH HAS STRIVEN TO FOLLOW GOD, NOT WAVERING TO THE LEFT OR THE RIGHT ...
LIKE AN ARROW, YES.
HE JUST WANTS ...

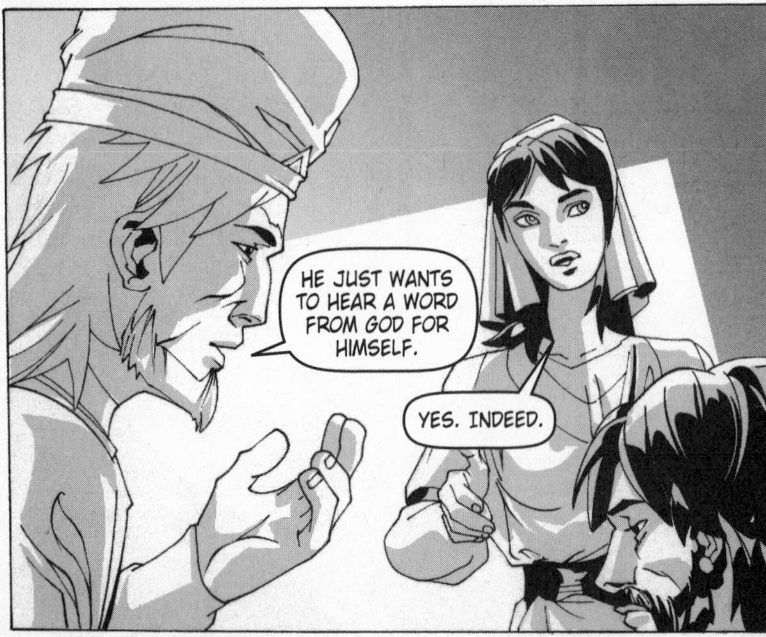
HE JUST WANTS TO HEAR A WORD FROM GOD FOR HIMSELF.
YES. INDEED.

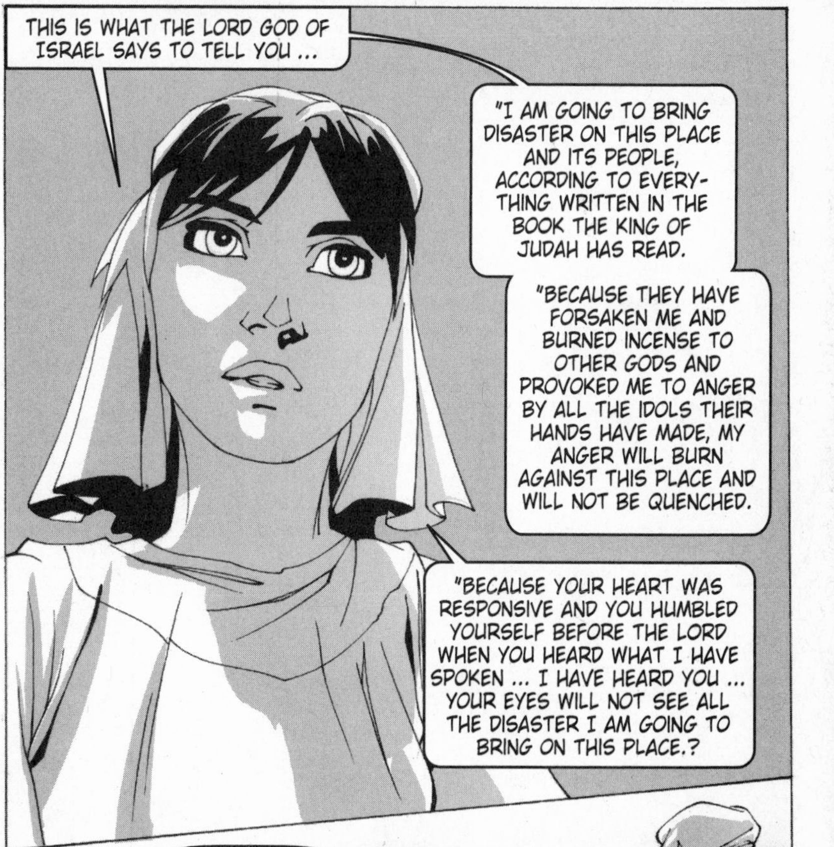
THIS IS WHAT THE LORD GOD OF ISRAEL SAYS TO TELL YOU ...
"I AM GOING TO BRING DISASTER ON THIS PLACE AND ITS PEOPLE, ACCORDING TO EVERY-THING WRITTEN IN THE BOOK THE KING OF JUDAH HAS READ.
"BECAUSE THEY HAVE FORSAKEN ME AND BURNED INCENSE TO OTHER GODS AND PROVOKED ME TO ANGER BY ALL THE IDOLS THEIR HANDS HAVE MADE, MY ANGER WILL BURN AGAINST THIS PLACE AND WILL NOT BE QUENCHED.
"BECAUSE YOUR HEART WAS RESPONSIVE AND YOU HUMBLED YOURSELF BEFORE THE LORD WHEN YOU HEARD WHAT I HAVE SPOKEN ... I HAVE HEARD YOU ... YOUR EYES WILL NOT SEE ALL THE DISASTER I AM GOING TO BRING ON THIS PLACE.?
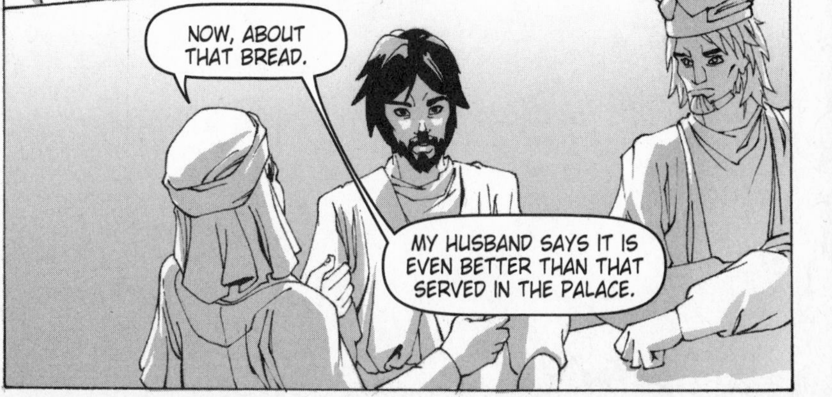
NOW, ABOUT THAT BREAD.
MY HUSBAND SAYS IT IS EVEN BETTER THAN THAT SERVED IN THE PALACE.

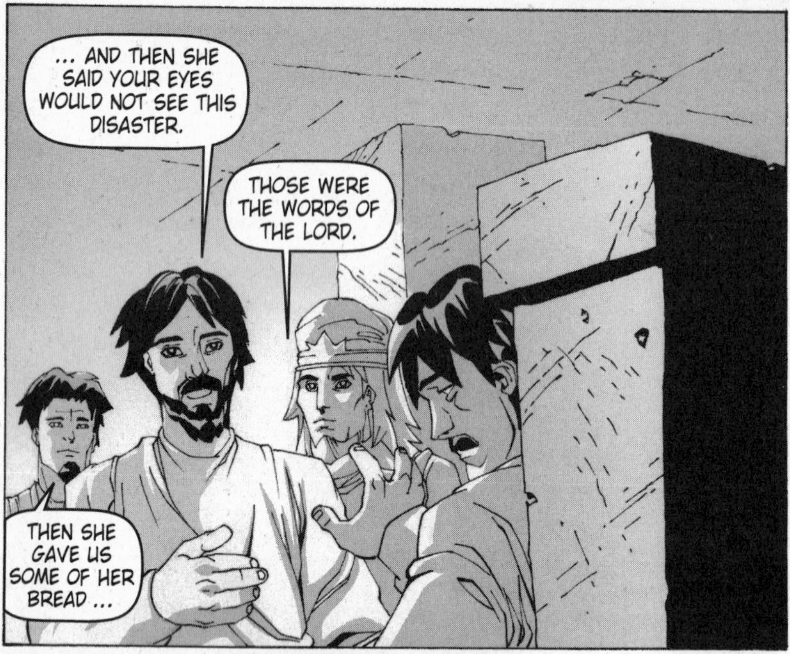
... AND THEN SHE SAID YOUR EYES WOULD NOT SEE THIS DISASTER.
THOSE WERE THE WORDS OF THE LORD.
THEN SHE GAVE US SOME OF HER BREAD ...

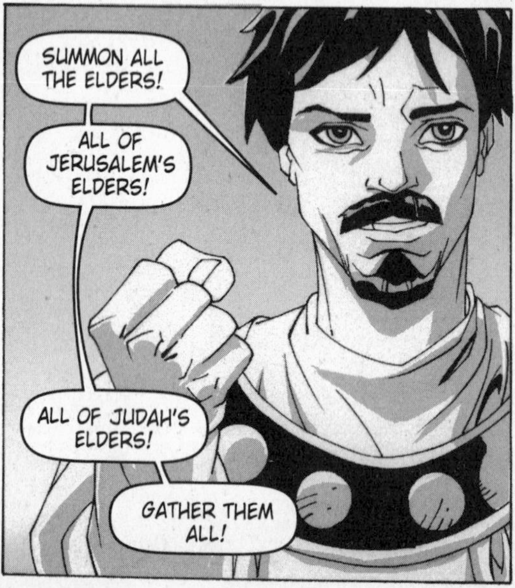
SUMMON ALL THE ELDERS!
ALL OF JERUSALEM'S ELDERS!
ALL OF JUDAH'S ELDERS!
GATHER THEM ALL!

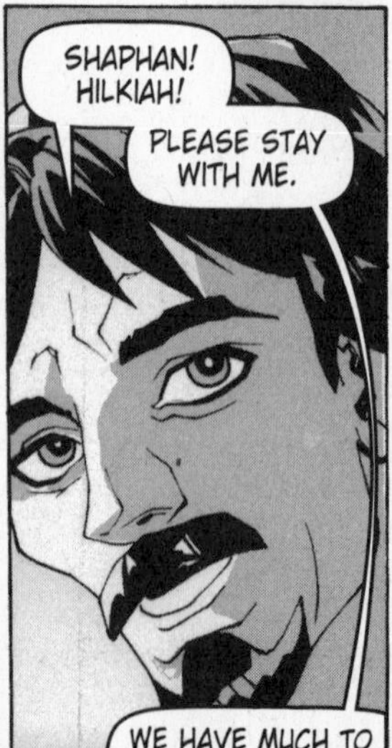
SHAPHAN! HILKIAH!
PLEASE STAY WITH ME.
WE HAVE MUCH TO DISCUSS ... MUCH TO PREPARE.

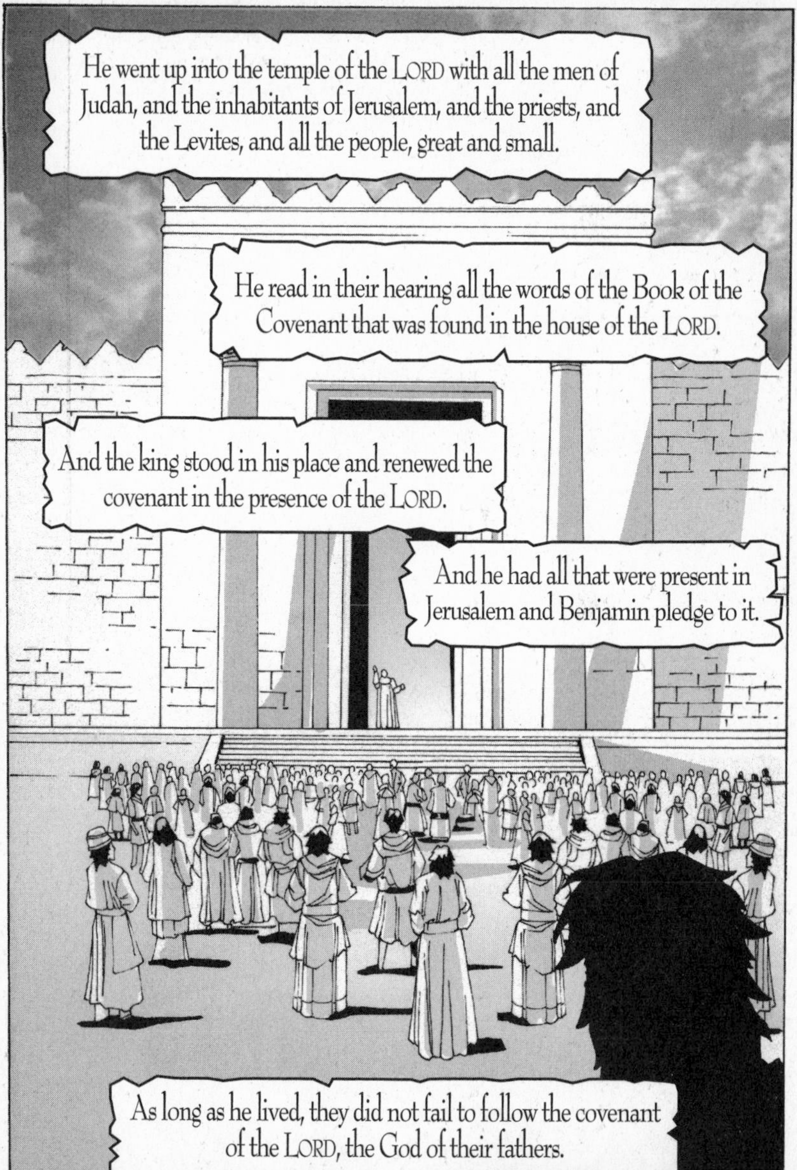
He went up into the temple of the LORD with all the men of Judah, and the inhabitants of Jerusalem, and the priests, and the Levites, and all the people, great and small.
He read in their hearing all the words of the Book of the Covenant that was found in the house of the LORD.
And the king stood in his place and renewed the covenant in the presence of the LORD.
And he had all that were present in Jerusalem and Benjamin pledge to it.
As long as he lived, they did not fail to follow the covenant of the LORD, the God of their fathers.

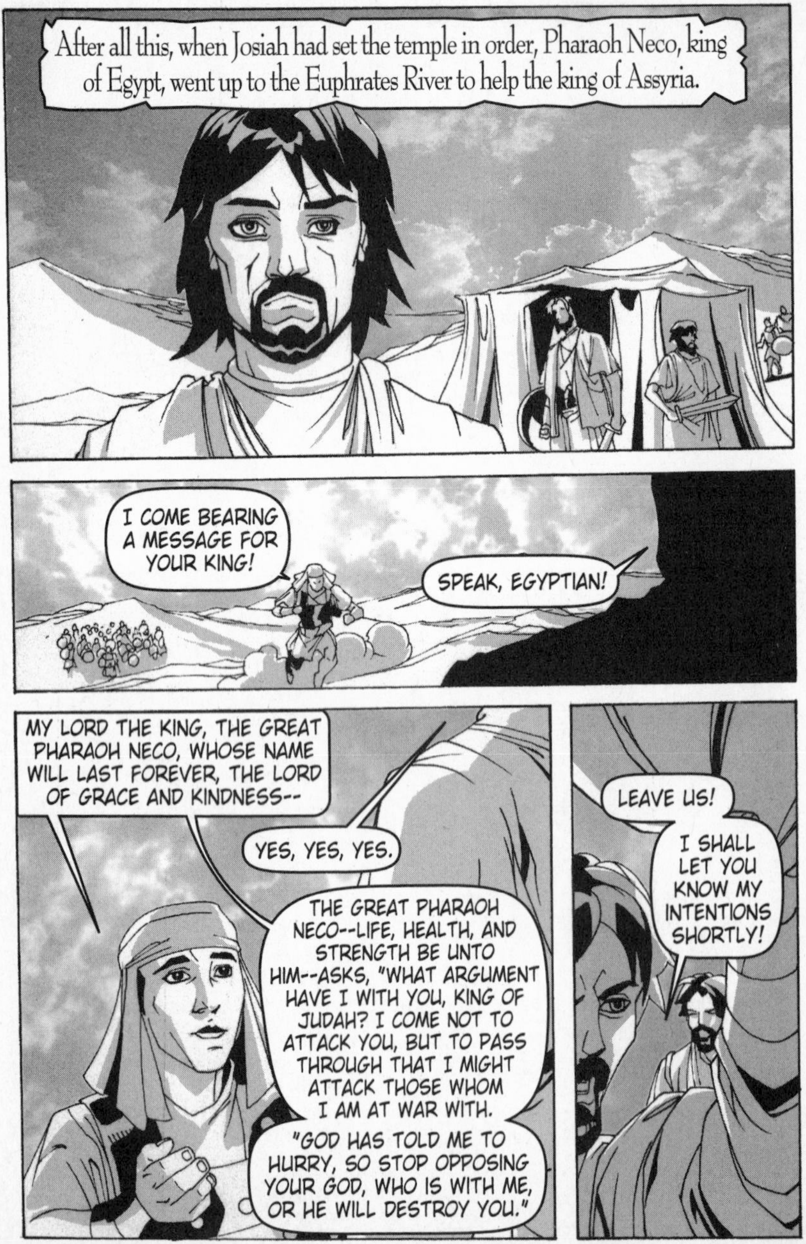
After all this, when Josiah had set the temple in order, Pharaoh Neco, king of Egypt, went up to the Euphrates River to help the king of Assyria.
I COME BEARING A MESSAGE FOR YOUR KING!
SPEAK, EGYPTIAN!
MY LORD THE KING, THE GREAT PHARAOH NECO, WHOSE NAME WILL LAST FOREVER, THE LORD OF GRACE AND KINDNESS--
YES, YES, YES.
THE GREAT PHARAOH NECO--LIFE, HEALTH, AND STRENGTH BE UNTO HIM--ASKS, "WHAT ARGUMENT HAVE I WITH YOU, KING OF JUDAH? I COME NOT TO ATTACK YOU, BUT TO PASS THROUGH THAT I MIGHT ATTACK THOSE WHOM I AM AT WAR WITH.
"GOD HAS TOLD ME TO HURRY, SO STOP OPPOSING YOUR GOD, WHO IS WITH ME, OR HE WILL DESTROY YOU."
LEAVE US!
I SHALL LET YOU KNOW MY INTENTIONS SHORTLY!

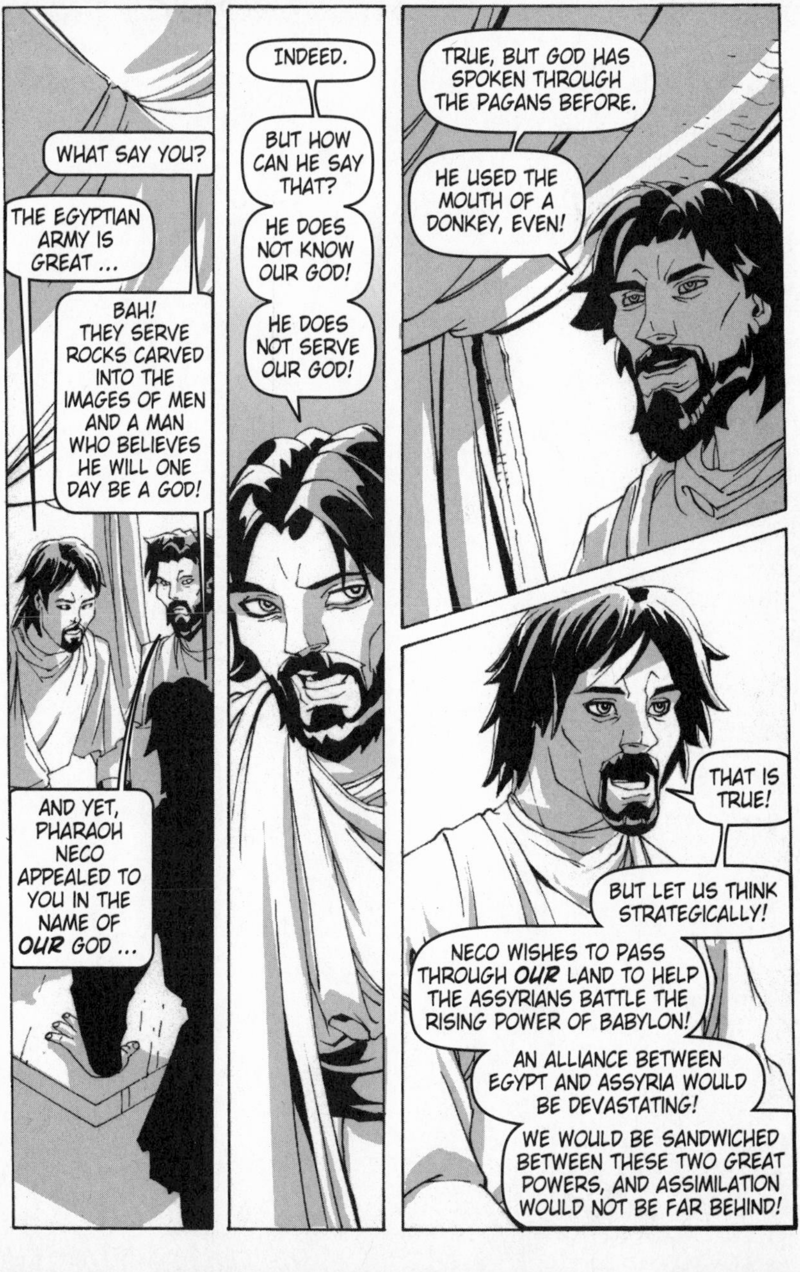
WHAT SAY YOU?
THE EGYPTIAN ARMY IS GREAT ...
BAH! THEY SERVE ROCKS CARVED INTO THE IMAGES OF MEN AND A MAN WHO BELIEVES HE WILL ONE DAY BE A GOD!
AND YET, PHARAOH NECO APPEALED TO YOU IN THE NAME OF ***OUR*** GOD ...
INDEED.
BUT HOW CAN HE SAY THAT?
HE DOES NOT KNOW OUR GOD!
HE DOES NOT SERVE OUR GOD!
TRUE, BUT GOD HAS SPOKEN THROUGH THE PAGANS BEFORE.
HE USED THE MOUTH OF A DONKEY, EVEN!
THAT IS TRUE!
BUT LET US THINK STRATEGICALLY!
NECO WISHES TO PASS THROUGH ***OUR*** LAND TO HELP THE ASSYRIANS BATTLE THE RISING POWER OF BABYLON!
AN ALLIANCE BETWEEN EGYPT AND ASSYRIA WOULD BE DEVASTATING!
WE WOULD BE SANDWICHED BETWEEN THESE TWO GREAT POWERS, AND ASSIMILATION WOULD NOT BE FAR BEHIND!

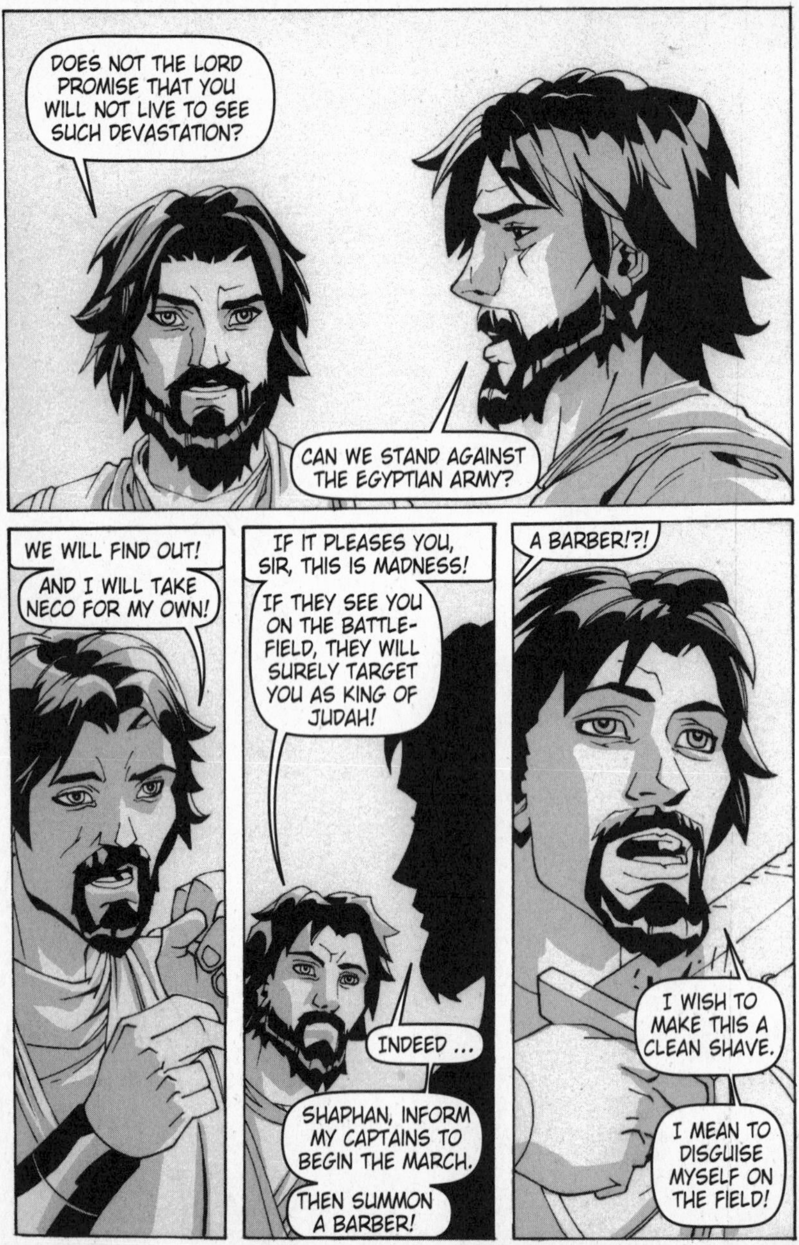
DOES NOT THE LORD PROMISE THAT YOU WILL NOT LIVE TO SEE SUCH DEVASTATION?
CAN WE STAND AGAINST THE EGYPTIAN ARMY?
WE WILL FIND OUT!
AND I WILL TAKE NECO FOR MY OWN!
IF IT PLEASES YOU, SIR, THIS IS MADNESS!
IF THEY SEE YOU ON THE BATTLE-FIELD, THEY WILL SURELY TARGET YOU AS KING OF JUDAH!
INDEED ...
SHAPHAN, INFORM MY CAPTAINS TO BEGIN THE MARCH.
THEN SUMMON A BARBER!
A BARBER!?!
I WISH TO MAKE THIS A CLEAN SHAVE.
I MEAN TO DISGUISE MYSELF ON THE FIELD!

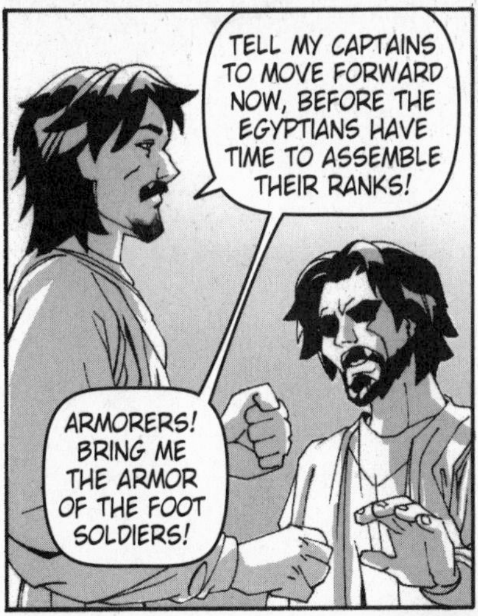
TELL MY CAPTAINS TO MOVE FORWARD NOW, BEFORE THE EGYPTIANS HAVE TIME TO ASSEMBLE THEIR RANKS!
ARMORERS! BRING ME THE ARMOR OF THE FOOT SOLDIERS!
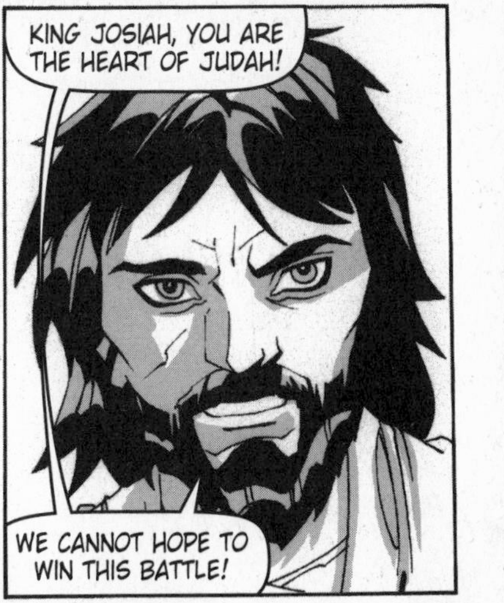
KING JOSIAH, YOU ARE THE HEART OF JUDAH!
WE CANNOT HOPE TO WIN THIS BATTLE!
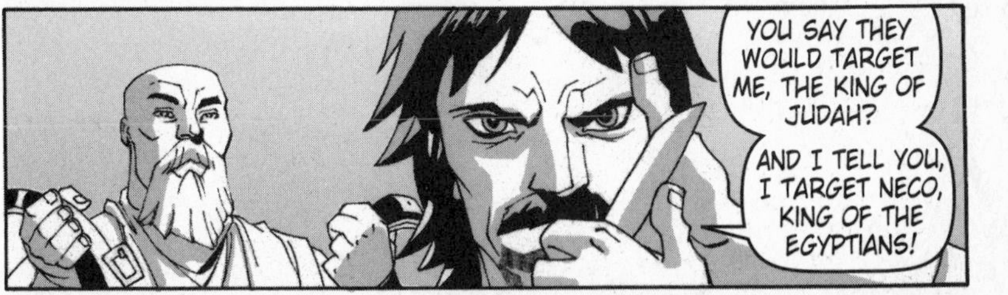
YOU SAY THEY WOULD TARGET ME, THE KING OF JUDAH?
AND I TELL YOU, I TARGET NECO, KING OF THE EGYPTIANS!
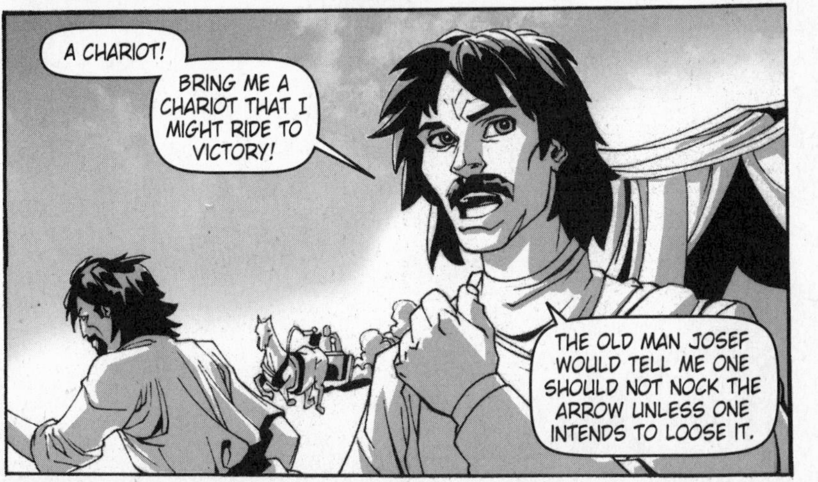
A CHARIOT!
BRING ME A CHARIOT THAT I MIGHT RIDE TO VICTORY!
THE OLD MAN JOSEF WOULD TELL ME ONE SHOULD NOT NOCK THE ARROW UNLESS ONE INTENDS TO LOOSE IT.

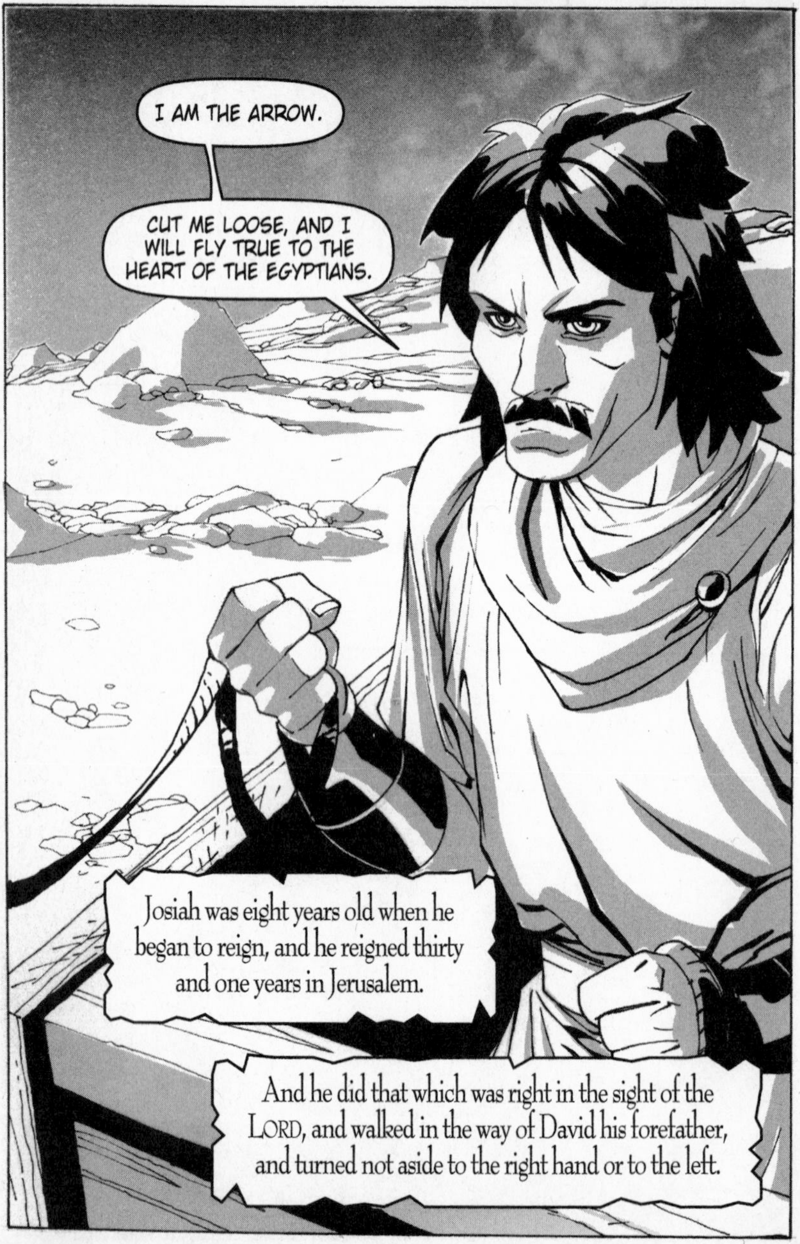
I AM THE ARROW.
CUT ME LOOSE, AND I WILL FLY TRUE TO THE HEART OF THE EGYPTIANS.
Josiah was eight years old when he began to reign, and he reigned thirty and one years in Jerusalem.
And he did that which was right in the sight of the LORD, and walked in the way of David his forefather, and turned not aside to the right hand or to the left.

CHAPTER FOUR
"SINS OF THE FATHERS"

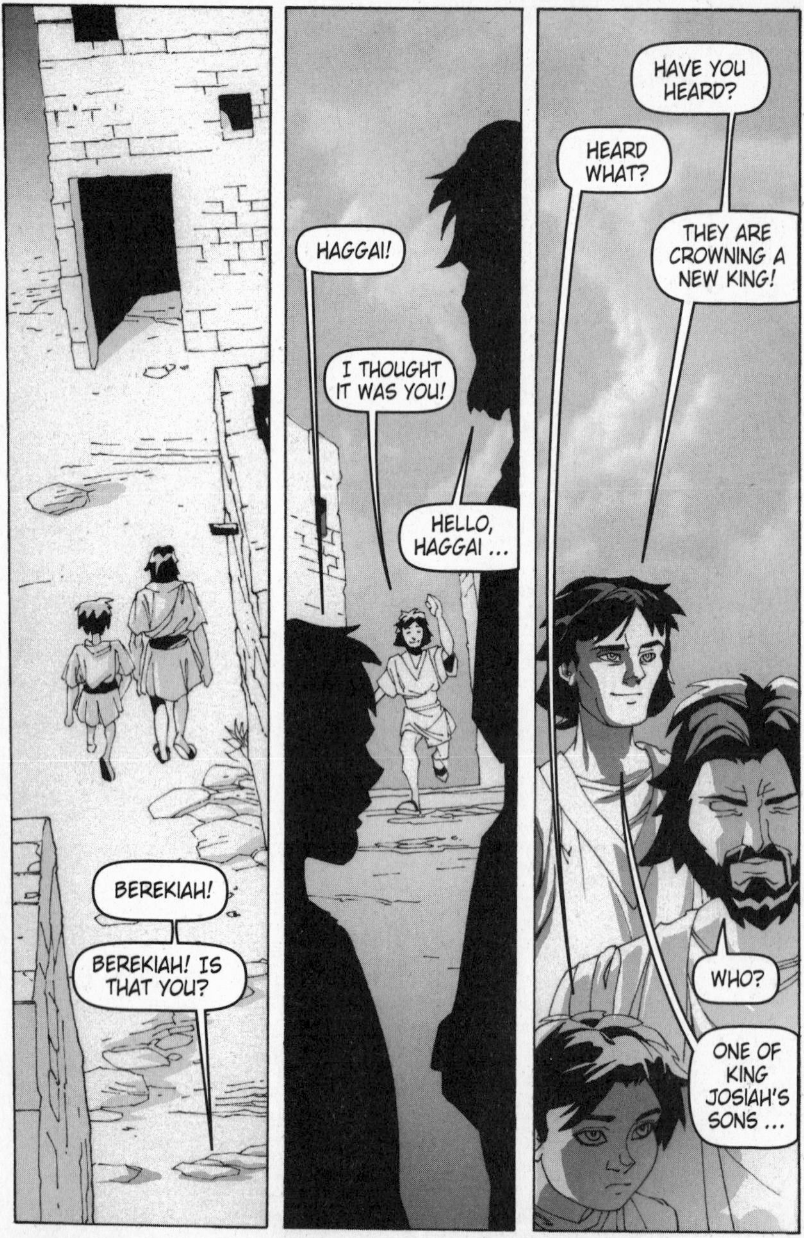
BEREKIAH!
BEREKIAH! IS THAT YOU?
HAGGAI!
I THOUGHT IT WAS YOU!
HELLO, HAGGAI ...
HAVE YOU HEARD?
HEARD WHAT?
THEY ARE CROWNING A NEW KING!
WHO?
ONE OF KING JOSIAH'S SONS ...

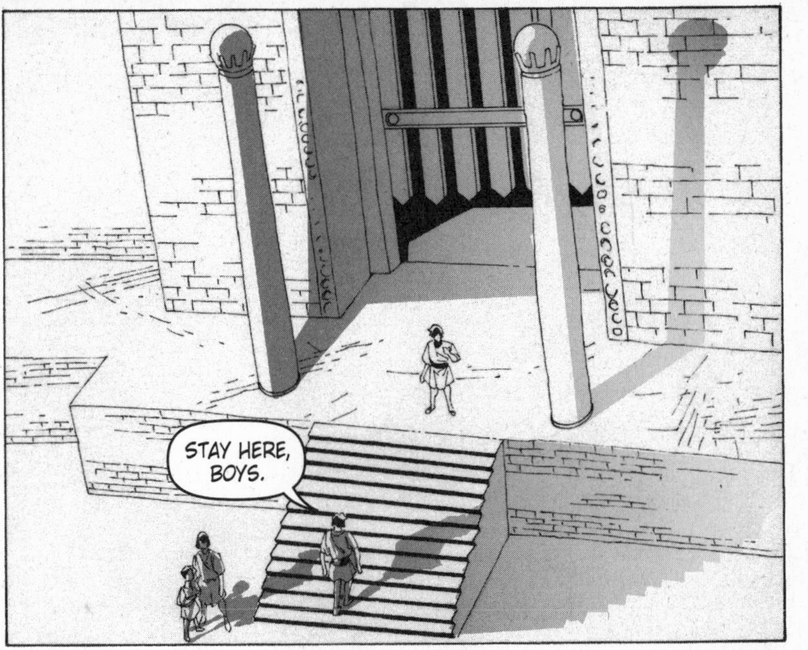
STAY HERE, BOYS.
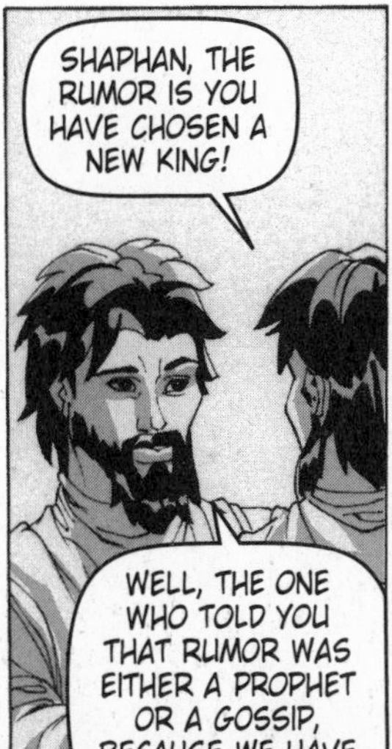
SHAPHAN, THE RUMOR IS YOU HAVE CHOSEN A NEW KING!
WELL, THE ONE WHO TOLD YOU THAT RUMOR WAS EITHER A PROPHET OR A GOSSIP, BECAUSE WE HAVE NOT DONE SO YET.
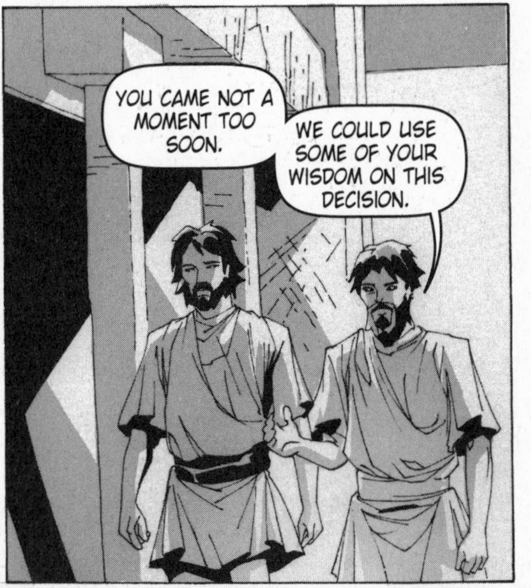
YOU CAME NOT A MOMENT TOO SOON.
WE COULD USE SOME OF YOUR WISDOM ON THIS DECISION.

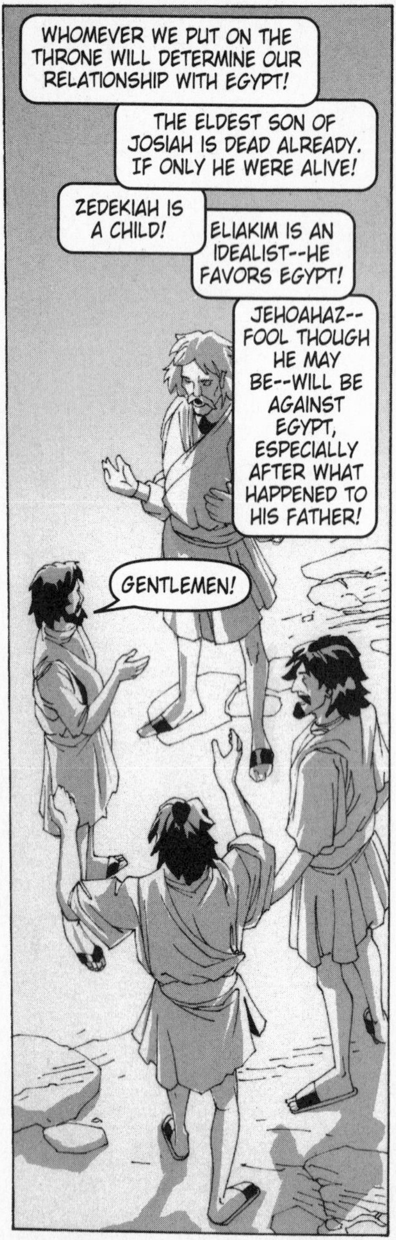
WHOMEVER WE PUT ON THE THRONE WILL DETERMINE OUR RELATIONSHIP WITH EGYPT!
THE ELDEST SON OF JOSIAH IS DEAD ALREADY. IF ONLY HE WERE ALIVE!
ZEDEKIAH IS A CHILD!
ELIAKIM IS AN IDEALIST--HE FAVORS EGYPT!
JEHOAHAZ--FOOL THOUGH HE MAY BE--WILL BE AGAINST EGYPT, ESPECIALLY AFTER WHAT HAPPENED TO HIS FATHER!
GENTLEMEN!
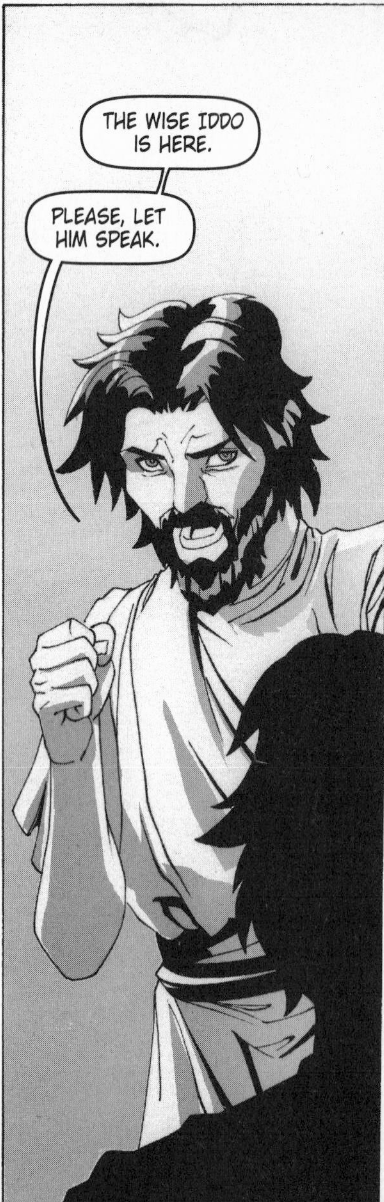
THE WISE IDDO IS HERE.
PLEASE, LET HIM SPEAK.

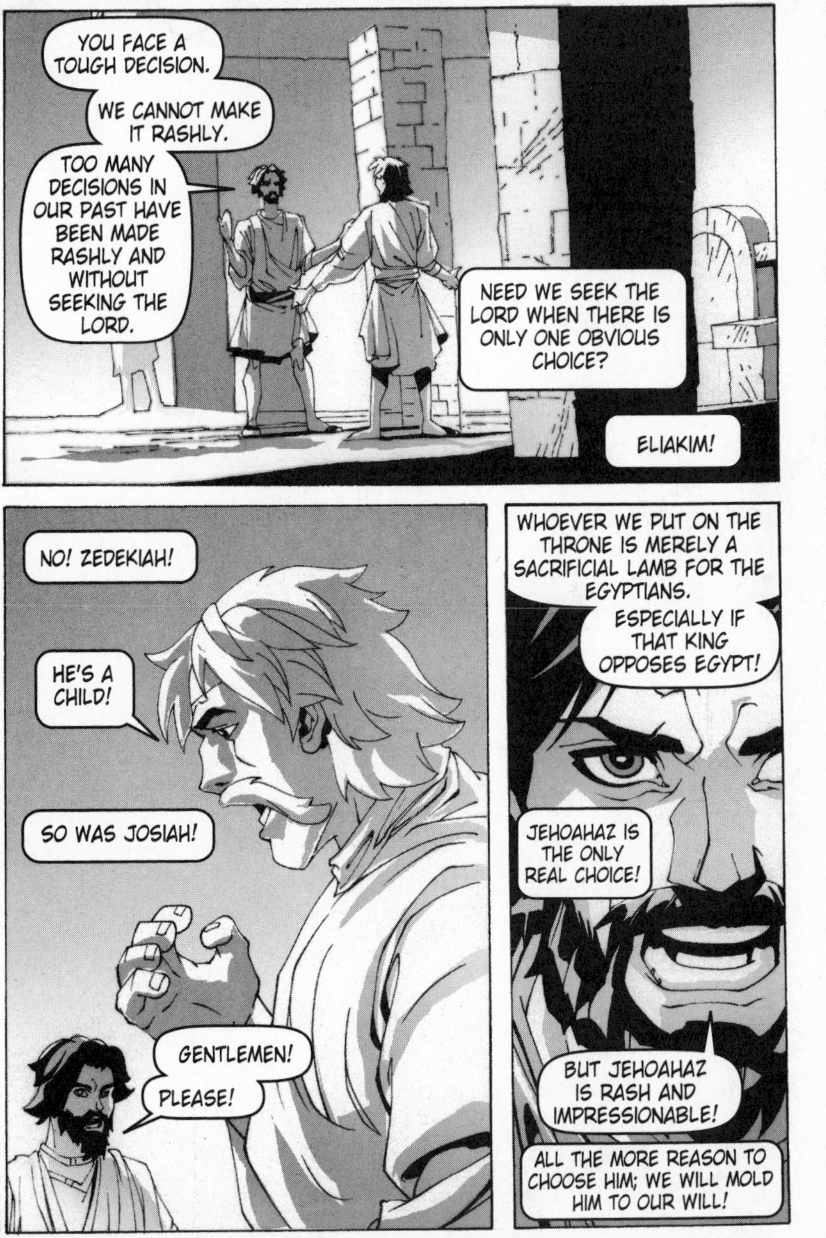
YOU FACE A TOUGH DECISION.
WE CANNOT MAKE IT RASHLY.
TOO MANY DECISIONS IN OUR PAST HAVE BEEN MADE RASHLY AND WITHOUT SEEKING THE LORD.
NEED WE SEEK THE LORD WHEN THERE IS ONLY ONE OBVIOUS CHOICE?
ELIAKIM!
NO! ZEDEKIAH!
HE'S A CHILD!
SO WAS JOSIAH!
GENTLEMEN!
PLEASE!
WHOEVER WE PUT ON THE THRONE IS MERELY A SACRIFICIAL LAMB FOR THE EGYPTIANS.
ESPECIALLY IF THAT KING OPPOSES EGYPT!
JEHOAHAZ IS THE ONLY REAL CHOICE!
BUT JEHOAHAZ IS RASH AND IMPRESSIONABLE!
ALL THE MORE REASON TO CHOOSE HIM; WE WILL MOLD HIM TO OUR WILL!

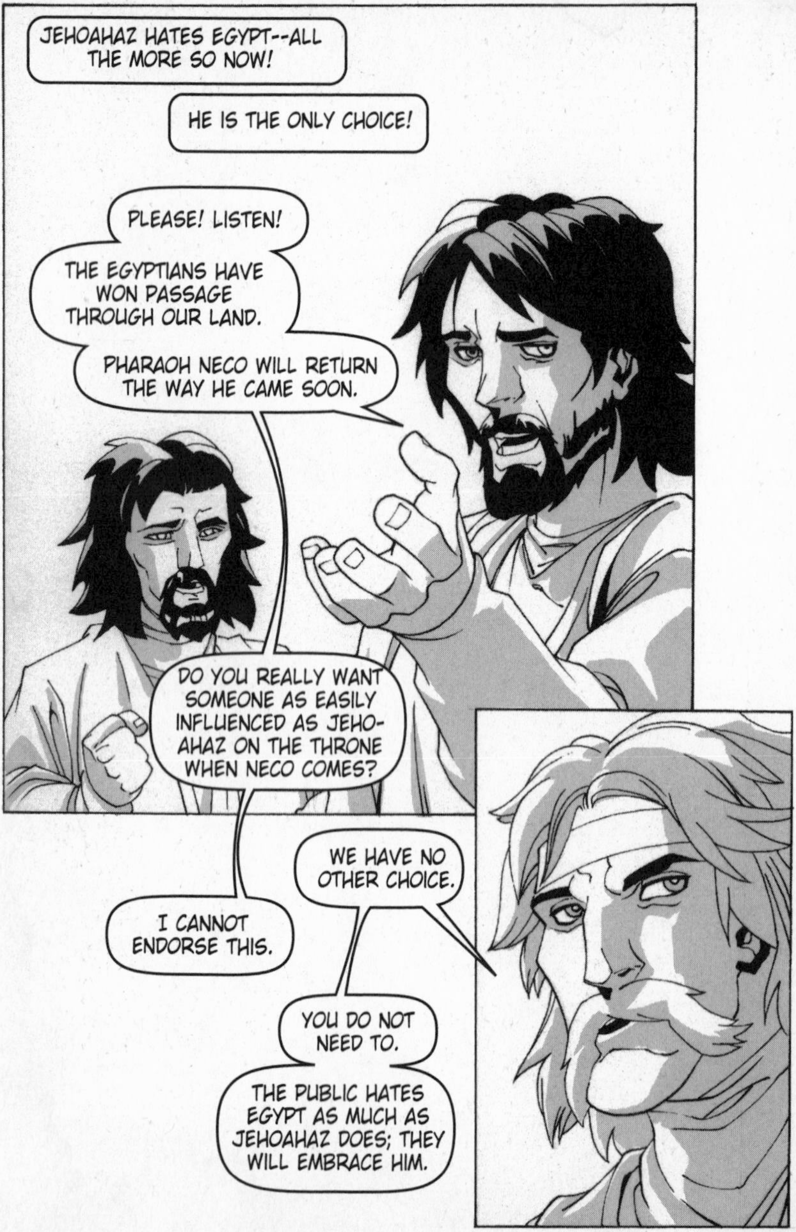
JEHOAHAZ HATES EGYPT--ALL THE MORE SO NOW!
HE IS THE ONLY CHOICE!
PLEASE! LISTEN!
THE EGYPTIANS HAVE WON PASSAGE THROUGH OUR LAND.
PHARAOH NECO WILL RETURN THE WAY HE CAME SOON.
DO YOU REALLY WANT SOMEONE AS EASILY INFLUENCED AS JEHO-AHAZ ON THE THRONE WHEN NECO COMES?
WE HAVE NO OTHER CHOICE.
I CANNOT ENDORSE THIS.
YOU DO NOT NEED TO.
THE PUBLIC HATES EGYPT AS MUCH AS JEHOAHAZ DOES; THEY WILL EMBRACE HIM.

AND WHAT HAPPENS WHEN JEHOAHAZ MUST NEGOTIATE WITH PHARAOH NECO?

WILL HE BE AS EASILY SWAYED BY NECO'S WORDS AS YOU EXPECT HIM TO BE OF YOURS?

WE WILL BE AT HIS SIDE.

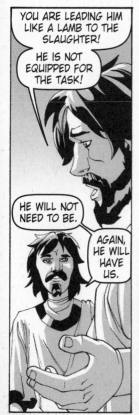

YOU ARE LEADING HIM LIKE A LAMB TO THE SLAUGHTER!

HE IS NOT EQUIPPED FOR THE TASK!

HE WILL NOT NEED TO BE.

AGAIN, HE WILL HAVE US.

HE WILL NOT BE ABLE TO PARLEY WISELY AS A KING SHOULD IN TIMES SUCH AS THIS!

WE HAVE DECIDED.

LET US GO, IDDO.

THE CROWNING CEREMONY WILL BE ON THE MORROW.

THIS IS NOT THE FIRST TIME I HAVE BEEN WITNESS TO THE PICKING OF A NEW KING ...

BUT THIS TIME, THEY ARE NOT PUTTING A NEW KING ON THE THRONE, THEY ARE PUTTING HIM ON AN ALTAR OF SACRIFICE ...

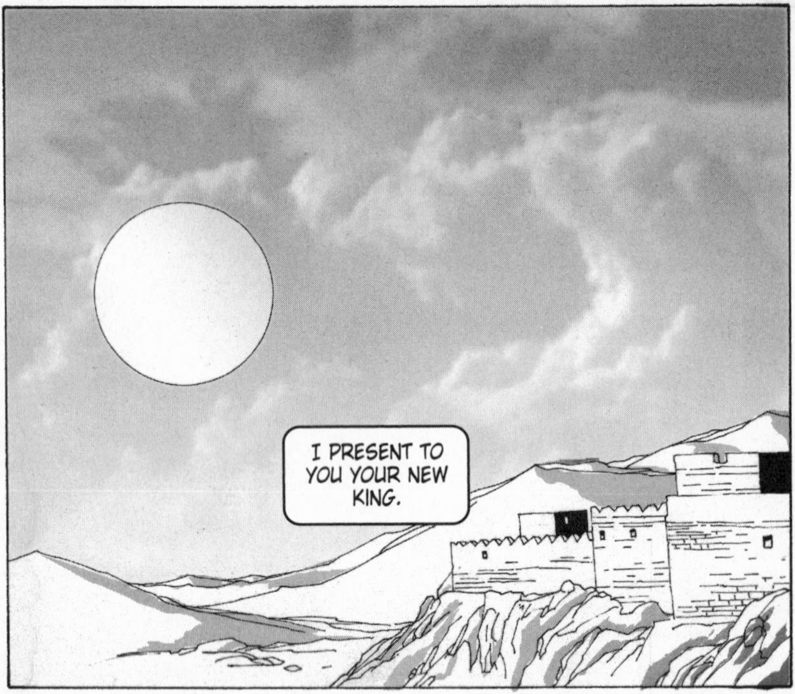
I PRESENT TO YOU YOUR NEW KING.

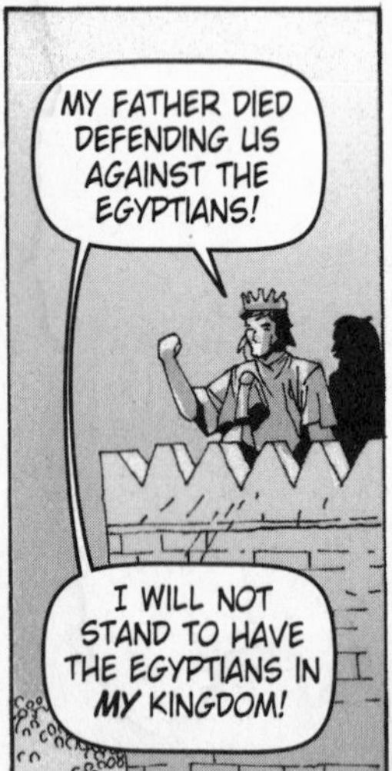
MY FATHER DIED DEFENDING US AGAINST THE EGYPTIANS!
I WILL NOT STAND TO HAVE THE EGYPTIANS IN *MY* KINGDOM!

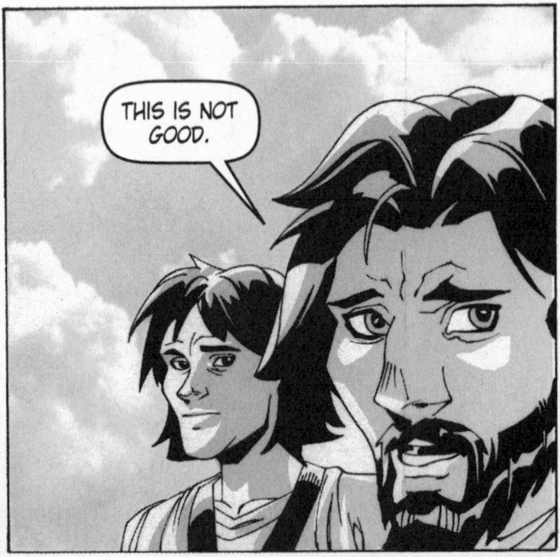
THIS IS NOT GOOD.

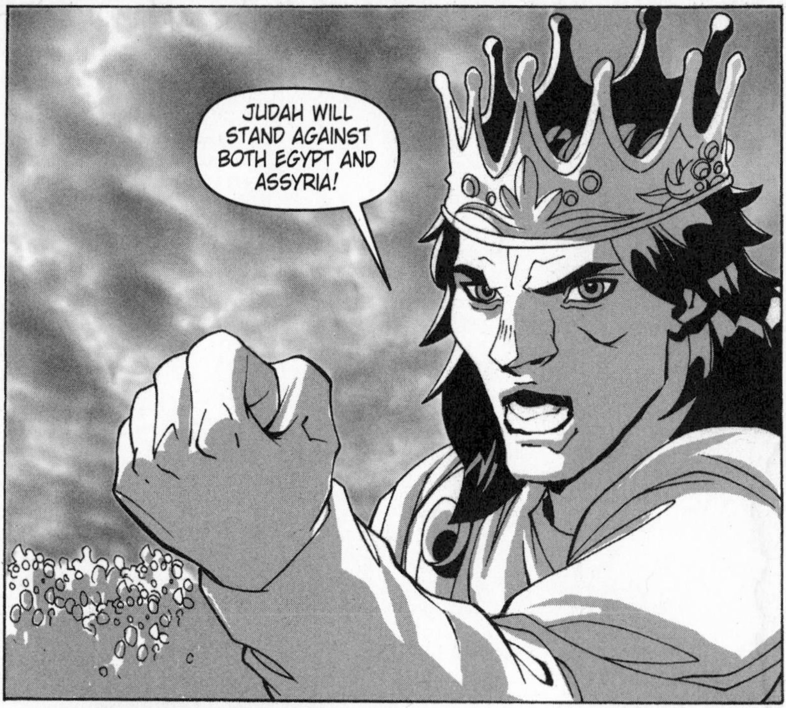
JUDAH WILL STAND AGAINST BOTH EGYPT AND ASSYRIA!

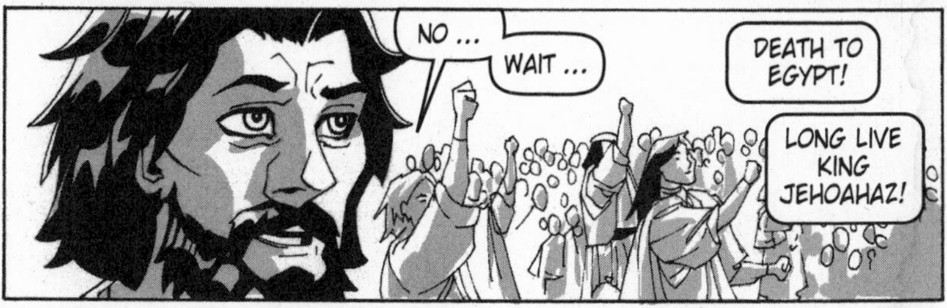
NO ...
WAIT ...
DEATH TO EGYPT!
LONG LIVE KING JEHOAHAZ!

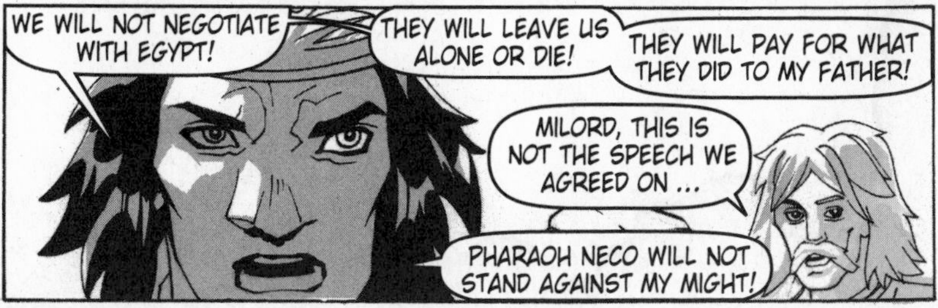
WE WILL NOT NEGOTIATE WITH EGYPT!
THEY WILL LEAVE US ALONE OR DIE!
THEY WILL PAY FOR WHAT THEY DID TO MY FATHER!
MILORD, THIS IS NOT THE SPEECH WE AGREED ON ...
PHARAOH NECO WILL NOT STAND AGAINST MY MIGHT!

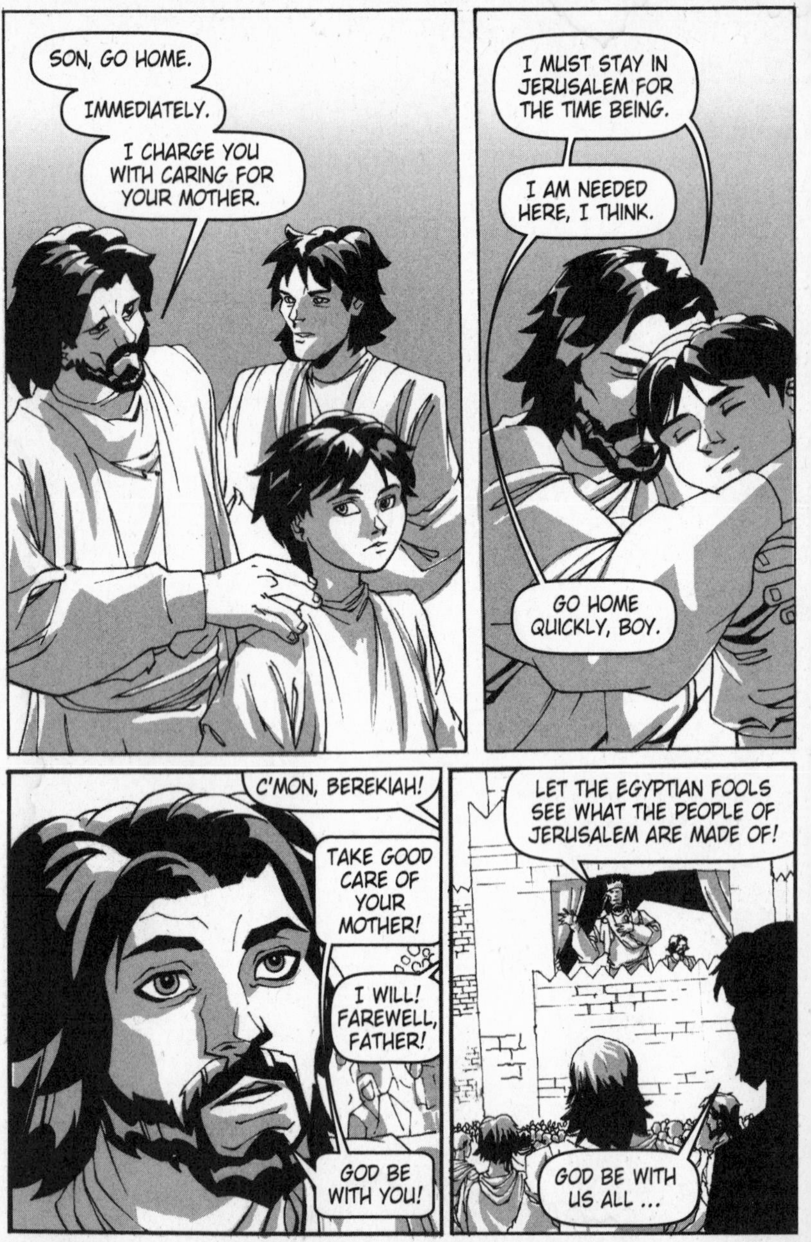
SON, GO HOME.
IMMEDIATELY.
I CHARGE YOU WITH CARING FOR YOUR MOTHER.
I MUST STAY IN JERUSALEM FOR THE TIME BEING.
I AM NEEDED HERE, I THINK.
GO HOME QUICKLY, BOY.
C'MON, BEREKIAH!
TAKE GOOD CARE OF YOUR MOTHER!
I WILL! FAREWELL, FATHER!
GOD BE WITH YOU!
LET THE EGYPTIAN FOOLS SEE WHAT THE PEOPLE OF JERUSALEM ARE MADE OF!
GOD BE WITH US ALL ...

TIME FLYZ
SHOOM

FLYING THROUGH TIME TO SAVE THE WORLD!

TIME FLYZ
PYRAMID PERIL

Pyramid Peril

Available Now!

TIME FLYZ
TURTLE TROUBLE

Turtle Trouble

Available Now!

TIME FLYZ
BERLIN BREAKOUT

Berlin Breakout

Available February 2008!

TIME FLYZ
TUNNEL TWIST-UP

Tunnel Twist-Up

Available May 2008!

AVAILABLE AT YOUR LOCAL BOOKSTORE!

VOLUMES 5–8 COMING SOON!

ZONDERVAN®